ALSO BY KELLY COLE

<u>Supernaturals of New Brecken</u>

The Maker

The Alpha's Den

<u>Blade of Traesha Trilogy</u>

Daughter of War

Weapon of Rulers

Speaker of Fates

<u>Standalone Novels</u>

Unmourned

THE COVENS

SUPERNATURALS OF NEW BRECKEN
BOOK 3

KELLY COLE

ISBN: 979-8-9910376-0-0

CHAPTER 1

Nora paused on the stairs leading to the second floor of the Alpha's Den. Over the steadily buzzing magic of the vines snaking down the railing, the beating bass of the lowest floor, and the cacophony of human noise, she picked the voices of her pack. The words made her go cold.

"—isn't up here. You can leave."

"Patrick…" Heather's voice was long-suffering but contained no bite.

"What? I don't care what's going on between her and Nora. It doesn't mean we have to play nice when Nora isn't around. It doesn't mean we have to be friends."

"But we *can* be friends," Colbie said, her sharpness dulled. Nora's heart cracked. It was the same argument Colbie had made with Nora in the beginning. Though their conversations had a vastly different undertone, Nora couldn't fathom how so many members of her pack were insistently rejecting Colbie. Nora hadn't held out nearly as long and hadn't had her alpha's encouragement to get along like they did.

"Why? Why would we want to be friends with you? You caused all of this. Nora left because of you. You destroyed our pack when New Brecken needed us most. You got into her head and made her side with your brother. If Gabriel was right about anything, it was what he said about him," Patrick sucked in a breath when Heather spoke his name again with admonishment, but she didn't protest enough to stop him. "West brought all this trouble to the city. He let Reelings walk away and then abandoned us in his mess. Where is he? What are *you* doing about any of this? New Brecken would be better off if you were making time for him and not our alpha. We have no idea where Reelings is, what the witches are planning, or where all the drainers keep coming from, and all you do is feed off the humans downstairs and distract Nora."

"It's not any of our fault. If I've learned anything in all this, it's that accusations like that don't help anyone. I don't distract—"

"You *do*. Constantly. She just became an alpha, and you have no idea what that means or how hard it is. Our pack needs her. She needs us. We *don't* need you meddling with our business, vampire."

"I only want to—"

Nora had never heard Colbie talked over so much. Never heard that lack of confidence in her voice. Everything in Nora ached to barge up the stairs and order Patrick to ease off. Order all of them to talk to Colbie respectfully and kindly with the alpha powering her voice. Make them give her girlfriend a chance.

But Colbie had asked Nora, very specifically, not to do anything like that. Colbie wanted to gain the pack's trust. She'd called herself likable and claimed it wouldn't be that hard. Nora hadn't realized how little progress Colbie had made. She didn't know it was this bad when she wasn't in the room.

Lupe cut in. "We don't care. It won't happen. You aren't part of this pack. We can't stop you from being part of Nora's life, but you won't be part of ours, you fucking leech."

Silence.

Nora didn't move. Her mouth had dropped open. Those

who had transferred to Nora from her old family didn't know what to make of Colbie's presence, but Colbie had promised she'd be able to handle it. These were supposed to be the more reasonable members. The ones who chose Nora over Gabriel. But they were still too caught up in their old ways. Nora was coming to understand the cruelty she'd been raised surrounded by. Cruelty directed at humans, other packs, witches, and vampires. Always vampires. It took Colbie being the brunt of the hatred to whip away the last of Nora's delusions about her past. She'd been right to leave. Right to choose Colbie and work for this burning emotion between them. As right as it all felt, the grief for her childhood remained. Had her father been this bad? Even if he changed his mind, was all this the foundation of her childhood? Of who she was today? If Luis Morales was here instead of Patrick, what would he say to Colbie now?

It wasn't Nora's entire pack, at least. Heather was kind to Colbie and carried too many memories of Topher as a human to hate him like the rest. Ricky didn't have a mean bone in his body, nor did he possess a confrontational one. Janelle was the best as an in-between, but of course, she was downstairs working the bar. She and Colbie got along like wolves on a full moon, and Nora consulted with Janelle and her pragmatism more than anyone else about the issue. Nora was tempted to raise Janelle's status in the pack for this reason alone but was hesitant to make any huge decisions with things so new and unstable.

For each beat that the silence stretched, Nora knew fiercer regret for agreeing to stay out of this. But Colbie had been adamant. "If you get in the middle or order them to like me, it'll never work out. It'll only breed resentment. I have to genuinely make friends with them," she had said. Nora heard in her tone that the dislike wasn't one-sided. Colbie had a hard enough time forgiving Nora for what Gabriel's pack did to Topher. She hated most of them for what had been said to Nora while she lived under Gabriel's roof. The fact that Colbie was upstairs, trying still, putting herself in the position to hear the poison being spewed, spoke to how badly she wanted to make this work for Nora's sake.

And Nora loved her even more for it.

The words almost slipped out when Colbie appeared at the top of the stairs. But the raw expression on Colbie's face before she spotted Nora made Nora's breath catch in the sweep of her anger. In a blink, Colbie cleared the hurt from her face. She smiled and bounced down the stairs, her breezy movements too forced.

"Look at us, making progress," she chirped before passing Nora. She turned at the base of the steps and headed for the outdoor space behind the building. She walked too quickly. Her shoulders too tight. Nora followed.

Outside, Colbie shamelessly charmed the humans milling on the patio back into the bar. Nora approached, searching Colbie's face for what she might need. There was a light summer rain muffling the world around them. Poppy's greenery burst with scent. Colbie hugged her arms around her middle, standing in the center of the lot. Only one parking spot remained after the renovations—Lana's sleek black car waiting on the other side of the short section of the picket fence. Flowers Nora couldn't name hummed with magic around the edges of the tall wooden fence. There were a few chairs, two picnic tables, and buckets for cigarette butts. The pebbles beneath their feet crunched as Colbie shifted her weight, tipping her head back to watch the rain fall through the fairy lights strung above. Nora loved the patio. Poppy spent a lot of time on the garden, and it was quiet during the day. Colbie didn't fit with those memories of daylight, of rolled shorts for tanning, and Oliver's intense popsicle addiction that had become a running joke within the pack. It made Nora's chest ache now as she looked at her girlfriend. Colbie missed so much of the joy that came with their friends and the heat of the sun and having a pack. She woke to shadows and cold shoulders but kept showing up here anyway for Nora. Colbie worried about Topher back at their apartment and still showed up.

Heart too tender with all the feelings, Nora shucked off her sweatshirt and tugged it over Colbie's head. The action prompted a real smile and a lopsided bun, but Colbie didn't bother snaking her arms through the sleeves. She continued to hug herself as Nora pressed in close. Colbie stepped back, out of the lights, until she'd allowed Nora to crowd her against the fence behind them.

"They'll come around," Nora tried instead of repeating her offer to get involved.

"I'm starting to think they won't."

Nora bent, pressing her nose into Colbie's throat, smelling herself on the damp skin there and humming with pleasure. "No one can resist you."

"I think you're the first person who couldn't, and that's why we're stuck in this mess."

Nora kissed Colbie's cold skin, the curls at Colbie's nape tickling her nose. "There is too much of me spread through the pack. They'll pick up on my affection soon enough through the bonds."

"I don't know what to think about that statement," Colbie said, laughing.

Nora's shoulders relaxed at the sound of that laugh. Everything and everyone was so unsteady these days. She didn't hear Colbie laughing nearly as much as she wanted to. Nora pulled back, looking her girlfriend in the eye. Colbie was still trying to hide the hurt, but Nora was very slowly unraveling all that went on in Colbie's mind. The bruises of past rejections. The self-consciousness underlying the boldest of statements.

The sweet need to be comforted that she let Nora see. That she only sought from Nora.

"It's growing pains. Learning. I wanted to kiss you the first time I saw you and it still took me far too long to learn what it means to like you as a person. Things are changing faster than I ever dreamed, but there will be bumps in the road. I could try to smooth—"

Colbie stiffened. "No, Nora. I want them to like and trust you. They won't if you turn into Gabe and start ordering them how to feel and what to think."

Nora sighed and let her head fall forward until she and Colbie were standing forehead to forehead. "Then tell me how to make you feel better about it all."

"Well, there was mention of kissing—"

Nora's lips needed no further prodding. This kiss started slow, a gentle, comforting brush. *I'm here. I'm with you. I'm not leaving.* Then Colbie responded, pushing into Nora's space and making a high, needy noise in the back of her throat. This, too, Nora had learned. When Colbie stepped forward to take, it was always rushed, always desperate, always hot. But when Nora took charge, all the doubt backing Colbie's movements became apparent as it vanished.

Colbie wiggled in the sweatshirt, attempting to free her arms. Nora reached up and fisted the tops of the sleeves, capturing Colbie inside and drawing the perfect sound of surprise, surrender, and relief as Nora tugged Colbie back against the fence. Pulse thundering in her ears, Nora broke from Colbie's lips to kiss her way down Colbie's cheek, jaw, neck, ending with a bite hard enough to make Colbie's knees momentarily give up so that Nora was holding her upright with the sweatshirt. Nora dropped the sleeves. Colbie snaked her arms out, wrapping them around Nora's neck and clinging while Nora's lips made their way back to the sweet bliss waiting in Colbie's mouth.

She moaned. The taste. The lightheaded sensations. The high that was kissing. It would never grow old. Nora needed more of it, completely and constantly. Colbie's breath hitched. Her legs came up. Nora grabbed her thighs, keeping Colbie off the ground, and pressed into the fence. Her mumbles against

Nora's lips shifted into incoherent pleas. Her hips began to move.

Nora was going to lose her mind.

The doors opened with a bang, jarring enough to turn Nora's head with a snarl. Janelle stood unimpressed at the top of the stairs. "You two really need some alone time," she said. Then, "Lana's asking for you."

Alone time, indeed. Between the pack, Topher, learning to manage a club, interruptions like this one, and the thin wall shared with Annaliese back home, this level of kissing was the furthest Nora and Colbie had gotten since officially getting back together two months ago. First, Nora was nervous. Colbie had gently suggested they take things slow. Now, the need for Colbie, bare and gasping as she had been moments ago, was a desperate thrum consistently in the background of Nora's world.

"Way to kill a mood," Colbie muttered, feet hitting the ground with two thumps. Nora agreed. They probably could have picked up again if Janelle hadn't mentioned the name Lana.

Colbie's face and mannerisms all pointed to her being completely fine once more as they walked back in, but she stuck close to Nora's side and clung to her warmth in a way that betrayed how shaken she was. How shaken she had been for weeks, if not months. Years. Being a source of comfort and strength…Was it wrong for Nora to enjoy it so much?

Julia's death had hallowed Colbie's laughter. Topher's suffocating grief had dimmed the spark in Colbie's eyes. The blood on her hands from killing Poppy's mom lingered and left Colbie constantly seeking warmth and affection. The fear from those nights—Colbie wasn't the same girl Nora had hunted in the Maker last winter.

But neither was Nora. All their broken edges fit together. They just hadn't figured out how to make their relationship fit into the world around them. But Nora had hope, enough for the both of them.

She was confident in the same way she was an alpha and the same way she knew her power now, that the two of them would make it through this and bring all their friends out of the darkness with them.

On the top floor and inside Lana's pristine apartment, the maker beckoned for Nora to join her at the table. When Colbie dropped onto the white, plush couch instead, it was far too tempting to ignore Lana's summons. The alpha in her still reared a stubborn refusal to Lana's every command, but Lana was her pack's landlord. No one paid rent; they simply worked downstairs to earn their keep. However, despite Nora's signature on the papers, she had no idea how to run a nightclub. How to own a building without someone there to hold her hand. They depended on Lana's goodwill until Nora learned enough to house and employ her pack on her own. The more spreadsheets they looked at, the further away that point in time felt. But Nora was learning, and Lana was unsure of her position without Topher around. They were in a wary peace where both sides benefitted. Even Patrick recognized this and simply ignored Lana when they were in the same room.

Colbie watched intently as Nora pulled out the chair across from Lana's, forcing Lana to turn her laptop screen so they could both see. A petty move not to sit in the chair that Lana indicated, but it felt good. Colbie twisted on the couch, crossing her arms over the back and resting her chin on her top wrist. Her eyes remained on Nora, but Nora knew Colbie was paying close attention to Lana. Julia had become an uncrossable rift between the West siblings and the maker. So far, nothing had come out of it, the tense peace existing even there, but Topher had also been keeping to himself. Nora hadn't seen him at the Alpha's

Den in weeks. He'd been too reluctant, drawn, and exhausted. Not even Annaliese could get him out of his room.

Nora looked at Lana now, wondering if Topher had weakened himself enough for his maker to be able to charm him into getting outside. They needed him. His knowledge of this fact only added weight to his depression, so they stopped reminding him, but his absence was a constant source of anxiety. Even Oliver was different now. His worry was constant that Zayn had finally agreed to a trip out of town to Oliver's parents and take a break from the city.

Something was brewing. *Had* been brewing. Ever since Topher was changed and Lana let him go home to attack Colbie. Ever since Lana began hanging on Topher, touching Topher, using Topher however she wished. Ever since she'd struck a deal and not held up her end. The Alpha's Den was a delicate thread holding them together. Holding the entire city together, it felt like at times. With human-supernatural relations at an all-time low but the line outside this particular club always long and impatient, this place was the one hope for a better, more cohesive future.

Just like Lana wanted, which meant even though Nora approved and wanted this club to succeed, she didn't trust this place either.

"We need to review last week's numbers and see if those drink specials were worth it. Then, check the schedule and make sure your wolves will be happy with it. There are a few doubles with Zayn gone, but I stopped scheduling the pack at the bar with my darlings, aside from Janelle and Ricky, so they can quit complaining about that. Then, we have a visitor coming in tomorrow that you'll need to deal with. He's coming too early for me to greet."

"Who is it?" Nora asked. She had very little interest in numbers or schedules despite her attempts to learn. As always, she would have Lana email her the pages and bring them down for Chase, the pack accountant, to look over and explain in a way that didn't make her skin crawl.

Then, if he were willing, she'd have Topher double-check. She trusted his knowledge of clubs more than Lana's or Chase's.

When Topher inevitably stared at her blankly, she'd ask Raven instead.

Lana frowned. Her red nails tapped silently on her crossed forearms. It was the most Nora had ever seen Lana fidget. This guest was a big deal. Instead of explaining, Lana opened her email. The situation was intriguing enough that even Colbie came around the couch, willingly approaching Lana to look. She perched on Nora's lap. Nora wrapped an arm around Colbie's waist and leaned forward, resting her cheek on Colbie's shoulder to read.

Dear Ms. Williams,

It is our understanding that you are in possession of a club on Twenty-Fifth Street that retains vampires in its employment aside from yourself. While not illegal, it had been previously agreed these vampire clubs would remain in the Fourth Street territory. We are not oblivious to the strife currently taking place in that section of our city and are opposed to any more violence; therefore, we are willing to overlook the location of your establishment should it pass an inspection.

You may question our authority to do this, as it is our understanding that with the passing of your late maker, you have not attended any City Leadership Meetings. It was during one of these meetings that our branch of the city government was announced and appointed. We head the Supernatural Mediation Division in the position of human assessors. While we strive to be understanding of supernatural ways, the violence occurring in our city is inexcusable. Our assessors are in charge of inspecting supernatural groups to determine whether the supernatural laws permitting activities such as feeding on humans will remain on the ballot for the next city elec-

tion cycle. While we have seen many benefits to having supernaturals out in the open, it is the role of our department to decide if the costs outweigh the benefits.

All this is to say you will receive an inspection on Monday, July 10th at five PM. I, Brett Campbell, will tour the premises and observe how your supernatural staff interacts with human clients, whether human clients understand the risk of frequenting your establishment, and attempt to unearth whether charm has influenced them illegally.

Any hint that your establishment has taken part in the murders of the last year will lead to immediate closure and legal action.

Regards,

Brett Campbell

Head of New Brecken Supernatural Mediation

"Well, that's intense," Colbie muttered before Nora had finished reading. "Also didn't know your last name before now." Even with her skin prickling with all the threats and what this email could mean, Nora smiled at Colbie, feeling pride for her bookish girlfriend and determined to read more as she slugged through the final paragraph.

Lana ignored Colbie's last comment. "I'm certain we will pass muster. Nora, you will give the tour with Raven, who knows what to say. We have mostly werewolves on the schedule, Colbie's paltry charm barely warrants mentioning, and Zayn and Oliver have tomorrow night off for their little trip." Lana was frowning, tapping red-tipped nails on the table. "It bothers me we had so little warning. One of us must make a place for ourselves in the leadership meetings."

No part of Nora wanted a seat at that table. "We don't need a warning. We aren't doing anything wrong. They're only worried about us because we're so much closer to downtown," Nora said. Fourth Street may not be entirely legal, but the clients are loyal. The humans there wouldn't be welcoming to these government figures threatening to shut down their clubs and would lie through their teeth to assure the assessors nothing was amiss. If Fourth Street had faced similar inspections, they no doubt passed.

"Regardless, I need you to get in this inspector's good graces. We need to be more informed."

Lana swiped quickly to exit the email, pulling up her spreadsheets. Colbie stiffened in Nora's lap. "Go back."

Lana raised an eyebrow at the order and made no move to do so. When Colbie reached to touch the computer, Lana bared her teeth, but the snarl that ripped through Nora kept the maker in place as Colbie clicked on the email tab again. "Why are you emailing Solas?" Colbie demanded. "You *know* she's under Reelings's charm."

"I don't know that. I have been trying to get a meeting to find out. As I *just* said, we need more information." But Lana sounded too defensive. They all knew that no matter the Alpha's Den's success, what Lana truly coveted was a club on Fourth and a position among the vampires who ruled that section of the city. She'd been a faithful lower to Connor Grace and losing him and their position on Fourth Street was a blow Lana was still touchy about when mentioned.

"Were you going to tell us about this? I thought we agreed to stay no contact until we figured out where Reelings went," Nora said, the snarl still in her voice. They'd worked hard to keep an eye on Lana without Topher and with Raven's loyalties uncertain. Nora didn't like this getting past them or what else Lana could be up to without their noticing.

"We're no closer to finding Reelings than two months ago. Topher has become useless t—" She switched tactics when Colbie snarled this time. "I thought you would appreciate me deepening the search."

"What we wouldn't appreciate," Colbie said, "is you going out there and getting yourself charmed like the rest of them.

For all we know, Reelings could be using Solas to message you! For all we know, he could be hiding in Blue Blood right now!"

"Blue Blood is Patter's club, darling."

"Don't call me that!"

Nora had seen Colbie upset, but she'd never heard that tone. Never felt this much tension. Her worry about Topher, Nora's pack, and Reelings's silent and untouchable residence in the background was getting to her. Lana studied Colbie through narrowed eyes, figuring out the best way to maneuver this conversation. Nora couldn't help but feel there wasn't a correct way to navigate this. As usual, Lana was in the wrong, and Colbie was far too tired of her manipulation to let her keep getting away with it.

Lana straightened. The alpha in Nora surged to match the maker brimming in Lana's haughty expression as she said, "We can't just hide here, hoping no one walks through our doors and disrupts the peace. We already have humans sticking their noses into our business. It won't be long until the other vampires tire of leaving us alone while we steal customers. Soon, Reelings will decide Topher got lucky and isn't that big of a threat or *is* that big of a threat and does something drastic to get rid of him. We need to stop acting on the defensive and waiting for shit to happen to us. I have been patient, but I need Topher, and you have to let me talk to him. If he would accompany me to Fourth Street, we could find out if Reelings has made contact without the risk of being charmed. If he hasn't made contact, we can take steps to ensure he isn't welcome there. If Reelings doesn't have Fourth and can't get Fourth, he won't get another foothold in our city."

"It's too risky," Colbie said, shaking her head.

Lana smacked a hand on the table. Nora jumped, more from the sudden show of stark fear in Lana's eyes than the noise. "Everything is a risk! We need Topher more than ever. We need to show the city that supernaturals belong, that we don't have to hide, and that our presence is a good thing. The laws, the future, and the beacon of hope New Brecken has become for our people are all on the line here!"

Colbie stood. She turned and paced but quickly whirled back, stooping into Lana's face. "Maybe we deserve to live in hiding! No matter what you preach, I haven't seen much good come from people like you. Topher is in this situation because of a witch and a vampire. One, who wanted to kill him, the other, who only changed him because she thought he had a pretty face. All supernaturals do is kill and fight for power and make anyone who isn't part of their population miserable."

"Does Henry's pack only do that? Does Topher only do that? Are you accusing your girlfriend of that? What about yourself, Colbie?"

"Oh, sure. Name a few people. For every one you mention, I can think of three times as many shady supernaturals, and you're at the top of that list, Lana. I think Henry, Topher, and Nora would all agree to lay low if it kept New Brecken safe from the likes of Reelings. Topher would pay good money to become a hidden creature of the night without worrying about you bothering him again."

Lana's lip curled. "Just because you and your brother are afraid of this, of change, doesn't mean it's wrong. Topher is weak but—"

But Colbie had enough. With a whip of movement, Lana was suddenly rocking back, a hand on her struck cheek. Stunned. Nora froze, too. Since when could Colbie move that fast? "You little bitch. You—"

Nora stood between Lana and Colbie, facing down the maker. "Be very careful what you say next, Lana."

Lana took a deep breath. "We are already out of hiding, Miss West. You're already a vampire and acting like one more by the day. There is a reason that for every book of lore about our kind, there's a human hero who hunts us down. Hiding *doesn't* work. Hiding after exposure certainly doesn't work. We are part of this city now. How we live in it is up to people like Topher."

"He needs more time."

"Out of all his gifts, time is the one thing he doesn't have, and you know it."

CHAPTER 2

Poppy shut the door quietly, staring at the empty sleeping draught in her hand. Could Topher tell she's been lowering the potency? Could he tell she'd been tweaking the ingredients? Would he be angry at her for doing it? Could he even feel emotions like anger right now?

She shivered. Hating this. Hating how quickly he'd succumbed. One second, he was a powerful vampire taking on the biggest threat to the city and trying to make things right; the next, they were given a chance to breathe, and it was like all the grief and fear in the air swallowed him whole.

What could any of them do? They gave him company, asked him to eat, and tried to be a safe place for him to talk, but it was like Topher was gone. Empty, bleak space stared back from his blue eyes, a hint of effort buried below when he tried to keep them from worrying. That was the hardest part to watch. Poppy had no idea where he went in his mind. Secretly, she hoped he was healing. The most positive spin she could put on all this was that Topher needed time to himself to feel these things, so maybe when, not if, he woke up or recovered or whatever word there was for his return, he would be ready. Every time she gave him a sleeping draught and left him to the darkness hanging in his room, she told herself he was preparing. Just like she was.

Ru turned from the kitchen counter, pushing Poppy's notebook away hastily. Trying to hide that she'd been reading Poppy's latest notes about her brews. "Did he say anything?"

"Just 'hello,' 'not tonight,' and 'thank you.' Same as always."

Ru nodded. She glanced away from Poppy's notebook to the binder on the kitchen island. She obviously wanted to get on with their plans for the night but felt she needed to give a moment to hurt with Topher.

A big part of Poppy longed to pull her notebook forward instead of her and Ru's binder. She was close to figuring something out with her latest brew. It felt big. So big she hadn't mentioned it to anyone yet. The implications of her brew succeeding felt nearly impossible. Too hopeful to hold in her head.

Poppy snapped, bringing the binder through the air and into her hands and breaking the moment of quiet for Topher. "Where do you want to start tonight?" she asked, thoughts forced away from ingredients and brewing.

She and Ru had been brainstorming, stalking social media and public records, and leaving messages for weeks. It was time to take action. After testing her and Ru's wards to the brink, Poppy felt they were ready to venture into the city. To look in person at places Poppy hadn't dared visit since she moved in with Topher and Colbie. The only exception was—

"Margot's," Ru said. "I want to see her shop."

Poppy nodded, chest smarting as she recalled her last visit there. The lack of life. Josh's presence at her back. The possibilities such a shop represented for witches in this city. Only, none of them were safe with Reelings dipping his fingers into New Brecken's business. The sole hint of Margot that Poppy had seen since that uneventful visit were the tarot cards sold in bookstores and gift shops around town. Margot was nearby. Her abandoned shop was their best place to start looking.

The familiar hesitance rose, but Poppy swallowed it and reached for her keys. "Let's do it then."

Ru's smile made every smothered fear worth it. This wasn't merely about making Ru happy, though. This was finding their people, finding answers, finding hope. Preparing for things to get worse and protecting what they had. Poppy refused to believe Mother Kallow, Beth, and Tiff Jennings were the best that witches had to offer. Guilt burgeoned at the thought of bringing their people out of hiding, but for the most part, witches were a peaceful and life-loving people. With Topher shut in his room and the packs of the city at odds, they needed real magic more than ever. Supernatural polls were at an all-time low with the humans. Maybe it would be witches who turned the favor and gained the support the supernaturals needed to keep the laws in place.

Not that humans had a great track record for their treatment of people they thought were witches. But times changed. Poppy had to believe in the possibilities. Magic stemmed from potential, from the hidden strengths of life and love. This could come from humans, too.

"Jay said to pick them up at Vegan," Ru said, head bent over Topher's phone. Poppy had yet to get Ru her own, but as neither she nor Topher complained about the current setup, there wasn't any rush. Poppy had brews and witches to worry about first.

Ru frowned. Her lavender lipstick was a new shade she was trying, matching the purple hue of her sharp eyeliner and the blush of glitter on her cheekbones. In these last few months, Ru had truly mastered the art of makeup and hair and online shopping. Poppy self-consciously tugged at the old ball cap she wore over her unwashed hair.

"I don't remember inviting Jay."

"We didn't," Ru agreed. "They texted me anyway." Poppy

and Ru shared a look. Jay talked with knowledge of the super-natural and had enough Sight to know about Gus, but maybe they hadn't been entirely forthcoming about their talents with the occult. The sisters had discussed involving Jay in their search a few times before, but in the end, they decided that the presence of a stranger in their search might be what kept the other Jennings witches in hiding.

Poppy shrugged. Margot's old shop was the least dangerous of all the destinations they had come up with to search for witches. If Jay wanted to come along, it likely wouldn't hurt. And as always, Poppy hoped Jay would let slip more about their witch friend and tutor. If that witch were willing to work with a human, they might be open to what Poppy and Ru had in mind.

Ten minutes later, Poppy was pulling into the diagonal space in front of Vegan Your Day. The cafe and bakery allowed regulars to leave their own coffee mugs on the shelves there, and Jay balanced Ru and Poppy's as they stepped off the curb and opened the back door.

"May the Mother bless you," Ru muttered reverently as she accepted her lavender-scented drink. Had Jay picked up on the color theme of the day with their Sight or foretelling? Poppy didn't like what that implied about Ru's wards. Hopefully, it was simply a coincidence.

Poppy accepted her drink, the tea bag string still dangling over the side. "Thanks, Jay. How did you know to text us?"

Jay gave Poppy a quizzical look, licking the splash of latte off their thumb. "We talked about meeting up today? When you said you would restock my plant water."

Ru giggled at the relief on Poppy's face. She twisted in her seat. "Poppy forgot. What's plant water?"

"It's nutrient-rich water, with some other stuff in it to help their plants grow," Poppy explained. "We can stop back at the apartment and grab it now. Do you want a ride home then?"

There was a beat of hesitation. "What did you think I Saw?" Jay asked carefully.

With a raised brow, Ru looked at Poppy. She'd been more in favor of involving Jay than Poppy, thinking Jay's witch friend was their most concrete lead. Ru hadn't backed down easily. She was impatient to start their search and wouldn't tolerate Poppy dragging her feet for much longer. Not as her wards and magic had surpassed Poppy's skills too obviously for Poppy to keep pulling the older, wiser sister card. Ru was in this. She was the trick up their sleeve, ready to go into play.

Poppy nodded, and Ru happily explained their errand for the day and their search.

"You think your sister will be at this shop?" Jay asked when Ru finished.

"Probably not, but…" another glance at Poppy, this one more wary. Poppy nodded again. They were in this. "But I think I'm probably stronger than Margot. I might be able to undo the wards on her impression and get an idea of why and when she left."

Jay went so still in the back that Poppy noticed it in the rearview mirror. "Did you say Margot?"

Jay didn't say it outright, but they didn't have to. Margot was their witch friend—the unnamed tutor just out of their mentioning and always in the background. Poppy's heart raced. She loved her sisters, but Margot had always been special. It made perfect sense she would be willing to help humans with their Sight. Margot was *kind*. She was the closest mother figure Poppy had growing up.

Margot's magic wasn't strong. Her Sight wasn't much better than Poppy's. Maybe she had discovered how to strengthen her gifts as Poppy had, or in comparison to humans, witches would always know more and be able to teach. Jay knew more than Poppy about the Sight and the veil. If that came from Margot, she too had studied beyond their mother's limitations.

Their mother. Poppy's stomach dropped. If Jay knew Margot, finding her was suddenly feasible, which meant explaining that Tiff Jennings was dead and how she died. Poppy glanced at Ru. She had forgiven Colbie. Ru believed Colbie had saved Poppy's life with her actions. Would Margot feel so favorably toward Poppy's roommates? Would they ever be able to regain Margot's trust? Even after Tiff's poor decisions, the witch had been their Mother. Their coven leader. A bond nearly as demanding as that of alpha with the werewolves and maker in the vampire community. Tiff had broken that bond, but Poppy and her friends had made getting it back impossible.

Ru grabbed Poppy's wrist, tugging her hand away from her mouth and forcing her to stop biting at her nail. Poppy shot her a tight smile and placed her hands firmly back on the wheel. In the backseat, Jay was texting, looking nearly as anxious as Poppy felt about the discovery. "We can take you back to Vegan," Poppy offered.

"No. I want to come, but I don't want Margot to think I led you to her and betrayed her trust."

"Are you texting her now?" Ru asked. "You could have her call Poppy, and we won't even need to track her down."

Jay tapped their phone on their thigh. "I've been trying to message her for days now," they admitted quietly. "It's not unusual for her to go quiet for days or even weeks, but with everything happening in the city, I have been worried. Maybe this is good. I'm glad I don't have to go check on her on my own."

A chill burrowed down Poppy's spine, but Ru wasn't deterred from her optimism. "Margot hasn't gone dark when I try to See her. Her wards are still up and that means she's okay. Even if she isn't in the shop, we can leave her a message if she returns."

"Right," Poppy forced cheer into her voice. "You can stay in the car, Jay. If Margot does happen to be there, we'll explain the coincidence. We'll make sure she knows you didn't lead us to her."

Jay nodded curtly, turning to watch the city pass outside the window. Poppy and Ru shared a look before Poppy returned her attention to the road, taking the familiar route to Margot's shop and pushing aside memories of coming here with Josh during her desperate search for Topher last winter. It was still shocking how quickly things between her and Josh had picked up and lost speed twice. Still smarted to know in both instances, it had been her fault things hadn't worked out. He'd always been right. About everything. All Poppy could do was accept he didn't want to stick around while she learned from her mistakes and do better in the future. She tried not to think about him beyond that.

But losing access to Henry's pack… that had been a blow. Lana constantly compared Nora's efforts to the pack she had lost an alliance with. Poppy knew it wasn't her fault, but she still felt guilt. Before she'd sent Gus to spy on Topher, their system with the drainers had remained undiscovered. Failing, but undiscovered. Then Poppy stuck her nose in it without permission or even warning Topher, and suddenly people were dead. Her mother. Quinn. Julia. And the drainers were still out there.

It wasn't Poppy's fault, but in all those cases, she couldn't shake the sense that she could have done more. Her thoughts went to her notebook, to plants and blood and portions.

She was so caught up in theoretical brews that they were in front of Margot's shop before Poppy realized she'd parked. Ru grinned, face pressed close to her window. This place looked so different in the summertime. Vines and trees and bushes and flowers were a riot of color against an impossibly more colorful Victorian home. Margot had been shopping for storefronts before Tiff had dismantled their coven. She'd shown Poppy her options. When they'd gotten to the current address, Margot's eyes grew soft and dreamy. "There are rooms upstairs. A whole apartment set up."

Poppy had been shocked. No matter her scheming to get into UNB, she still hadn't imagined leaving home. "You want to *live* there?"

"Well…" Margot had shrugged. "At some point, children leave home, right? Even witches."

"When their Mother decides it's time," Poppy had said, but it had sounded like a question. She had never considered leaving the protection of their coven, especially not without Tiff Jennings's approval. A coven was a special thing. Few witches grew up in a complete one like theirs. How could Margot think to leave for a clever shop idea of selling fake but sometimes real magic?

But now, Poppy looked up at what Margot had built. The life she'd created outside of their coven. Had Margot made more human friends than Jay? Did Margot date? Could she explain to Poppy what had gone wrong with every romantic endeavor she embarked upon? Did Margot know enough about the world and magic to be the older sister Ru truly needed? The older sister Poppy wanted?

Poppy felt herself rising with excitement for this mission she and Ru were on. Without Tiff, could they have a better foundation for sisterhood? It had happened with Ru. Why not Margot? Maybe this was about more than uniting witches against the threats rising across the city. Maybe Poppy could be as optimistic as her younger sister and hope to rebuild her family.

The thought rang as faintly disloyal. Topher and Colbie had become a better family than the coven had ever been. But things were complicated now. So complicated.

"Shall we?" Poppy asked.

Ru nodded, though she looked a bit pale. A sudden case of nerves vanishing her smile. Poppy couldn't remember Ru and

Margot being close. Margot and Poppy had bonded over being disappointments. What would Ru, whose father stuck around longer than anyone's and who had their mother's adoration, have needed from Margot?

They stepped out of the car and walked up the brick path. While the world had bloomed to life around them, the building had the same air of disuse Poppy had felt the last time she was here. Her hopes began to crumble, at least regarding finding Margot today.

"It feels…" Ru paused, and Poppy waited with anxious breath. Through their lessons, Poppy had taught Ru to feel and listen to magic rather than just bending it to her will with the ease of snapping. She had slowed down and noticed pockets of magic or little spells nearly everywhere. Most of which Poppy herself missed. "It feels fake. Put on."

Poppy raised her brows toward the overly witchy atmosphere of the shop, including the crystal balls displayed in the window to the left.

"No, not the products. The abandonment."

"You think she's home?" Poppy asked, breath quickening.

Ru hesitated only briefly before nodding. "Either Margot's home or someone else who can cast lives here now."

Gently pushing Ru behind her and ignoring the ensuing noise of protest, Poppy stepped up to the front door. What if Margot had been here last winter? What if they had gotten so close to crossing paths, only for Poppy to fall for the spells Margot had cast to throw her off the scent? Had Margot realized Poppy came to her in need of help? Had she hidden specifically from Poppy?

Could any other witch have picked apart the spell as effortlessly as Ru? Poppy's cheeks burned as she knocked and then tried the handle.

"Maybe I was wro—" Ru cut off when the knob turned under Poppy's hand. The door swung open to reveal an empty hall.

Poppy's confidence fled, but Ru pushed past, muttering to the magic and reaching back for Poppy's hand. Poppy let herself be pulled into the house. With Ru's magic flowing into her, she could see all the impressions set to misguide other witches or humans. She could see the life of the place under the gloom and dust.

More importantly, as they came to the base of the stairs, she could hear a conversation quickly cut off. Ru threw back her shoulders. "Margot? It's Ru and Poppy. We need to talk to you!"

"Who the fuck are Ru and Poppy?" A voice upstairs asked, but Margot didn't answer. She was already at the top of the stairs, eyes blown wide with shock. Then, she was running to them. Poppy's hope shattered into reality even more sweet as Margot engulfed them in a hug.

CHAPTER 3

Topher groaned and pulled one, two, three blankets off his head. And yet, still, he felt a chill deep under his skin. He sat up, turning toward his door as it opened slowly. Oliver's worried eyes peeped out of the crack before he was pushed inside by Zayn.

Zayn didn't take on the same hushed tones and concerned eyes as everyone else. In Topher's post-sleeping draught state, the world was muted. Soft gray light and a heavy pull back toward sleep. Zayn's ability to act normal was appreciated enough for Topher to force himself awake.

"Hey." Topher's voice scratched past disuse. He cleared it, but it was so dry…

Zayn stepped firmly in front of Oliver, smile sharpening. "How has tonight been?" He never asked *how are you?* It was a shame Zayn was covering for Topher in his absence from the world and Alpha's Den. His was the easiest presence to swallow these days. But that was a selfish thought, wanting Zayn around to make Topher feel a touch of the normal.

Topher shrugged in response. He'd woken from a nightmare of shadows shoving down his throat while he was too thirsty to stop gulping them even as he couldn't breathe. Poppy must have heard something. He remembered her waking him gently and offering a sleeping draught, then nothing until Oliver knocked at his door.

"Are you sure you'll be okay?" Oliver asked. The opposite to Zayn in his visits, rare as they were with Topher refusing to feed. Oliver was in full support of Topher "taking this time." He didn't think it was Topher's new constant, which was a hopeful thought. Yet he hated that Topher was going through this at all. His eyes always careful, and the distance they had to keep hurting him.

Making the room darker with guilt. Topher couldn't get it together to be the friend Oliver deserved.

His brain took a second to parse Oliver's words. When he caught up, he nodded as enthusiastically as he could. It did nothing to ease the tension that crept into Zayn's shoulders or the poorly disguised hope in his eyes. He didn't want to leave New Brecken. Zayn's world had been Lana and the supernatural politics from too young an age. He didn't want to leave the Alpha's Den. Didn't want to be so far from Fourth and the threat of Reelings. He didn't want to leave Topher in this state.

But Topher would do anything for the chance of escape Zayn had before him, even for a few days. If he had the energy to summon, he'd ask to go with. "This trip means a lot to you, Oliver. Of course, you should go." Topher focused on Zayn. "Stop putting off meeting his parents. Go have fun."

Zayn pulled a face that he quickly flattened when Oliver glanced up. He wrapped an arm around Oliver's waist, sighing as he pressed his face into his boyfriend's neck. "Fine," he muttered into the skin there.

Oliver smiled, patting Zayn's head. "You won't even have to deal with them during the day, only the nighttime campfire fun stuff."

"*Nighttime campfire fun stuff,*" Zayn mocked Oliver's cheerful tone. Oliver rolled his eyes, but he was fighting a grin. It died when he focused back on Topher.

"You'll call us if anything changes? You know we'll drop everything and come back if you need us."

Topher tried to clear his throat again. "I know. Thank you." It was getting harder to keep his eyes open. Sleep tugged at him as he reassured them a few more times, and they reluctantly left him to his isolation. Topher fell back into the mattress as soon as his door closed behind them. He pulled the three layers of blankets back over his face.

Topher woke gasping. The dark apartment pressed in. The only light was the soft red glow from the alarm clock, and he blinked at the numbers, searching for something, anything to ground him after another nightmare. This time Julia. Dylan's laugh in the background as her hands tightened around Topher's throat.

It was only midnight. How was it only midnight? Why did it matter either way? Colbie wasn't home. Poppy and Ru were still out. Mouse made a squeak of protest as Topher pulled back the covers and stood, squeezing his eyes shut against the sweep of lightheadedness. He would only leave his room long enough to grab another sleeping draught. In the kitchen, he caught sight of the note Ru had left on the counter.

Gone witch hunting. Will hopefully be back tonight. I took your phone. Please try to feed—Roux like the sauce

Topher almost felt like smiling at the note, but, as with the last few weeks, any hint of good feeling was quickly snuffed. He sighed and grabbed the draught, stopping to pet Mouse at his food bowl before sitting back on his bed. Twirling the corked vial between his fingers, Topher tried to make himself see reason. He couldn't be sad everyone else was out in the city or on a camping trip when he couldn't get himself to leave the apartment. Topher couldn't wish for them to hide with him so that he didn't have to deal with loneliness on top of everything else. They had tried to do what he wanted. Even after he went silent under the weight of guilt for pausing their lives, too. They'd holed up with him much longer than they should have, patiently keeping him company in the darkness. Maybe they needed the quiet as much as he had at first. But they had all recovered. From Reelings. From Tiff Jennings. From Julia. From Gabriel. From Quinn. From Annaliese nearly being turned into a drainer. Standing in that circle as Topher pounded on the walls, begging this darkness inside him for access—Topher shook off the memory.

Maybe they didn't make a full recovery, but they had overcome grief and fear long enough to leave Poppy's wards. To come home laughing and find interest and talk in hushed tones about the future.

Why couldn't he? Not for the first time, Topher seriously wondered what was wrong with his mind. Nothing, nothing had ever been easy. Not middle school crushes or high school love. Not parents or siblings. Not expected losses or the ups and downs that came with human life. And definitely not being a vampire. He just… couldn't. Not right now, not yesterday, not the past week or month or however long he'd been in this state. Not since he stupidly told Reelings to fuck off and didn't bother to tell him where or how or not to come back. Because of Topher, Reelings was out there, and the only place Topher was safe was in his bed. The only place Topher was safe from the feelings was in his sleep.

Topher stared at the vial in his hand. Maybe it was an indication that he was finally getting better in that the thought of more sleep filled him with boredom. He didn't want to feed, he didn't want to leave the house, and now, his desires were so minimal he didn't even want to sleep. Maybe it was an indication that he was getting worse.

He was lifting the vial to his lips when someone knocked on the door. For a fleeting hope, Topher thought it might be Annaliese, but she hadn't been back since… well, he couldn't remember the last time he'd woken at night to her warmth beside him. There'd been an argument about feeding, about the smell of her blood being too much, but he couldn't seem to recall exactly what had brought on her silence. He couldn't bother to call her to ask what happened. It was better this way.

When the knocking sounded again, Topher realized the rapping was too soft to be Annaliese. The wards had let whoever it was this far, so it must be a friend.

Even though he had just been wishing for company, faced with the threat of it, Topher couldn't find the will to go to the door. Only when the person knocking called out did Topher find the will to stand, stumbling until the black spots cleared enough to walk normally.

"Hey, Topher? I know you're home. I was hoping we could—"

Topher yanked open the door. "Josh? What are you doing here?"

Josh's expression shuttered, and Topher regretted opening the door immediately. Josh was here for something. Something that needed Topher's *gifts*. He had nothing to offer, but Josh had spent the last weeks grieving, same as him. Topher didn't have the heart to shut the door on his withdrawn face. Josh had always been calm, easy. But now, beneath the stillness, it wasn't a content and confident sense of self. It was a tiredness that Topher recognized.

He opened the door wider and turned to go back into his room. Josh followed. Soon enough, he would understand how pointless this visit was and report Topher's uselessness to his alpha.

Maybe it was rude to climb into bed, but Topher was still so cold. He pulled up the covers like they were a proper barrier to protect his battered soul. He could guess what was coming with this conversation and didn't want to be physically uncomfortable for its duration, at the very least.

Josh waffled in the doorway. It had been weeks since Topher had seen or heard about the werewolf. He inhaled deeply, reacquainting himself with Josh's earthy scent. Pulling on the hood of his sweatshirt for an extra layer of armor and settling back into his pillows, Topher held Josh's eyes and waited. There would be a request. A demand, maybe? A message from Henry. The last thing Topher wanted to do was make an enemy of Henry's pack, but the exhaustion sat so heavy. The will to do anything, let alone get involved in supernatural politics, wasn't there.

"How long has it been since you've eaten?" Josh broke the silence. He moved into the room and perched on the foot of Topher's bed.

Topher dropped his eyes. He wove his fingers through the crochet blanket on his lap. "I don't remember." Maybe when he fed from Annaliese before they confronted Reelings. Lana brought in bagged blood, and he'd forced that down when Colbie looked too upset. He knew, like with Julia, it wasn't enough, but thus far, it had kept him from completely wasting away. He'd done it to the drainers long enough to survive on the bags when Colbie asked until something within him finally shifted for better or worse.

Josh worked his jaw, resting his elbows on his knees and looking down at his feet. "Why don't you eat? It doesn't hurt humans."

"Can we be sure of that? What are the psychological ramifications of being literally fed on? What if the positive side effects have long-term consequences? We don't know. No one has ever studied it."

Another thick silence fell. Josh rubbed his eyes. He looked nearly as exhausted as Topher. "Why are you here?" Topher asked. The sleeping draught he'd dropped onto his nightstand beckoned with promised escape. Sleep suddenly appealing yet again.

"I..." Josh paused. Shook his head. "Henry mentioned

you, and I realized how long it's been since I'd seen you out. We see everyone else going in and out of the Alpha's Den."

Topher turned to look out the window. The sky beyond was fully dark. Cloudy and threatening yet more rain.

"How long has it been since you left the apartment?" Josh asked next.

Topher shut his eyes, so tired. "I just… can't."

Josh sniffed, and the salty tang of tears reached Topher's nose. Josh was crying. Hiding the view by dropping his head into his hands. "I just can't either. I… It's so fucking hard. Everyone says it is, but no one talks about how tiring it is to grieve. How long it lasts. I thought—I don't know. I guess I thought I would be stronger. We live dangerous lives as werewolves. We knew the risk of coming to such a volatile city, yet… I see Quinn in everything. My mom had no desire to be a high-ranking pack member. She likes living on the outskirts and only shifting with the moon. My dad's a human. Quinn taught me so much about being a wolf. She was always there when Henry was busy and she made him so relaxed and happy despite all the pressure to lead. Seeing him change has almost been as hard as losing her. Everyone is on edge now…"

Topher braced, waiting for the load of Josh's grief to add to his own. Waiting for the need to comfort to sweep in and take from all the effort he was using to keep himself semi-functioning. But that didn't happen. For whatever reason, the instinct was different with Josh. It was a sharing. An unburdening. He found himself asking, "Do you think there's anything that makes it better?"

Josh shook his head in his hands. Then he took a breath and, with a final wipe of his eyes, looked at Topher. "Maybe. But I've tried hiding away long enough to know it isn't this. I feel better in wolf form. When I run, especially under the moon."

"I wish I had another form."

"Well, don't you?" Josh asked. His heat was seeping

through the blankets, weighing gently on Topher's feet. He wanted to move closer. It had been so long since he'd felt anything but empty cold.

Topher tilted his head, distantly realizing this was the most interest he'd shown in a conversation in weeks. "What do you mean?"

After a hesitation that had Topher bracing again, Josh said, "How often do you let your vampire out?" When only stillness answered, Josh kept going. "Are you miserable and feeling grief when you're feeding? When you're using your charm? When you're pushing your physical vampire body to the limits? Right now, this is about as controlled and human as you can get, and humans feel too much. Maybe you do have a release."

Topher shook his head, throat closing with the thought of letting himself fall back into the monster. Josh only watched with sympathy. He kicked off his shoes and turned on the bed, hiking up a knee and resting his chin on it. His thigh rested on top of Topher's feet, and the nausea subsided in the face of blissful warmth. "I think the other part that's supposed to help is finding a purpose. I want to make sure what happened to Quinn doesn't happen to anyone else."

More than any of Josh's previous words, this one sent a chill down Topher's spine that had him shifting. He pulled his knees up to his chest, undeserving of Josh's comforting weight. "The only way to ensure that is to take control."

"Were you not ready to do that when you confronted Reelings?"

Topher fidgeted, picking up the sleeping draught and longing to put it to use to avoid this. "I… Julia was dead. I'd killed her. Poppy was in danger, and everyone around me stepped up to help. I might be a monster, but I couldn't sit back and *let* another friend die. Even in my lowest moments, I couldn't allow that. But now, for the moment, they're all safe. Nora is building a pack and will protect Colbie. Poppy is finding her sisters, and it'll be unprecedented what a group of witches could accomplish with Poppy to lead them. Annaliese never needed or wanted protection, and she certainly doesn't now." In short, no one needed him to step up. Not really. No one needed Topher. He wasn't worth the risk.

They stared at each other for a long moment. Topher couldn't read Josh's face. He felt too raw under the werewolf's scrutiny. Like he'd said too much.

Eventually, Josh sighed. "Do you want to go on a run? That's harmless, right?"

Topher winced. He didn't get winded anymore, but getting up for the sleeping draught made his body feel sluggish and heavy. It had been too long since he'd fed to summon that amount of energy.

"He'd have to eat first," Nora said in the doorway.

Josh yelped, nearly falling off the bed as he twisted to see her. Topher was surprised neither of them had heard Nora enter, too engrossed in their conversation, but he was beyond reactions.

"How the hell did you do that?" Josh asked, panting with a hand on his chest. So dramatic. For a moment, he seemed back to his old, buoyant and borderline silly self.

Nora shrugged. "How the hell did you not hear me?"

"What are you doing here?" Josh asked as if it was strange that Nora was here and not himself.

Nora hesitated. Topher answered with a sigh. "She's checking on me. They rotate to make sure I haven't completely wasted away."

Choosing to ignore that, Nora stepped further into the room. "A run is a good idea."

"You mean feeding so I can run is a good idea."

Another Nora shrug. "Sure, but running off your guilt after doing so might be healthy."

They looked at Topher as if it made all the sense in the world, but in what other situation would two werewolves be ganging up on a vampire trying to convince him to feed on humans? It caught Topher off guard enough that he didn't fight it when Nora approached, took the sleeping draught from his hand, and tugged him to his feet. Josh followed behind them as she drew Topher from the room. "See? You're too tired to even fight this."

"I'll hurt someone." One taste of blood at this point, and he wouldn't be able to stop.

"You think Josh or I will let you drink too much?"

Topher didn't have an argument for that. His vision was going a bit funny. Nora grunted and he realized how much he was leaning on her, but he couldn't find the strength to straighten. "How do you still weigh this much?" she muttered as Topher shifted to slide on the sneakers Josh had grabbed.

This was happening. He didn't have the energy to argue or get back to bed on his own. Maybe he'd reached his limit in fighting his thirst. Maybe it was the combination of Josh's worried eyes and Nora's determined jaw. He didn't resist as they carted him out of the apartment. "I don't think I can charm anyone right now," Topher said, already mourning the loss of freedom to speak openly. But it wasn't as if he'd been talking with anyone he was at risk of charming anyway.

"We'll just ask. I've done it for Colbie," Nora said.

Topher tried to meet Josh's eyes over Nora's shoulder. He only read relief in the soft brown. Nora had swept into Topher's room like a solid storm of energy to spare. It lifted the burden of decision-making for both of them.

In little time, the super of their building was offering his neck and Topher was biting his wrist instead. He hated that he used his fangs as soon as the blood touched his brain and lifted some of the fog. When Topher could stand on his own, Nora left Josh to supervise. Just as Josh tugged Topher off the man's wrist, another human offered their hand. Blood had drenched reasoning and negative feelings. The bliss of feeding nearly the equivalent to what Topher's saliva did to humans. A slice of his nail, and Topher was drinking more. Then, from the next wrist. And the next. Blood filled Topher's veins, warmth and life nearly overwhelming after so long starving. He couldn't get enough. As long as he didn't stop, the thoughts would be held at bay. The hall on the first floor of the building was filled with giggles and sighs and Nora's commanding presence organizing it all. Doors opened and closed. Excitement filled the air as Topher's neighbors caught wind that a vampire was feeding *right there.* He caught the slight buzz of nicotine. Someone had been drinking whiskey, and it hit him right between the eyes before he quickly healed their skin and moved on.

Topher had no idea how long he fed. How many wrists were thrust at him. It was like he was refilling his deadened veins completely. Drinking to replace every skipped meal. He could practically hear his heart thundering with vitality. Then, the supply was cut off, and Topher was led out into the night by both hands. The fresh air hit his face in a wave of smells. Senses dulled for weeks were nearly too much to bear now, but as he was fed, no impulses accompanied the influx of information.

"Follow us," Josh said, voice soft. Not wary, but also not entirely trusting. When they shifted to four legs and took off into the night, Topher focused on following them. He didn't allow any other thoughts, but the competitive instincts of his vampire let loose. The shadows would smother him later, but he ran as if he could outpace them forever.

CHAPTER 4

They ran. If Nora were human right now, her grin would be smug at Josh's labored breathing behind her. The wolf, the alpha, loved the competition and the winning. Topher, being a vampire, was so *other* in this body that she didn't even care he was neck and neck, his breathing unchanged and showing no sign of slowing. She was in her human mind enough to note his face seemed to be clearing. The tightness in his brows that had been there, even in sleep, since he'd banished Reelings had finally eased. He ran like putting one foot in front of the other was all that mattered.

He ran like he understood the wolfish urge. Like the moon sang in his ears, too, pushing him forward and reveling in the strength of his limbs.

Maybe vampires weren't so different after all. Josh might be on to something.

And then, without Nora—or Josh judging from his startled yelp—noting the time, the moon retired and the first rays of sunlight reached through the branches. Topher abruptly stopped. He looked back at Josh and then crumbled with an alarming amount of bonelessness.

Josh shifted to human, crouching in the dirt. "Um…"

That was all he had to say about Topher's lifeless body collapsed among the pine needles and foliage. Nora snorted, still a wolf. She approached Topher, nudging his limp arms until Josh caught on and helped her get Topher slung across her back. When he stepped away to take in their handiwork, he laughed. "A year ago, would you ever have imagined yourself in this situation?"

Nora let out another snort and waited for Josh to shift back. They had a long trek to the road. Even further to reach the city like this. At the edge of the trees, Topher made the first sound since falling unconscious—a pained hiss that prompted Nora to dart back into the shade. She shifted quickly and began pulling Topher's hands out of his hoody while Josh waited. "I don't think we can bring him into the city like this. The sun hurts him too much." Nora remembered how red and angry his skin got through the sunlight coming in through the basement window at her childhood home. She hated thinking about that time.

Her heart squeezed, knowing Colbie was likely terrified of Topher's absence. She should have brought her phone. Should have texted to let Colbie know Topher was with her.

"I can watch him while you get a car," Josh offered.

Nora hesitated. She liked Josh. She wanted to trust Josh, but Josh had left them in this. Josh wasn't pack. He wasn't even close anymore. And Topher was in a way that was as shocking as it was unshakable. He deserved Nora's protection and Colbie's loyalty. He didn't deserve to be left in the forest with someone they formally called a friend.

Josh's expression shuttered, reading all this in Nora's face as she finished pulling off Topher's sweatshirt. Luckily, it would be big enough to cover her most important bits once she returned to the city and needed to get into the apartment, but as she freed his head and it dropped back into the dirt, Nora studied Topher's face. Helpless. Motionless. Creased brow the only hint of life. Honestly, not so different from his waking affect since he'd fallen into this fugue state of grief.

Could she leave him like this?

"He'll be fine with me," Josh said, an undertone of frustration in his voice.

"He's literally the key to saving the city, Josh. And more importantly, he's my girlfriend's brother. Abandoning him isn't something I take lightly, even if you find it insulting."

Josh glared but didn't have a response.

Nora sighed. "Where have you even been?"

It had been bothering her. A lot. Losing that connection to Henry and, therefore, the city leaders. Nora looked into the trees. What if that one conversation about building a pack had been Nora's only chance to ask about her mother? Had Topher and Lana burned that bridge when they hid the drainers? Had Poppy ruined it by not giving herself wholly to whatever she and Josh once shared? Had Nora ruined that chance by picking Topher and his people over ending the drainers?

"I…" Josh sighed, rubbing at the back of his neck. He searched for words, and Nora waited, knowing well how grief and fear could keep them hidden.

Josh never got a chance to explain. As they crouched in the shade of the trees, a car pulled into the clearing. Nora quickly donned Topher's sweatshirt, relief flooding her in a cooling wave as she recognized the small, black vehicle. Ru stepped out from the passenger's side, talking to Poppy as she did so. "I don't know what it is, but I know we should be here now."

"Well, I, for one, am thrilled you are," Nora said, stepping out of the trees. Ru's face lit with the delight of being proven correct. She looked smug as she turned back to the car.

"See? My Sight is getting better."

Poppy was stunned. Margot and Jay were stunned. Margot was justifiably more so, considering she was shocked by the appearance of two werewolves and the slumped vampire, let alone Ru's show of power.

Earlier that night, after Margot greeted them at the shop and Jay came inside with the coincidence explained, Margot had ushered them into the tearoom. She'd look continuously up the stairs, maybe waiting for whoever had been with her to make an appearance. Whoever it was had never come down. Late into the night, the four sat and talked over cups of tea. Poppy was too fearful of spooking her sister to ask who else was hiding in the apartment above the shop.

Catching up had been a long, painful process. Margot admitted that she knew when someone first came looking for her, but she hadn't been able to tell it was Poppy. "Your wards." Margot shook her head. "I've never seen anything like them. You aren't even hazy; you're like a black hole. An absence of a presence. And you taught Ru…" Margot hadn't finished the sentence. The unspoken question hanging in the air. *Can you teach me?*

Poppy explained her wards, sparing no details or tips even if they ruined their chances of finding her again should she break contact. Jay had already told Poppy their witch friend had to conserve magic to hold their wards during the full moon. Poppy would do anything to keep Margot safe from the demons and Beth.

Beth, the sorcerer. The demons. The shadows hanging over New Brecken. All of these issues edged their conversations, but Ru and Margot were smiling and so happy to be reunited that Poppy couldn't bring herself to address what had spurred Poppy to begin the search for the other Jennings witches. The threat Poppy believed they could expel through the combined strength of their magic. Through the witches stepping forward as a group that, for the most part, always valued life. The supernatural group that predominately had the bigger picture in mind and no deep-rooted enemies or hatred, only fear of exposure and being used.

Used like Poppy wanted to use them. But the outcome had to outweigh the risks. New Brecken wouldn't survive a full-out supernatural war. It wouldn't survive supernaturals at all without a proper check and balance, something only witches could monitor. Gabriel and his killing of innocent vampires proved that.

When Ru fell asleep, Margot told Poppy and Jay to stay. It was late enough that the decision was easy. Poppy only remained awake long enough to reinforce Margot's wards, wishing Nora was around to lend her strength.

Then she'd awoken to Colbie's frantic phone call. Both Nora and Topher were missing, and the apartment smelled like Josh. Poppy had been quick to defend Josh, but it wasn't until Ru woke up, looked at her tea leaves, and declared everyone was fine, but they needed to head to the national park that Colbie calmed.

Now, they sat in disbelief as Nora, dressed in only a sweat-shirt, and Jay angled Topher into the backseat of Poppy's car. They found an old blanket to cover him with as Poppy drove them back toward the city, shaking her head occasionally. Ru sat in the back, taking most of Topher's weight and checking the blanket blocked all the sun. Margot twisted to address her. "Ru. How in all that is darkness did you See two werewolves and a vampire?"

Poppy saw Ru's shrug in the rearview. "It was mostly Topher. When he and I are home alone, I practice Seeing him. He asked me if I could try to figure out how."

"What?" Poppy didn't mean for the word to come out so incredulous, nearly angry in her surprise. This had to be a recent development, which meant Topher wasn't as contained to his room as they thought. Why was Ru the one gifted with his wakefulness?

"He's not like normal vampires. You know that, Poppy. There are enough shadows twisted up in Topher that he isn't as...opaque as most vampires when I try to See him. It's almost like looking through the veil to summon a specific spirit."

Poppy didn't know Ru dappled so much in summoning, but now wasn't the time to ask about that.

"What do you mean?" Margot asked. She was only growing more bewildered as Ru talked.

Poppy and Ru shared a glance. "It's complicated," Ru said, carefully adjusting Topher's head on her shoulder and no longer looking at Margot. She wouldn't give up his secrets, not even to one of the sisters she had been desperate to find. Poppy relaxed in her seat.

"I had no idea werewolves were so fast," Jay broke the silence that fell. They were looking out the window, craning their head to keep track of Josh and Nora in their wolf forms blurring through the trees.

In the quiet, watching Josh playfully nip at Nora's heels, Poppy felt a surge of hope. Topher had left the house last night. Ru could See better than any witch Poppy had heard of. No matter what she said Topher was shrouded in, Poppy was no closer to Seeing him than she'd ever been. Poppy's understanding of magic and ability to pierce the veil would never compare, but Ru wasn't going anywhere. Nora had protected Topher and made sure he was fed, judging by the returned color and fullness to his cheeks. Josh was…back? And Margot sat taking it all in, but not looking nearly as afraid as Poppy might have thought she'd be to share a car with a vampire.

Between Ru's growing knowledge, Nora at their back, and Topher possibly making a recovery, Poppy *knew* things would finally shift for the better.

Colbie remained awake, waiting until they returned and she saw Topher safely tucked into bed. Josh said nothing, ignoring the looks and remaining in wolf form as he jumped up and curled into a tight ball at Topher's feet. Poppy felt too much seeing him there. He used to do that with her. More cuddling, but equally as protective. Now, he refused to look at Poppy. Why was he suddenly here? His reasons seemed to revolve around Topher, giving Poppy a bad feeling. Had Henry sent him? Had Josh missed Topher's flirting and power? Were the wolves attempting to pull Topher away when his bond with Lana was weakest?

Nora followed Colbie into her room, quietly telling her about the night with Josh and Topher. They'd gotten Topher to feed for the first time in… another flare of guilt accompanied Poppy not knowing. She'd been consumed with brewing and her search for witches. She thought he needed time. Colbie had said he'd acted similarly in the weeks after his being changed and Dylan's death. Poppy made him draughts and napped with him to share the warmth both her vampire roommates craved, but she hadn't thought to push him to eat. Hadn't thought to do anything but speak gently and follow his lead.

When what he needed this whole time was werewolf company and some extra assurances and protection.

After Topher fed, Nora claimed they simply went running. Poppy couldn't imagine wanting to do such a thing, but she didn't have the stamina or the senses it took to run like that and find it entertaining. Topher had been in bed for weeks, and his body probably needed it. Exercise helped human mental health. If Poppy had attempted to find solutions rather than provide comfort, she might have thought to try it.

She sighed. What's done was done. If it brought Topher back and returned Josh to their lives, Poppy would be glad for the werewolf's help.

Colbie's door shut behind her and Nora. Margot walked the perimeter of the living room, shaking her head at their photos and notes to each other while Jay rustled through the fridge. Since their apartment had become a home base of sorts, Poppy kept the food well stocked—Oliver's favorite ice cream, kombucha for Ru's latest kick, Annaliese's supply of grapes. Poppy loved the community of it. She loved having a piece of everyone here.

But, when Annaliese arrived and Nora came out of Colbie's room to greet her, Poppy realized they would need more space soon. Especially if Nora invited more of her pack, if Poppy found more witches, if Josh was truly back, and when Oliver and Zayn returned. Their group, the family they were building, kept growing, and the apartment seemed to shrink with each addition.

"Alright. First, these wards, Poppy." Margot shook her head again. She'd been doing that a lot. Her brown curls bounced and green eyes, like Poppy's, like Tiff's, alight. "Stunning. But I don't think you told me enough last night. I did most of the talking. What the fuck is going on here?" A wave of her hand encompassed Annaliese, Jay, Nora, and the vampires' shut doors.

They all shared a look. Annaliese sat forward. "You're Poppy's sister?"

Margot nodded.

"Are you at all associated with Reelings or Beth Kallow?"

Margot was startled at a human knowing those names. She bit her lip, and Poppy's heart dropped at the hesitation in Margot's eyes. "Not Beth. But her sister, yes."

Annaliese looked at Poppy. "Kallow wasn't part of Reelings's shit, right? So her other daughters should be fine?"

"Should be. But so should Beth."

"What do you mean by Reelings's shit? What are you all involved in?" Margot turned to Poppy. "Why does a human know any of this?"

Annaliese's nod was the encouragement Poppy needed to tell her sister everything. The ad in the paper that led to Poppy living in this apartment with two vampires, how they grew to be close friends, and how Topher had supported them after the Maker opened. She explained how Nora had shown up, and their lives were turned upside down by Gabriel and the appearance of drainers and demons. Nora and Annaliese jumped in then, the whole story unravelling between the three of them. Ru contributed when Poppy described the first demon attack and how the youngest Jennings had needed help after losing Jane. Margot's eyes filled to hear of Jane's death, then their suspicions that Natalie had also fallen to the sorcerer plaguing the city.

When they finally reached Reelings, Gabriel, and Beth and the standoff of last spring, Margot was sitting ramrod straight on the armchair. "Someone needs to tell Mother Kallow."

Poppy shrugged. "I don't know if she would care. We told her Beth was behind the Maker burning and the vampires being kidnapped for Nora to kill, and she refused to act."

"Killing witches throughout the city and controlling demons is very different than—" Margot cut off, noting Ru's glare.

"Killing witches and trying to kill vampires isn't different. One supernatural is not more important."

"Right," Margot conceded quickly, but they could tell in terms of crime one was still on a completely different level to their sister. "I just think Mother Kallow will feel killing witches is another issue now that we know why. Her daughters have come under attack. Are we certain it's only Beth? I can't see a witch killing her coven and the youngest Kallow, well…"

Poppy and Ru shared a glance. It wasn't so hard to fathom for Poppy, not after their mother's treatment during their last interactions. Not after breaking their coven left all her daughters deeply weakened and vulnerable during the most dangerous time the city had faced. Made even more hazardous by her determination to summon and control the demons before Beth could get to them, which led to far too many demons currently running amok throughout the streets, up for grabs.

"It wouldn't surprise us," Annaliese said, expression hard. "We've seen werewolves betray their alphas, Mothers abandon their covens, and vampires break from their makers. If we're going to make any progress as a city, it's about time each group recognizes their ties are as fallible as any other relationship. It's better to align yourself with the people who want to see the same progress you do. Are you happy with how the city is functioning currently?"

Margot lifted a brow, sitting back in the armchair and studying Annaliese. It was far too similar to the look Tiff had given Annaliese for asking questions. "And what's your solution? You are familiar with what happens to witches when we declare ourselves in their world, right?"

"You scared of a witch hunt in New Brecken? We told you it was already happening, and a former witch is leading it. You have been in hiding too long. Mother Kallow is known and respected. Poppy has faced no backlash for warding the Alpha's Den. I'm not saying it isn't without risk, but it's the same risk every exposed supernatural faces. Do you think I don't know fear as one of the few humans involved? Times have changed. Exposure is still dangerous, but the laws mean the payoff is far greater than it's ever been. It would be better to show the city you aren't all as bad as Beth."

Margot cringed. Ru nodded in silent support. Usually, Annaliese's influence on Ru was cause for concern, but now Poppy was grateful that Annaliese was here to speak eloquently for their cause.

"So what's your plan, Poppy? You came looking for me. What do you want us to do?" Margot was considering this. She wasn't running.

Fighting a smile, Poppy answered. "For now, I need help brewing. We have humans aligned with us and weaker magic at night. I've been brewing nearly constantly to build a supply of potions to help us when the time comes. To help everyone caught in the crossfire. We don't need you to declare a side or claim that you're a witch, but there's no way to tell what's to come." Then, if Poppy found she could truly trust Margot, she might ask for help with her other brew, the one not even Ru knew she was close to figuring out.

"That and you could help me try to See what is to come. Poppy isn't very good at it," Ru put in, frank enough that Poppy snorted.

Margot nodded. She glanced toward Jay. "What's your place in all this?"

Jay shrugged. "Annaliese and I are trying to get more humans informed of what's going on. Mostly, it's been kids we know from high school who are willing to hear us out, but our social media page for the Alpha's Den is getting real attention."

Nora stiffened enough for Annaliese to turn with a questioning look. Nora cleared her throat. "I also have an update on the human front. You two and Oliver aren't the only ones getting more involved."

CHAPTER 5

Nora fought against her instinct to keep the new supernatural department secret from Annaliese. Last spring, Nora and Topher had proven they could keep Annaliese safe from supernatural threats in the city, but things could have gone so differently that night. They still didn't fully understand the effects left over from the summoning circle she'd been stuck in. Annaliese's resistance to charm had given her a confidence that couldn't be healthy when dealing with vampires, but Nora also swore Annaliese squinted more in the sunlight and stayed up late more than she used to. Annaliese wore Ru's bracelets every day. Her skin shimmered faintly from the protective powder Poppy mixed into her lotion. Nora's best friend was safer than ever before. Then, there was Annaliese's continued insistence that she no longer be left out. Nora had seen how quickly she'd allowed Topher to push her away. Annaliese was tired of fighting to be let in and taken seriously. If Nora tried again, she might be dropped as quickly as the vampire sleeping in the other room.

But when would any of the protections feel like enough? Would getting involved with human assessors make Annaliese safer or lead to her sticking her nose into even more dangerous situations?

Either way, Annaliese was far too intrigued by this new branch of the city government. She and Jay ducked over Annaliese's phone, looking at their homepage and wondering if it would be helpful or just a bunch of men sticking their noses into the world they knew little about and trying to find control.

Nora interrupted their musings. "Brett Campbell is inspecting the Alpha's Den tonight. He's scheduled to arrive before Lana wakes up, so I don't think he knows much about vampires."

"Or he's trying to see the place without her influence," Poppy guessed.

Annaliese nodded. "She wants you to talk with him then?"

"Yes," Nora said.

Her reluctance made Annaliese grin. "Don't worry. I can do the talking."

Nora bounced her knee as she considered. With a sigh, Nora agreed. "That would probably be for the best."

"I can be there too," Poppy said. She glanced at her older sister, but Margot appeared undecided and said nothing.

As if confirming Nora's thoughts, Margot stood. "I need some time to process," she admitted. "Can I get a ride home?"

Ru wilted with disappointment, but Poppy was quick to agree, understanding softening her tone. Just like that, the witches left the room, Jay at their heels as Margot leaned in to talk to them quietly.

Only Annaliese and Nora remained in the living room. With the gentle morning breeze and yellow sunlight coming through the curtain, Nora felt transported back to the days after she had broken from Gabriel's pack. When it was the two of them filling quiet mornings with shared air and familiarity. Nora had been grieving and miserable during that time, but she found herself missing the simple quiet now.

Annaliese flopped back on the couch, head tilting to take Nora in. "Well, alpha, it's been a minute since I've seen you without a pack member or Colbie attached to you."

Nora fought a smile at their shared thoughts. "Yeah, sorry. It's been..." Nora didn't have the words to describe the whirlwind and balancing act that was her life lately.

"A lot?"

"A shit ton. All the Morales pack members hate Colbie and being connected with vampires. It's all I can do to keep them from blowing up at each other. Janelle is so over it. Ricky is a ball of anxiety, trying to keep everyone from fighting. He loves having a new family, but the tension is ruining it for him. Heather is too pregnant and miserable to use her energy policing Chase, Lupe, and Patrick. Lana thinks their discontent is funny, which doesn't help anything. I know they hope this alliance is temporary. That the Alpha's Den will either be mine soon when we take out Lana or that I'm going to officially challenge Gabriel and win us back the Den. They don't think my relationship with Colbie will last much longer than that, no matter what I tell them."

"Have you ever said challenging Lana or Gabriel was your intention?"

Nora rubbed at her eyes hard enough to see stars. "No. It's just what any other alpha would do. They're waiting for me to adjust to my new position. To *grow up* and start acting like other wolves. They don't understand how intentionally I made this alliance and that this is what I had in mind." Nora dropped her voice to a whisper. She felt guilt-ridden over this, yet... "Sometimes I wish they hadn't broken with Gabriel and immediately joined me. I wish we'd had time to discuss things like I did with Janelle. Even Ricky got the full story before he shifted, even if it was that same night. It's a huge honor they trusted me enough to yield to my alpha, but they aren't listening to me. They still keep thinking I'm 'little indecisive Nora.' I know

Patrick is regretting his decision. I think he only joined me because Heather did."

"What are you going to do about it?" Annaliese asked.

The question felt like too much. Her answer felt like she was letting her proactive and pragmatic friend down. "Can I complain without a solution right now? It's too overwhelming."

Annaliese's grin was unexpected. "Oh, I'm down for a whining session. How annoying has Patrick been?"

It was like a weight lifted from Nora's chest. She launched into his and Colbie's interactions, how Nora could tell Colbie was more sensitive about it than he would ever be and was turning into a completely different person around him. "She wants to be accepted. She's so social and loves having friends and being surrounded by loved ones. I think the pack appeals to her in that aspect, but they're all rude to her because she's a vampire, and they won't give her a chance."

"Maybe it's not that she's a vampire, but that she stole you away."

"And then I stole them away, but they chose it. Why can't they just lay in the bed they made?"

Annaliese laughed. "If only it were so simple."

"It's better when we're all wolves. It works so well."

"And it worked last night? You really ran with Josh and Topher?" Annaliese asked, pointing toward Topher's closed door. They could hear Josh's large wolf body snoring on the other side. And Annaliese looked… hopeful? Hurt that she wasn't in there, too? Proud? Betrayed that she wasn't who Topher called when he decided to leave his room? Too many conflicted emotions played across Annaliese's face for Nora to read them accurately.

Nora felt the urge to defend the situation and put Annaliese at ease from any hint of jealousy. "Yeah, I think Josh showed up at the right time. Topher was so hungry he couldn't get out of the apartment on his own two feet. Then, we made sure he didn't feed too much from anyone and made him run before he could feel any type of way about it." Nora shook her head. "I thought I understood vampire abilities by now, but I had no idea they had the same kind of stamina wolves did. I don't think he would have stopped if the sun hadn't dropped him."

Annaliese looked a bit sick. "He was that hungry? How long has it been?"

Nora shrugged. It had taken them a bit to realize he was lying about eating. Raven dropped off the blood bags, and occasionally, they got him to drink those, but the grief had gradually pulled him under. He'd begged to be left alone enough that it seemed pestering him to care for himself was doing more harm than good.

Was he finally on the mend? It felt like too much to hope for, but Nora saw it on everyone's face this morning—especially Colbie's tentative smile. Nora had enough conversations with Lana and Poppy that a selfish part of her was ready for him to return to the fray. To rid New Brecken of Reelings once and for all. If anyone could find the hiding maker, it was Topher.

"Anyway, I asked because it gave me the idea that Colbie might be able to run with you all. I know you said no solutions right now, but that seems like a simple first step, right?"

Nora felt her shoulders relax a bit. "Right. I like that idea. Maybe we even just start with Topher since it seemed to help him. The pack hates him more, so when they see Colbie again after, she won't seem as bad."

Annalise laughed. "We can dream."

She yawned. They were both exhausted. The summer had stretched long and tense. Days were spent sleeping more than nights with most of their active hours spent at Alpha's Den. "I might go nap with Colbie."

"I might go—" Annaliese looked at Topher's shut door, lips twisting when Josh blew air from his snout with a dream-induced, high-pitched bark. It didn't sound like a happy dream, and Nora felt for him. She understood. "—to sleep here,"

Annaliese finished, reaching for the blanket draped over the back of the couch.

"I believe this is the first step to Topher getting better, Annaliese. I really do."

She nodded, fiddling with a newly done magenta braid. "Maybe, but… it's been months since we met. Too much has happened, and I'm kind of tired of waiting. Does that sound incredibly selfish?"

"No, no, it doesn't. After what Topher's been through, it'll probably be even longer until he's ready for more with you. If you don't want to wait and know you can't rush him, maybe you…" Nora didn't finish. This conversation, though maybe realistic, did feel slightly cruel.

Annaliese nodded with a sad smile and settled back on the couch, pulling the blanket over her head. Nora felt for her friend, but there was nothing better than entering Colbie's room and shutting the door to the rest of the world. She climbed under the covers. Her heart swelled as Colbie immediately rolled and tucked herself in close. Colbie breathed Nora's name, and for a second, Nora thought she might cry from the stunning happiness one word summoned.

Poppy gritted her teeth. They sat at the Alpha's Den cocktail bar, but Nora was fidgeting so much Poppy was ready to tell her to go for a run and let her, Raven, and Annaliese deal with the assessor. They had already decided Poppy wouldn't reveal herself as a witch unless the situation demanded. Raven and Annaliese could speak for the club as humans well enough to avoid problems. All Poppy had to do was nod along.

It was a Tuesday night. Only a few couples sat at the high tables. Two girls laughed over a phone displaying a dating app at the other end of the bar. One of said girls had been coming in regularly, and there was a running bet for when Ricky would realize she was flirting with him during her visits. He was so distracted with his new life as a wolf he barely noticed her extra attention, but Poppy had seen him turn once with a confused look and check his teeth in the mirror behind the shelves of alcohol after she'd stared a beat too long. She was pretty sure that Janelle held the bet he wouldn't notice longest and kept redirecting him and leading him astray.

Janelle stood behind the bar now. She was commonly found serving the higher shelf drinks with an expertise that bordered on artistic. She had been the perfect hire and pack-mate. Whatever fate had brought Janelle into Nora's life knew precisely what it was doing. Janelle was the only pack member that Colbie felt comfortable approaching, and Colbie talked about her often enough that Poppy had hope for Colbie to make a place for herself in Nora's pack.

There was a questioning tug on the wards a second before the door opened, and Annaliese asked, "Do we think that's him?"

Poppy twisted on her barstool. "I don't think anyone else would come in here with a clipboard," she said. The three of them stood.

The human assessor was a tall, bald man with bronze skin and full sleeves of tattoos disappearing into his polo shirt. He was younger than Poppy expected, maybe in his late twenties or early thirties, but his expression was severe.

Nora wiped her palms on her jeans and approached first, sticking out a hand in greeting. Annaliese, Poppy, and Raven flanked her. Janelle and Lupe paused where they worked behind the bar, watching their alpha's back with preternatural stillness. Ricky was coming down the stairs, starting the girls at the bar whispering, but his eyes were only on the assessor. Then the door to the speakeasy opened, spilling out Chase and Patrick. Somehow, they all knew when to monitor this new person in their territory.

The human seemed unaware of all the wolf eyes on him as he shook Nora's hand, looking distinctly unimpressed.

"You must be Mr. Campbell," Nora said. She channeled Lana in her smooth, relaxed tone but not her tense posture.

"Yes, I'm here to speak with Lana Williams."

"She's still sleeping. She asked me to be here when you arrived."

One of the man's eyebrows rose. "If Lana couldn't make our meeting, she should have informed me. Or responded to the email I sent at all. I'm sorry, but I'm a very busy man. I don't have time to meet with bartenders and children."

Poppy snorted. Loudly. She couldn't help it. After everything they had dealt with, it had been a long time since she'd felt like a child. Even Nora, not yet twenty-one, seemed like a seasoned adult in their supernatural world these days. The last year had aged them all.

Annaliese matched Brett Campbell's unimpressed air. "Well, you're welcome to wait, but if you want to get to know the supernatural community in New Brecken, I wouldn't recommend blowing Nora off. I would also recommend studying vampire sleeping habits. I thought it was common knowledge, but…"

Brett Campbell blinked. "Nora? As in, Nora Morales?"

Nora crossed her arms. Her chin tipped up with a hint of pride at being recognized. Poppy fought a smirk.

"Would you have time to answer a few questions about your former pack and alpha?"

Nora looked affronted, lip curling up slightly. "I think we should stay on the topic at hand. I'll answer questions about my current pack, Alpha's Den, and our goals for the city."

Campbell sighed. "Gabriel himself has met with me. I want to make sure his stories corroborate with—"

"Would you like a tour or not?" Annaliese stepped forward, voice flat. Nora was struggling with her expression, pain blinking through.

He wasn't deterred. "You won't answer any questions about the other packs or how you gained your own pack?"

"No. I won't. Maybe someday, but I don't know anything about you or your organization. The building of trust here has to be mutual, and we aren't on an equal playing field at this moment with your presence here threatening my pack's livelihood."

Nora then took the human assessor on a monotone tour of the Alpha's Den. She explained the setup, the hours, and the clientele.

"And feedings? How often does that happen?"

Raven cleared her throat. Thus far, she'd been quietly studying Campbell, no doubt looking for motivations and tells to report to Lana. "Feedings are done willingly. No full feedings occur except in the case of a vampire who works here and only feeds on his boyfriend. We only have four vampires on staff, including Lana. Two feed from the clientele, but neither are potent enough to cause incoherence."

"And Christopher West? We know he works here under his maker."

"Topher hasn't been in the club for weeks. He's on mental health leave."

Campbell snorted. As quickly as that, Nora was tense again. She whirled. "That's funny, Mr. Campbell?"

"You expect me to believe the most potent and powerful vampire isn't using this club at his disposal? That vampires need *mental health* days?"

"Yes." Nora crossed her arms again.

Campbell waved a hand in dismissal. "Fine. Either way, I will need access to your cameras to decide whether they comply with city codes on feeding."

"We don't have security cameras," Raven said. "Like most supernatural-based clubs, we rely on wards."

"Explain." Campbell was writing rapidly on his clipboard. He didn't look happy.

With his attention diverted, Raven glanced at Poppy before

saying, "We employ witches to ward our dwellings and businesses."

"We?" Campbell looked up sharply at Raven's use of the word.

She straightened with pride. "I applied to become a vampire. As I'm sure your research into Lana has made you aware, she is suspended from making at the moment, but once she can again, I'm the first she'll turn. My application was accepted months ago."

"Why not be turned by another maker?"

Raven curled her lip. "I don't trust Solas or Patter."

"What makes Lana trustworthy? She is currently the only one with her maker status revoked."

"For standing up to the corrupt vampires on Fourth who are in the city leaders' pockets."

"Do you have proof of Solas and Patter's corrupt dealings?" Campbell asked sharply.

Raven gave a sweet smile. "Just my opinion. But we were talking about this club."

"How regularly are you fed from here?" With his question, he gestured to all the humans present, including Poppy.

"I ask to be fed from about once a week. Usually at the end of my Friday shift," Raven answered readily. "Lana does it."

"I've only been fed from once," Annaliese said.

Nora came to a standstill, barely controlling her features as she turned to her best friend. "What? Who fed from you?"

"Topher. Who else would I let do that?" Annaliese asked, eyebrow raised in challenge.

Nora clearly had as many questions as Poppy, but Campbell jumped in first. "You feel Mr. West is trustworthy? Accounts of his vampire charms are not flattering."

"He hates his power as much as anyone. I haven't met a vampire less inclined to use their abilities."

Campbell frowned doubtfully but wrote more notes on his

paper before turning to Nora. "And the wolves? You keep the vampires in line?"

"We are willing to if it comes to that, but they haven't even toed the line of our alliance."

"How many of your pack work here?"

"We all do, and the pack lives in the rooms upstairs. There are eight of us total."

"And how many witches?"

"Only one in our employment currently," Nora said. Poppy could feel how badly Nora wanted to make eye contact, but she resisted.

"I'll need to speak with her," Campbell stated like it was asking nothing. He jotted down another note.

"Witches are very private. We'll have to—"

"Your club's license is at risk," Campbell interrupted Nora with a no-nonsense tone. "We have to ensure the humans are safe. That you don't deal with the demons or unclaimed. Witches have moved into place as our top suspects regarding these monsters. I need to ensure your club isn't *corrupted*, as you say, beginning with the curses or wards placed on the building. The fact that I haven't found a single witch willing to speak with me only raises my suspicions."

They all tensed. Words floated in Poppy's head. They suspected witches were behind the monsters in the city now. They were looking into witches. Looking into witches. *Witch hunt.*

"Maybe you haven't found a witch because they're hiding from the demons more than anyone. Because they need protection too, and we will provide that for our witch friend." Annaliese broke the quiet.

Poppy wanted to hug her. They all waited, watching Campbell intently. His brown eyes took in the space. The humans at ease. The werewolves at attention. A group stumbled out of the speakeasy door, giggling and making plans to go to Hill's Brewing next. They asked Chase to escort them, something the humans had quickly learned the wolves were willing to do. Even Henry's pack was becoming recognizable, walking the streets and keeping the humans safe when asked.

There was nothing here that wouldn't pass inspection.

"Well, I'll expect at least a phone call with the witch and a meeting with Lana. There will be further inspections, but we can start with cameras—"

"The footage could get tampered with."

"Not without leaving a trace." He looked down at Annaliese, but as ever, she stood with a confidence that made her small stature vanish. "The vampires have their bliss and charm, the witches have their magic, the werewolves have their strength and numbers, but humans have our technology. It evens the playing field more than anyone gives us credit for."

"Maybe, but everyone can learn to use a computer."

Campbell shook his head. "They don't. Never met a tech-savvy supernatural. It's not a biological imperative to gain power with technology. They depend almost entirely on instincts, magic, and animal desires."

Annaliese made a disgusted face. "Let's not talk about biological imperatives. We've evolved, all of us. We can live together and find peace without trying to determine what's right or natural or how to strip people of power to feel powerful ourselves, don't you think?"

"That would be nice, but—"

"But that's the goal of your branch, right? Or are you just a group of humans trying to compete with people you don't understand? That you're not trying to understand aside from threat levels?"

Campbell studied Annaliese. "That is… an interesting take. Do you work here?"

"Sometimes. Mostly, I care about my friends here. Supernatural and otherwise."

Campbell reached into his back pocket. "We could use a voice with your… more *hopeful* perspective." He handed

Annaliese a card, then Raven and Nora. "Tell Lana she has two days to get her cameras up and running. I'll be waiting for updates."

Nora and Raven both looked unhappy, but they nodded.

He turned back to Annaliese. "I hope you'll be in touch…"

"Annaliese."

"Annaliese," he said like he was agreeing. They shook hands. "For the moment, nothing looks amiss."

"Great," Nora and Raven bit the word out simultaneously.

Campbell's eyes swept over them. He'd softened after Annaliese's tongue-lashing. "For what it's worth, I am impressed by what's being attempted here. If the goal is truly as Lana implies, it seems like a business of a better future."

And with that, he swept out. Poppy studied each of her friends' faces. No one seemed more affected than Annaliese, staring at the business card in her hands and mouthing *New Brecken Supernatural Mediation.*

"Are you going to answer that?"

Josh's voice startled Topher awake. He gasped, jolting upright, then flinching away from Josh's too-close face and smacking into the wall. Instant concern crowded Josh's features. He reached to grab Topher's arm but thought better of it. "Sorry. I thought you were awake."

Topher clutched his chest. It was too human a reaction. It only reminded him his breath didn't heave in moments like this anymore. His heart didn't pound. He dropped his eyes to his ringing phone. He'd grown so used to ignoring Lana's calls that it didn't wake him anymore.

"No. I'm not going to answer it. That's Lana's ringtone."

Topher dropped back into his bed, pulling the blankets, still warm and smell of Josh and the forest, over his head. Even in the darkness, he found the image of Josh sitting in his bed, wearing Topher's clothes, looking sleep-ruffled and better than he had last night, remained imprinted on his vision.

"You were getting lots of text, too," Josh said.

Topher grunted. Why didn't Ru have his phone? This was why he preferred it in her hands. She jokingly called herself his secretary in exchange for access to the social media accounts she'd set up and tutorials she watched.

"Should I check them? It might be important."

"If you want to," Topher grumbled, and he rolled toward the wall, cocooning himself tighter in the blankets.

The fog had cleared with the feeding last night. The high of human blood and running through the trees left him bereft. There wasn't anything here but Josh's presence and Julia's absence. Listening for breathing and heartbeats, the rest of the apartment was empty. Why was Josh still here?

"There's a new governing branch in the city," Josh said, voice lifted in surprise. "Lana said a member went by the Alpha's Den today to do an inspection. Henry mentioned this guy—I think he's coming to our apartments soon, too, but Henry wasn't worried. He appears to fall among the humans who support werewolves. Lana wants you to discuss it all at a team meeting after closing tonight."

Topher wished he was unfed and unfeeling. He wished the heaviness of responsibility wasn't pressing down. Josh had shown up and gotten Topher out of bed and now the real world was knocking on his door again. Josh was still talking, reading Colbie's reaction and Nora's assurances.

He couldn't. He just couldn't. His grip on the blankets at the base of his throat made his voice sound strangled when he whispered, "Josh. Will you please leave?"

Josh fell silent. Topher pulled the blanket tighter around his head. The sound of a sigh, but Josh didn't move. "Did last night help at all, Topher?"

Topher didn't answer. He heard the disappointment in Josh's words. He had thought himself brimming, overflowing, and incapable of more emotion. Now, he felt guilty, too. Josh was only trying to help. How to tell him that feeding made the feelings stronger? Only reminded him of what he was? Because now that he'd recently fed, all he wanted was more. His charm was dancing beneath his skin, begging for release. Vampire instinct and foreign desires urged him to leave bed. To hunt anyone that wronged him. To go to the Alpha's Den and ensure Lana didn't mess this up. To act. To gain power.

Josh wasn't leaving. He waited for an answer. "It helped in the moment," Topher conceded. But now he felt worse than he had upon waking last night.

"We can go run again tonight if you want to." Josh waited a beat, then, more softly, "Or we can stay here." *But I'm not leaving either way.* The words unspoken and calming. Topher's grip loosened on the blankets.

Topher considered. It meant no talking. No feeling once his muscles began to burn again. It meant new smells that weren't human. Trails and shadows that didn't hold unpleasant memories. He sat up, waiting for the lightheadedness, but it didn't come. He'd drunk his weakness away.

"There's food in the kitchen," Topher said. "You should eat before we go."

Josh shook his head. When had he become stubborn? "We'll go after we both eat." He left the room before Topher could argue.

CHAPTER 6

Topher's absence was keenly felt when they met after closing that night. Lana was unhappy, Colbie solemn, Poppy biting a thumbnail, Annaliese scowling, and the pack kept exchanging looks. No one panicked over his being gone, but no one told Lana that this was because Josh had texted Nora. He was with Topher again in the forest.

Nora recalled Topher's face last night while they ran and found herself glad for it. While they needed him and wanted him here for this, it wouldn't do anyone good to force Topher back into the city before he was ready. So far nothing had helped as much as Josh. Nora resisted texting Josh back to ask if he'd gotten Topher to feed two nights in a row. She'd decided it wasn't her business and Josh's focus should remain on Topher, but it would be a relief to know and be able to tell Colbie.

They were all upstairs in the conference room of the Alpha's Den. Poppy and Colbie looked lonely without Topher, Zayn, or Oliver on their side of the table. The pack was still too tense in their company, although Janelle tossed Colbie a note that made her snort upon reading it. Chase sent a glare down the table at the sound, Heather elbowed him in the ribs,

Annaliese rolled her eyes across from him, and Nora tried to swallow the sense of hopelessness that most of her pack and the vampires would never get along.

Lana was still talking. The humans in attendance were exhausted after the unexpectedly busy Tuesday night, yet somehow, Human Josh, Iris, and Mik appeared the most stressed about Lana's news of the inspection and interviews. Mik went so far as to protest, the first words of dissent Nora had heard one of them voice. Nora was only scratching the surface in her knowledge of what working on Fourth Street had been like for the three humans, but she knew they were committed to Lana for offering them jobs and a home after the chaos Grace's death caused in his former club, Happenstance.

Annaliese had done most of the talking when they updated everyone about passing the first steps of the inspection. Lana seemed content with how it had gone but went over important activities they should avoid when the cameras were up and inspections occurred. Most of her points were so obvious that Nora knew she wasn't the only one tuning Lana out. When she mentioned keeping Poppy's identity secret, Colbie's eyes glazed over so severely that the slight cross-eye she got when she fed on too many drunk humans made an appearance. Nora glanced nervously at her pack. It looked as if they were paying attention and she knew they would do what Lana said when Nora backed her orders, but how many of them wanted to see the Alpha's Den closed? How specific should her commands be? Were they grateful enough to have jobs and board to stay loyal to Lana? A lie during an inspection would be the easiest way for them to remove the vampires from their lives. Nora had never seen anyone at Alpha's Den step out of line. If anyone were to come close to inappropriate behavior, it would be Lana. But Colbie fed as often as the maker. To judge Lana would be to condemn Colbie, and Nora had never seen either vampire approach an unwilling human or take more than two swallows of blood at a time. Neither of their saliva was potent.

Nora had spent a couple of weeks watching humans after Colbie fed. Within fifteen minutes, her victims were clear-eyed and searching for more drinks because Colbie had taken the edge of their drunkenness that quickly. Nora had never spotted any harmful side effects. Not from Oliver or the three human bartenders. They regularly requested to be fed off of and never seemed any worse for wear when they did or didn't get blissed. Nora wasn't sure if things had been different on Fourth Street to make the three of them seem so haggard when they first began working here, but from the vampires of Alpha's Den, Nora had never seen any harm inflicted.

Were her pack members similarly assured after working here for weeks? They might not like Colbie, but did they hate vampires as much as they had under Gabriel's thumb? Nora needed to find out before it was too late.

Once Lana had given her expectations and told them where the cameras would be placed, she concluded the meeting.

"My pack, stay behind," Nora said, voice practiced and steady despite her nerves. She and her pack didn't talk vampires, and she was terrified. The subject was so touchy they somehow got around it for weeks. Even when her pack complained about Colbie, her supernatural affiliation was never explicitly mentioned. The pack knew Nora's stance and held all the boundaries she'd set but preferred to act like the vampires around them didn't exist. They were all so busy and simply happy to be together during downtime. Or they were running as wolves, where Nora ruled with only snarls, barks, and snaps of her jaws if needed.

Life was much more straightforward on four legs.

There wasn't even a grumble at being asked to stay up later. The only reaction came when Colbie paused by Nora's side at the head of the room long enough to kiss goodnight. Even then, Nora probably wouldn't have noticed how Chase, Lupe, and Patrick stiffened if she hadn't been looking for it.

Colbie winked when they separated and slipped out the door, but Nora hated her stiff shoulders.

It was enough to bolster Nora's resolve as she turned to address her pack. She wasn't only doing this to ensure the Alpha's Den stayed open. She needed her family to stand behind her. She needed their love and support. She needed them to accept Nora's choices and to give Colbie a chance. Nora had explained it all when they first became a pack, but clearly, they didn't get it. They didn't understand who and what Colbie was. They thought Colbie was getting in the way of Nora acting like a true alpha when Colbie was the only reason Nora had accepted the title in the first place.

"We haven't done a check-in in a while," Nora began, trying to find the right words. They were eluding her, so she took a deep breath and continued without thinking them through, hoping instinct would guide her correctly. "I want to know how everyone is feeling about working and living here."

There was a moment of quiet, and then Ricky raised his hand. Chase laughed at the action, and Nora fought a smile. She felt like a high school teacher as she nodded for Ricky to speak. "I like it," was all he said, and he joined in the laughter his simple words spurred.

A tension fell immediately back over the pack once the laughter died. Nora's heart dropped as she waited for someone, anyone else, to speak up. She made the mistake of glancing at Janelle and found pity on the girl's face. Janelle knew what Nora wanted, and she must understand better than Nora how far the pack was from that goal.

"Is it so awful?" she asked, voice quieter than an alpha should be. "Living with them?"

Shifting along the table. It was Heather who sighed. She placed a hand on her protruding stomach and turned in her chair to face Nora. "I think we're wondering, is this the end goal?"

"What do you mean?" Nora asked. She had a feeling she knew.

"You challenged Gabriel," Patrick said. "I thought the pack would stay together when you were so obviously stronger than him. I thought you were going to take your place as your father's heir. When I broke from Gabriel, I expected everyone to. That's not on you, but you *could* have brought them along. You should have broken all the ties and taken Gabriel's place. We don't work split like this."

Nora's heart was pounding up in her throat. Her body rejected Patrick's words, but she couldn't say why yet, not with everything in her reacting in a cringe away from his disappointment. "So it's not about Colbie?"

Patrick's eyes dropped. It was about Colbie, too.

"We just…we need an alpha," Lupe said too gently.

Nora flushed with swift and sudden anger. Her hands balled into fists and she looked Lupe in the eyes. "If Gabriel had fallen in love with Colbie, how would you have reacted?"

Silence. Nora realized she'd never said she loved Colbie to them, had never admitted her feelings ran so deep.

"Gabriel wouldn't, though," Lupe tried. She was still speaking so carefully.

"If Gabriel was gay, how would you have reacted?"

"That *isn't* the problem, Nora," Chase said.

"A real alpha finds a mate, though, right? A real alpha contributes to the pack with their mate. A real alpha sticks to tradition. A real alpha kills vampires." This was all about Colbie. "You saw me with her before you accepted my bonds, but maybe you didn't realize how important she was. Maybe you didn't realize how important progress was to me."

"Is it so awful?" Patrick asked, throwing Nora's previous question back at her. "Tradition?"

"*Yes.*" Nora's answer was fast and vehement. Patrick blinked. "I grew up thinking the highest I could ever go was a beta. Was being Gabriel's mate. When he ordered me, I pretended I could submit. When he touched me, I convinced myself I liked it. It wasn't until Colbie touched me that I understood freedom and attraction. I made myself small for Gabriel and Matt told me I still wasn't acting small enough. We still don't know what Gabriel is planning because I let them push me out of the pack my father made. *Tradition* led to Gabriel aligning with Reelings. To what end, I don't know, but the laws have helped us. They have enabled me to figure out who I am and what I'm capable of. The laws, Colbie, and Annaliese are the only reasons I'm happy and functioning. Tradition kept me afraid and powerless. Hanging onto it will do the same to you. But, if you regret your choices, I can live without the past."

Henry had never told her it was possible, but Nora found her ties to the people around the table and let the knots weaken. It was easy—her knowledge of how to control her pack bonds innate and simple. Everyone gasped. Ricky shook his head quickly, and she felt him pull the thread, tightening the knot again immediately. After a moment, Janelle did the same, brows furrowed in concentration. Heather next. Nora narrowed her eyes at Patrick. "If you accept me again only because of Heather, we *will* have problems."

He hesitated, glancing at his mate and then dropping his eyes to the table. Thinking. Heather's eyes widened with horror, glancing between him and Nora. Maybe she hadn't realized his discontent ran so deep. Nora only crossed her arms and waited, the loosened bonds wavering like ropes in the wind between them. She felt them so acutely that she could practically see them. A different shade and texture for every wolf, all created of her power and hold, but also her love. She didn't want to lose her family again. She desperately wanted them to choose her.

Their shoulders relaxed as if feeling the sentiment. Patrick looked up first. "What did you mean when you said Gabriel touched you?"

Nora swallowed. "I wanted to be his beta. To have power like my parents did. I never imagined I could be like my dad, so I thought I would be like my mom. I just… wanted a true place in the pack. I wanted the standing to act and make them proud. I thought the only way to do that was to be his mate. When Matt found out, he was so cruel. And then, after they took Topher, and Colbie ended things for not telling her, I went to Gabriel, and he…" When had the memories of this night become something Nora feared? She'd been so out of touch with what she wanted, with her very body, that now that she was fully inside of herself, her breathing hitched. Her hands began sweating, thinking of the kisses, the gripping, the feel of her parent's room, and memories crowding in so that only her tensing and squeezing her eyes shut had stilled Gabriel. She should have said something to stop it sooner, but words had been so difficult back then, even worse than now. "He said he would take me as his mate. He said after I killed a vampire, he would let me into the pack and make me his beta. Then, he chose Colbie as one of the vampires I would have to kill. It took me too long to accept, but in my core, I knew long before that moment that Gabriel's version of a pack wasn't something I was interested in, but it took him putting Colbie in danger for me to fully realize how wrong he was."

"But he didn't know you loved Colbie, did he?" Lupe asked.

"Matt knew. Maybe not that I loved her, but he knew I was friends with them. But even then, after all these weeks of living amongst the vampires, of getting to know Zayn and Colbie and Oliver, do you really think anything justifies Gabriel sending me to kill a bunch of innocent people to be *allowed* into my father's pack?" Nora didn't wait for their answer. "Colbie never feeds long enough to hurt. Zayn doesn't feed from anyone but Oliver, who I know has explained to all of you the benefits he's enjoyed through the relationship. But also, the moment Gabriel sent me down those stairs and I saw Colbie, I knew he wasn't the alpha of my father's pack anymore. He wasn't living within the bounds of my father's memory. He'd created something different and dark. And now, I know my father was in support of the laws. He was planning to stop the initiation process, a process even Henry finds monstrous, by the way. I *am* the Morales pack now. I'm leading in a way my father would be proud of. Upholding memory and tradition of good, kind, but powerful leaders. Now, fucking *choose.*"

Nora was careful not to back the order with the alpha, but the bonds hanging between her and her pack still snapped to attention at her sharp words. Patrick's hands fisted on the table, and Chase's jaw clenched. Lupe looked pale, but she straightened, and with the motion, the bond between them went taut. Slowly, one by one, Nora relaxed as the bonds solidified once more. She softened her voice. "I *believe* in what I'm doing here. Maybe not in Lana, but I love Colbie. I liked Topher even before I was certain of his sister. I trust Poppy and Zayn and Oliver. They've all been kinder to me than Matt or Gabriel ever were. They made space for Annaliese when Gabriel told me I had to let her go. I like being an alpha, and I'm desperate for you all to accept me in that role, but if it gets too much, or you hate what I'm working for, I'll do that again for you. I won't keep you here against your will. I have no idea what's going to happen, but it'll likely be violent and messy and scary. If you change your minds, I won't hold you to any decision made when you realized Gabriel's betrayal or tonight."

"Fuck Gabriel," Patrick bit out. Nora realized the clenched fists weren't due to anger toward her, but what she'd confessed happened with his former alpha. She blinked rapidly, not wanting to cry right when they had resubmitted to her strength.

Nora nodded and then motioned for them to get up. "That's enough for tonight. Let me know when you have questions. And I think we're due for a run tomorrow. I'll tell Lana to make sure the schedule allows it."

There were cheers but a muffled version of the pack's usual exuberance. Somehow, the tempered reaction felt all the more authentic.

"Nora, wait!"

Nora turned. She'd been texting Colbie, seeing if her girlfriend was home and if Nora could join her to sleep this morning. She thought the pack likely needed time to talk and process away from her. Janelle would tell her later what they discussed without Nora nearby. "Hey, Lupe, what's up?"

Lupe waited for the rest of the pack to pass on the way to their rooms. Lupe was fifteen years older than Nora. She was a "cousin" in that she was her father's cousin's daughter from her first marriage. Lupe had come to live with the pack when she was eight. Her mother remarried, and Lupe showed signs that she wasn't entirely human. Lupe's mother and stepfather rejected her and sent her to live with Nora's father and Tio Marcus.

Lupe had embraced pack life, changing her name from Penelope to Lupe to fully step into her new identity. Nora had always respected it, but Lupe hadn't given Nora much time when she was growing up. Heather once told Nora that Lupe was jealous and would grow out of it. She'd been one of her father's most loyal members. It hadn't been a surprise she was one of the first to grab Nora's tethers when Gabriel's hold loosened, but it also wasn't a surprise that she was resistant to the lifestyle Nora modeled.

"I wanted to come clean about something," Lupe said, eyes downcast.

Nora's shoulders tightened, but she nodded, inviting Lupe to continue.

"I've been texting Marcus. He isn't sure he made the right choice and is asking about you. I haven't told him anything about the club or Colbie, but I kind of think I should. He would pick you if he had another chance. I didn't realize you had so much control over the bonds. It was you who loosened them with Gabriel that night, wasn't it? Maybe you could help him? At least hear him out? I think he stayed with Gabriel for reasons beyond loyalty. He cares about the Den and all the other members of your father's pack. He didn't want to leave *them*."

"He told you that?"

"Not in so many words. He's careful with his texts."

"Alright." Nora tried to think about this logically, but the hope that her uncle could still care and be willing to talk with her was sweet. She missed him. She missed everyone who stayed behind, even Adriana. "Make a plan to meet him, but don't tell him I'll join in case Gabriel sees the message."

"When?"

Nora was tempted to give a time late enough in the day to bring Colbie for support, but she resisted. There were some things she would need to do alone now—though she would probably bring Annaliese. Tio Marcus always loved her, and it was hard to break old habits. The plan was set to meet around noon the next day.

Colbie still hadn't answered by the time they were done planning, so when Nora left the Alpha's Den, she turned herself south toward her and Annaliese's apartment. It was closer to jog there, and Nora couldn't remember the last time she'd slept in her own bed. She hated the thought, but it might be time she and Annaliese talked about finding someone to take over their lease. Or at least Nora's half.

She and Annaliese hadn't exactly drifted apart since Nora made her pack, but there wasn't the desperation behind their time together that there once was. For years, Annaliese had been Nora's only friend outside the Den, and Nora was Annaliese's only close friend, period. Now, Annaliese hung out regularly with Oliver, Jay, and Poppy during the day. She even had coffee with Molly once a week. She came by the Alpha's

Den to hang out with the pack and often spent nights dancing with Colbie. She and Nora weren't attached at the hip anymore. It felt mutual and, if she was being honest with herself, healthier, but there were times when Nora missed the simplicity of only having one person to be held accountable to.

Nora entered the apartment and found Annaliese still awake. She was eating some leftover Thai food at the kitchen island. Brett Campbell's business card face up next to her plate.

Nora leaned a hip against the stone counter and tried to make her voice nonchalant. "So… you let Topher feed from you?"

Annaliese snorted, a smirk lingering on her lips. "Is it driving you crazy to know I let myself get blissed?"

"Yes, yes, it is."

"You're handling it much better than I expected," Annaliese said.

"I… I guess it would be a bit hypocritical for me to freak out. I hate that he fed from you but," Nora winced, "when Colbie and I kiss—"

Annaliese's eyes widened. "Nora! You get blissed? Regularly?"

"It's not as potent as being fed from!" Nora said, too defensive. Annaliese was laughing now, covering her mouth to keep from spraying rice on the counter. "But, yes," Nora admitted, disgruntled. "There is a high."

Annaliese rolled her eyes. "I can't believe you've made such a big deal out of me being fed from when you're casually—"

"It isn't casual!"

"Alright, seriously and intentionally letting yourself get blissed on the regular."

"Whatever." Nora waved a hand as if she could clear her past judgment and Annaliese's amusement from the air. "Just know you have to be careful, letting them feed from you."

"Right. I wouldn't want to end up like Oliver or Raven.

Never getting sick and fully functional and way less stressed about life."

"Or like Julia," Nora added, though she felt like an asshole as soon as the words left her mouth. "Especially with Topher, you have to be careful."

Annaliese's amusement fled. Nora was relieved when her friend nodded, looking down and fidgeting with her chopsticks. "I *will* be careful. I wouldn't want to do that to him. But I am excited about this." She touched a finger to the card. "What do you think?"

Like Annaliese's meetings with the other humans associated with the supernaturals, it seemed like a better option than anything else she could be doing to get involved with the supernatural community here. "I don't trust him, but humans should have a bigger place in supernatural discussions. I think they've earned that right and, being the majority, they should have a say in how their city is run. It seems like a position that could be targeted first if things take a turn for the worst, but I also think you'd be good at it."

Annaliese smiled. Nora was getting better and better at saying the right things. "I think you're right. It'll be good to have something new to focus on." Her dark eyes turned sad.

This prompted Nora to say, "Topher went running with Josh again. It's a good sign that he's getting out of the house."

"And yet I still haven't heard from him." Annaliese stood. "I'm going to bed now and only thinking about things I will be doing for myself to give me purpose and happiness."

Nora smiled. "And I'm going to finish your curry."

"I figured."

CHAPTER 7

Margot called. After the silence since dropping her off at the shop, Poppy and Ru had nearly given up hope. Ru was certain it was their living situation that had chased Margot off. Poppy thought she might be right. When they'd dropped off Margot and walked her to her door, Margot had stopped Poppy with a hand on her arm. "Are you sure you know what you're doing? Letting Ru run around? Living with *vampires*?"

Poppy hadn't been able to answer. She didn't know what she was doing. Hadn't known since Tiff Jennings broke their coven's wards. But her confusion and the feeling of flying by the seat of her pants for the last year did not mean she was wrong. In fact, after everything, her friendships were the only thing she felt sure about in her life.

But the doubt and worry in Margot's eyes had been deep enough for Poppy to falter. She'd nodded once and pulled out of reach, following a dancing Ru to their car. Ru had been so excited to have another sister back, but since then…nothing.

Poppy carefully eased out of bed, careful not to jostle Ru. If Margot was calling to say she didn't want to reconnect further, Poppy would have to figure out a way to break it to their little sister. The living room was calm, cast in morning shadows. There was still movement behind Colbie's door, but she wouldn't stay awake for much longer. It was dead quiet in Topher's room. Was Josh there? So close, yet still as far away as he could get from Poppy?

Focusing on the task at hand, Poppy answered her phone with a tentative, "Margot?"

"Hey, Poppy." It was so bizarre how Poppy had gone from hearing Margot's voice every day for years to finding it unfamiliar and jarring over the phone. "Is it a good time to talk?"

"Sure, what's up?" Poppy lifted her thumbnail to her mouth, already bracing for the worst.

"I… I have another friend. A witch friend."

"Okay?"

"We were talking and she told me she knows about Topher. Or, she's heard of Lana and what his maker wants for the city."

Poppy swallowed. She knew what getting into business with Lana would mean, but her cheeks heated at her sister knowing about Poppy's association with the maker. They hadn't spoken about Lana, but Topher's name was known enough for Margot's friend to have made the connection.

"Poppy, the wards around Alpha's Den, was that you?"

"Yes."

"Without Ru's help?"

"I didn't want her traced."

"Poppy, those wards are incredible. Jay asked me to check them out when you first put them up. My friend and I went by one morning when no one was around. Neither of us has felt any magic so layered and intentional."

"I had a lot of help. Werewolf power and my plants and brewing."

"You did all that without casting like Mother taught." It wasn't a question, just a statement full of wonder. Poppy squirmed. This wasn't something she was used to. Praise from a fellow witch. Her roommates, yes. Her little sister, sure. But an elder witch? Poppy felt herself rejecting the compliment, wanting to explain how the wards weren't that complicated and assure Margot it was all Nora's brute strength behind the magic's power.

Poppy resisted the urge, leaving Margot to fill the quiet. "It's incredible, Poppy. I think it might even be safe enough to risk meeting regularly."

"You'll come see us there?"

Now Margot's tone shifted into that of an older sister. "You let Ru hang out at a club?"

Poppy laughed. "Not often, but sometimes it's safer than leaving her alone, and she can't hide here all the time. The rooms upstairs are apartments, and the top floor is always empty when Lana's awake. Ru likes being up there to study and hang out with anyone not on shift."

"Study?"

"To get her GSE. She wants a high school diploma."

Maybe more, but those hesitant conversations about going to college had fizzled when Josh cut off Poppy and Ru lost contact with Daniel and his plans to enroll in UNB openly as a werewolf.

"Like you," Margot said, and Poppy couldn't read her sister's tone to know if Margot thought this was a good or bad thing.

"Yeah." Poppy winced. She'd ripped off a hangnail. Popping her bleeding thumb into her mouth, Poppy scrambled to think of what to say. "So, you'll come to the Alpha's Den, then? When?"

"Can we meet you there tonight?"

"Yeah. I'm not on the schedule, so we can talk." Despite her trepidations, Poppy's heart raced with excitement. She wanted to show Margot her club. Wanted her older sister to see this world she had discovered, full of friends and brimming with life and dancing. Poppy looked to Topher's door. Would he leave his room if she asked him to come and meet Margot?

Then, Poppy remembered how this conversation started. "Your witch friend will be with you? Why is she interested in Lana? In Topher?" Poppy's protective instincts came to attention. Somehow, most people didn't seem to have heard of Topher's interaction with Reelings. Gabriel, for good reason, hadn't come clean to the other city leaders about his betrayals, and Beth had gone into hiding so deep they struggled to find even the remnants of her summoning circles. Until Reelings forced everyone's hand, they were at a standstill, no one wanting to expose their power or associations.

"My friend is, ah, interested in getting involved in supernatural politics. In learning what's been happening in New Brecken to put all the witches in hiding. Her mother has stepped back quite a lot, and she isn't ready to do the same."

Poppy smirked. "Would she be a daughter of Mother Kallow?" The witch had dropped out of the race for city major and hadn't been heard from since. With witches dying more than any other supernatural group, Mother Kallow had pulled in her daughters and wards. She hadn't accepted a single call from Lana.

Margot went quiet for a beat before clearing her throat and admitting, "Yes, she is."

"Which one?"

"I won't say more than that over the phone."

"But Topher might already know her. He said Mother Kallow would attend leader meetings with her daughters."

Another beat. "She did?"

So, Margot didn't know this friend all that well. Or the friend was keeping secrets. Poppy didn't like it. "I won't let her in if she's up to something involving Topher."

"She's not. She wants to see the club, ask a couple questions. I promise, nothing weird."

How quickly they had gone from Poppy searching Margot out and hoping to be let in to Margot asking to be allowed into Poppy's life. Maybe she hadn't thought all this through. Poppy hesitated, but a glance toward her room and Ru's sleeping face decided her. "You can come by tonight, but I doubt Topher will be there. You can meet everyone else."

"That's… fair. Thank you. I'm excited to see you again."

Poppy nodded. Her "you too" sounded forced. She wanted to see her sisters, to build a community of witches to have at her back, and to help her finalize and then distribute this brew she was working on, but she wasn't sure about meshing that group with her friends.

The look was fleeting, but Tio Marcus didn't seem especially pleased when Nora and Annaliese crashed his lunch with Lupe. Maybe Nora had only imagined it. When he stood with his arms open, the smile that split his face was as familiar as the taste of Nora's father's carne asada in the Den's backyard. Drizzled with extra lime, just for Nora, it was the taste of home and childhood memories and games and squealing laughter. She fell into Tio Marcus's arms and willed herself not to cry.

Tio Marcus stepped back first, holding Nora at arm's length. "Look at you, mija. I can't believe it. Your energy… it feels like Luis's."

That set Nora blinking again. People had said she was powerful, but thus far, few had compared her to her father and his strength. Few of the people she spent time around had even met her father. "Thanks. How are you?"

Tio Marcus shrugged, his smile dimming. "Maybe we should sit down first."

They all took their seats. They were closer to the Den's side of town at a small sandwich shop Tio Marcus had frequented for years. Annaliese went to the counter to order for her and Nora, giving the werewolves a moment alone.

"Things are… they aren't great. A lot of infighting. Gabriel still won't tell us all that he's up to, only that we need to trust him. I never doubted he had New Brecken's best interests at heart, but I don't know that he's going about it the right way."

"How could you stay with him, Tio?" Nora couldn't stop the question. "After learning what he did to my dad?"

"I—" Tio Marcus paused, glancing around the shop and sniffing the air. The hair on Nora's arms rose. "I knew you would need someone. Someone to keep an eye on him."

The breath left Nora's lungs in a rush. "You stayed behind to spy on him for me?"

"I didn't know what else to do! Lupe was the only one who would answer my messages, but I had to reach out. That *bruja*, *sorcerer*, Beth comes by the Den far too much. Whenever we ask about the unclaimed, they insist the people they work with now are all willing, and no one innocent is getting hurt. And there haven't been as many attacks. They say," he dropped his voice and switched to Spanish, an extra step to keep any listening ears in the dark. Nora's concentration strained in a way that made her heart sink. How long had it been since she'd had a conversation in Spanish? "They say the only way to stop Reelings is to keep working with him for now. Gabriel will only tell us his goal is to shut down vampire clubs and stop vampires from feeding on humans."

Nora winced. Her tongue tripped over itself as she asked, "Does he plan to kill them all then?"

She was grateful that Lupe and Tio Marcus pretended not to notice her stumbling accent. "Not kill them all, but there are too many. It shouldn't be so easy for vampires to build their numbers and feed. It isn't the natural order."

"In your opinion or Gabriel's?"

Tio Marcus raised his hands. "Gabriel's, I swear. Your father and I helped dream up the laws together. *I* think they've been working and helping the city."

"Then why are you still with Gabriel?" She didn't need a spy. She needed support and a large enough pack to face the city. Whatever her tio's intentions, with Gabriel holding the bond, it would only take one command to ruin Marcus's plans.

"To let you know when he gathers us to make his next move." Tio Marcus's eyes, the same color as Nora's father's had been, held her steady. "I don't trust what he's doing. I don't understand it either, but I won't let your father's pack fall into disgrace because of him. I'll stop him if I need to, or I'll call for you when it's time for you to challenge him officially. You need to challenge him, Nora. The pack, the Den, it should be yours."

"And you'll help me? What if Gabriel orders you not to?"

"He's too afraid right now. The pack is too shaken. He doesn't give orders like he used to, but we aren't allowed to go out much. Matt helps him keep tabs on us. I shouldn't even be here right now. Gabriel says it's for our safety, but he's too distracted to watch us. To care what we get up to. He didn't even notice when I fought his order enough to come here today. He's slipping. When the time is right, you need to take advantage of that."

Tio Marcus reached for Nora's hand across the table. "We are still the Morales pack. Your father's pack. Yours. You need to do your part to prove it to everyone loyal to Gabriel. You need to take your place and *show* us you aren't the little girl we remember. Build your strength, build your pack, and prepare for whatever Gabriel and the witch are brewing."

Tio Marcus stood, kissed Lupe and then Nora on the forehead, and swept out with only a nod to Annaliese as she came back with the wrapped subs.

Nora was too lost in her thoughts to answer when Annaliese asked her how it went with any more than a confused, "I don't know."

CHAPTER 8

"Poppy. You said I could be involved now. Margot is expecting me! Don't change your mind now. My wards are good. My magic is under control. The Alpha's Den is the safest place in the city."

"Yes, when Nora and her pack are there! Tonight, it'll just be the humans, Lana, and Colbie. Not even Zayn will be around and—"

"And it's still safe. *You* made it safe. Do you not trust Margot?"

"I don't trust Kallow's daughters." Not after Beth. Not after Kallow refused to help.

"But do you trust Margot?" Ru insisted. Speaking as if she were making a winning point in the argument.

Poppy shrugged. "I don't know, okay? I don't know if I trust any of our sisters except you. I definitely couldn't trust Mom. No one even looked back when we fled that night. Jane took you with her, but… I was the last one out of the house. I knew it wasn't protected, but I thought someone would have to get over the initial fear and come back to check that everyone was okay. No one did, Ru. No one cared. I went to Margot for help last winter. She *had* to feel me in her wards, but she didn't

even check who was there. She stayed hidden until you dismantled them. Would she have even come out that day to see us if
you hadn't figured out her impressions? *She* doesn't trust us. I
don't know how to feel about her."

Ru looked stunned to see how deep Poppy's hurt went
regarding their family. "But you said—"

"I know. And I still think finding our sisters is the next best
move, but we have to be careful. We have to prepare to debate
our cause and be ready for it not to work. That means taking
precautions with our safety, even around our sisters."

Ru considered. It was clear that she didn't like thinking
about their sisters as threats, but at least she was listening. After
a moment, she nodded. "Okay. I see your point. But I think
everyone is afraid, and the precautions come in meeting at
places like the Alpha's Den, where our allies are close. Not in
me hiding away as if Margot doesn't already know I'm with
you."

In the end, Ru won the argument. She ducked into Colbie's
room to get ready for the night. She made more use of the
vanity in there than Colbie ever had and often riffled through
the vampire's closet. While Poppy waited, she readied her latest
potions and spent a bit of time on her own appearance in the
bathroom, edging her eyes with a brown liner to make the
green pop and twisting her hair into two French braids. After a
time, Ru and Colbie's laughter floated out of Colbie's room.

By the time they left, Colbie was still dozing, and Ru's
cheeks were dusted with tiny, sparkling stars. She used the
makeup Poppy had made her, a mix of sparkling liner and
daylight brew that glowed softly all night. Poppy hid her proud
grin, ducking her head until it was under control. She hadn't
been sure how her younger sister would feel about the stick of
makeup when she'd gifted her the container, but Ru had
squealed with glee and used it most nights since.

They were quiet in the car. Ru fiddled with her bracelets,
soft waves of magic brushing over Poppy with the movements.

Mother and Life, Ru was so powerful. It was intoxicating to sit near her sometimes. Poppy tightened her grip on the wheel and smothered the faint blue glow that began at her fingertips.

It was early enough in the night to find a spot in the diagonals in front of Alpha's Den. They shared a look when they recognized the bike chained up in front of them. "Does he know Colbie and Topher won't be in until later?"

"Probably not even Topher," Poppy reminded Ru.

Ru grabbed Poppy's phone from the center console to check it. "He didn't text the group to warn anyone."

"I guess it's a night for the estranged siblings," Poppy mumbled as they got out. Chance had been in and out of their lives so inconsistently the last few weeks that Colbie complained about whiplash.

They walked inside, the wards a comforting embrace, and immediately caught sight of Jay and Chance sitting at one of the high-top tables along the wall. They both wore black t-shirts and jeans, something Ru noticed right away as they approached. "Why are you two matching?"

Every now and then, Ru's lack of social awareness came out. Poppy didn't have much more time than her sister in social situations, but the months Ru had spent living in the forest with Jane certainly counted against her. Jay blushed immediately. Chance looked down in surprise, faint amusement lighting his features when he saw how similar their t-shirts and jeans looked. "Down to the white shoes," he realized aloud.

"What are you two doing here?" Ru asked. They were sipping on sodas. Chance was still too uneasy around the supernaturals to have ever let loose at the Alpha's Den the few times he visited.

"Margot asked me to come," Jay said. "Chance was already on his way here. Colbie said Lana might have a job for him."

Poppy's stomach tightened. She hadn't wanted to bring Ru even. "I don't think Topher would like this."

"Well, Topher isn't here, is he? He hasn't been around in weeks," Chance said. He tried for indifference, not even looking up from his drink, but his tightened jaw betrayed his real feelings on the subject.

"He's grieving," Poppy reminded him.

"He's falling into old, unhealthy habits. If he wants to keep hold of Julia's memory so much, he should do something about what happened to her."

"That's not—"

Chance threw his hands up. "I didn't come to fight about him and whether or not he needs some tough love. I came to talk to Raven and now I have to make sure you getting witches caught in this mess won't make it worse for him." Chance crossed his arms like that was all there was to say, abruptly switching into the Colbie half of his personality.

Poppy might have argued further, but the wards twinged with Margot's presence, wary of letting her and the other witch in.

Ru actually rubbed her hands together. "It's go time."

"You nerd," Chance teased, abruptly all Topher. Ru sent a thread of magic that nearly unseated him, making him laugh. Poppy blinked. When had she missed them growing so friendly? The lingering look Chance cast over Ru made Poppy's stomach clench, and that was before she noticed Jay's wounded expression.

Poppy didn't have time to process this startling development before the front door opened. Margot and the other witch stepped cautiously inside.

Margot's friend didn't look like her mother at all. Where Mother Kallow was charismatic enough to involve herself in politics, her daughter was already scowling. Her hand sported a slim, silver ring for nearly every knuckle, her wrist twisting as she read the magic. Ru did that too, sometimes. She described it as feeling the threads, untangling them with her fingers. Poppy could barely *see* the threads of spells, let alone touch them. Mother Kallow was tall, with big, too-styled hair. Her daughter's brown hair was hacked into a layered mullet, showcasing the silver studs going up her ears. Her green eyes shifted constantly, taking in the cocktail bar like a cat about to pounce.

For some reason, she made Poppy nervous, but when Ru fearlessly stepped forward for introductions, Poppy had no choice but to follow.

Margot also appeared to be experiencing some nerves. Her smile was slightly stiff as she gestured at her friend. "Hey, y'all. This is Vivienne. Viv , this is Poppy, Ru, Jay and… I don't know you."

Chance's smile was easy as he offered his hand. "Chance."

Vivienne tilted her head. "You look just like Topher. Brother? Cousin?"

Chance's eyes widened with surprise. Vivienne had caught the resemblance faster than anyone else had. "You know Topher?"

"I've met him a couple times. It's the dimples and those eyes."

"Where were you seeing Topher while he was smiling?" They all turned at Annaliese's sudden appearance. Her arms were crossed, examining Vivienne while she waited for the witch's answer.

"Happenstance. Once at Blank Space, but mostly at the Maker after it opened." Vivienne craned her neck, looking around. "Where is he?"

"Not here," Annaliese said curtly. Poppy had no idea what was going on between her and Topher these days. The part of her that remembered being in love with Topher was glad for the new distance. The part of her that worried about Topher was pleased to see Annaliese still possessed enough care to feel jealous of him. Annaliese's presence always seemed to bolster Topher. Poppy firmly and begrudgingly believed he needed Annaliese back in his life if he was going to get better.

Vivienne's eyebrow rose, and Ru jumped forward to diffuse

some of the tension. "I'm not supposed to hang out down here. Do you two want to go upstairs to chat more? Or it's nice out. We could go sit on the patio?"

"Let's go upstairs," Margot said with a relieved smile. It was the beginning of twilight outside, and Poppy could tell Margot was looking for vampires. Likely wary of the night and demons, too.

Ru led the way to the conference room, trialing her fingers on the vines growing up the wall and letting them drink from her magic without thought. At least she'd mastered giving the magic without leaving her mark. Poppy was grateful for Ru's offering. It saved her from pouring magic into the wards to recharge them that night.

But checking over her shoulder confirmed that Vivienne was watching Ru's magic spilling so effortlessly. Her green eyes were wide, and she hesitantly reached to touch a leaf, pulling back with a hiss at the force of power contained within. Poppy smirked and turned forward again.

The Alpha's Den was their place. No amount of scowling or claiming to know Topher would give anyone a leg up on them. This meeting would be fine, and if Margot needed to feel safe around Poppy and Ru, Poppy could prove they could be sisters again.

Topher woke up yet again to Josh's voice. This was beginning to get ridiculous, but he couldn't complain. He'd come to depend on Josh's steady company, even in wolf form. Josh was close, Topher's back pressing against his warm side with Josh's arm under Topher's pillow. Topher could hear Nora on the other end of the call. "—will also be in the forest. Will that be a problem?"

Josh snorted. "You know we don't have a problem with your pack, Nora. Just Lana."

"I am allied with Lana. Same with Topher."

A beat of quiet. Topher found himself wishing he could pry open Josh's head to read his thoughts and figure out why he was giving Topher so much of his time the last three nights. It made no sense, but Topher wasn't sure he wanted the answer. Maybe Josh needed someone also drowning in grief to keep him company but couldn't handle the layers of grief within his pack. Maybe Josh wanted to push himself to physical extremes, and racing a vampire every night worked for him the same way it had been working for Topher. Maybe Josh longed for silence like Topher did, silence in and outside his head.

Maybe Henry had sent Josh to warm Topher up, get him out of bed, and return him to the streets to fight for New Brecken with his pack.

"I know that. But you didn't know about the drainers in the apartment, and Topher was in love with one of them. I can't blame him for trying to save Julia. I can't blame you for what happened because you didn't know. I just… hate myself for it. For being convinced to be part of it. I hate Lana. I hate her so much. But I don't hate you guys."

"What about Poppy?"

Topher was pretending to sleep, but he nearly gave himself up with a cringe at Nora's question. "Poppy doesn't and never has had space for me. I don't blame her any more than I can blame myself, but…"

"But you blame and hate yourself for what happened?"

Damn. Was Nora spending too much time with his sister?

"Yeah," Josh choked on the word. He cleared his throat. "We need to get going. See you all in the forest."

"Okay. Um, will you warn Topher I'll have my pack? They still aren't great with vampires, but I'm going to shamelessly use him to get them more used to vampires in wolf form instead of risking Colbie."

Josh snorted. "He's listening. I'm sure he's fatalistic and loves Colbie enough that he's fine with it."

Topher rolled and opened his eyes to the sight of Josh's subdued smirk. He didn't disagree.

Twenty minutes later, they were fed and waiting in a dirt lot for Nora and her pack. After the first night of getting trapped in the forest by the sun and being rescued by Ru's Sight, Josh started driving them and Topher now ran with a backpack containing a change of clothes. In a rare moment of his old humor, Josh had also slipped some sunscreen in. "Maybe that'll help you next time," he'd said.

The growl of two engines on the inclined dirt road rumbled up the path. Topher braced himself as Nora and her pack came into view. He was surprised they opted to drive, but Nora was probably as nervous about being caught by the sun again as he and Josh were. Faces stiffened and eyes widened as the pack saw Topher and Josh waiting.

So, Nora hadn't warned them. Sneaky. Topher almost felt like smiling, but seeing their faces took him back to the night they confronted Reelings. Topher hadn't seen much of Nora's pack since. Occasionally, Janelle or Ricky stopped by to check that Topher was still in bed and breathing, but no one from Gabriel's pack. Topher wasn't prepared for the wash of horror that swept over him at seeing them again. The memories of the Den's basement made his mouth go dry. The snarls from the warehouse. The emptiness they had put in Nora's eyes. He stuffed his trembling hands into his pockets as they unloaded. Josh took a step closer, far too perceptive.

It was Heather who broke the tension. She crossed the clearing and threw her arms around Topher. "I'm so, so sorry," she whispered.

It was strange that she was one of the few people who knew of both Dylan and Julia. Topher had talked to Heather for hours about his dating life during his drunken nights at Hunter's warehouse parties. She'd been the first to question his morals as he snuck around with Dylan but told everyone he had a girlfriend. He broke up with Julia when Heather told him the girl deserved better. He should have remembered that when he let Julia back into his life. Heather had been all too right. He had ruined Julia's life, demolished her future, and then killed her.

He shrugged out of the hug he didn't have a right to take comfort in, making someone snarl in the group surrounding Nora. Likely Heather's mate. Heather ignored it all, stepping back but touching Topher's cheek. "You are a victim here, Topher. You've always done your best to do what was right."

"I killed Julia, Heather."

"No. It's all on Reelings. Whatever you did, it saved her from the life of a monster."

"And if there was a cure?"

"There isn't one. Not yet. If you want to find one, do it in her memory, not to torment yourself over what could have been."

The sound of gentle brewing each time he woke haunted him. Topher suspected Poppy was working hard to do just that. It was the epitome of how low and horrible he was that he couldn't stomach the thought of her succeeding. Topher looked away, finding Josh's eyes and stepping closer. "Can we go now?"

Josh was quick to nod, though he hesitated to shift. Topher waited impatiently for Nora and her pack to follow suit. Standing over six feet, Topher usually felt tall, but now, he felt a strange mix of too small yet too upright. The wolves *felt* bigger than him, though he didn't know how weight or actual body length compared, but he stood amongst them at least two heads taller. He didn't know what to do with his awareness of his body in that moment, and was grateful when Nora slipped out of the huddle and moved forward to lead them. A few of her pack members growled as they passed Topher to flank her. One wolf, Ricky if Topher had to guess, gently booped Topher's thigh with his wet nose, but the rest were unwelcoming. Topher bared his teeth, his own monstrous side closer to the surface this far from humans, but he needn't have bothered. A quick bark from Nora, and everyone fell in line. They slipped into the trees' embrace, Josh and Topher bringing up the rear.

They ran hard. An underlying sense of competition backed the force of their steps. Nora's pack wanted to be faster than Josh, a member of another pack, but they needed to be faster than Topher. The smugness that flooded him when he easily kept up was the most feeling Topher had let himself experience in days.

Time passed as it did in the forest: trees and scents and trails and careful feet. Topher had never pushed his changed body so hard as he did within the trees. Sometimes, he found himself remembering a wild run to the park to save Ru from demons. Josh, barely more than a stranger, had been at Topher's side then, too. Had fought just as well. Maybe that was the difference. Running with werewolves this far from the city, no one around him was in danger.

Topher leaped over a felled tree, a wolf in front of him looking back with a snort, clearly having hoped the obstacle would slow him. But this was night number three, and Topher had barely brushed the edges of his limitations. He was starting to grow fearful that, like his charm, his stamina would know no bounds.

They cleared a small stream, and Topher caught his train of thought. Maybe it was the other wolves, but Topher had been *thinking* more during this run. Thinking too much. Was it no longer helping? Or had it helped? It was like poking a healing bruise and wondering if it would hurt—if he wanted to press hard enough to make it hurt. Thoughts would quickly lead to memories, to pangs of grief, but being numb wasn't an option after Josh's constant company keeping him present and full three days in a row.

Topher felt like he'd returned to his body, and it was thrilling as much as it was terrifying. Maybe he was done hiding… though running in the forest was very different from stepping back into the supernatural world of New Brecken.

Nora took a sudden turn, her energy shifting as she lay on a sudden and shocking burst of speed. Her pack began to fall behind, and Topher pushed himself to overtake them and keep up, sensing their confusion at his back as Nora put her nose down and *sprinted*. It felt important not to let her out of his sight, so Topher stayed right there until a white-blond wolf came into view. He almost stumbled. Henry's pack or Gabriel's?

The Nora shifted in a flurry of movement he couldn't follow. She stumbled from her momentum and landed on her hands and knees. A cry tore from her throat.

"Mom!"

CHAPTER 9

I t wasn't thought; it was pure desperation. Nora turned to Topher, the only one who kept up with her. The only one who could help. "Please, ask her to stay."

She saw the conflict in his eyes as he understood what she meant. She needed Topher. She needed his charm. How had she not thought of this sooner? He broke her from Gabriel. Maybe he could break her mother from her grief long enough for Helen to shift.

Nora almost took back her words when his entire being dimmed at her request. She hadn't even realized how much life had returned to him until that moment. Topher hated his charm, but Nora had to believe it wasn't all bad. There must be good uses of his power. She looked back toward her mother. Would Helen Morales feel this was a good use? Would she hate Nora for ripping her from the comfort she'd found in wolf form? Or would this be saving her from a position she was stuck in?

"It might not work, Nora. Charm works on humans, and I don't feel a lot of human in her."

"Please. Topher, it's my mom. Please try. I need her."

"Okay, Nora. Okay."

Topher gently touched Nora's shoulder as he passed her. Helen waited, crouched, teeth bared, but she hadn't run. A growl answered Topher's brief touch from behind, alerting Nora to her pack's presence. They had caught up. They had heard her ask a vampire for this. Nora found she didn't care what they thought about it. Not with hope rising almost violently in her core. She might vomit from the force of it. Every raw nerve buzzed, and all the progress through grief she'd made was suddenly stripped.

Topher approached Nora's mother slowly, his eye contact intense. The hope grew more acute when holding her eyes was enough for Topher to keep Helen rooted in place. Nora remembered the force of that blue gaze. She remembered how it felt to drown.

The forest around them stilled. Topher's charm filled the air. Helen made a keening noise in her throat. Patrick shifted forward anxiously but settled when Nora sent him a look.

The hand Topher lifted to Helen trembled as he knelt to her level. Nora felt Topher's charm but no untethered bonds of the alphaless. Her mother truly was entirely wolf. No, mostly wolf. If anyone could find her mother, it was Topher. It had to be Topher.

The shadows stretched. Everything watching and reaching toward Topher's power, and he hadn't even summoned his voice yet. He must be digging deep, searching for the part of Helen he might command.

Finally, finally, his voice rang out. It held enough charm that even Nora came to attention. He glanced back at her, eyes unfocused with charm, but just beneath, he seemed to ask *are you sure?*

"Please, Topher."

He nodded. "Helen, shift long enough to talk to your daughter."

Nothing happened. Nora held her breath, her head swimming. A human yelp sounded behind her when Ricky accidentally shifted from the force of the command. Topher's brows furrowed. He was wincing. Channeling so much fucking power.

"Helen, talk to Nora."

A few things happened at once. The pack behind her shifted. Each protested what Topher was doing or saying Nora's name, whatever it took to fulfill Topher's charmed order.

Then, Topher collapsed.

And… Helen shifted. "Nora," she breathed, trying to rise on unpracticed human legs. Tears were already streaming down Nora's cheeks as she ran into her mother's open arms, steadying her and holding her so, so tightly.

They settled in around the table on the second floor. Ru set a ring in front of her and kept spinning it with her magic. Jay and Chance didn't even blink at the show of power displayed in Ru's nervous tick.

Margot and Vivienne sat next to each other. There was something in the way that Margot scooted to put more space between them, and Vivienne's hurt look quickly concealed that tipped Poppy off. Maybe the label "friend" didn't cover what Vivienne was to Margot. But, if Margot wasn't comfortable explaining the relationship, Poppy wouldn't pry. She took her eyes off the space between them and asked, "You have questions?"

Vivienne sat forward. Now that Poppy had her suspicions, the hostility in Vivienne's gaze rang more toward protective. Was she checking the safety of the situation for Margot? "How many times have the wards here been breached?"

Ru laughed. She didn't mean to; it was obvious from the speed with which she slapped her hands over her mouth, but the sound still filled the space between them all.

"They haven't."

"I mean, when you two aren't here."

"The wards are sustained off more than my and Ru's magic. They never falter."

Vivienne leaned back, eyes narrowed, arms crossed. Poppy glanced toward Annaliese. The two were mirror images. "Explain," Vivienne said.

"Most of what I contribute to the wards these days is redirection if one of the spells woven into them is getting stronger than others. Like, the one that keeps out malicious people didn't let a girl in the other night because she was meeting up with someone who was not her boyfriend. Lana wasn't happy about losing that business, so I've had to adjust there. The wards are fueled by the magic contained in its plants, in the human energy, and in the pack. They draw from the wolves here, especially Nora, now that she knows how to feed them intentionally."

Poppy also felt Topher in the wards after he visited. Some of that darkness he'd shared with her a couple times to help her deal with Gus. Poppy had never heard of a vampire giving off life energy, but it wasn't exactly life. Whatever he exuded, her wards liked it, but Poppy couldn't be sure how it worked. It shouldn't be possible. She'd never told anyone about the shadows woven into the protection here, and Ru had never mentioned them either.

"But... how?" Margot asked, eyes wide.

Poppy opened her mouth to explain the intricacies of her casting and crutches, but Ru jumped in first. "You have to see it, right? Poppy figured out how to be a conduit for magic and how to make even her spells and impressions do the same. Sometimes, she starts glowing when she's in the basement with the humans dancing and their life energy is too strong. Her spells soak up magic the same way. It's incredible. It's like she channels power. Makes it do what she wants and draws it from the world around her. Poppy can cast using a plant and none of her own power. Why didn't any of you teach me to do that? Jane never even mentioned it."

Margot's mouth was agape. Vivienne's eyes were huge. "You cast without using your life energy?"

"But isn't that like…" Margot trailed off, uncomfortable.

Ru knew where their sister was going and snorted. "No, it's not like sorcery. It's life energy." She glanced at Poppy then, unspoken words between them—except what Poppy pulled from Topher. Or Topher gave her. They didn't know what it was, but neither suffered any consequences, so it was nothing like the sorcery Beth committed while leaving a trail of dead witches in her wake.

"And your wards, even on full moons, they stay strong? They hold?"

Poppy almost laughed. "Nora Morales has more power than she knows what to do with on full moons. I'd say the club is at its strongest then, and that's just from the burst she feeds the wards before she leaves to run."

Vivienne leaned forward, her scowl breaking completely. Something like hope lit her eyes. "When can we move in?"

Ru's brows furrowed. "Are you that afraid? How many times have *your* wards been breached?"

"Three times. The last two were too close together. Margot and I were still healing from injuries during the second demon attack for the third. It got… scary."

Ru's face drained of color. "Even being together? Your wards weren't strong enough?"

Margot shook her head. "Our magic's don't weave together very well."

Ru looked to Poppy. "Jane's and mine didn't hold when we were attacked."

"The only places in the city I thought were safe were the covens, but of course, I couldn't bring Margot to my Mother's." Again, Vivienne hinted at more. Margot blushed, looking away. Why was she so uncomfortable? Poppy looked at Ru and knew it hadn't slipped her younger sister's notice either.

"So witches are only safe within their covens or with

Poppy," Jay said. "Why aren't more staying in their covens then? How is Beth finding so many witches?"

Vivienne flinched. Margot finally shifted closer to her. Hand on Vivienne's arm, she answered without mentioning the sorcerer. "True covens are rare. All the daughters have to be near. The Kallows are growing weaker, and as far as we know, there were only three complete covens in the city at the time of the laws. There were more witches, but only those with the protection of a coven were willing to speak up. The Rosenfield coven didn't even come forward, only sent messages."

"A witch alone shouldn't have been able to make it this long," Vivienne put in, eyes narrowing on Poppy.

Poppy shifted under the scrutiny. Even Chance, who understood little of what was going on, looked impressed.

"The only thing that throws me is your friendship with the vampires," Vivienne said. "I don't understand how you can trust them."

Poppy crossed her arms. "I think that, at least in the early days, Topher and Colbie kept the demons away. I didn't even start putting wards around our apartment until I was sure it was safe and permanent. I'd been living there for a month. Likely, Lana's constant presence here is a deterrent, too. No one gets attacked on Fourth Street by demons. Mom even survived there at her weakest. But, in terms of how I can trust them," Poppy shrugged, "Topher and Colbie were my first friends. The first people to accept me when I never fit in with our coven. They're my *best* friends. And if you want to stay here, we have to clear it with them first. But they let me in. They'll probably help you too. Because they're great people."

"Maybe Topher and Colbie would, but are you forgetting who owns the building, Poppy?"

Poppy whirled. Ru swore and dropped her ring with a clatter. With vampire quiet and hearing, Lana had interrupted their meeting. Her fangs were dropped when she smiled at Margot and Vivienne. "Vivienne Kallow, good to see you again. And you, I don't know, but I'm guessing you're a Jennings?"

Margot and Vivienne shared a look before nodding.

Poppy tried to shift attention away. "You own half the building, Lana. Nora will let Margot and Vivienne stay here if Colbie asks."

"And why would Colbie ask?" Lana asked. She was still constantly pressing them for details about their dynamics.

Poppy shrugged. "She owes me." After killing her mother, Colbie would do whatever it took to keep Poppy from losing more family—unless said family put Poppy in danger or hurt her, as Tiff had. Colbie would put Poppy first. That's what all their conversations and Colbie's apologies had led to Poppy knowing. For Colbie, it was Topher. Then maybe Chance. Nora, who needed no protecting. Then, Poppy. Zayn and Oliver were close after her. But Colbie thought in steps, in black and whites, and priorities. Poppy now knew exactly where she sat in that list and how Colbie could justify killing Tiff Jennings to save Poppy's life.

Poppy had thought about that night over and over. She'd even gone back to examine the summoning circles and the imprint of the spell. Colbie was right. If she hadn't done what she did, Annaliese would be a drainer. Poppy would have died in the process. Tiff's life had released barely enough potential to keep them both utterly fine.

Well, aside from Annaliese's new resistance to charm. Maybe more. Annaliese hadn't asked, and Poppy was too wary to delve deeper into the effects of Beth's spell.

"We can rely on Nora's generosity, or we could add more witches to the payroll," Lana said. "Any interest in joining our cause? It's been a great time and means free drinks."

Margot stiffened. Vivienne's face scrunched like the idea was repellant, and Poppy knew Lana would not be what drew them in. "This is a private conversation," Poppy said, as firm as she could.

Lana's smile was fake and too wide. "Alright. But if they want to know more, they know where to find me."

Lana turned from the doorway to help the humans working the bars below, but they didn't resume their conversation until Annaliese made sure the maker had gone downstairs and shut the door behind her.

Margot leaned forward. Thus far, she'd let Vivienne lead the conversation, but this was important to her. "I get it. The West siblings are your friends, but Poppy, why *her*?"

All eyes were on Poppy, but it was Chance who spoke up. "Lana is horrible, but so are almost all of the other leaders in the city. So is pretty much every politician. At least her goals align the most with Poppy, Colbie, and Topher's. And as horrible as it was, as much as he didn't want it to happen, she did save Topher's life after Tiff Jennings tried to steal it. She did protect Colbie and give them a place in the supernatural world."

Poppy turned. "She only did all that to benefit herself."

"And no one here has benefited from her selfishness?" Chance shrugged when Poppy didn't have an immediate answer. "I'm not worried about Lana gaining too much power. Topher is in a bad place right now, but he'll step up if she tries to mess with us. I don't feel bad about benefiting from her for the time being."

"What are you getting out of this?" Annaliese asked.

"Right now? A job. Colbie asked if I would set up the security cameras. Apparently, I'm the only person anyone around here who knows even the slightest bit about tech. Jay and I were here looking at outlets and good places to set them up."

They fell into a contemplative silence. Vivienne was the one to break it. "Is there even room for us here? At least to pass the full moon?"

"That would be when the wolves are out running," Poppy said. "But, I do think things might be getting tight. Nora is nervous about accepting more pack members because they ran out of beds. We can see if you two can crash at our place, though."

"Four witches in one apartment? In normal wards?" Vivienne asked. She looked ready to get up and leave.

Poppy hated the way Margot's face was dimming. Ru spoke up, "We can figure things out. Nora would help us strengthen the wards. We can find somewhere else to set up, too. For now, there's room here, even if it's tight. I'll talk to Nora."

"Yeah. Hang out until she gets back. It'll be fine," Poppy said, latching onto Ru and Margot's hopeful expressions. "At least rest for a bit. We can have a drink and catch up some more."

Vivienne reached for Margot's hand. "Let's do that."

Margot nodded, squeezing Vivienne's fingers before dropping her hand. Curiosity burned in Poppy as she stood. "What do you want to drink?"

CHAPTER 10

Topher wouldn't wake up, but concern for him was beyond Nora right now. Only Josh's palatable fuming kept bringing the vampire's state to Nora's awareness. She was far too swept up in her mother's presence as they sat in the clearing. The shadows had given way to the nearly full moon overhead. The night was perfect, bright and crisp and full of the impossible.

"How long has it been?" Helen asked carefully. She kept looking at Nora like she was a stranger. Was it the years as a wolf making Nora unfamiliar? Nora's new age? Was it her alpha status coming through and distorting Helen's memories of her daughter?

"Almost three years," Heather answered gently when Nora remained tongue-tied.

Her mother went quiet, hands on Nora's arms, taking her in. Nora had gotten very used to being naked between changes with her pack, but she felt so vulnerable under her mother's scrutiny. She fought the urge to curl into herself.

"Where is everyone else?" Helen asked.

Lupe answered. "They're still with Gabriel."

"Gabriel? What do you mean?"

Nora exchanged a look with her pack, twisting on her knees to take them in. She sucked in a breath when she saw that Josh had changed into the clothes in Topher's backpack and had a phone in hand. Without meeting Nora's eyes, he hefted Topher onto his shoulder and put the phone to his ear. Nora knew she owed Topher for this, but she also trusted Josh to get him revived and fed safely. Topher would be fine. He would tell Nora to stay with her mom.

"What do you remember from… before?" Lupe asked carefully. With Topher and Josh gone, the pack condensed around Helen. They eased into their natural state when alone. Affection and touches and relaxed shoulders and smiles. Hands on Helen's back. Heather's head on her shoulder. Ricky and Janelle at Nora's side.

"I remember Luis dying." As soon as the words left Helen's mouth, all color drained from her face. "I shifted, but I was untethered. It was easier, and then, I couldn't stand being human anymore. I forgot…" She sucked in a breath, tears filling her eyes. "I left. I left you, Nora. God, I'm so, so sorry."

Nora let her mother pull her back into a hug. She didn't realize how much she had numbed herself against the betrayal of her mother leaving. Almost every time the sting came, she turned off feeling and told herself it was just her mother's reaction to her father's death. She didn't let herself feel it personally.

Until now.

All the walls and repressed feelings came out in a near-violent sob. Shoulders heaving, breath impossible, vision blurred to black. Her mother murmured comforts and regrets. At first, she was gentle, but then she grew panicked as the tears wouldn't stop. Nora had no control over all the feeling, not as fear began to crowd in. How badly had Nora craved her mother's voice? Her touch? Now that it was here, Nora couldn't trust it. She had to force herself not to cringe away, and that made it even worse.

She didn't know how to reconcile the guilt it brought. Didn't know how to let her mother's embrace comfort her when she was terrified of it disappearing again as soon as she learned who Nora had become. She didn't know how to stop *crying*.

Nora was cold and breathless and unable to calm herself. Maybe the lack of air would lead to her passing out or throwing up, and she wouldn't have to focus on how much this all *hurt*.

But then, cold hands were on her cheeks, blue eyes breaking through her tear-filled vision. Air filled Nora's chest as she lunged into Colbie's arms. Colbie held her so tight; it was like being pressed back together. "I'm here. It's okay, Nor. I'm here."

Colbie's voice. Her lips in Nora's hair. Nora buried her face in the safe place that was the curve of Colbie's neck and breathed in her own scent lingering there. Nora focused on inhaling the familiar until the tears finally slowed. Colbie didn't loosen her grip or stop whispering reassurances until Nora moved to pull back. Not very far, only enough to look into Colbie's face. Colbie immediately tugged down her sleeve and set to work, drying the tears and even snot from Nora's face. How had she even found her this deep in the forest?

"Is Topher okay?"

"Yeah. Of course. Josh is taking him to the club. Poppy and Annaliese are there. They'll all get him sorted out."

"You came here instead?" Nora whispered, so emotionally stripped that the words threatened to bring even more tears.

Colbie rolled her eyes and kissed Nora's nose. "Of course. Now, if you're better, introduce me to your mom."

Nora turned. In her crashing sobs, Colbie had somehow maneuvered Nora until she was sitting in her lap, bracketed by her arms. Helen was staring at them, shocked and teeth bared. Nora stiffened and swallowed, but Colbie's hold didn't let up. It brought confidence rather than the shame she'd once felt. In

Colbie's arms, Nora thought maybe she could handle her mother's disappointment. Maybe even her leaving again.

Nora had done this already. She could do it with her mom. Pulling in a shuddering breath, Nora looked down at Colbie's forearms and launched into her story. All that happened after her mother vanished. Nora didn't remember her grief well, and the years leading up to her first shift were relatively uneventful. She skimmed over them and truly began with the night she met Colbie, determined to kill a vampire.

Maybe she hadn't told this story before as thoroughly as she thought. Never with Colbie there. Nora realized sometime between describing her second meeting with Colbie that her pack was listening intently. Not only that but listening with far more open faces than they had sported even last night. With Colbie's chin resting on Nora's shoulder, whispering words to remind Nora of details, the story spilled out of her effortlessly. There were points in which Nora turned her head to talk to Colbie specifically about what things had been like for her, especially during those dark weeks after Nora lost both her and her pack.

The wolves remained silent. They stiffened when Nora described her side of the story during the confrontation with Reelings with only Ricky and Janelle at her side. Nora explained what she had seen of the magic, the bonds, and how she had thrown her power over Gabriel's so that Nora's strength went to Annaliese and Gabriel's was lost to the shadows, making him weak enough for the bonds to break and Nora to challenge him partially. She explained how Colbie had saved Poppy and Annaliese, killing Tiff Jennings and starting Poppy on the path to find her sisters. She left out Ru and Margot's appearance yesterday, still careful of the witch's privacy, though most of her pack already suspected or knew who Ru was.

"The city is going to be unstable for a while. I understand if you don't want to be part of it. But I need to talk to you,

Mom. I have to know—" Nora cut off, too afraid of asking the question. Too afraid to find out how thoroughly she had disappointed her father's memory. But there were too many gaps in her knowledge. Was her father really going to stop the initiation process? What happened to the other packs that had once lived here? How had Gabriel gained control, and what happened to the other pack members who didn't accept his bonds? Did her mother even know?

Nora finally looked up and found Helen watching her with a hint of a smile. "He was going to stop the vampire killings. He wanted that tradition finished, yes. He never would have imagined this," Helen gestured awkwardly to encompass Nora on Colbie's lap, "But he would have come around. He would be so proud."

Nora didn't have any tears left, but her throat still tightened. She could only nod. With so much out in the open between them, Nora was beginning to tire. Like the sun dragged a vampire to sleep, the talking was wearing on Nora.

"We should head back," she said. They still had a few hours until sunrise, but she knew Colbie would want to check on her brother. "Are, are you coming with, Mom?"

Helen looked into the trees. There was longing in her gaze, a hint of dread when she turned back to Nora. But her nod was resolute. "I have much to tell you, too."

The blood tasted like a familiar smell, but it didn't taste good. Like the difference between the aroma of freshly brewed coffee and the bitter tang of it on your tongue. Topher jerked away from the wrist pressed to his lips, blinking up past through a blinding headache.

"Thank god, you're awake."

Topher might have replied, but the words were beyond reach. He couldn't wrap his head around the pain or the fact that he'd just drank Josh's blood. Now, Josh was tugging at him, trying to get Topher to his feet. He was dressed and human, but they were still in the forest. Josh's cheeks were flushed, the smell of his healing wrist potent in the air around them.

"We just have to get to the car. Are you better now? Good enough to feed without draining someone?"

"Blood." Later, Topher would be ashamed of how desperate he sounded for the word.

Josh's voice was quiet for a beat. He tightened his grip on Topher's arm. "Alright. We'll be careful."

The hike to the car was a blur. Topher felt weak and, for once, hated it. So quickly, he'd grown used to being fed. He wanted to keep running through the trees and hated that the option had been taken from him.

"Do you need more of my blood?" Josh asked.

Topher wrinkled his nose. Josh's laugh was more an expulsion of anxious air. "We're close, hold on."

Somehow, Josh got Topher to the car. Darkness swept in as soon as he was seated again.

Topher woke with a vengeance when they returned to city limits. Josh had to reach across the car and physically stop him from opening the door and loosing himself on the nearest human, all while Josh spoke to someone on the phone.

Topher couldn't help it. He was so fucking hungry. With Josh leaning across him to hold the door shut, the sweep of his neck was right there. Josh only grunted when Topher's teeth sank in, bitter blood flooding his mouth. He swallowed twice before the taste overpowered his desperate hunger.

"I'm sorry," Topher gasped, wrenching away and covering his face.

Josh's hand fell to Topher's knee, squeezing. He was focusing hard on the road, words out of reach between his concentration and Topher's bliss, but the hand was reassuring. Josh wasn't mad. Topher held his breath and squeezed his eyes closed.

The warm grip on his knee didn't let up as they drove the

city streets. The car finally jerked to a stop. Josh's breathing was ragged. "Topher, look at me."

He did as he was told. Since converting the back lot of the Alpha's Den into a patio for their patrons, there was only one parking spot available. Usually, Lana's black car was parked there. Josh had cleared the spot for them, out of the street and slightly safer from all the humans out on Twenty-Fifth, but Topher's eyes still narrowed on the back doors. If he could get inside…

But Josh's blood was holding him over. Keeping him in charge of the monster's impulses. For now.

"I'll be right here, okay? It won't go too far."

"What won't?"

Josh looked past Topher's shoulder. His heart sank as the doors opened, Annaliese's delicious scent gripping him and wiping out all other thoughts.

CHAPTER 11

The bloodlust faded on the fifth wrist. Josh had figured out how to maneuver this side of Topher flawlessly. He couldn't remember Josh getting him out of the car, but when he came to, Annaliese, the bartenders Josh and Mik, and Raven were leaning against the brick wall. The last three were happily smiling, far too used to bliss. They regularly asked Topher to feed from them, but he'd refrained for so long—all that effort for nothing.

Topher looked up from the wrist his lips were clamped on, starting when he saw Jay staring down at him. Wonder widened their eyes behind their green glasses. They had a hand in Topher's hair, holding him more firmly to the cut in their skin. Topher stopped drinking and only took the time to lick the wound to heal it before wrenching back. He covered his face with his hands, the blood filling his stomach turning viciously, but his vampire would never go so far as to vomit and lose the precious contents. What would Chance have to say about this?

They all waited for Topher to collect himself. Annaliese's scent swept in close again, and she grabbed his wrists. Topher couldn't fight her as she lowered his hands. His breathing hitched.

"We're okay. You're okay." She narrowed her eyes at Josh, who didn't even seem concerned anymore. Only relieved, leaning against the wall and enjoying his own lingering bliss, fingers on his neck where Topher bit him. "What the fuck happened?" Annaliese demanded.

That was enough to light the darkness in Josh's gaze again, eyes snapping between Topher and Annaliese's grip on him with something unreadable in their depths. The door opened and shut as the bartenders and Raven returned to the club and their positions. Without Nora's pack on shift, they couldn't stay away from the bars for long. Josh admitted in a low voice, "He charmed a werewolf. That shouldn't be possible... he can't... how?"

Annaliese turned back to Topher. She knew it was possible, he could, and how. "Who did you charm?"

The blood was pounding in Topher's veins, taking the edge off his shame as it replenished him in a hot, comfortable spread even as he tried to deny himself the enjoyment of it. "Nora's mom. Nora asked me to."

Annaliese froze. "Did it work?"

When Josh and Topher nodded, Annaliese dropped Topher's wrists and turned away. She pulled out her phone. He missed her tight grip holding him together.

Josh stepped in closer, replacing her warmth and pressing their shoulders together. "Why isn't she surprised?" he asked carefully.

Topher met his gaze. He struggled for a moment. Josh was part of another pack. A pack that was no longer allied with their cause. Werewolves were confident in their immunity to vampire charm. It gave them power that no one else had inherently. It kept balance.

Werewolves were all about balance. They did everything they could to keep it in place. It was why Gabriel took such an immediate offense to Topher's existence. What would Josh do, knowing how big of a threat Topher was? He wouldn't keep another secret from his alpha after what happened with the drainers.

Topher swallowed and stepped away, ducking his head. It was too late. Josh had seen what Topher did to Helen. He would make his conclusions anyway, and Henry would act in whatever way he saw fit.

"That night, in the basement last winter, when Nora attacked at Gabriel's order, I, I told her not to listen to his commands. I think she let me break the bond. It couldn't have been that strong to begin with, but…"

Josh's face paled. "You… *you made her an alpha?*"

"No, she already was one. I just, I had to save Colbie and Zayn," Topher whispered, eyes down. He didn't want to see Josh's face. It likely matched the expression Gabriel had when he looked at Topher. The look of all the werewolves who had questioned him in the Den basement. It was the look Reelings had when he realized he was being charmed. The look of everyone in Happenstance when Topher charmed Mary, the first vampire able to touch a drainer with his power.

It was a look that made Topher want to claw off his own skin. Sink his fingernails into his eyes and remove his ability to perceive that fear and scrutiny. Someone sizing up a monster, a piece of horror that should only exist in the imagination. Something that shouldn't exist, but you suddenly found yourself face to face with and tasked with the need to reinspect your reality.

Topher hated that look. Almost as much as the submission that filled humans' faces when his charm slipped.

Not even the warm flush of recent feeding could keep Topher strong enough to see it on Josh's face. He felt himself trying to get smaller, shoulders curling in. It was a relief when Annaliese hung up her phone and broke the moment. "We should go in," Annaliese said. Her brows were furrowed, taking in Topher's stance.

Annaliese had never once looked at Topher like he was something she couldn't fathom. She'd never once been afraid when she met his eyes. He took a step toward her but faltered. The smell of the club, the sway of the music inside, the evidence of the life his friends and sister had been living without him...

Topher wanted to go back to bed.

But then, Josh's hand was at his back, his body too close to Topher's. Why, *how*, was he touching Topher after learning that?

Josh didn't want to go inside either. Topher knew that, but his following words brought a wash of cold. "Henry wants me to ask Lana—"

"About the new supernatural office?"

"Have you already been visited?" Josh asked. He was still touching Topher, Annaliese a familiar presence on Topher's other side. They were determined to keep him from leaving. Maybe trying to stop him from spiraling by including him in the conversation but needing nothing from him in terms of contribution. That, or they were both fearful of letting Topher go into the city so soon after he'd lost control.

They entered the club, and Topher's head snapped up, yanked from his wallowing with whiplashing force. He stepped out from between Josh and Annaliese, Josh's hand following him with a brief touch, and stalked into the cocktail lounge.

Chance sat at one of the high tables, cables and black squares of uninstalled cameras strewn about. His brother was barely paying attention to Poppy, Jay, the two others sitting there. An empty seat spoke of Annaliese's recent presence. There was barely enough room for them, their drinks, and Chance's equipment at the table. A tension hung in the air, but Topher was too focused on Chance being here without himself, Zayn, or Colbie to parse that out yet. Nora wasn't even around with her pack to keep him safe. What the hell?

"What's going on?" Topher demanded as soon as he was within hearing range. "What are you doing here?"

Chance didn't start, but the person beside him did as she turned. Topher blinked. "Viv ?"

"Topher, finally. I need to talk to you."

Poppy groaned, maybe trying to lighten the moment. "Why did he say 'Viv ' like he said Brady, and Tamara, and Rico and—"

"Please don't talk about my brother's sex life in front of me," Chance said, eyes firmly fixed on his laptop screen. "I heard way too much about it in high school."

Speaking of expressions Topher didn't like—Poppy, Josh, Annaliese, and the stranger at the table looked at him in different shades of personal injury. Topher's eyes caught on Josh, confusion ringing as to why *he'd* be hurt until Topher realized it was likely on Poppy's behalf.

"Just one time," Viv muttered to the person next to her. A witch, Topher presumed, when her wards kept him from picking up a scent. Poppy's sister? Viv stood from the table, grabbed his arm, and pulled him toward the stairs, where it was quieter. Topher felt everyone's eyes, but no one moved to stop Viv from dragging him away.

"First, I need to know if you have any issues with me after what Beth did," Viv said.

Seeing Chance here, the events of the night and all the looks had exhaustion falling over Topher. Beckoning him toward dissociation and calling for him to return to the uncomplicated shadows found in his bed.

He raised an eyebrow at Viv in response, too tired to reassure her.

"Okay, good. Margot and I need a place to stay."

"And Margot is…"

"Poppy's sister." Viv gave Topher a look. He was taken back to his room at the Maker, the darkness outside, the cigarette smoke in the air as they passed the stick back and forth. Viv complaining about a girl, Topher complaining about Lana. An agreement that the release they'd found hadn't been what they needed and no more texts to follow that night. "Poppy said we can stay here, but I'm not holing Margot up in a vampire den without knowing you'll be around to make sure nothing happens to her."

The air squeezed from Topher's lungs. He wanted a cigarette. He wanted to feel the effects of a cigarette. He couldn't... "Viv . Everyone I promise to protect ends up dead or in danger. I, I can't... Poppy can—" He cut off his stuttering, eyes unable to focus on the witch in front of him or the room around him or anything but the memories. The memories.

The memories.

"Leave him alone."

Topher jumped. Chance was there, gripping Topher's arm and maneuvering him so he stood a step behind his younger, human brother, who could apparently still read Topher's face. "With or without Topher's promises, you'll be safe here. The fact that I'm standing in this building should be enough proof of that. He's got enough on his plate."

Viv scowled. This had drawn Topher to her when she came by the Maker with Beth that time. The total lack of kid gloves, the refusal to fall into pity. Their night had been over as soon as it began, but it'd been exactly what Topher had needed at the time. Where had the person he once was gone? The boy who could be handled without delicacy? Topher found himself too glad for Chance's interference as Viv spoke, "I know he's been through it, but we all have. The difference is the city needs him."

The weight on Topher's shoulders was stacking again. He had hidden from it, buried himself in shadows, and cut himself off from the world, but within seconds of reentering, there were the reminders. The demands. The tugs at Topher's conscience that didn't care about his tired, ragged soul. He still cared, but he *couldn't*. A contradicting state of being that left him empty.

"Witches are dying," Viv continued. "There are still drainers out there and new ones being made. Beth needs to be stopped. The humans shouldn't have to be the ones stepping up. They're over it and the most at risk, but they're doing what they can to solve the problem. Why can't he? He isn't the only one to lose someone here," Viv said. Her eyes were shining. Tears threatening but not falling. She must have lost a sister. It was enough to make Topher recoil.

Beth was the one using witch life energy to keep from facing the consequences of sorcery. Had she used her sister? Sisters?

Or was Beth the one Viv had lost? The two had been close.

"This isn't all on Topher. He can take time to grieve while the city is—"

"Is what? We know something is happening, but no one is looking because no one is strong enough to stick their business into it and not end up killed or charmed. Reelings could be up to *anything* right now, and we're letting him. The drainer attack last spring might only be a shadow of what he's capable of, and no one has seen Topher since. Some of us consider him the last hope. Some of us are barely holding on to that. To our lives here. To our loved ones. To the city."

Chance stilled. At some point, Josh came to stand beside Topher, too. He wasn't breathing. Viv let a tear fall, but it did nothing to muffle her fierce expression. She jabbed a finger into Topher's chest. "The last thing I expected in the midst of all this was to figure out there are some things you just *can't* bear to lose. I get it. That's what happened to you, but I have a chance here to keep it from happening to me and so many other people. *Do* something, Topher. Do it for us. I don't care that I'm being selfish. I can't care about anything but keeping my people safe. And I know if something ever happened to them, I would burn down the world to make it right. If you can't do this for the living, do it for the dead. Revenge is a great motivator, and wouldn't they have done it for you? Would they have hidden from this? Seriously, Topher, what the fuck do you have to lose?"

"Viv ..." Margot was there. They were all there. Too close. Too alive. All of them stunned by the speech. That was all Topher could read of their faces through the panic. He grabbed Josh's hand, only thinking about the release of running and having someone there to the people Topher passed protected. Towing Josh behind him, he pushed his way out of the club. Annaliese's sharp voice was behind him, but she didn't follow. Topher stepped back into New Brecken, the city seeming to brighten with his presence, welcoming him with open arms.

"Toph..." Josh's voice was retched, but he agreed with Viv . Topher knew Josh was tired of the running. That he was trying to get Topher into the streets again because Josh wanted revenge as much as Viv . As much as Topher probably would if he hadn't been broken by what happened.

There was nothing in Topher's voice when he spoke. He would stay firmly in the emptiness. "Tell me what to do, Josh."

A long pause. Josh tried to read Topher's face. Topher could feel the scrutiny, but he kept every thought under lock. Finally, Josh said, "I want to find him. I want to stop him from doing this to anyone else."

"Let's start looking then."

CHAPTER 12

Nora walked into the Alpha's Den with her mother on one side and a sagging Colbie on the other. Though the air inside the bar was solemn, Annaliese beamed at the sight of Helen. Nora and Annaliese had become close after Helen had left, but she knew what this meant to Nora. She'd called earlier to ask if it was true and see how Nora was. When she heard Colbie was there, she'd been relieved and told Nora to head to the club as soon as possible.

Things were finally happening now that Topher had left his room. Nora just didn't know what.

It was nearly dawn outside, the club long since closed, but Chance was there on a ladder, screwing something into the far corner of the wall while Raven stood below. She held the base still and watched him closely. "He's putting in the cameras," Annaliese explained. Her voice was muted after the initial excitement of Helen's return dimmed. Everyone seemed off. Nora was putting it together that it might have something to do with more than her mother's appearance.

Nora hated the thought of cameras watching. She understood the usefulness for a business, but this was their home, too. Her pack constantly went up and down those stairs, hanging out in the lounge during closing hours to share takeout meals on the tables. She didn't want Lana to have access to their daily lives. Didn't want some new city government branch watching them interact.

The tension rising in the pack at Nora's back said how much they agreed.

Nora turned to nod at Heather and Chase. They stepped forward to show Helen to the rooms upstairs. Returning to her human body had quickly become overwhelming. The emotions too raw and forceful after all these years. Nora's mother was nearly asleep on her feet as she was guided upstairs. Annaliese stepped closer, voice barely above a whisper, "Did she say if anyone survived that we didn't know about?"

Nora remembered the glimpses of people she thought were aunts and former pack members who she'd been told had died with her father. Nora shook her head. "We didn't get that far. I hope sleep will help, but it was all… a lot. For us both."

Annaliese nodded. They were no strangers to *a lot* when it came to big, emotional moments.

"What happened while we were gone?"

Annaliese stiffly turned to introduce Nora and Colbie to Margot and Vivienne. She informed them of what happened with Topher when Josh brought him here. Colbie hadn't stopped glaring at Vivienne since hearing how Topher and Josh left. Colbie's scowl grew as Poppy explained how her sister and the other witch needed somewhere to stay.

"Colbie. Stop." Those words and one look from Poppy eased the expression, though Colbie couldn't resist one more eye roll in Vivienne's direction.

Nora almost smiled. She didn't understand Poppy and Colbie's complex friendship, but it was fun to see how easily the people Colbie cared about could soften her. Colbie was all blunt words and glib attitude until Oliver gave her puppy dog eyes, Poppy looked mildly disappointed, or Topher's eyebrows bunched, then she was big hugs and attempts to make things better. Nora loved the sweeter side of her girlfriend. Loved how she didn't share it with everyone. It made it all the more special to be on the receiving end. She pulled Colbie close, still marveling that it was something she could do, and pressed a kiss into her girlfriend's neck. She felt eyes on them and couldn't care.

In the end, Janelle and Ricky went with Nora and Annaliese to their place to sleep. Nora's head was swimming with questions as she settled into bed for a nap next to Janelle. She wished she'd thought to go to Colbie's, but her and Annaliese's place was closer to the Alpha's Den and Helen. She hadn't thought twice when Poppy helped a flagging Colbie to her car, the two of them whispering about Topher's whereabouts while Nora turned to focus on her pack. Now, she wished she'd had more space to join them and that conversation. She owed Topher a huge thank you. Janelle had asked to talk, though, and as she'd given up her bed for Helen, Nora went with her to the apartment on campus, discussing the position of head bartender Lana had offered.

And days spent with sleeping arrangements like this were why hardly anything more than kissing had happened between her and Colbie.

The sun was bright on the other side of the curtains, and Janelle was a restless sleeper compared to Colbie. Nora wished the brightness would pull her under like it did vampires. Instead, after the emotional roller coaster that had been her night, Nora's thoughts were swept in a restless whirlwind. Where had Topher gone? Had Josh forgiven them? Was he back? Was her mom doing okay with the new pack? Was she comfortable? Did she miss the forest? Could she switch back to her wolf form without leaving Nora again or needing Topher to return her to human? How would they find room for everyone if they began housing witches, too? Nora needed to keep building her strength and her pack for what was to come, but they didn't have the space.

Nora's thoughts flitted to the apartments Raven had suggested they use a month ago. The drainers's building had sat empty since the night Reelings showed himself, but Raven had offered to go over and clean it up for them. Lana's smile had been tight, but she'd agreed it was perfectly serviceable for the pack's needs and only asked she be informed if anyone wanted inside. Nora had been angry and thinking primarily of Topher when she snarled at Lana and told her to sell it. Maybe Nora had spoken too soon.

And what would her mother be like after resting and learning all she had missed? Nora tried to imagine her interacting with the city once more and froze. The Alpha's Den was down the street from Josh's pack. *Helen would see Henry.* And soon, especially if Josh was interacting with them again. Josh wouldn't make the mistake he had last spring of keeping secrets from his alpha. What would Helen and Henry's reunion look like? Nora no longer needed him to tell her what her mother had been like before joining the Morales pack, but why had both she and Henry split from their childhood pack? Did that pack still exist?

On the tail end of all these exhausted, spiraling thoughts was the question that had been nagging at Nora since she'd gotten involved with the supernatural groups of New Brecken. Where had all the other New Brecken werewolves gone when the laws were being debated? Why was it just the Morales pack after they were passed and before Henry got to town? Did her mom know?

Nora huffed quietly and slid out of bed. Sleep was beyond her reach. Janelle, exhausted from the night as Nora should have been, stirred only enough to shove her head under the pillows. After pulling on her baggy, worn jeans and a sweat-shirt, Nora left the apartment.

The world outside was so different than the one she lived in. Nora couldn't remember the last time she was awake this early. It was the middle of the summer, and sunlight was already glinting off windows and casting shadows from the buildings. As Nora left the campus area and ventured through downtown, buildings grew taller and the people out at this early hour were more professional. Manilla folders, black suits, phones to ears, and coffee cups in hand—the mob was very different from the people she experienced on Twenty-Fifth, yet this was New Brecken still. People walked with confidence with the sun out, but they eyed each other warily. The humans seemed almost muted in their exhaustion. This city had been through so much. An economic depression, the rise of gangs and mayhem, the supernatural law debates, the supernaturals gaining their power, the acceptance of supernaturals, and now the plague of demons and drainers that none of these humans knew enough about. The story was still mostly contained, but someone had debunked the rumors of a serial killer when they escaped a demon attack with video footage on their phone. Now, the nights were filled with the scent of fear. Some chose to exclusively frequent the vampire clubs as a result, feeling safer there than in the streets. Other humans thought they would rather face a demon than a vampire and blamed Fourth Street for the city's woes. The call had gone out for were-wolves to step forward as protectors, and Nora knew Henry and Gabriel's packs were making a killing acting as drivers and security guards, but that only protected those who could pay.

Nora's pack swept the streets, scenting for summoning circles and trying to find demons before it was too late. But her pack was still small and disorganized. They had kept Twenty-Fifth from attacks, and thus far, that street hadn't suffered any business losses, but New Brecken couldn't take much more.

Nora needed more werewolves. She needed a home base that didn't have Lana popping in all the time. Nora needed to learn how to manage her money to afford such a place, balance all the pack contributions, and find somewhere they could be together. A woman walked by, practically gliding despite her heels and tight pencil skirt as she rattled off figures into the phone at her ear. *That* was the energy Nora needed.

But still, the only woman Nora knew who compared and who could teach her was Lana.

Nora sighed at yet another completed circle of thoughts, going back to how they were stuck at Alpha's Den until she figured something else out. Annaliese had offered her stepdad's services, but Tim didn't know Nora was a werewolf and had spouted justified but unkind feelings toward the supernaturals as of late. He was probably in one of these skyscrapers now, standing around a coffee pot and talking about supernaturals and the state of the city.

It took Nora an hour of walking, but she wasn't in any rush. She couldn't remember the last time she had strolled and enjoyed her city. It had taken hits, but it functioned and breathed. New Brecken still churned out business. Families went to the library, and tourists visited the museums. Construction sites clanked and shouted. Buses navigated traffic as if by magic. Cyclists sounded their bells, and cafes with outdoor seating clicked with mimosa glasses and silverware. Things grew quieter as Nora ventured further north. She passed Twenty-Fifth, growing more comfortable on the familiar block. She crossed the pedestrian bridge, and from there, it was twenty more minutes before she entered the apartment building with Colbie tucked safely within the wards.

When Nora opened the front door, Poppy looked unsurprised to see her. She sat on the floor in front of the coffee table in the center of the living room. A scale was before her, some light blue powder mounded on top and more waiting in a mason jar to her left to be portioned.

"Couldn't sleep?" they asked each other in unison. Poppy's smile wasn't quite all there as she turned back to her task.

Nora took the armchair, eyes straying to Colbie's door. It was ajar, practically beckoning her with invitation. Yet Poppy looked so small and alone on the floor, toiling away at her potions while everyone else slept. Nora sighed and her gaze went to Topher's closed door next. "What's going on there?" she asked, tipping her chin in that direction.

The haunted, weary look in Poppy's green eyes deepened. "I wish I knew. They came back right before sunrise. Josh was practically dragging Topher, but he shifted before we could talk. I think Vivienne got to Topher. He might be leaving his room more."

"A good or bad thing?"

"Again, I wish I knew." Poppy put the mound of powder in a little baggy with a furrow of her brow and wiggle of her fingers. Nora let her power sweep out, easing the effort Poppy used to transport the powder with her magic. "Thanks. What's keeping you awake?"

"Space. I need to keep building the pack, but we need to protect the witches and I'm twenty years old and have no idea how to find housing for so many people."

Poppy drummed her fingers on the table, considering Nora's problem as if stepping back from her issues was a relief. "Without Margot and Vivienne, you had enough room at the Alpha's Den?"

"Now that my mom is there, it's tight, and that's with people sharing rooms. I know Patrick and Heather wish they had their own space and are worried about room for the baby."

"What if some of your pack looked for apartments nearby?"

Nora felt her body cringe from the suggestion before she could respond. The only apartments nearby were Henry's. Poppy nodded. "Alright. What if you took the Den from Gabriel? Now that your mom is back, it's got to be in her name, right? You can call the cops on them for trespassing."

The idea didn't sit well, but Nora forced herself to consider it. "I mean, I can talk to my mom about it once she feels more—"

Poppy's eyes widened, an idea striking, but she quickly blinked and cleared her throat, returning to her powder. "What was that?" Nora asked.

"Nothing."

"Poppy? Penelope? Popcorn?"

Poppy finally smiled a bit. She scrutinized Nora with a familiar look. The one that was shared by supernaturals of different groups trying to decide if they could trust one another. Nora had looked at Lana like that so often she thought her face might get stuck.

"Okay. I had a thought."

Would the flush of warmth that came with being trusted by the inhabitants of this apartment ever diminish? "What was your thought?"

"You don't know this, but we grew up down the road from each other. We stayed hidden in our coven, but it was the lavender house—"

"You grew up in the haunted mansion?" Nora asked, straightening.

Poppy rolled her eyes. "It's not haunted. Those were our wards keeping people out. Impressions of dark shapes in the windows and a feeling of unease for anyone who got close. Anyway, it feels hypocritical for you to go digging into the ownership of your old home if I'm not willing to do the same. Maybe, now that we're finding some of my sisters and my mom is gone, it belongs to one of us."

"You want to go back there? And you wouldn't mind my pack moving in there?"

"Same as with the Alpha's Den, we need the protection. If we're going to house multiple witches in one place, we need a big deterrent from attention. It worked for us growing up. No other supernaturals set foot on the Morales's street. It could work now, but proximity to Gabriel might be a problem. I can do some casts to hide your scents and tint car windows, but you guys all run and go places on foot so often I can't promise it won't cause trouble."

Nora considered for a long beat. "We should at least check up on it. It's an option and I didn't have any before except seeing how the sale of the drainer building was going, and I really didn't want to have to go there."

Poppy nodded. "We should go check the wards. They crumbled and morphed when my mom cracked them. We might not even be able to get in anymore or it might have messed with the house itself. We should check before we float the idea."

"Want to go now?"

Poppy looked at her powder, opening her mouth to answer, but Ru, stepping out of Poppy's room, eyes shining with the thought of going to their childhood home, beat her to it. "Yes, please."

"I feel like I can't look at it straight on," Ru said. "My eyes keep skipping over it." She seemed as discomfited as Nora did to have the wards on the Jennings house still in effect. Neither of them was accustomed to magic working on their beings. Poppy stayed quiet. It was another reminder of how powerful a full coven was. Even broken, the wards they had woven held. Different and less effective, but still there. One coven with this capability in magic could have helped them so much in this fight against Reelings.

"It seems so empty and abandoned," Nora added.

"I don't know what the wards turned into when Mom broke the Coven. They could be… not good."

"I don't see much maliciousness, but you're right. We should be careful," Ru said, unbuckling her seatbelt.

They stepped out of the car and onto the cracked overgrown sidewalk. Nora glanced down the street before she caught herself. "Let's go before someone sees me," she said, grabbing Ru's hand and tugging her up the walkway. Poppy followed, her magic flowing as she felt for any threats.

Nora and Ru glanced back from their place on the porch. They both gaped. Poppy followed their eyes, her own jaw dropping.

She knew this house. She knew every inch and, more importantly, every source of light and strength. She'd spent her childhood pulling from the plants inside and out to try and keep up with her sisters. She spent her nights trying to funnel the magic back outside so she didn't kill the yard or wildflowers.

The greenery remembered. With every step Poppy took toward the door, the grass she passed straightened with life. Weeds and flowers bloomed. The leaves on bushes and trees swayed in Poppy's direction. Years and years of shared life energy answered to her presence, and beneath it, Poppy felt her contributions to the coven's wards. All seven daughters and their mother had been building the wards as they lived there. It was why covens were so hard to breach—all the raw magic of childhood and the force of the seven daughters. The life bursting out of the mother with each birth within the walls. And… Poppy practicing her warding by weaving it into the plants. No matter what Tiff had done to the magic of the freestanding wards, it hadn't touched Poppy's. She suddenly felt safer, even this close to Gabriel, as she continued up the path.

"You're still here," Ru murmured, feeling Poppy too. "It's like your magic in the yard kept it all from imploding."

Poppy nodded. It was an excellent way to describe what it had felt like when Tiff collapsed their coven. Like the wards had been sucking in, pulling at their magic and life. Poppy remembered nothing but panic and the need to get away before she was emptied. But it would appear that wouldn't have happened. The wards had settled into a much less powerful but contained force. Supported by the magic *Poppy* had left behind.

"Do you think we could wake them back up?" Poppy asked Ru. If anyone could read through the jumbled mess of magic surrounding them, it was Ru.

Her brows were furrowed, and her eyes unfocused slightly as she examined the yard and walls of the house. Her hands lifted, bracelets clicking faintly as Ru wrapped threads around her slim fingers. "I think… this is all that's left. But something has been feeding what's remaining. I don't see why we shouldn't be able to build them back up, but I don't understand how they're holding steady."

Ru, bent on solving the mystery, went to the front door. As was a habit born from a childhood of entering these wards, she placed her hand on it and whispered, "Let me in."

The magic answered with a click of the lock; the door swung open with a rusted creaking. They exchanged glances as Ru stepped inside, Poppy on her heels and a very tense Nora bringing up the rear, muttering something about the house still *feeling* haunted.

Nora closed the door behind them and waited patiently as Poppy and Ru took in the front room. Emotions tugged at Poppy's throat at the sudden wash of acute recognition. Ru must have been experiencing something similar as she stepped into Poppy's side and wrapped an arm around her sister. Poppy hugged Ru back and looked her fill.

The front room had been Natalie's favorite. The shelves of books their mother felt most useful lined the walls. A cushioned bench was nestled in the bay windows, and Poppy could have sworn she caught a glimpse of Natalie's impression there.

The rug of muted pinks and oranges was the same, one corner folded as if one of them had tripped on it while scrambling to leave the wards. There was a mess of papers in the corner and a half-empty water glass on the coffee table between the armchairs.

Nora reached and tried out the light switch. They blinked when the chandelier above flickered to life. It illuminated the stained and scuffed wood floors and dust particles in the air. Ru went to the windows, opening the curtains to let in even more light as if it could chase away the darkness that was their last moment in this home.

"Someone has been here," Nora whispered. Her eyes were on the half-empty glass of water. Poppy blinked. She had dismissed it as another hint at the abandoned decor of the room, but Nora was right. The water would have long since evaporated in the year since the coven had been broken.

Ru walked up to the glass carefully, eyes again searching for magic. "Whoever left it was warded," she whispered. Her eyes went to the pothos plant on the table, widening as she watched the leaves rustle, moving again toward Poppy with more life.

"It's like you're the sun," Nora said. Poppy was slowly growing used to people admiring her magic. She straightened, bolstered. She had Ru and Nora, two of the most powerful supernaturals in the city.

"Hello?" Poppy called, startling her companions with her sudden loudness. "Is anyone here?"

Hope rose like it had in Margot's shop once they realized all the impressions were fake. There were still wards, weaker but tailored specifically for the Jennings coven. If there was a witch here, it had to be one of them.

Silence answered Poppy's question. Nora sniffed rapidly, but if the witch's personal wards were too strong for Ru to see who they were, they would also be blocking the witch's scent.

"It's Poppy and Ru," Poppy called. It had been enough to summon Margot. The youngest and the weakest of their coven. Less threatening than anyone else by far.

There was a crash in the kitchen, and Poppy took off down the hall without thought. "Wait!" she cried as the shadowed figure yanked open the back door. She flung out a wall of magic, thoughts desperate as she tangled the cast. Poppy hadn't counted on the enthusiastic response from the shrubbery outside. It willingly hurled its strength toward Poppy, and a sharp wind caught the witch inside, slamming the glass door. A crack swept up one of the panels.

It was too dark in the kitchen to make out the figure's features, but the stance and mannerisms were still the same. The hair shorter. A glint of a piercing in the nose. Poppy began to relax, opening her mouth to greet her sister, but…the face wasn't quite right. A shadow of stubble and a hard, walled-off expression. This wasn't—

"Rayna?" Ru asked. She'd stepped up to Poppy's side and took in the windswept figure without fear.

"I go by Ryan now," the witch answered, voice too deep for the memories.

Ru blinked, her only reaction. Poppy smiled, rightness settling. Ru didn't hesitate a second longer before throwing herself into Ryan's arms. His eyes widened with surprise, and Poppy wondered if he'd been running, hiding, from their response to his transition, not them. It softened Poppy toward him. Another of Tiff's children, repressed and freed by her breaking the coven. It was little wonder why Ryan would hide from his sisters, likely fearing the break from femininity would be met with the same disproval Tiff had always shown when he fought against the braids, skirts, and blouses Tiff wanted her daughters dressed in.

Poppy wasn't certain when she started crying, but by the time she'd joined Ru and Ryan in the hug, her cheeks were soaked, and their childhood was making a lot more sense.

CHAPTER 13

"You two look more like siblings than we do," Ru said, eyes bouncing between Nora and Ryan on the couch. Then at herself and Poppy. Poppy snorted, and Ryan almost smiled, but he was still too tense and reeling from his sisters' sudden appearance with a werewolf in tow.

They'd made their way from the kitchen back to the "front room," as the siblings called it. Nora could only assume that meant there was a living room situation somewhere in the house as well. This place was similarly structured to the Den, but in Nora's childhood home, this room was larger and more open. There, the space spilled into the kitchen without the hall connecting to a dining room and closed-off kitchen like here. The doorways were begging to be explored as Nora realized how much bigger this house was, but she'd have to wait.

Ru's joke was her attempt to break the silence that had fallen. Ryan's eyes were bouncing between his younger sisters. His gaze was still guarded, but he was slowly softening. "You really don't have a problem with this?" Ryan finally asked, gesturing to his buzzed hair and flat chest.

Poppy quirked an eyebrow. "Do you have a problem with

the fact that we live with vampires? One of whom is a lesbian dating the werewolf beside you on the couch?"

Ryan's head snapped in Nora's direction. She smiled at him.

"Mom taught us lots of shit we don't agree with," Ru said. "She tried to mold us into people we didn't want to be. If any good came from her breaking the coven, it was the freedom to find who we are outside her limits."

Poppy nodded, and Ryan finally relaxed, slumping back into the couch with a heavy exhale. "Alright," he said. The room became cozier as he looked between them all. The chill left the air. "I want to hear how you ended up living with vampires."

Poppy cleared her throat. At this point, she sounded well-rehearsed as she launched into her tale. Nora half listened. Her eyes kept straying to the view outside. She could barely see down the street, but still, she looked for any sign of her childhood. The Den's van driving past. Someone going for a run. Any glimpse.

She still missed it. The Den. Her father's pack. Even with half of them under her charge and her mother returned, Nora felt torn in two. She was finally growing through the grief that had muffled her relationship with Matt, finally found the power he didn't think her capable of, finally able to see Gabriel's toxic hold and how young they were when he took charge, and yet couldn't do anything to use this knowledge to help them. Nora was ready to move forward. She even thought she could forgive Matt and the others for choosing the wrong alpha, but there wasn't a chance. She hadn't seen or heard a peep from those still living at the Den. Even Tio Marcus had failed to respond to the updates about Helen. The street outside felt too quiet.

But maybe having her mother back would help. Maybe Marcus hadn't seen the messages and this new contact with her tio would lead to him breaking from Gabriel and joining Nora. Maybe, maybe, more of them would see how wrong Gabriel was for joining Reelings, for his role in her father's death, and Nora would get her people back. But she also knew they would have to come to her with no ties remaining to Gabriel. Out of all of them, all the hurts, there wasn't any space in her left to forgive him. Nora wasn't willing to make things right between their packs. She wasn't willing to negotiate with him. She only wanted her family back, and in the last months, Gabriel had lost his position as part of it.

Gabriel wasn't her family. He'd once been accepted, but he'd ruined everything. Only Nora could make it right. With Poppy and Topher and Colbie, she was making steps in that direction. Once Helen made a public appearance, everyone would realize how much Nora and her friends were capable of.

Confidence was a heady drug, and Nora let it fill her. Poppy could build her coven, Nora her pack, Topher his charm. They would save the city.

Around Nora, the conversation shifted to the present. Ru was crying a bit, hopeful tears that made Nora's chest ache for similar reunions with her family. They all started when someone knocked. Poppy checked her phone, then opened the door with a wave of her hand. Margot entered, eyes seeking Ryan immediately. Nora hadn't noticed how much he'd warmed until a chill breeze swept the room, and he straightened, chin jutting forward.

And in a reaction that didn't surprise Poppy or Ru, Margot burst into tears. She nearly kicked Nora as she threw herself into her brother's arms. Vivienne followed Margot in, cautiously shutting the door behind her.

Abruptly, Nora became aware she was the only non-witch in a very witchy place—the atmosphere changing with Ryan's moods, Poppy's plants inching toward her without her noticing, Ru's unfocused gaze and shifting fingers, reading threads of something in the air that Nora would never see. The very air was charged with heady pulses of magic, making Nora dizzy if she didn't actively try to ignore it. That was with only five witches in the room. What would an entire coven feel like?

Everyone but Poppy and Ru cast looks in Nora's way. Undoubtedly, they wanted to talk openly about what finding each other here would mean. What having their childhood home meant. About continuing their search for the last Jennings.

"I might go check on my mom," Nora said, standing.

Poppy followed her to the door. "Can you help me strengthen the wards before you go?"

Nora was exhausted from lack of sleep, but she agreed. She shifted into her wolf, and they went out and casted for a good hour before Nora finally left, going out of her way to avoid passing in front of the Den. She ran straight to the Alpha's Den, scratching at the backdoor until Lupe let her in, then up the stairs. Nora shifted and pulled on one of Ricky's sweatshirts and a pair of shorts before searching for her mother. She found Helen still sleeping in Janelle's bed.

Helen stirred when Nora lowered herself onto the mattress. They faced each other, Helen blinking sleepily and brushing Nora's hair from her face. The touch as soothing as it was when Nora was a child.

"Are you going to leave again?" Maybe it wasn't fair to ask, but Nora was raw and tired and needed a warning if it was going to happen.

"No. Even if the emotions weren't as strong as a wolf, I still felt them. I still healed. But by then, I was lost. I'm so glad you found a way to pull me back."

Nora felt it between them then. The thread of magic that only she could see. Relief filled her core when she reached for her mother and offered to tether her. A beat passed before Helen accepted her place in Nora's pack. "We'll make Dad proud," Nora whispered.

Helen smiled. "We already have, but we do need to kill the motherfuckers who murdered him."

Topher groaned as he woke. Night had settled almost entirely outside. His body hurt from the activities of the night before and the heavy slumber of the sweltering day. His mouth was dry, brain sluggish, everything struggling against the sun-induced sleep's hold.

He used to love summer. Soccer games in the intense heat and ice cream and jumping into the lake in the Park. It was the happiest he felt as a human. When the sun chased away shadows and brought out smiles and interaction.

Julia was summer. Trampoline jumping and bike riding and growing up together. Then, kissing during a camping trip and experimenting without adults around. Their love had been easy like a summer's day. No hurry, no pressure. Barely even a commitment to anything but learning what it meant to date. There was heaviness in their time together, but only when Topher's bad habits and school got in the way. During the summer, Topher had been at his best, and their relationship consisted of ignoring the nightfall. Julia had been so good at blocking out what she didn't want to see. What she didn't think made her life bright and shiny.

Topher hadn't gotten a summer with Dylan. It had only just dawned when Dylan died, ruining the season forever. Their relationship was all fall leaves, shortened days, cold nights. They'd spent their time cuddled up and hushed, muffled by snowfall, and kissing in the shadows. Maybe that was why the darkness called to Topher so much now.

He was alone, but Topher forced himself out of bed. Out of his head. Out of the heaviness of his body.

It was so hard without Josh there. The wolf must finally be done holding Topher's hand, like everyone else. And right when Topher dared hope that they were making progress. The previous night, they had hunted for a scent. For any trace of Reelings to point them in the right direction to start their search. Topher had reacquainted himself with the city. Filtered out what was new, what remained from the spring. A few more werewolves were in town, but Josh hadn't seemed worried about them. Topher had caught the metallic buzz of multiple witches' wards, but Josh hadn't picked those up. It would seem the city was drawing in more supernaturals despite the turmoil brewing. Topher didn't know if this was good or bad yet.

In the early morning hours, Topher scented his first drainer, but he'd faltered. Stood frozen while Josh broke away to hunt it down. That was when Topher went home. Alone. Unable to face the task Josh was completing for him.

But Topher knew where they should start searching today. Or where he would if Josh was done with him. Dread coated his tongue at the thought, but he had to get it over with. Topher dressed and opened his door, stopping short when he found Colbie and Josh in the living room. Waiting. For him.

Topher thought he was doing a good job staying out of his head, but he hadn't even noticed Josh's smell in the apartment. He'd just taken in his empty bed and succumbed to loneliness. The balloon inflating in his chest was terrifying, but he went straight to Josh's side anyway.

"So, what did you smell last night?" Josh asked. When Topher sat next to him on the couch, Josh lifted his arm to rest it on the back of the cushions as he angled toward Topher.

Last night, Josh remained a wolf the entire hunt so they hadn't compared notes on their search. Topher cleared his throat. "Lots of supernaturals, but nothing of Reelings aside from…"

Josh and Colbie nodded, knowing what he couldn't say. Josh must have told her how Topher had reacted to finding a drainer.

"We've been smelling more wolves," Josh said. "Nora is probably drawing them in, but since no one is approaching her or Henry, we think they're trying to get a feel for the city first."

"What are you doing tonight?" Colbie asked. She didn't seem surprised about the werewolves flocking to Nora's power.

Josh said carefully, "Henry wants to talk with Topher if he's up for it."

Topher shrugged. If he was going to come back and actively search for Reelings and alliances, it would take conversations with all the city leaders. This time without Lana at his side. Why not start with the kindest among them? "Sure. Then I thought we'd go to the warehouse. See if we can pick up a trail or learn anything more."

Colbie's brows pulled together. Topher knew he sounded as flat and empty as he felt, but this was what they wanted, right? Even if Colbie would never ask more of him, she'd gotten involved with the supernaturals. Her girlfriend wouldn't stay away from the conflict. Colbie had to want Topher to act.

"You sure?" she asked.

"I should feed on the way," he said, still sounding wooden. "Where are Poppy and Ru?"

A beat passed as Colbie decided whether she would let herself be redirected. "They're at their childhood home. They found another one of their sis-siblings, I mean."

Topher noted the gender-neutral term and filed it away. They weren't called the Jennings sisters anymore. Noted. "That's great."

Colbie's brows knitted further. "Maybe we should go out another night," she said. Even when he tried to sound happy for Poppy, the tone had been robotic and cold.

He swallowed. "Colbie, I don't think laying in bed is helping. I don't think anything will help. Maybe I need a distraction. A purpose."

"Do you want to be distracted? Do you want a purpose?"

Topher didn't want to tell his sister what he wanted most of the time—the quiet of sleep. Sleep, sleep, and more sleep. Sometimes, in the darkest moments, a never-ending sleep. But... He had Colbie. And Poppy. Annaliese and Josh. Even

Chance was cautiously trying to fit himself into their strange world. Topher had points of light that he could focus on in the worst moments. And they were in this. Whether he was part of it or not, the people he loved were at risk.

Some of his old determination swept in, unexpected and only slightly unwelcome. He had to *try* to keep his people safe. It didn't always work. The disastrous results broke him, but sometimes he did okay. No one but Grace died in the basement during Nora's first change. Because of him. Topher was the only person who could have convinced a recently changed Nora not to kill Zayn and Colbie. She'd even forgiven him for what he'd done to her pack bond.

That was the moment Topher clung to. Even when Nora hated him afterward, he had to hold on to that one redeeming moment and hope there might be more.

"Let's go talk to Henry."

They drove to Twenty-Fifth Street, and Topher felt strange the entire time he sat in the backseat of the car. He rarely did anything so human. *Driving* through the city now felt foreign. Colbie insisted, though, saying Topher needed new shoes before he kept up his nightly runs. It was only then he'd noticed how true the statement was.

Henry's apartments had no unassigned parking, so they found a diagonal spot down the street a bit. Vegan Your Day was dark, Hills Brewing bustling, the entire street busier than Topher could remember it ever being.

"It's the safest place in the city these days," Colbie said in response to Topher's attention.

"Why?"

Colbie shrugged. Josh smirked, turning in his seat so Topher got the full effect of it. "Some of it is knowing about the packs in this area, but mostly, the humans are starting to hear about you. They come this way hoping for a glimpse of Topher West. You even have a fan page on most socials."

Colbie nodded. "You should see the edit this one person put together of you bartending." She mimed shaking a drink and then flipping it as if that was ever something done with a full pint glass.

"Should I really?" Topher asked, this time purposefully flat. "I'm guessing Lana was behind it?"

"Well, initially," Colbie said. "She thought it might annoy you enough to get you out of bed. But humans picked up on it. Then Annaliese didn't want Lana controlling the narrative." Colbie winked at Josh. "So, she started telling stories to her friends from the university. Oliver has shared some videos and pictures with her to post, too. Your fame is growing to mythic proportions within our New Brecken bubble. Also, when I said this one person made a thirst-trap edit of you bartending, I'm sure that person was Annaliese. She keeps denying it, but I know she took at least one of the videos in it."

A frown tugged Topher's lips. He trusted Annaliese and probably hadn't been answering her calls when she started this, but he might have appreciated a bit more of an effort to get his permission for this kind of publicity. "I didn't know anyone was filming me."

Colbie shrugged and opened her door, turning to face Topher when he joined her on the sidewalk. "You haven't gone unnoticed, Topher. People went to the Maker to see *you*. A lot of stories have cropped up. So far, none of them bad. Were-wolves might still hold the humans' favor in polls, but as an individual, you outrank every supernatural person in the city." Colbie looked smug. "Nora's annoyed. She keeps coming in second."

"You shouldn't look so happy about that," Topher said. "She *is* your girlfriend."

"Maybe I think her ego is getting a bit big since she's gotten the pack and the girl," Colbie said, but the joke sounded forced.

Topher's chest squeezed. It had been too long since he'd been able to show interest in Colbie's relationship. All was not as well as he'd assumed. But from the way Colbie's face lit with delighted surprise when Nora approached from the direction of the Alpha's Den, the problem must not stem from Nora herself. At Nora's side was a very different version of her mother than the one Topher had seen briefly last night before he collapsed.

He tensed. Waiting for Helen Morales to recognize him. Josh stepped in closer. All Topher could think about was the devastation on Nora's face after he charmed her. After he'd taken her pack from her. He'd taken Helen's coping mechanism and thrust her back into the city he couldn't stand himself. He'd done it for Nora, but the guilt was—

Helen stepped forward and wrapped Topher in a tight, unexpected hug. He stiffened in her embrace, body locking into place and confusion stilling his mind.

"Thank you for bringing me back to my daughter."

Helen was undeterred by his tense posture. The hug lasted so long that he pulled in a breath and cautiously relaxed. He knew his human self would be blushing over how much it meant. How much it affected him. He felt warm and contained, squeezed back into nearly normal a version of himself. He'd forgotten what this felt like. His arms came up and hugged Helen back, but not for long because he didn't trust the settled feeling it brought on. Topher stepped back.

Helen allowed him the space but rubbed his biceps as she looked at Colbie. "Hello again."

"Hi, Mrs. Morales."

Topher couldn't hold in the snort that escaped at Colbie's sudden sweet manners. Colbie glared at him and muttered, "Don't embarrass me."

"You do it on your own."

Helen smiled again, but Topher saw how it didn't quite reach her eyes. She returned to Nora's side, tipping her head back to take in the red brick and gleaming windows of Henry's main apartment building.

"And you're sure Henry Gould lives here?" she asked.

Josh stepped forward. "He's my uncle."

Helen hadn't noticed Josh. This new reality was too overwhelming, and his scent blended with his pack's territory. "My god. You look just like Stacia."

"So I've been told. Come on. Henry's very excited to see you." But Josh seemed nervous as he turned to lead them inside. Topher knew on some level that he was watching everyone else too closely. He was parsing out their every facial tick and tense muscle and doing his best to ignore his own discomforts. But it was no small thing when an alpha entered another's territory. Nora had come here before but with only Annaliese at her side and no pack under her care.

This was different. It was big. And Topher couldn't help but notice Annaliese was nowhere to be seen.

He fell into step beside Nora and tried to ask casually, "Where is Annaliese tonight?"

Nora fidgeted. "She's meeting with Brett Campbell. It was supposed to be over by now, but she texted and said it was going well. She's going to do an internship with them."

Topher didn't know what to think about that. He'd ignored most of the conversations about the assessor and was regretting it now. They stepped inside. Josh explained the layout of the apartments to Helen as they walked. Nora kissed Colbie's cheek and then hurried forward to stay at her mom's side. Leaving Topher and Colbie, the two vampires, in the rear. Topher had been here before, but weeks and Quinn's death lay between his visits. The looks he received weren't the same ones he'd gotten the last time he was here. Topher hadn't anticipated the disappointment on their faces. The distrust. The exhaustion he felt mirrored in the wolves' eyes. When Henry's pack first arrived, nothing could shake their confidence. New Brecken and its accepting laws were a beacon of hope, exactly what a large, progressive pack like Henry's was searching for in a home.

But had the price gotten too steep? The roots were laid down, but it wouldn't take much for them to leave. Just like all the other New Brecken packs had.

Then, there was the attention Colbie was getting. The shock of seeing the relationship confirmed said enough about how rare Nora and Colbie's love was. If Henry's pack hadn't seen the like, they may be the first. Or the first to proclaim their relationship. Werewolf and vampire. Alpha and someone of the same gender. They'd dismissed every line tradition drew.

They climbed the stairs to the top floor. The office/penthouse fell silent as Josh led them inside. Like the last time they met with Henry here, the alpha sat behind the grand desk against the far wall. Henry looked up with confusion, the furrows deeper in his forehead than the last time Topher had seen him. At first glance, the alpha appeared to have aged ten years, but all that cleared when he saw Helen. Recognition brightened his face. "Thank god," he said, rising from his leather chair. "I thought you were lost to the animal."

Helen's response was a near-hysterical laugh. Out of everyone, Henry appeared the least surprised by the reaction. He came forward and wrapped her in a tight, tight hug. Topher could see how his knuckles whitened where he gripped Helen's sweater.

Nora's face wasn't exactly pleased. Enough pain flashed behind her dark eyes that Colbie stepped into her girlfriend's side, linking their arms and dropping her head to rest on Nora's shoulder. They stood like that as they waited for Helen to catch her breath.

CHAPTER 14

After all this time and the lack of information she'd received, Nora had begun to minimize the connection between Henry and her mother. In her head, it was only a shared bond in a large pack. The way Josh talked about his pack members like they were relations, not the tight-knit, immediate family like her childhood pack had been. But... no. It was clear Helen and Henry were close. Had been close. Theirs was a story from before Luis Morales entered the picture. Nora found herself hating it. As if her father's memory wasn't in the room. Like Nora was the only one holding space for him. And maybe that wasn't fair, but there was more than friendship in that damn hug. Nora smelled and saw it, and only Colbie's reassuring presence kept her from bolting.

Topher stood expressionless, not quite focusing his gaze on anything. Colbie often complained about the distance he had placed between himself and everyone else. How not even she could read his face lately. Josh slipped away, still uncomfortable in their proximity despite the time he'd spent with Topher. He went to sit on a low couch, resting his arm on the wolf sleeping there. Daniel, Nora realized. The last time she'd seen him in wolf form, his face had been soft and almost puppy-like. He'd gained the ability to shift earlier than most. Now, he looked older. So similar to Henry with deep, pink lines running down his face. Fingernails raked hard enough to scar a werewolf.

The work of the drainers that Reelings had released. The drainers that killed Quinn. The roiling in Nora's stomach settled, sympathy taking its place as she realized there must be room for her father in the embrace Henry and Helen shared. Luis *and* Quinn. They were hugging and now crying over the years between them. It wasn't just relief. Had they been young and untouched by grief the last time they'd seen each other? Following some alpha who took every choice from them and left them blank, innocent canvasses that the world had dirtied in their time apart?

She would get her answers. Henry stepped back. He had barely cried, but his voice was rough when he spoke. "I haven't told Nora anything of how we know each other. Maybe now would be a good time?"

Helen agreed, and Nora found herself bracing as they all found a place to sit. Colbie stuck to Nora's side, exactly where Nora wanted her.

Helen began speaking. The entire room listened. Nora couldn't believe how little she knew of her mother's past. Each word was unfamiliar as Helen spoke. "I grew up in northern Montana, mainly the Canadian border, though we didn't pay much attention to our location. The pack I was raised to join had a more traditional alpha. He was strong and demanding. His presence drew wolves from all over."

When Helen paused, Henry stepped in. "Stacia and I grew up in Washington. We were adopted and had no idea that werewolves might be real. I ended up going to university in Montana, and one night, while I was feeling like I could crawl out of my skin and trying to party the feeling away, I wandered away from the town. I kept walking even though it was freezing. All I could do was follow the path of moonlight and this smell in the air."

Helen nodded. "Our paths crossed, and my alpha brought Henry in. He helped him make the first change. We were a very nomadic pack. We didn't like to interact with humans or other wolves. If we ever caught the scent of a vampire, well, my alpha enjoyed a challenge. A hunt, he called it. We went on one shortly after we accepted Henry to the pack."

Colbie made a face, but Topher didn't blink. He was sitting on an armchair, head angled to look more out the window behind Helen than she and Henry. Nora had no idea what was going on in his head. Josh stared at him as if he could figure it out if he looked hard enough.

"The hunt drew us further south than we had gone in years. We finally found the vampire, but he was young. Too young to have been changed. Vampires don't usually make teenagers; they have their own codes against such things. When my alpha still… well, that was the first time Henry and I found ourselves at odds with the pack. We started spending more time in our human bodies, discussing the aspects of our pack that rubbed us the wrong way. Then Stacia made her first shift and joined us, and Henry grew even more concerned when our alpha took a liking to her. Our alpha heard us talking and decided the words were a challenge. He and Henry fought; it was the first time I recognized the alpha below Henry's skin. When Henry broke free, I also took the opportunity to break away. I remember watching Stacia and Henry go one way, but I ran the other. I was foolish and tired of living under a man's rule. I was tired of being told to keep out of my weak, female human body. I wanted a home and to set down roots. I kept going south, and eventually, I ended up here. Then, I met Luis, and I think he might have been the only man who could sway me into joining another pack. The shift was already growing difficult for me after being without an alpha for so long, but Luis took the time to convince me. He introduced me to the other alphas so I would have an option, but during those weeks, we fell in love."

As events became more recent, Topher started paying attention. His blue eyes were focused on Helen as if he were silently charming her to tell him something he needed to know. "New Brecken was different then, but the makings of the city it is now were obvious. Supernaturals were drawn in. At the time, the economy was barely surviving. No one had enough space in their worries to pay attention to us. Not when the nights were full of people hiding in their homes or leaving the warehouses with contraband. It was a delicate balance, but Luis loved it. He loved the challenges of protecting humans, especially from themselves. So many had been losing jobs and homes, but we did our best to keep the streets safe. Us and the other packs, but then, to the north, the vampires started gaining power. Those without homes found themselves on the other side of the river, chasing free lodging and giving up their blood freely. The people forgot all the werewolves had done for them. Without people to protect and with no thanks for the balance maintained, a few packs started to leave, but then, well, we don't know what chased the others away." Topher's eyes dropped at that unsatisfactory answer. "But by the time Luis had agreed to endorse the laws to keep balance and help the situation, a solution that would help everyone, the last of his allies had left."

Helen stumbled there. Her features tightened with anger. "They left him after all the years of working together, and he died."

"But you don't know why yours was the last pack in New Brecken?" Henry asked.

Helen shrugged. Looking haunted still. "No. I assumed Reelings was behind it. He was never in favor of balance—our biggest threat. I don't... I was consumed with helping Luis figure out the right wording for the laws, how much power to give each group, and what would have to change in the pack to make it work. I wasn't paying much attention after Luis said he was sure he could convince his friends to vote in favor."

"He did want change?" Nora couldn't stop the question. "Beyond the initiation?"

Her mother smiled at her. "I can't tell you what he would have thought of this," she said, gesturing to Colbie and her, "but Luis had been breaking the traditions set by his previous alpha for years, starting with accepting a woman as his beta."

"And Gabriel? What was his relationship with Dad?"

"More distant at the end. We all knew Gabe had the alpha in him, but Luis wanted to wait for you to mature and give you the choice to run the pack. It was so special that you—"

Helen tapered off at the shock on Nora's face. "He thought I could be an alpha?"

"He dreamed of you taking over for him, Nor."

He knew before Nora had shifted. That meant the others had sensed it, too. Every time Gabriel and Matt told her she was too weak, that she wasn't holding up her father's memory, they were doing so to make her believe it. Every moment of doubt suddenly felt like a wasted use of her time and energy. Her father had believed in her. He had prepared a pack for her. He was changing the entire city for her. He had wanted this life she was living now.

The Morales pack was hers. The Den was hers. Nora had practically felt the building whispering in her ear earlier that day. Gabriel had tried to take everything. He had done everything to keep her small and under his thumb when she'd been destined to lead.

Henry questioned Helen about her time as a wolf, but Nora barely paid attention as her resolve grew. She should be listening, learning all she could about the rival pack in town, but Nora didn't think of Henry like that. Especially not now, with the warm friendship all too obvious between him and her mother.

Henry turned to Topher as he and Helen finished catching

up. "Mr. West," he started, his tone colder than it had ever been with Topher. Nora felt her hackles rising, and Colbie straightened. "Josh has informed me you feel ready to rejoin city life now?"

Topher didn't deny it, but the words of confirmation seemed stuck in his throat.

"Do I have your word no harmful secrets like last spring's come to bite me and my pack again?"

They waited as Topher collected his thoughts. "If I can help a drainer, I will. I still have hope there is something human in them, but I didn't intend to put anyone at risk, and I will be more careful." He dropped his eyes, shoulders pulling in.

"It isn't Topher's fault," Colbie put in, exasperated. "The drainers were contained. Reelings let them out. And it isn't as if we were in the wrong to keep them secret. No one in this city asks questions before killing the drainers they come across. Topher is already suspected of making them; if he started defending them publicly, that would only make it worse. We handled everything in the best way we saw fit. Maybe *you* would have listened, but don't pretend that if our secret had gotten out any of those drainers would have survived. We aren't the villains for trying to find a cure and keeping quiet, especially not when our good friend was at risk. Now there's no one trying to help."

Silence fell over the room. Nora tensed. The expressions all around were stony. Nora suddenly very much felt like an intruder in another pack's territory. But Colbie wasn't fazed. Her expression didn't falter as she defended their actions and Topher. Topher, who was staring at his sister. He hadn't questioned the blame Henry placed at his feet for what happened. As if speaking to her brother directly, Colbie said, "What happened to Quinn lays fully on Reelings's shoulders. Nearly everything bad in this city goes back to him. The laws were working. The alliances were steady. We can bring that back as long as we don't let him tear us apart. We have a shared goal, a shared enemy. We have to focus on that."

"Are you telling me to reform my alliance with Lana?" Henry asked.

Colbie snorted. "Of course not. She led me and Topher astray. Again, maybe not the villain, but she's a silly person to trust. If Topher is ready to get back into New Brecken and the politics, he's the one you want an alliance with. Josh knows that already. I know that. Nora knows that. Even the humans know it. So what will it be?" Colbie asked, but the question wasn't directed toward Henry. She was looking at her brother.

The room went quiet. All breath held. Topher met his sister's eyes, jaw clenching. Nora saw it in every line of stiff muscle. He didn't want this. But he didn't protest. When Henry cleared his throat, Topher met the alpha's eyes and spoke, quiet but steady. "I'm going to find Reelings and stop him. It'll likely involve me taking Fourth."

Another silence, brimming with shock. "Why would you do that?" Henry asked.

Topher stood. He paced, agitated and finally showing something of what he was feeling. "What's my other option, Henry? Fourth Street is Reelings's goal! He wants to return the city to what it was before the laws when he owned north of the river. You know Solas, Patter, and Grace's seconds are battling for Happenstance. You know they aren't going to be a unified front when he attacks, and he may not even have to with his being their maker. He just has to say the word. *What's my other option?* Somehow, I've been granted a reprieve, but we all know what comes at the other end of this. I'm either removed as a threat or put into power."

"You'd declare war on all the vampires?"

"I'll see how talking works first." Topher shrugged. He stopped by the window, staring outside. Hands clenched, jaw bunched, eyes unblinking. Entirely still. Inhuman.

Henry considered him. Josh was pale. Nora felt herself

getting angry the longer they watched him silently. Topher was drowning. He'd been drowning for a long, long time.

Colbie knew it, too. She addressed her brother in a low voice. "If you don't want that, Topher, we can leave."

He blinked at her like he never considered the option. Or, never thought that Colbie might go with him. He took a shallow breath. "I think the problem here, Colbs, is that I don't want anything these days. I can do this. I don't want to, but…" He shrugged and turned back to the window.

Helen rose and went to Topher, leaning close and giving him a side hug. Impossibly, his posture stiffened further. "You know they always say those who don't want power are the ones that should have it. Maybe this is a step forward for you. Maybe it'll be good."

"Maybe." He gently untangled himself from Helen. "I'll give you all some more time to catch up. You want to come, Colbie?"

A quick kiss on Nora's cheek, and Colbie was at her brother's side. "Where are we going?"

"If I'm making my official come back, I'm going to need a phone," he said dryly, waving goodbye. With that, the vampires swept out of the room. Leaving Nora and her mother with Henry's pack. There was a beat, and then Josh followed the vampires. He nodded at Henry on his way, and Nora frowned. She knew trust was a long way off, but the blatant spying was insulting.

"Tell me everything, Henry," Helen bid.

And Henry did, launching into the story of leaving after challenging their old alpha, finding Quinn, and building a pack. How they wandered from place to place, mainly in the Midwest. How they eventually ended up here. This was the life most werewolves lived. Nora's childhood home and its permanence were an anomaly. New Brecken was an anomaly. How different her life would have been in a nomadic pack. Nora knew it likely wasn't, but that sounded so *simple*. Most of them lived their days as hearty wolves, their main preoccupation hunting vampires and hiding from humans. What a gift the laws and dynamics of New Brecken were. And with so many other cities and towns looking their way, Nora needed to keep peace and show that lives like this were possible. It was an option. Living in peace, embracing the human half of their beings. This was a form of freedom, and Nora wanted to make it available to everyone.

So did Henry. He loved New Brecken. Shining through his grief and hesitance to rejoin the fray was his devotion to this place and its people. He hadn't left. He housed humans and werewolves in harmony. When their eyes met, Nora saw everything she felt mirrored in his gaze. It was the werewolf's duty to protect humans from vampires, but they aspired to become so much more.

CHAPTER 15

There was a knock at the front door of the Jennings house. They all jumped, expecting no one else to join them. Ru stood to answer it, but with a grunt, Ryan pushed her back into her seat, muttering to the wards as he approached the entry. He turned, brow furrowed. "No one's there."

Poppy snapped, opening the door for her roommates and making everyone jump again. Topher scowled. "It might have been another vampire, Poppyseed."

"She knew it was us," Colbie assured him, walking inside. "I followed Nora's trail to get to the right house. Who else can sniff out my girlfriend so creepily?"

Poppy smirked. "My thoughts exactly. What's up?"

Ryan stood by the door, watching their easy interaction with raised brows. He always had the most expressive eyebrows. When Ru was a baby, they'd entertained themselves by watching her try to copy him even before she could talk. Margot and Vivienne were less surprised by the appearance of vampires, but Vivienne looked wary after what she'd said to Topher the night before.

Topher ignored the witches entirely and went up to Ru. "Phone, please. I think it's time we got you your own."

"Amazing! Thanks, Dad!"

Topher made a gagging noise, and the weight of worry crushing Poppy began to ease. It was the most he'd acted like himself in weeks. "Don't, Rhubarb. Just don't." Topher turned to Poppy. "Can we talk?"

Poppy led the two of them upstairs. It felt strange and full circle to bring them to her first bedroom, the place she had fled before ending up with them.

As soon as the door shut behind them, Topher opened his arms. Poppy wasn't sure who he was comforting or seeking comfort from, but she and Colbie stepped into his embrace and remained there until his grip loosened. He sat heavily on the lower bunk bed, head dropping into his hands. "Will you two tell me what to do? I'm tired of thinking."

Poppy and Colbie exchanged a look. Maybe they were finally getting Topher back, but he wasn't the same. "What have you been thinking up to this point?" Colbie asked carefully.

Topher's knees bounced under his elbows. "I smelled Reelings a bit last night, but he must still be with Beth, and she's warding him. It was nothing very recent; only his smell left on things he touched that she must not have noticed." Topher pulled a face. "Just in a couple of random neighborhoods. I don't know what he's doing."

"Only that he's still in the city," Colbie said. She and Poppy shared a look at that. Most people believed Reelings must have left New Brecken to lick his wounds. Only vampires can smell other vampires, and none had as strong of senses as Topher. He'd learned more in one night than anyone else had figured out all summer.

"Yes. I need to go check on Solas and Patter," he said. "I want to see if—" Topher's voice faltered. The bouncing of his knees worsened until he stood, pacing the room, eyes taking nothing in. Those shadows of his, the ones Poppy was becoming adept at seeing, swirled out. They reached toward the walls, the wards, but there was nothing sinister in their darkness.

Poppy suspected they were half the reason her wards always worked so well against demons. The darkness counteracted the life of Poppy and Ru's magic, concealing it better than anything else. After tonight, thanks to Topher and Nora, the wards around the Jennings house would be stronger than anywhere else. Hopefully, strong enough to protect all the witches gathered within.

Poppy couldn't take her eyes off the slithering shadows now that she knew to look for them. They weren't like the haunting quiet of darkened alleys. They were like the stillness that hung around Ru and Poppy when they stayed up whispering late into the night. Topher's shadows spoke of what flickered around the light cast off a fire in a mantle. His shadows were the black between stars, supporting the pinpricks of light and making them look all the brighter against its solid, unyielding presence.

Topher's shadows weren't sinister. Ru believed they were some kind of impression left by Dylan. Whatever magic their mother wanted to draw from Dylan's life and their young love, Dylan had somehow imbued in Topher's change instead. A piece of his first love, always a bit out of Topher's control, reaching to protect him, giving him so much power that Topher was untouchable.

Poppy was grateful to Dylan, this boy she'd never met.

Topher hadn't calmed. He didn't appear able to, but he forced out the words in a rush, "I'm going to have to see what charm Reelings put on them and if I can undo it. I was trying… when I snapped Julia's mind, that's what I was trying to do. I'm scared I'll do it again. I'm scared I'll accidentally kill them, too."

Colbie stilled. The shadows rushed out of Topher faster now, anxious alongside him. Poppy cleared her throat. "I think whatever charm Reelings used on the drainers is something different. It's tied with the cast that turns the humans into

drainers, placed in their head when they're most vulnerable."
Like how Dylan's strength wound with Topher's being during
his change, but Poppy didn't say that. "I bet whatever charm
he put on Solas and Patter is standard. Maybe very strong, but
I doubt removing it will hurt them, Topher."

Topher stopped pacing, eyes searching Poppy's face. He'd
asked her before to speculate what charm was, what was in a
vampire's saliva, and the effects he'd have on the life force of
humans around him. Poppy knew he didn't always believe her
answers, but it meant a lot to her that he listened and valued
her words. It made her stand straighter now. "You won't hurt
them, Topher. Especially if you take someone else to stop you
if things get bad."

Topher nodded. He went to the window, gaze dropping to
the lawn below. "Josh might come. He seems pretty good at
handling me when the m——when I lose control, but I would
feel more comfortable if he had charms too. It's, it's getting
easier. To charm werewolves. I'm scared I'll get good at it. And
if Reelings is as strong as he seems, maybe he can do it too."

Poppy nodded. "Ru will help Josh with that."

"I'll take some, too," Colbie said, tipping up her chin. "And
Nora."

"I don't want——"

"Too bad, Topher. I have your back. We'll meet with the
vampires and set the tone for what they can expect."

"Then I'll come too," Poppy said, though the thought was
terrifying.

Topher considered and finally nodded. He picked up the
pacing again. The meeting with Solas and Patter was not his
only source of anxiety. "I'm going to try and track Reelings,
but I need to be in a position to step forward before I find him.
I'm going to talk to Campbell. I'm going to tell him I'm a
maker." Topher looked at Colbie. "Do you want to be registered under——"

"Yes. God, yes. Take Lana's name off anything to do with me."

A ghost of a smile from Topher. "Alright. I... If I get cleared, I'll offer to turn Raven."

That was unexpected. "Why?"

"She wants it. She's had years to think about it. If I'm going to compete with the makers, I need vampires under my name to seem legitimate. And Lana will hate it."

Colbie's brow furrowed as she considered all this. "They might not clear you after you've kept it a secret for so long."

Topher nodded. "I know. I'll have to be *persuasive*."

Poppy's heart dropped. Topher was prepared to charm to get his way. He was in this. All in. Ready to play the game like a vampire, as much as he hated it.

"They'll have cameras set up. If you charm them, they can watch it back and know what happened."

Topher considered that. "Then, I think we need to call Chance."

"To hack the cameras?" Colbie asked, eyes widening with far too much excitement at the thought.

Topher snorted, shaking his head. "I want to set up a similar situation and see if my charm will work over technology. I don't know if anyone has ever tried that."

"I never thought of that," Poppy said. "You think it could work?"

Topher only shrugged. "If it does work, I doubt any vampires who figured it out are advertising the fact. We'll need to ask Annaliese what the setup of the office is."

Colbie's attention snagged on her name and the forced casual tone Topher used when he said it. "What *is* going on with you and Annaliese?"

The shadows seemed to gather behind Topher's eyes at the question. "I don't know. I don't trust myself with her. I don't like how I am with the people I'm—" Topher cut off, glancing at Poppy and then the floor. Then he hid his eyes completely, pressing his palms into them.

"Go ahead, Topher," Poppy said, surprised by how little it stung. No matter who he liked, it was Poppy in this room. Her and Colbie and Topher. A little family they had made, and she'd worried she'd lost when Topher couldn't get out of bed. Yet, as soon as he left it and started thinking about the future again, Poppy and Colbie were the ones he sought. That was enough.

Topher dropped his hands and nodded slowly, reading all this in Poppy's face. "It's like my body wants to be attracted to people at all times. It feels so wrong now, but it's like... it's this big way I find comfort. Has been. I cheated on Julia with Dylan. I went back to Julia when Dylan died. I went to so many other people every time I've been upset. I just... I hear about love and loyalty and lack of interest while mourning, and I don't know what's wrong with me that I... It's like I need someone touching my body to escape it all." He sighed, voice cracking. "What the fuck is wrong with me?"

Colbie stepped forward, taking his hands. "I do think it's different for you, Topher. I think it's comfort, but I also don't think you mean it maliciously. I also have noticed it seems to go both ways."

Topher's brows bunched. "What do you mean?"

"You don't seem to get jealous. Like ever. Like, do you even know what it feels like?"

"I mean, I've been jealous of Chance before. Of Oliver and Zayn having each other."

Colbie let out a little laugh. "But, romantically? Do you know what people mean when they worry about being cheated on? Would that bother you? We know you cheat yourself, but I'm wondering if it's because you don't think it's that big of a deal. I've been thinking you might be poly."

Topher's brows pinched. He knew the term, but it was like

he couldn't apply it to himself. "I was monogamous with Dylan."

"And Dylan was special and yours. But what if he'd had a hookup that wasn't you?"

Topher didn't blink at the question. "If he wanted to, it would have been fine. I know what he felt for me wouldn't have changed."

"See?"

"I don't think so…"

"What I'm trying to get at is maybe you aren't monogamous. Maybe you and Dylan, years down the road when things were less new and intense, would have opened the relationship, and you wouldn't have had a problem with it. Maybe your heart and body don't have issues with spreading the love. Maybe you know and understand that your love for Julia and for Dylan were completely different, and you had space for both. Maybe you don't feel that has anything to do with the attraction you might feel for Annaliese. It sounds like you can separate it all, and you're more worried about what happens to the people you love than betraying their memory or something like that."

Topher had stopped pacing again, lost in thought. Poppy was impressed. That did make sense for how Topher moved through the world. "But who would be okay with that?" Topher asked, heartbreakingly solemn. "Who would want to be with me knowing even a few weeks after their death, I would be heartless and disloyal enough to sleep around to make myself feel better?"

"Do you feel like that's what you did after Dylan?"

"Dylan was different. He would get it."

"And Julia wouldn't, so you hid yourself away and fell into the depression she would want."

Topher looked a bit sick at that. "Colbie. Don't."

"You grieved for her appropriately, Topher. That's all I mean. Not that it was fake grief or forced. But, now you have to do what you can for yourself, especially as you go into the city for all of us. You need to be strong. You need to find the support you crave."

"It's too selfish," Topher whispered.

Colbie wrapped him in another tight hug. "Just think about it and know I would love nothing more than for you to be more selfish."

Topher heard the commotion first. The witches, whether they wanted to or not, were getting accustomed to late nights. Or unused to being able to sleep period when night came. Poppy was basically nocturnal at this point and kept the same hours as Topher and Colbie most of the time. Because of this, they were all awake, sipping tea in the front room and discussing living situations. Heather and Patrick would have first dibs on the main bedroom as none of Tiff Jennings's children wanted to take over her space. Vivienne hesitantly asked if Margot expected to share a room, and Margot answered too quietly for even Topher to hear. Ru was excited to have her old room back, even if she'd have to share the space eventually. Topher noted how Poppy tried to force enthusiasm, but she loved having Ru nearby. There was a vague plan for Poppy to stay here a few nights and ensure the wards were strong enough, but Topher was fairly sure she'd be coming home soon. Poppy didn't view this old Victorian with the same nostalgia Ru possessed. Topher felt proud that he and Colbie had made a place they considered home.

He'd ignored the shuffling on the other side of the window at first, knowing who was out there. But when the first yelp sounded, it was a sudden rip in the night. Topher stood, sharing only a glance with Colbie before he ran for the door. Outside, it was too still and quiet, but Topher knew he'd heard something and… there. A soft snarl. Topher ran around the house toward the sound, keeping in the shadows. At his back,

Colbie stuck close. He could nearly hear her focus as she kept her steps silent. It was no longer something he thought about as Topher willed the shadows to conceal them. In the back-yard, two wolves circled.

Josh was the one snarling, but his eyes, the same color as a wolf or human, held the tension of someone who knew they were where they didn't belong. The other wolf took Topher a moment longer to recognize.

Topher's memories flashed to Pressing Park. Ru in a dying ring of light and Poppy's screaming. Both these wolves had been there. Colbie too. A strange reunion without the glue that had joined them all at the time. Nora was still at Henry's for all Topher knew. Josh was on his own, far too close to Gabriel's Den. He was in the wrong territory, and he knew it.

Matt let out another growl. Not for the first time, Topher wondered how detailed communication was between were-wolves. It would seem some form of conversation was happen-ing. Though his reluctance to do so was evident, Josh was making himself smaller. Less threatening. As if to say, I know I shouldn't be here, and this is a misunderstanding. But his pride was singing, too. His hackles too far raised to be in submission, his steps too forceful.

It was a stalemate. Matt likely didn't want to threaten a member of Henry's sizable pack. So far, the two packs had kept a strained peace. To disrupt it, when Nora and Henry were once again aligning, wouldn't do for Gabriel's pack.

Topher took in all this, watching for either wolf to make any sudden moves. It was like he watched them so intently that he forgot to take stock of his own feelings. Forgot to smother them as usual. The building anger at the sight of Matt kindled to a roaring blaze, and Topher couldn't stop the hiss that left his lips.

He didn't like this. Didn't like Josh and Matt facing off and threatening a fight. Didn't like that Matt was so close to Colbie, Poppy, and Ru. Didn't like that Matt, no matter his proximity to his Den, would dare think he had the upper hand in this. That last thought was full vampire.

Matt heard the hiss and turned to him. Josh's growling spiked, but Topher was removed from any fear he maybe should have experienced with a werewolf stalking toward him and his sister. All Topher knew was the anger he'd felt the last time he'd seen Matt. At Gabriel's side, defending Reelings while Annaliese was in that summoning circle. There was some relief at having Matt focus on himself, not Colbie or Josh.

Topher never let his fangs slide free, but he did so now as he bared his teeth. Without thought, his charm began to gather and the shadows thickened, dimming the light of the moon. And Topher knew this situation was in his control. He was strong, fed, and angry. He'd never tested himself against a werewolf, but it would have to happen soon enough. Why not now?

Distantly, Topher was aware of a car door slamming. Matt's ears perked in that direction. Topher stepped forward while the wolf's attention was split. Matt lowered his body, his snarling rising in volume. He was going to pounce. Topher braced. The monster within him thrilled, readied, smiled.

Then, Annaliese was there. Jumping in front of Topher with her hands outstretched. "Go away, Matt," she said. Bored, like she was shooing a troublesome but harmless stray cat.

The tension between them released into shock. Topher darted forward, grabbing Annaliese's arm and pulling her to his side. "What are you doing?" he asked, words not quite right. Topher didn't realize why until Annaliese's eyes widened at his mouth. He ran his tongue over his teeth, retracting his fangs, though the monster within loathed to do so.

Topher pushed it down. Dredged up his human side, though it was heavy and laden with loss and pain and anxiety at seeing Annaliese. Josh had been so right when he theorized about Topher having two sides as much as a wolf.

"Stopping you two idiots," Annaliese answered, shaking off

Topher's grip. She turned back to Matt. He was still lowered, ears flat on his head, but confusion had replaced the hostility in his eyes. "Leave Josh alone, or you'll have to deal with Henry and Nora. Just go home. I'm sure Gabriel's wondering where his goodest boy is."

Matt's eyes narrowed, the expression all human on the wolf's face. Annaliese waved Josh closer. "Come on. Let's go inside."

Josh gave Matt a wide berth but came to a halt at Topher's side. By then, Annaliese had turned from them all to yell at Colbie. "You were going to let them fight?"

Colbie shrugged, stepping out of the shadows and glaring at Matt. "It's been boring for weeks. I wanted to let Topher have a little fun. He's got plenty of scores to settle with Gabriel's pack."

"Topher does, or you do?"

Colbie slung an arm around Annaliese's shoulders. "We both do, but between us, I'd let Topher be the one to fight a werewolf."

Josh snorted. He butted his head into Topher's hip until Topher moved to follow Colbie and Annaliese inside. He couldn't help looking back long enough to ensure Matt had slunk away into the night. No doubt to tell Gabriel what he'd seen here. There would be eyes on the Jennings house now. Would Beth be among them with her shadows and the demons she controlled? Would Poppy's wards be strong enough to keep them all out?

Ahead, Colbie was already on her phone, calling Nora. Between them all, the Jennings home would be safe for the rest of the night.

CHAPTER 16

I t was late in the night. It was so late that the Alpha's Den was closed, and they had all ended up in Poppy's childhood home. Nora looked around the space. They'd tumbled into the basement, the largest area for them all. It looked and smelled like it hadn't been updated since the eighties: wood paneling, worn gray couches, crates of books, and old DVDs around the wall. Concrete floors were covered by rugs so old Nora couldn't guess their original coloring. It seemed this was the only space that hadn't been touched by Tiff Jennings's refined taste.

Nearly everyone Nora enjoyed interacting with outside her pack was here. Oliver and Zayn's absence was keenly felt, especially when the space around Topher remained empty. But then Josh settled in next to him. He huffed a breath through his snout as he rested his chin on Topher's shoe. Was Josh that reluctant to talk to Poppy? To speak to any of them? Or did he prefer being a wolf these days to deal with the emotions? Nora knew werewolves who chose to stay a wolf more often than human. From everything she learned, there was no danger in it as long as they had an alpha to help them back to their human body. Without that, the wolf could get lost like Nora's mom.

Except—Nora glanced back toward Topher—now, not even that was a life sentence.

Topher stood against the wall, but there was a circle of chairs and couches set up. Margot said they used to do classes down here, explaining the burn marks and occasional strange smell as she and Nora had moved the couches into a circle. Now, Margot sat next to Poppy, Ru, and Ryan. The four of them had squeezed themselves onto the longest couch. Perched on the arms were Vivienne on one side and Jay on the other. Chance sat on the loveseat, a space next to him as they waited for Colbie to come back downstairs. Janelle and Ricky were in another loveseat. They were the only pack members Nora had brought tonight. Annaliese was in an armchair. She was the subject of their questioning tonight. They all wanted to know what the humans were planning, how the new city government branch was structured, and how much they should trust it.

Colbie came bouncing back down the stairs. Having Topher out and about had done wonders for Colbie's mood.

"No wolves around the house," she reported. "I think the wards are deterring them well enough, or Gabriel's too much of a coward to try anything." Nora pushed off the wall where she'd been waiting and sat down next to Chance, opening her arms for Colbie to fall into her lap to sit. Colbie wrapped an arm around Nora's neck, tucked her feet under Chance's thigh, and let out a contented sigh.

Vivienne stared at them from her elevated seat. She kicked Margot to get her to follow her line of sight. Nora and Colbie had been through this before. Usually at Alpha's Den, but once when they met Annaliese at Hill's Brewing. Colbie wasn't surprised and laughed at Nora's suspicion when she caught a couple looking at them. Colbie had explained, "You don't get all happy and want to be friends when you see other lesbians? Of course we stare at each other." Nora hadn't been about to deny it.

When Nora raised an eyebrow at Colbie now, Colbie was already looking at her with a knowing expression. From what Nora gathered, Margot wasn't proclaiming any type of romantic relationship with Vivienne, but maybe with Ryan now out, with Jay there, and with Nora and Colbie modeling just how safe a space this friend group was, Margot would get more comfortable. *If* that was even the problem.

"What was it like?" Topher asked Annaliese. He was still stiff from the near confrontation with Matt outside. Nora had some words with her best friend for putting herself between the two of them. Annaliese should know better than to reach between fighting animals, and at that moment, that was basically what Topher and Matt had been. Nora was certain only Topher's extreme control had kept the situation from escalating.

"Just your normal office building, but I did like the people. They're rightfully suspicious, but they formed their branch to keep the laws and think we can find peace in the city. I talked to Brett mostly. I told him what it was like being around the Alpha's Den and its inception. I didn't tell him anything about last winter, and he only seems to know what the humans who attended leadership meetings can remember. He knows about you, Topher, but no specific stories. He seemed to want those from me, but I only talked about how you're trustworthy and haven't been around lately, then mostly talked about Nora and my friendship. I told him I know you all from when she and Colbie started dating. He had *lots* of questions about that."

"Gross," Colbie muttered.

"It wasn't fun," Annaliese agreed. "But then I started in with my questions for him. It sounds like his branch was mostly started to appease scared humans. Too many people are calling for supernaturals to be kicked out and get rid of the laws. It sounds like everyone high up in the city is still benefiting from the tourism, increased interest in UNB, and Fourth Street, so they made this mediation branch as a show that they're handling the drainers and any other discontent. But I don't think there's any real reason to fear Alpha's Den will be shut down or that the laws will change. The money-hungry humans in charge are still on Fourth Street's side."

Nora didn't love the sound of any of this. She didn't want to benefit because power-hungry humans were on her side. She didn't want her werewolf status to be a money grab, but knowing the assessors weren't the threat they could have been with real backing was a relief.

Colbie seemed to feel the same. "Well, that's something."

"Could be worse," Topher agreed.

Annaliese wasn't looking in his direction, but everyone else in the room kept glancing Topher's way. All of them attempting to read his closed-off features. How okay was he? Was it good that he was here? A sign of healing? Or bad? Was it repression and denial and acting only for them in a way that would lead to resentment? How would any of them discover one way or another until it was too late?

A cool press of lips to Nora's neck calmed her thoughts. A hint of bliss. "You're thinking too hard," Colbie murmured.

"Just worried."

"What else is new?"

Annaliese gave more details about the meeting and what her internship would look like, then Colbie brought up their half-formed plans to, apparently, try charming Brett Campbell. Chance didn't think the charm would translate over camera, but they would try it tomorrow night if they had time. The plan lighthearted and without much weight. Annaliese's assurances about the assessor's lack of power had eased some of their apprehensions, though Topher still needed them to like him enough to grant him his title as maker.

"Maybe they'll just like you, Topher," Nora suggested. "Maybe you wouldn't need charm to do whatever you're planning."

Topher's eyes dropped. Colbie sighed. "I mean, Nora is

right. It's not like it's your fault you're a maker. You'd be following the law by coming out as one, and you can blame Lana for taking so long to do it. Maybe they won't punish you for it."

That was throwing kindling into the fire. Everyone had an opinion about how the humans would react to Topher waiting until now to get registered, let alone going on to register anyone under his name. Topher didn't contribute to the debate, and Nora didn't love the topic much either. Now, Annaliese was watching him intently.

Nora hoped Annaliese wasn't thinking what Nora thought she was. For the most part, Nora was used to and okay with Annaliese's fascination with the supernaturals. But occasionally, Annaliese seemed to want more. Like now, when she was considering Topher as if the possibilities were endless. Like she might want to be made.

But Annaliese didn't want that…right?

Nora needed to have a long talk with her best friend. In private. She had thought being stuck in Beth's magic last spring would have removed this fascination, not spur Annaliese to want more.

A quiet descended. There was a soft rumbling at Topher's feet, and Nora realized Josh had fallen asleep. Even though having so many people invade his space had made Ryan nervous and fidgety all night, he didn't look far from following Josh's lead. Poppy offered everyone rooms in the house, and Ru moved to magically remove dust from blankets and beds. Margot and Vivienne slipped upstairs and in less time than Nora would have imagined, everyone was settled. Even Topher had simply closed the blinds on the ground-level windows and stretched out on the couch, Josh on the rug beneath him. Topher stared at the ceiling, sleep at least half an hour away. Nora waited on the stairs as Colbie asked him if he was sure he wanted to stay there for the day. He raised an eyebrow and whispered too quietly for Nora to hear. Colbie straightened up like a rocket and turned for the stairs. She grabbed Nora's hand and tugged her up the steps.

"What's the rush?" Nora asked, laughing at Colbie's sudden enthusiasm.

"Topher's staying here."

"Okay?"

"Ru's staying here. Poppy's staying here. I love this house."

"I don't—" Nora tripped on the stairs, suddenly understanding what Colbie was implying. Her mouth stilled, tongue heavy with sudden nerves and anticipation. Nora picked up the pace.

The apartment door slammed behind them, Nora falling into Colbie against it. Nora could practically taste her pounding heart in the back of her throat. Colbie was similarly frantic in her movements. Only their practice kept their kissing pleasant and in check, though teeth still struck and lips would be bruised by the end of this. All Nora could think of was what was coming next. How little experience she had. How much more of this Colbie had done.

Nora speared her fingers into Colbie's hair, nails catching. She mumbled an apology, and the words seemed to bank the fire. Nora ached for more heat even as relief allowed her to pull in a full breath when Colbie backed away the slightest bit.

The apartment was lit by the stove lights Poppy had left on. Mouse padded near, meowing until he realized neither of his two favorite people was in the room. He turned and went right back inside Topher's cracked door.

In the dim, orange glow, Colbie held Nora's eyes. When they first started dating, Nora always got the sense that Colbie was learning her. Trying to learn to read Nora's expressions as clearly as the text in a book. Parsing each twitch or relaxed feature until she could guess what Nora was thinking underneath. Nora had the sinking feeling that Colbie had finally figured her out. Understanding broke through the glimmer of lust in Colbie's eyes.

She reached up, cool palms cupping Nora's cheeks. "Take a breath. We can slow down."

Nora didn't think she wanted to do that. Her nerves made her feel the need to rush, to rip off the bandaid that would be her awkward fumbling. Nora almost laughed. This was how Colbie seemed to feel underneath their kisses. The kisses Nora had learned to control. She'd mastered putting Colbie at ease in those moments but had known how far things would go before. Now, they had an empty apartment, and the only upcoming event was the sunrise, but even that sometimes failed to bring Colbie down immediately. The lack of parameters was messing with Nora's ability to take control. She couldn't put Colbie at ease when she didn't know what she was doing.

"Nor, remember when I mentioned breathing?"

Nora sucked in a breath, groaned, and dropped her forehead to rest on Colbie's shoulder. "I'm so fucking nervous. What if I'm shit at this?"

Colbie shrugged, bouncing Nora's head. "I'll probably not find it adorable at all and break up with you."

At least Nora was confident enough in the relationship to bark out a laugh at that. She straightened and took in Colbie's beautiful face. The gentle smile that might be Nora's favorite if only because it was just hers. "You wouldn't dare."

"I wouldn't," Colbie agreed. She played with a lock of Nora's hair, suddenly calm and idle. Herself. Like she'd been when they met in the sweaty darkness of the Maker. This moment had been building since then. "I wouldn't leave you, Nora. I wouldn't embarrass you. I wouldn't make you do anything you don't like. I wouldn't ignore you if something made you uncomfortable."

"What would you do?" Nora whispered. She'd shut her eyes at some point during Colbie's promises. Sometimes, her face was too much to take in.

"I might start with something like this," Colbie said. Her voice was different. Husky. Full of feeling. A breathiness in the words that ghosted over the skin at the base of Nora's throat before Colbie pressed a kiss there.

Goosebumps erupted from that soft contact, the slight tickle as Colbie traced her lips to the side of Nora's neck. She bit at the curve leading into Nora's shoulder. Not enough to pierce skin, but enough for a concentrated flare of saliva to make Nora's heart calm momentarily. Colbie hummed with encouragement, licking the small hurt to soothe it with more bliss.

Nora was holding herself up with Colbie's shoulders now. Her head swimming, her knees too relaxed to fully support her. There was a warmth building in her core and that was taking all of Nora's attention.

Colbie's tongue traced to Nora's ear, her breath cool in the trail of wetness. Nora shivered, and Colbie pressed closer as if to help warm her. "Should I stop?"

"No." Nora's voice was rough around the word. It was dragged from that hot place that begged for more. Nora tipped her head back, fully exposing her throat, asking when the words were too hard.

Colbie's cold fingers made contact with Nora's stomach under her sweatshirt. With a question in her slow movements, Colbie began to pull the thick fabric up.

Nora was bare underneath. Bras were the worst part of swift shifts, and in the months since she'd gained the ability to turn wolf, Nora opted to forgo them more often than not. She nodded eagerly nonetheless. Colbie's pupils seemed to widen with every inch of skin she exposed. Her mouth dropped open when Nora's breasts were suddenly between them. With a growl, the sweatshirt was tugged over Nora's head, and Colbie's lips were back on Nora's neck, tonguing the pulse point before Colbie promised, "Unless you stop me, I'm going to make myself very familiar with your chest."

Nora didn't stop her. Only watched, mind empty of thought and consumed with feeling, as Colbie started with her collarbones, hands trailing up and down Nora's waist. Nora thought she knew Colbie's lips, their firm pressure. Colbie's saliva, the warm bliss incongruent with her temperature. Colbie's touch, always too gentle or too hard, always perfectly unpredictable. Previous touches didn't compare to this.

Colbie's hands and lips were greedy. So eager, Nora knew that if Colbie hadn't let Nora set the pace, they would have done this weeks ago. Even so, Colbie's movements seemed like she was holding back. Keeping herself from rushing. Closer and closer, her fingertips inched upwards while her mouth made a slow trail downward. Nora was squirming now, word-lessly begging for the contact her body craved. This inching, cautious speed was for Nora's benefit, and it only stoked the heat more to see Colbie keeping herself in check. Seeing how Colbie was trying to care for her made everything so sweet.

And when Colbie finally found her breasts, her *nipples*, so hard and peaked, all the anticipation… well, Nora could never have guessed she'd react the way she did. Gasping, arching, crying out Colbie's name. Just from contact with her nipple. From the one Colbie rolled between her teeth, easing any pain from the pinch with her freely flowing bliss.

Nora felt it all the way between her legs. Nothing had ever done this before. She squeezed her thighs together, trying to soothe the ache, but Colbie growled and shoved her knee between Nora's. Her hands clamped on Nora's shoulder, pushing her down onto Colbie's thigh, and the pressure was *right there.*

"Colbie!" Nora was still making noises she'd never let out before. It only got worse when Colbie's hands went to Nora's hips, encouraging her to rock on the firm line of muscle Colbie provided. Nora's hips jerked, movements so frenzied that Colbie had to stop using her teeth, sucking and licking and following Nora's movements with her head bobbing. Fingers at work, encouragement murmured. Nora was only vaguely aware that, over the sound of her harsh breathing, Colbie kept moaning, too. Using Nora's thigh in the same tangled way. Nora tugged on Colbie's hair, bringing her head back up and their lips together as they used each other's bodies to chase pleasure.

Getting there was so easy. Nora had no idea how long it took, only that it was less work than ever before. Or the work was more enjoyable than anything she'd ever done. She didn't get in her head about the timing either, not when Colbie was enjoying herself equally. The rush wasn't impatience to move to the next form of pleasure. It was thrilling that it was fun and so fucking sexy. That bubble of hot tension in Nora's core *burst* with the rush in a fast, sweeping, shivering haze. Colbie made happy noises throughout, kissing her neck again when Nora's breathing got too labored. She came down slowly in Colbie's arms. Colbie's eyes bright and focused on Nora's face.

Colbie's breathing was steady, but that was the vampire in her. "See?" Colbie asked. "Nothing to it. I'll show you more. Pants off activities, although I've always been a fan of the seams here." Colbie dragged a finger down Nora's zipper, then followed the seam underneath with her knuckle, the pressure suddenly more focused and right where Nora was reeling and sensitive. The touch made her hips buck, and Colbie smiled—a wicked, heart-stopping grin.

Nora happily followed Colbie to her room.

Colbie had been more patient than Nora realized. As they tumbled into Colbie's bed and fell to kissing, it took Nora a moment to notice the frenzy had left Colbie's movements. At first, she assumed Colbie had also found release, and her body was relaxed and momentarily sated, but when Colbie's next mumbled words were an incoherent jumble, Nora lifted her head and noticed how bright the room had gotten.

"Nimfinekeepgoin," Colbie tugged Nora's head back down, and Nora kissed her but repositioned them so they were both lying on their sides under the covers.

Colbie could never resist a cuddle. She sighed, breaking the kiss to glare at the window and the brightening sky outside. "I hope I dream of this continuing."

"Then do. I'll be here when you wake up." Nora tightened her hold, pressing her knee between Colbie's legs and making her gasp.

Colbie blinked up at her. Cheeks flushed with Nora's warmth, eyelids drooping. "You will?"

And then Nora felt like a shit girlfriend. When was the last time she'd been here while Colbie woke? The last time Nora had come to meet Colbie, not the other way around? "I'll have to go check on my mom and the pack. Make sure Gabriel hasn't done anything after what happened with Matt and Josh, but I'll come back tonight."

"At twilight?" Colbie asked, grinning at the reference.

"Shut up." Nora kissed her and knew the exact moment the sun claimed Colbie. She let the exhaustion drag her under, too, tucking Colbie in close for some much-needed sleep.

Nora woke, already annoyed, to the front door slamming. Her ire calmed at Ru's happy chatter as she and Poppy moved about the apartment, heating water in the kitchen for tea and then migrating into their shared bedroom. Packing up Ru's things. Nora gave Colbie one last squeeze, knowing she was sad for the girl to leave, before she rolled out of bed.

The chatter stopped when Nora shut the door of Colbie's room. Poppy stepped into the main room with a knowing smile. "Did we wake you?"

Nora squinted toward the clock. It was already one in the afternoon, the longest she had slept in a while. "Yes, but I should have gotten up a while ago. Did you hear anything today from Gabriel or his pack? Did anyone approach the house?"

Poppy shook her head. "I'm still trying to figure out the wards, but it seems my mom tailored them especially to keep the werewolves from paying attention to us since the magic can't do much to keep them out. There are a lot of imprints of fake walls and empty windows. Hopefully, they'll be more interested in the fact that Josh was in the area. Gabriel could complain if Henry encroaches on his territory, but Topher is free to go where he pleases. I don't like that they saw him at all. It might make Reelings even more careful to know that Topher is back out and about."

"You *want* them focused on Josh?"

Poppy shrugged. Nora was even more confused about what was going on between the witch and the werewolf. "Not really, but while he can complain, Gabriel wouldn't mess with Henry. No one would at this point. He's got the most supporters. He hasn't even pissed off the vampires yet."

Poppy crossed the room when the kettle began whistling. "And Josh is smart. He's getting Topher involved again. If Topher does unite the vampires, I can only see him continuing to work with Henry. From the way Topher acted last night, he'll have Josh's back."

Poppy held out a cup of tea for Nora. She accepted it with a smile of thanks. "We have lots of space at the house," Poppy said. "With you helping to strengthen the wards, your werewolves can get in and out if they still want to stay with us. Can they keep away from Gabriel, though?"

Nora considered. Ricky and Janelle wouldn't be a problem, but she had no idea how the others would react. They already wanted Nora to take the Den from Gabriel, and she wanted to do that, but she needed more time to figure things out. Maybe being so close would only fuel their impatience with Nora. "I'll talk to them when I go over there today. When I texted the group, they were excited about more space, but packs are usually opposed to living so far apart."

"Are they? Some of Henry's pack still isn't in New Brecken, but it makes more sense with such a large pack. Well, let me know what they say. I'm going to go over there and clear out some rooms. Get Jane and Natalie's stuff into the attic." The witch blinked at her mug, the only indication of her grief.

"Are you going to keep looking for more witches?" Nora asked.

"Vivienne might talk to her sisters about at least getting in contact, but we might have to start with Mother Kallow. She's the only person who might know how to find other witches in the city." Poppy glanced toward the jars lining the counter. All shades from neon to buttery yellow, with sticky notes attached describing the differences in the brews. Nora had no idea what any of it meant.

"Well, you know I'll help you if you need. Topher and I can talk to Kallow with you." It would probably be a good move if the two of them were serious about joining the ranks of city leaders. "What about your last sibling?"

"We still don't know where Amelia is, but Ryan got weird when she was mentioned. I think he knows but wants to make sure it's safe. He and Amelia were closer growing up. It would make sense that the two of them kept in contact." A hint of bitterness crept into Poppy's voice.

"What's it like seeing them now?" Nora asked.

Poppy shrugged, eyes down. "It's different without our mom. There were a few moments when Ryan or Margot questioned me about enforcing the wards but Ru is clearly the strongest of us. Witches tend to get hierarchical like every other supernatural group. Without our mother, she's the best of us and since she's welcomed me, I feel more welcome than I used to in the house. It still brings up old hurts to see them. To realize they kind of kept in contact. I knew about Margot's shop, but she made sure I knew not to go to her unless it was an emergency. Ryan kept mentioning the shop and how he'd liked a certain pack the last time he was there. Apparently, he didn't get the same warning to stay away. So yeah, it stings, but it doesn't feel like something we can't work through. Eventually. Maybe."

"That seems good. Not great, but like it could be worse."

"Could be worse," Poppy agreed. She looked so tired.

CHAPTER 17

When Topher woke up in the basement of the coven, he wasn't alone. Again. He kept his eyes shut, trying to block out the immediate rush of happiness chased by a gut-turning sweep of fear. He was getting used to Josh being there. He was terrified of the day Josh got what he wanted out of this and left. He was more afraid of Josh staying long enough to regret knowing Topher.

Once he'd found that emptiness of feeling, Topher opened his eyes. Josh sat at the end of the couch on top of Topher's feet. Watching something on his phone, he played with the strings of his hoodie with one hand. Topher's hoodie. The sight made Topher's chest squeeze. He knew they'd grabbed it from Topher's room in case Josh made the change. It was just what was available to Josh. But… Colbie's words rang in Topher's head, and he couldn't decide if it was horrible for him to like the sight so much.

Something must have changed with his breathing because Josh glanced over. "What's the plan for the night?" he asked. Warily. Josh didn't want to be here. He was done spending their time running from their problems in the forest and didn't want to stay in Gabriel's territory. But he would do whatever Topher wanted.

Since when could Topher read the wolf so well?

Topher had a long list of things that needed to be done. Each item glaringly important. He needed to talk with Brett Campbell and get registered. He needed to take Fourth. He needed to call Zayn and Oliver and see how their trip was going like a real friend would. And yet, "I want to find Matt and see what he gets up to," Topher said.

Josh perked to attention, phone dropping into his lap. "Wait, why?"

"Because he smelled like Reelings. Not much, and not recent, but it's better than nothing. He's our first lead, and we can't let the trail get too cold."

It was rare to see Josh so still. "You almost fought him last night. Was that why? Because he smelled like Reelings?"

"No." Topher didn't offer an explanation. He stood and found his shoes, stomping into them before moving toward the stairs. Josh's heart was beating faster than usual as he followed. Following another pack, *finding dirt on another pack*, was appealing to Josh's werewolf instincts. Tonight, they would finally start working toward finding Reelings. Toward stopping him.

"Oh, good. You're up!" Ru called as soon as Topher touched the top step.

She came out of the kitchen with bracelets in hand and a smile on her face. "Are you going out?"

Topher nodded. Ru checked the front room. Viv was sleeping on the couch, so Ru dropped her voice. "Poppy told me you picked up Reelings's scent in a few places where Beth didn't hide it, which made me realize you need a witch friend doing stuff like that for you."

"I don't think—"

"Relax. I know I couldn't keep up with you two on foot, and Poppy would never let me go 'hunting' with you. I charmed these to hold your scent in." She shook the beaded bracelets, the clicking glass beads loud enough that Topher checked if Viv was still sleeping. "It'll keep your essence contained, like a protective bubble around you. I'm confident it'll work even with your resistance to magic, but tonight will be a trial run. I'll keep working on other things. Josh, yours might be tight, but I wanted it to stay on when you shift." Ru somehow got the bracelets on the backs of her fingers on both hands and opened her fingers up for the two of them to slide their hands in. Topher did so, interlocking their fingers and bending to kiss her forehead once it was on. "Thanks, Poutine."

She laughed. "It's close, but I don't think it works." Ru shook the rest of her bracelets down her wrist. "Nora can sniff around for you later and see if she can find your trail tonight. If they work, they should help her pack come in and out of here without Gabriel's pack noticing."

Josh ruffled her hair in thanks. "You're brilliant. Hopefully, we won't have to worry about Gabriel's pack soon. Henry said he can tell when alphas are brewing closer to a challenge. This proximity will only make it come to pass that much sooner."

"Good," Ru said, surprising Topher with her viciousness. "Gabriel doesn't deserve a pack."

She turned back to the kitchen table, where she had beads and strings scattered. The metallic scent of magic hung over her workspace. "You're going to save this city, one bracelet at a time," Topher called as he and Josh turned to leave.

"I'll leave the saving the city to you guys," she returned. Her cheerful words sent a chill of ice down Topher's spine.

Josh still didn't shift as they walked down the sidewalk toward Gabriel's den. He appeared to be contemplating something serious, maybe a task that was made too difficult in his animal form. Topher quickly picked up Matt's most recent trail, and they turned toward downtown to follow it.

"Is there any more of Reelings?" Josh asked, sniffing as if this time he would be able to pick out the vampire's smell.

Topher shook his head. "I can barely even smell him. Probably this will be another dead end."

"Better than sitting around or aimlessly wondering the city," Josh said. He still sounded distracted.

A curiosity that Topher hadn't felt in a long time began tingling in his head. He wanted to ask what Josh was thinking. Wanted to pick apart his brain and find out every turn and alley within. Topher had been too tired for a long time to make himself care, especially in an instance like this where Josh's thoughts were probably laced with grief. Could Topher even handle someone else's grieving?

Topher didn't want to test himself. He spurred them into a jog, moving more quickly through the streets. They went south, then south some more, until Josh's breathing grew heavy. He didn't complain or shift. They passed campus, then Annaliese and Nora's building, both of their scents indicating neither had been there in hours. And yet… Topher and Josh shared a look. Matt's scent was more potent. He'd spent time outside this building recently. Waiting for one of them? Trying to talk to them or spying for Gabriel? Was he angry about Annaliese getting involved last night?

In an unexpected and only slightly welcome burst of sensation, Topher's heart lurched. Worry for Annaliese had him picking up the pace. If Matt hadn't found her here, where else was he looking? They followed Matt's fresh trail around the building, down the street, and then around another darkened corner before nearly running directly into him and Gabriel. Topher halted in barely enough time to grab Josh and push him into an alcove, refusing to think about how the shadows seemed to reach out and shield them eagerly. He worried about the breeze and their scents giving away their presence before remembering the bracelet on his wrist. They would be put to the test tonight.

"I told you to stay away from here, Matt," said Gabriel.

Josh stiffened, hearing the alpha in Gabriel's voice. It rang out like charm.

"I know, but shouldn't we find out what Annaliese was doing in our territory? Nora's scent was there, too."

"And you think you can waltz up to their apartment and ask them? They aren't your friends, Matt. Not anymore. Maybe once everything is settled, they'll see what we're doing and be more willing to talk to you. I know this hasn't been easy—"

"Do you? Do you know that, Gabriel? I haven't seen you in days!"

"Lower your voice." There was a beat. Topher pressed in closer to Josh as if that would muffle the sound of Josh's heavy breathing and racing heart. "We should get going. The gathering is about to start."

"I can come?"

"This time. It'll be good for you to see our progress."

By unspoken agreement, Topher and Josh ducked to follow as Matt and Gabriel moved down the block. Josh tugged Topher across the street as they kept on the werewolves' trail. Eventually, skyscrapers shrank into old neighborhoods. Three-story homes that had been converted to apartment buildings with bay windows and plants flourishing in windows. Gabriel and Matt walked into one of these buildings, barely pausing to knock before they were let inside.

Josh and Topher exchanged a look. The only smell here was of humans. That didn't mean Reelings wasn't nearby with Beth masking his presence, but Topher felt the air was too hushed. He didn't think the maker was here.

Maybe it was reckless, but they needed to be closer. They ran across the street and ducked under the windows, shadows again helping to hide them from view.

"—that Gabriel is here, we can get started," a woman was saying. She was standing directly above them and addressing what smelled like a room full of humans. "Our maker grows concerned. It seems we haven't been doing enough to prepare the city for his return."

"*What the fuck?*" Josh barely breathed the words, only for Topher's ear.

Topher nodded in agreement. The way the lady was talking it was like a religious ceremony. A creepy professor preaching to a room of impressionable undergrads in a movie. A cult leader addressing their following. As she continued speaking, Topher couldn't help but feel the last description seemed to fit best for what was happening here.

"It's been reported that polls for vampires are down. Lana Williams isn't the only maker with her privileges suspended. It's unnatural for humans to dictate how a vampire moves in the world. It's unnatural for humans to think they have any control over the night. While concerning for those in this room who still wish to become made, these polls aren't all bad. It could mean it's the first step in the humans realizing what their true place in this city, in this world, is. Of course, there will be resistance; there always is to change, but change is always good. This is only bad because it brings in fewer people to our gatherings. You were each supposed to bring two friends tonight." A significant pause. The sound of shifting bodies discomfited by being called out. Then footsteps and it was Gabriel standing right there above them, facing the room with his back to Topher and Josh.

"We believe it will help if next week, the meeting is framed more in association with us, the werewolves. We are still highest in the polls as a group. Use that to bring more friends."

"And association with werewolves will make people more comfortable discussing our true leaders," the woman said. From his vantage point, Topher saw the muscles in Gabriel's jaw bunch.

But he forced a calm nod and added, "Reelings should be able to attend, but the city is getting tense. Last night, we were nearly attacked by the West boy in our own territory. He must be stopped. We can't have him influencing people like Henry Gould."

Someone cleared their throat, sitting further back in the room. "But aren't the vampires all on the same side? They're all under Reelings? What makes the West kid bad? He's got the highest rating on the Bliss App, and people only ever say they wish he'd drink more than he does."

Topher must have made a noise. Josh put his hand over Topher's mouth, but his body trembled. Topher looked to him in concern.

Josh was fighting for his life against laughter.

The night air was cold, and the situation above confusing but Topher felt Josh's shaking and couldn't stop the smile that spread under Josh's hand. Couldn't stop himself from leaning back, just a touch, into Josh's warmth.

They sobered quickly enough at Gabriel's following words. "Is this your first meeting?"

"Yes."

"When you see Reelings, and he explains it all, you'll understand."

Josh's grip loosened, and Topher twisted to face him. They were thinking the same thing. Reelings had been quiet, but only because they were watching the supernaturals so closely. Not the humans. The humans above must be under Reelings's charm.

They went on to discuss their socials, how to talk to their friends about Reelings to get them to agree to meet with him next week, the goals for their "club," and how they would change the future under Reelings's guidance. An age of health through access to bliss. An age where real change could happen with the slightest nudge of Reelings's charm against the unreasonable. An age where they could encourage people to educate themselves, to better themselves, to do right by all, and fix the poison that had crept into society. Topher hadn't been involved in human politics much lately, but he could hear the racing hearts and the desperate voices inside the house.

He remembered when his personal life wasn't quite this horrendous, and he'd had space to look beyond himself. Topher two years ago might have attended this meeting. Even now, he could see the appeal. He hated thinking about what he could do with his charm and who he could brainwash, but Reelings didn't feel the same way. He could broker this promised change if only to better his position in the city.

Josh tugged on Topher's arm well before the meeting was over. Gabriel hadn't spoken in a while and might leave before the rest. Anyone could see them where they stood in the light of the windows. They walked away, shoulder to shoulder.

"At least we have a lead on Reelings. We know his next move," Josh said.

Topher nodded.

"We could interrupt the meeting or get someone to go in and see what he has planned. Maybe try to talk to him to find out where he's hiding."

Topher nodded again.

"It can't be Annaliese, though she'd probably want to. Maybe we can ask Jay or one of the humans in my pack."

Another nod.

Josh slowed, and Topher turned to look at him. His thoughts were a spinning, dizzying mess. "This is progress, Topher. This is a leg up on Reelings. If he's using his charm on all of them, we know we can fight fire with fire. You can undo it."

"Can I? I couldn't undo what happened to Julia. We don't know if I can undo what happened to Solas and Patter."

"Well, I'd rather we try things out on those two first. Then we'll have answers. Answers are important. It's good to know this shit."

Topher just nodded again.

"*And* now we know you have the highest rating on an app

called Bliss," Josh said. He sounded far too serious and that was enough to have Topher fighting a smile.

Josh saw him do it and let out a laugh. "The noise you made…" Josh started laughing in earnest now. "It was like you choked on your fangs."

Topher let himself grin as they walked. Josh continued to laugh, grabbing Topher's arm for support. He entertained himself by trying to mimic the noise Topher had made and looking up the app on his phone. "I've got to make an account! I can rate you after the incident with Helen!" Josh was way too happy about it.

Listening to Josh's laughter and light steps was the most normal Topher had felt in a long time.

"Oh my god, look at this review! It's so horny."

"Did you just write it?" Topher teased. He took the phone, eyebrows inching upward as his own laugh bubbled. He ignored Josh's blush, but Josh's lingering look warmed the side of his face. Topher desperately wanted to know what Josh's actual review might say.

CHAPTER 18

When Topher and Josh walked into the Alpha's Den that night, Colbie instantly came alert at Nora's side but didn't move from under Nora's arm. Though the two of them hadn't been chilly toward each other in a long, long time, it was like the night before had thawed something integral. Something Nora hadn't even realized was preventing closeness. Nora had been there to wake Colbie, but their lazy kisses in bed were interrupted by Josh's text asking on Topher's behalf to meet at the club. Even with Nora's pack watching, Colbie hadn't stopped touching Nora since they'd walked through the door. Playing with Nora's braid, holding her hand, touching her cheeks, leaning in closer than necessary to talk to her.

Nora couldn't be happier or less willing to leave her girlfriend to perform even one of the tasks waiting for her in the city.

With Nora's recent talk hanging over them, the pack tried to keep their expressions neutral. Still, with most of them working the basement, Nora had positioned her and Colbie in the cocktail lounge where Ricky and Human Josh bartended.

"Werewolf Josh!" Ricky said. Nora didn't know what it was

about Ricky, maybe his newness to being a werewolf or his human upbringing, but he lacked nearly all the territorial nature found in other werewolves. It was at once endearing and concerning.

Josh's smile was forced, but he lifted a hand in greeting before Topher steered him toward the stairs. Without a word, Colbie and Nora went to follow them.

Topher was waiting in the stairwell. Quickly and quietly, he explained what he and Josh had heard that night and their half-formed plans to find a human to infiltrate Reelings's new cult.

"Shit," Colbie breathed out the word.

"So Annaliese was right to turn to social media," Nora said. Pride for her best friend straightened her shoulders. "We should call her."

"Where is—" Topher broke off when the door to the lounge banged open.

In the quiet that followed, Ricky burst out with an "Oliver!"

Nora barely had time to note the relief on Topher's face before he was back downstairs, and Oliver let out an "oof" as he was engulfed in a hug.

There hadn't been so many smiles in the Alpha's Den in weeks. Even Zayn's mouth was perpetually quirked to one side, listening to Oliver catch everyone up. His parents had been much more accepting of Zayn than he had thought they would be. They'd missed Oliver since he went to school, but he also hadn't cared about what they thought as much as he expected.

"But enough about me. Seriously, T, how are you? When did you leave the cave?"

Topher rolled his eyes. Oliver punched him in the shoulder. "Don't act like this isn't big! I need to know if it's a good or bad thing."

Zayn nodded. They huddled around the bar. Colbie and

Nora at one end, Josh seated next to Topher with Oliver on his other side. Zayn had placed himself behind the bar and was wiping the counter. He always seemed more at ease when he had something to do with his hands.

"I mean, I'm not… great. But Josh was right that having something to distract me makes things easier. Having a purpose and all that."

Nora's heart squeezed. Topher wasn't looking at any of them, playing with a beaded bracelet he wore instead.

"And what *purpose* is that?" Zayn asked, now still as he watched his friend.

Topher met Zayn's eyes. "We have a lead on finding Reelings and think we know his plan." Dropping his voice so Oliver had to lean in to hear him, Topher once again explained the cult meeting.

Zayn picked up a pint glass and began buffing it so forcefully that Nora braced herself for it to break. Ricky wasn't even pretending to work as he listened, face paling the more Topher talked. A man at the opposite end of the bar snapped to get his attention. Human Josh rushed over instead, but the date was already ruined by the customer's rudeness. The woman beside him was collecting her bag and rolling her eyes. But Nora didn't let herself get too distracted by the drama, forcing her attention back as Topher finished.

Oliver had almost the same reaction that Nora had. "Annaliese will be happy to hear she's on the right path trying to get human support up."

"Now we have to find a human to go in," Ricky said, fully joining the conversation. "I could ask some of my friends—"

Oliver scoffed. "Please. It should be me."

Zayn set the glass down with a resounding clack. "Not happening. You have feeding scars. They won't think you're in there to get connected with a vampire. They'll know you know one."

"Makeup exists for a reason, love."

Zayn's jaw worked, but it was Topher who spoke up. "You smell too much like Zayn, Oliver. Any vampire would know that you're regularly fed from and live with him."

"But I know the most about all this! I've made half the captions for Annaliese's posts!"

"And you're good at that!" It was the closest Nora had ever heard Zayn come to raising his voice. "If we know that Reelings is targeting humans, we need you and Annaliese to spread awareness now more than ever. Focus on that."

Nora was grateful that Zayn included Annaliese in this. Oliver's eyes widened with an idea, already moving away from his argument. "Whoever we send in should wear a camera! Then we can post the meeting. Especially if Reelings is charming people, it won't come across the recording."

"Won't it?" Topher asked.

Oliver frowned. "Well, I guess I was going off experience. The way it feels to be charmed is almost like something physical reaching out and infecting me. I can't imagine the same happening over a screen."

"It's time we tested it," Topher said, standing. He once again went toward the stairs. Chance's scent drifted from that direction. With a sinking stomach, Nora noticed the cameras blinking from the corners of the ceiling. Chance must be here setting them all up.

The patrons of the cocktail lounge watched with interest as the six of them went to the stairs. Topher sighed before pausing to look at the humans in the room. Josh reached and squeezed Topher's arm. Topher turned back and approached the full high-top table. "Is anyone interested in being fed on?"

The four twenty-somethings seated nearly fell over each other to be the one Topher chose. He only reached for the nearest willing wrist and made a quick, neat cut with his nail before lowering his head. Nora gaped. She'd never seen Topher feed so openly. It was such a careful process. Basically the opposite of how Colbie fed with shameless fangs and moving bodies. Topher was careful and mechanical. His face void of expression. None of the pleasure and satisfaction Colbie showed. None of the love and gratitude Zayn exuded when he leaned over Oliver's neck. None of the smug control Lana flaunted.

Topher moved from wrist to wrist with quick efficiency. No more than a couple swallows taken from each, yet by the time he turned from the table, all four were glassy-eyed and grinning.

"Five stars," Josh said as Topher rejoined them.

"Shut up," Topher replied, but Josh's words eased the troubled tension in his eyes.

Chance knew they were coming. He was turned to the door when Oliver pushed it open at the head of the procession. The cameras must be up and running. "Watching you feed is probably the most boring supernatural occurrence that ever occurred," Chance said blandly to Topher.

"Sorry to disappoint."

Chance sat on a black swivel chair at the new desk in the corner of Lana's apartment. Of course, Lana would want the computers in her space where she could be in charge. It would have made more sense to put them in the conference room or somewhere the wolves would also have access, but at least she wasn't currently in the room. In front of Chance, two screens displayed alternating views of the club. One of the patio, two in the lounge, one in the stairs, and four in the basement. Raven lounged on the couch, looking over some spreadsheets and watching Chance's progress. More papers were discarded on the table next to her. Topher knew a twinge of guilt. She and Nora had taken over his position of helping Lana run the place. He felt bad for the added work he'd given them, but no part of him wanted his old responsibilities back.

Relief and guilt. Constantly coiling together. Topher wondered if they evened each other out eventually or if he would simply drown in the feelings.

"Where's Lana?" Nora asked, voice coated in suspicion.

"She had a meeting."

"A meeting with whom?"

Raven frowned, a hint of her agitation clear. "She wanted to talk with Brett Campbell. She was pissed Annaliese had already gone in and met him first."

Colbie nodded. "Trying to control the narrative."

Raven shrugged. "I suppose. It's something Lana would do."

"Do I detect a bit of resentment in your tone, Ray?" Oliver asked. He went to sit on the arm of Raven's couch, reaching over to awkwardly hug her from behind in greeting.

"Let's just say I'm glad you two are back. And Topher," she said, but her voice lifted with his name, making it a question. She sounded too hopeful.

Topher opened his mouth, but he didn't have a response. He was going to take this night by night.

"We want to test if charm works over camera," Colbie said, dropping onto the couch next to Raven and dissolving the question in the air.

"So use your phone," Chance said, turning back to his screens.

Colbie looked as if she'd genuinely never considered using the camera she carried around every day. "But… we have to immolate the circumstances at the human mediation offices."

"Why?" Chance asked.

"Just because. What if cameras like yours pick up more?"

"You make no sense," Chance said, but he was bent over, digging in his backpack. He pulled out a handheld camera and spun around on the chair, lifting it and pointing it at Topher's face. "And action."

Topher rolled his eyes. "You should leave. I'm not charming you."

"Who are you charming?"

Colbie turned, looking at the two humans on the couch beside her. "Are you willing?"

Raven barely took her attention from the papers. "Sure, fine."

"I want to stay," Chance insisted. He crossed his arms. The stubborn tilt of his chin and the narrowing of his eyes were all so familiar. Topher knew that look. His human self had always been more willing to let Chance deal with consequences than argue with that face. His vampire self two months ago would have said no and stood his ground. His current self had too many other issues taking up his spare energy. Maybe he would just try to keep the charm pointed at the camera, not his brother.

Zayn cleared his throat, breaking the standoff that no one knew Topher had already shied away from. "You sure you want to start feeling like you'd give anything for your brother to bite you?"

"It's really quite—" Oliver cut off when Zayn shot him a look daring him to finish that sentence.

"Irresistible," Raven finished it with a grin. She looked almost excited about this. It had been a long time since Raven had been on the receiving end of Topher's bite or charm.

"I have a bracelet," Chance said, shaking Ru's handiwork in the air.

"And you shouldn't waste the cast in it," Zayn said.

Chance's jaw worked. Topher was too tired to figure out why staying was important to him, but Chance's stubbornness reminded him painfully of Annaliese. This seemed like something she should be here for, but being uncharmable, no one had called her to be the test subject, and Topher didn't know how she spent her time anymore. Aside from running social media accounts for him. "Topher isn't telling me to go," Chance said.

"Didn't he?" Zayn asked. "He's probably not arguing because it's taking everything in him to even be standing in this fucking room preparing to charm someone purposefully." It was like everyone sucked in a breath and held it. Topher stilled, every raw inch suddenly exposed even as he kept his expression carefully blank, fearful of confirming Zayn's words. But Zayn wasn't having it. He turned to Topher and squeezed his arm. "I shouldn't have left. I'm sorry," he said, cutting a glare toward Josh as if blaming him for Topher's discomfort.

Until Topher told Zayn straight up that he was doing what he wanted to be doing, Zayn would hate the situation. The problem was that Topher didn't want to be doing this, but he didn't want to hide in bed either. Being willing to charm and embrace his vampire self at least meant he wasn't alone in his room. Zayn turned to him when Topher remained quiet. "I won't tell you to go home, but if you don't want to do this, we got it. I can charm them, and Colbie can film."

"But what if only my charm is strong enough?"

"Are you saying you *want* to test it yourself?"

Topher nodded. He felt almost childish as Zayn tried to coax words out of him that he couldn't form.

"But not with Chance here?"

"I'd rather not see him under my charm," Topher mumbled. It was bad enough when he charmed Colbie.

"Then Chance will hand me the camera and come back in when we're done," Zayn said.

Colbie gave a mock gasp when Chance did as Zayn said so quickly it was almost like he had been charmed anyway. "Chance listening to directions? Never thought I'd see the day."

Chance stuck his tongue out at her. "I'll wait out in the hall. Let me know when you're done," he said before pulling the door shut behind himself.

Topher crossed the room, clearing himself a spot on the coffee table in front of Raven and Oliver. "You two sure about this?"

"Of course. It's not like you'll make us do anything bad," Oliver said easily.

"It'll have to be something you'll be willing to repeat watching the film back if the charm works through the screen."

"Tell us to high-five or something," Raven said, bored now. She'd seen Topher's reluctance and knew not to expect anything exciting out of this.

Zayn turned on the camera and approached, standing close to Oliver in silent support. "Should I have you all in the shot or just you, Topher?"

"Do it on Topher," Colbie said. "If it's going to work at all, him looking into the camera would be the most potent."

Topher nodded, more relieved than he could say that everyone else was making the decisions for him. He waited for Zayn's nod, then dove into his charm, gathering it effortlessly up to the surface. It nearly choked him on the way out. He hated the taste of it so much, but there, underneath, was the warmth that made Topher fear he could grow addicted to using his power. The strength and love that seemed never to dim, and that felt like it could flow and flow until the entire world was under Topher's command.

Topher felt a hand on his shoulder, Josh, and a foot press into his knee, Colbie. Even Nora's face was without judgment as they all felt Topher's charm in the air. No one thought him a monster but himself as Oliver and Raven's expressions turned submissive and wanting. Oliver touched the two scars on his neck, looking dreamy and dazed. Topher cleared his throat and spoke. "High five."

The humans did so quickly and loud enough that Josh jumped behind Topher. Topher winced at the force of his charm and how their hands had to be stinging. "Give me your hands."

A quick lick to each of their palms and the redness vanished. Topher let the charm go. Both Oliver and Raven closed their fists as if they could keep in the pleasure of his saliva there. They made no move to wipe it off.

Colbie clapped. "Let's watch it back then, shall we?" she asked before anyone could think too long about what Topher had done, especially not himself.

The apartment was far too quiet. Poppy glanced at her phone where Colbie's location was still on the screen. She was at the Alpha's Den. Ru still had Topher's phone and was at the Jennings house. Poppy couldn't remember when she last had the apartment to herself without someone at least sleeping in the other room. The absence of Ru's belongings stung. No shoes by the door. No mugs with tea grounds on the bottom scattered around the room. No blankets in disarray or cross-body bags hanging from random doorknobs. Colbie's room was almost always a disaster, but Poppy hadn't realized how clean they were in the shared space until Ru swept into their lives. No one had minded her small messes, and now Poppy missed them enough that she had to fight the temptation to leave the apartment in search of company.

But she hadn't had this kind of privacy to work on the potion for too long. It had been ages since she'd had a break-through. This was probably an indication she needed to pull in some fresh eyes. Actually ask the witches in her life for help like she'd intended all along. But old wounds were freshly smarting after spending time with her siblings, and Poppy was more determined than ever to figure this out for herself. To go to her people with a solution and ask for help making it a reality, not come to them with a problem beyond her intelligence.

It would also help to have a test subject. To note any progress with tests beyond the small samples of data she'd collected. Poppy winced, thinking about that and looking at

Topher's supply of sleeping draughts. He hadn't taken any this week. Just when she thought she was close to figuring this out.

Poppy's goal was to figure out how much life and sunlight it took to keep a drainer down. To subdue them until witches stronger than her could study and attempt to unravel the dark magic within them. The current potions had given Topher longer-lasting and dreamless sleep compared to sleeping draughts tailored to humans and witches for centuries. He was unharmed and never complained about a different taste or color, but Poppy cringed away from the fact that she hadn't entirely told him what she was doing, only that the dosage was more potent.

Stirring and counting how many times she did so, Poppy added a few roots and muttered to the brew, telling it exactly what she wanted from it. When the roots dissolved faster than usual, she turned to cut some more. There was a sudden crash from Topher's room, and she jumped, swearing loudly.

Poppy had yet to admit it to anyone, but such noises were not out of the ordinary. Gus had vanished from her life for the most part, but he wasn't happy about it, and his impression was far too strong with Poppy's blood powering their bond. Poppy refused to acknowledge what just happened further, turning to the stove once more. She paused at the sight of her blood welling on her finger. Holding her hand out, she waited for the pain. Her knives were so sharp she hadn't even felt the slice when she jumped.

Attention fixated on the pooling blood, an idea began to blossom. Blood magic was so frowned upon it was rarely considered an option, but... sorcery was even worse, and that was what Poppy was up against. Poppy had used her own blood when she'd brewed that potion for Julia. Maybe... maybe brewing by day or full moon or adding more life from plants wasn't the solution. Vampires hated witches' blood, and it had been enough to subdue a poltergeist into following Poppy's commands.

Shrugging, Poppy decided it couldn't hurt to try it for one batch and tipped her hand so the blood slid off and into the buttery yellow liquid below. She watched, transfixed, as it turned white. Or, more accurately, lost all color. The shift was so fast. She couldn't smell the steam any longer. Whispering and squeezing out another drop of blood, Poppy felt that tug of fate in her core. She was on the right path with the potion. Now, she needed a way to test it.

CHAPTER 19

Nora's head still felt a little lightheaded from the charm that had swirled in the air. She hadn't expected to fear it, but the entire time, she'd known that if Topher turned that power to her, she could end up as helpless as the humans. Colbie's hand had twitched at his command, her eyes blinking now as she fought off the lingering effects. Nora caught Josh's eye, and knew he was thinking the same thing she was, yet he remained by Topher's side as Oliver hooked the camera up to Raven's laptop. Everyone stood back while he pulled up the video. Topher too still. Zayn shooting him looks, then glaring at Josh until Josh sighed and slung an arm around Topher's shoulders. "Just breathe, man."

Topher did. Zayn turned his attention back to his boyfriend. Nora and Colbie exchanged a look. "Okaaaaay?" Colbie muttered for Nora's ears.

Raven turned up the volume, and the video began. Nora couldn't see the screen and was relieved she didn't have to watch Topher's face again, the tinge of disgust. The reluctance in his eyes. Then, as he opened his mouth, that air of confidence. That must be what Topher hated most about his power.

That the vampire within him luxuriated in it, enjoyed it, and wanted to let it all loose.

They all watched Raven and Oliver intently as Topher spoke on the speakers. They frowned and glanced at each other, confirming as the sound of their palms slapped on the video that the charm did not affect them now.

"Give me your hands," Topher said on the computer.

Oliver laughed. "Oh my god! You *licked* us!"

Topher winced, but he looked more relieved than anything. His power had boundaries. Reelings's power had boundaries. Zayn went to the door, and Chance came in. "Did it work on screen?"

Topher shook his head.

"Is this good or bad news?" Raven asked.

Topher shrugged. "It means I have to convince the assessors to support me without using charm."

"You were planning to charm them?" Raven asked, confused. It was out of his character, but none of this was something Topher would typically do. The Topher in front of them was someone entirely different from the one who still possessed hope that Julia would survive and didn't know Reelings was plaguing the city. Maybe this new Topher had looser morals if it meant protecting the people he loved. Maybe he had looser morals because he couldn't be bothered to care as much as he used to. Maybe this Topher really was ready for the power at his fingertips, and it would merely take shaking off his old self for progress to happen.

Nora felt the old Topher wasn't a healthy version. This one at least ate and let Colbie in. Everyone in the room seemed happier for the changes, except Zayn and his suspicions, but there was no way of knowing the long-term consequences for their group or their place in the city.

Raven spoke again before Topher could answer. "Wait. Why? Do you want to rejoin the city? Officially?"

Topher met her eyes full-on. There wasn't any charm in

the air, but his power was right there. "Yes. I have no other choice at this point. I don't know what it'll look like, but the vampires need a leader, and they'll only bow to someone more powerful than they are. It can't be Reelings. Or Lana."

"Are you going to become a maker?"

"If I can convince the assessors to register me."

"Will you make me if that happens?"

Nora was ready for hesitation. For reluctance. For Topher's guilt to soften his shoulders and make him glance at the were-wolves in the room to see that someone shared his harsh judgment of himself.

She wasn't ready for his quick nod. "Yes."

Raven's smile was brilliant before she lunged and threw her arms around him. And that was when Annaliese walked into the room, Poppy on her heels.

"Ricky said you'd all be up here," Annaliese said, unaffected by the strange sight that greeted them. Poppy had never thought Raven much of a hugger, and her sudden comfort with Topher reminded Poppy of old jealousy. Back when he spent far too many nights without her and Colbie in the Maker with Lana's other seconds. It had been like he had a secret life he wanted them to have no part of.

Suddenly, Poppy was struck with a new fear. If Topher truly made moves in the city to become a maker, possibly even gain control of Fourth Street, would he invite her and Colbie into that world? If Topher did this, would they lose him completely?

Raven sat back on the couch, staring at Topher with an intensity that Poppy had never seen from her before. Topher cleared his throat and leaned away from her searching gaze. Into Josh. That made Poppy stiffen. She's been so surprised by Raven's affection, so used to Josh popping up around their group, she hadn't noticed he was in human form for the first time in her presence.

Josh's face wasn't nearly as difficult to look at as the last time Poppy had seen him, sitting on the steps of the apartment, angry at them both and devastated. It had been shocking and painful. She'd never expected him to look at her that way. There was still a hint of it in his eyes now, behind the walls that had been erected. Josh had hardened. He'd changed. New Brecken had sunk its claws into all of them.

As Annaliese passed, she ruffled Josh's hair and then sat on Topher's other side on the coffee table. Between the two of them, Topher's shoulders softened. Poppy entered the room, taking a seat on the other couch that met the first at a ninety-degree angle.

"Did the charm work?" Annaliese asked.

"Nope," Colbie said. "Topher has to raw dog it." At Chance's horrified look, she clarified, "Go in there and hope they like him for his personality."

"Which is charming enough as it is," Oliver said, nudging Topher with his foot. "You'll be fine. Things have been so turbulent since you were changed. I'm sure they'll understand if you go in and explain everything. And if you assure them you have the humans' best interest at heart, they'd be idiots to refuse you anything but an alliance."

"That's true enough," Annaliese said. She kept turning her head enough to cut glances at Topher. It was like she was trying to be sneaky about it, but she was also surrounded by supernaturals who missed no details. If Poppy caught the looks, there was no way Topher was unaware. But his attention remained on his hands in his lap. One knee was bouncing. Either a sign of his anxiety or the energy from a recent feeding. He suddenly turned to Josh.

Raven suddenly sighed. "I hate that Lana got there first now. It would be nice to know what she'd saying about you."

Chance fidgeted in front of a computer and the monitors

showing the Alpha's Den. He spun suddenly, fingers clacking on the keys. "What building were the offices in, Annaliese?"

She turned, surprised to be addressed by the youngest West sibling. Usually, when he was in their presence, he acted like he wished he were anywhere else. Never trying to make any friends with them, but always keeping a sharp eye on Colbie and Topher. Annaliese told him the address of the downtown building. Not quite in the town hall, but on the second floor of a nearby office building. Chance nodded, fingers flying. "I can try to use Mom's credentials to see if she has access to their feeds, and then we can watch Lana's meeting."

Everyone stared at the West siblings. Poppy's eyes bounced from Chance to Topher (found nothing in his expression) to Colbie. Colbie looked mildly impressed. "Please tell me Mommy dearest uses my birthday as her password."

Chance snorted. "Please. Right now, it's Chanceis-myprideandjoy."

"Really?" Oliver asked.

Chance gave him a look. "No, Oliver."

Josh snorted, a flash of his old self. He was the first to ask the question on everyone's mind. "What does your mom do?"

Poppy forgot how easy his voice was to listen to. How had she never appreciated his calm? The slight rasp? The slightly ridiculous Midwest accent?

Josh was looking at Topher when he asked the question, but Colbie answered. "She runs security for the government buildings here. Mostly in the mayor's office and such."

Annaliese's eyebrows rose. "Is your mom a badass?"

"That, and a narcissist and a tech-wiz like Chance. It's why they get along so well," Colbie said with a sweet smile.

Chance scowled at his sister. "I'm not a narcissist."

"Focus on your hacking, nerd."

Chance rolled his eyes as he spun back to his screens. Colbie might have fooled most of the room, but Poppy could see the tension in her posture. "He has files on all the supernaturals," Chance said. His clicking was rapid now, the cameras momentarily forgotten. "They don't have much on you, Topher. Nothing about you being a potential maker." A few more clicks. "Huh."

"What is it?" Annaliese asked.

"There's nothing on Reelings or Gabriel."

"What does that mean?" Annaliese asked.

Chance shrugged. "Maybe an administration error. Maybe they're still building their records. I'll keep looking for them to turn up." Chance clicked away for another moment before pulling up the video recordings from earlier that night, fast-forwarding until he found the view of Lana entering what looked like a small corporate interview room: a small table in the center, blue carpet, and soft gray walls. Someone set a cup of water in front of her, and her red lips quirked in smug amusement.

By now, everyone stood to surround the computer except Josh. He'd gone to the door, listening carefully for Lana's arrival. They should probably be doing this in a more secure place, but Poppy threw up a sound-blocking ward as Chance upped the volume just to be safe.

They listened, and Poppy's heart fell. Lana was more interested in endearing herself to the assessors than the Alpha's Den. She explained charm, makers, and the power system along Fourth Street, answering all of Campbell's questions with mostly truth. She declared no vampires could charm someone outside the bounds of hierarchy. That no drainer was susceptible to charm and, therefore, couldn't be vampiric. She painted Topher as entirely within her control and her exile from Fourth as ridiculous. The aim of this interview was clearly to gain human support behind her return to that block.

"She's using charm," Topher muttered.

"How can you tell?" Chance asked.

Zayn answered. "She always tilts her head like that when she's charming."

"She always has her head tilted," Poppy said. Then she scoffed. Right. There was always an undercurrent of charm to Lana's actions. It was how she made humans listen, how she wove authority. Even if the charm wasn't working, it would continuously needle. Charm had to be brushed off and actively blocked even by a witch's wards. Maybe Annaliese and those wearing Ru's protection were the only exceptions, but it meant that it took some level of concentration in all situations for someone to filter through Lana's charm. A tactic to get her way, to keep focus split from her words. Even if it was subtle, it was an upper hand that aligned with Lana's personality.

"Along Fourth, most of the makers are constantly using charm," Zayn said. "The amount of practice is half the reason they're so strong."

Campbell asked Lana about making Topher, and they stopped talking to listen. "It's not illegal to make a human into a vampire if they are dying and give consent. It was one of the aspects of the laws that swayed your kind in our favor," she said when he hinted that Topher had been illegally changed.

"And his sister?"

"I don't like repeating myself," Lana said.

"Why was Christopher dying?"

Lana shrugged. "Found him in an abandoned warehouse after he'd been attacked. Looked like a werewolf attack."

They moved on when Lana stubbornly kept playing dumb. Topher ground his teeth. He'd have to undo all of Lana's charm and tales when he went in. Campbell asked about the Maker and the Alpha's Den. Poppy and the rest collectively lost interest as they heard the same persuasive story about alliances and the future that had gotten them into this business. Lana even had to be truthful about losing her partnership with Henry, as he would tell his side if asked. She never once brought up the drainers or Julia. Never hinted that she knew Reelings was causing trouble in the city.

Finally, she left. A woman stepped forward and into the

camera angle. She must have been directly beneath it the whole time. "Well?" Campbell asked.

"She was using her charm. I was practically choking on it, but I couldn't tell if she was lying or trying to sway you to act a certain way."

"I couldn't either. I still don't trust her anymore than I did when she came in," Campbell said, rubbing his forehead and looking dazed. His attention was still on the door Lana exited.

The screen froze at the end of the recording. Topher sighed. "I won't have to contend with many lies at least. I can fill in the blanks that will help my story."

"What story is that?" Poppy asked.

Topher took a breath. "The truth? Maybe. I need to think more about it first."

He didn't say anything more before leaving, Josh on his heels. Poppy found herself examining Annaliese's face. Did she imagine it, or was that a flash of hurt in her eyes at the lack of goodbye? The exclusion they were all feeling? They had all gathered here to help Topher, yet Josh was the one privileged with any insight into where Topher went or what he was thinking. Annaliese turned away before Poppy could tell if she was the only one bothered. Everyone else was so used to Topher's moods that they didn't even notice.

CHAPTER 20

I t was no longer surprising to find Josh and Colbie hanging out in the living room when Topher woke up early that night from the blaring of the second alarm he set. The expectation was beginning to be terrifying. The two were bent over a stack of Colbie's books, one in Josh's hands as Colbie explained the recommended order to read the series. She plucked the book out of Josh's hand, replaced it with another, and went on to explain *her* preferred order. Poppy was studiously measuring potions at the kitchen counter, her back to the two of them, but her huff of laughter indicated she was listening.

"Do we know when the assessors leave their office?" Topher asked.

"Oh! Good morning to you, too!" Colbie glanced at her phone. "Annaliese said they have a late start so they can monitor vampires better. They're probably still open."

Josh's gaze was assessing, but his face relaxed at whatever conclusions he drew upon seeing Topher. Without thought, Topher took a seat next to him on the couch. That low rumble of anxiety and dread he constantly lived with settled into a purr.

"I'm going to go in tonight," Topher told his sister.

"Are you sure?" Colbie asked. She set down a book, watching Topher intently. His maker registration didn't just affect him. Lana had given Colbie plenty of freedom to keep Topher happy, but in the eyes of the law, she would be one step further removed from Lana after this became official.

Poppy had turned from her task when Topher came in. He faced her now, noting the pinch in Poppy's brow and the white vial in her hand. It didn't look like any potion he'd seen her brew before. "How has the sibling life been?"

Poppy shrugged. "It'll be hard to get used to. Margot still jumps at every little sound. Vivienne won't leave her side, but she is also moody about hiding away from her family. Ru is roping them all into making her bracelets, but no one can quite do what she does, and I can tell Ryan is frustrated by it. The city is quiet, so at least everyone feels safe."

Topher was glad for the daytime update, then surprised that Poppy had known he was curious what their days entailed when he wouldn't have said he was minutes ago. Josh shifted, pressing his thigh into Topher's and pulling his attention. "Just in case they leave the office soon, we should probably get going."

Poppy's eyes dimmed as she turned back to the stove, but Topher only saw the progress they were all making as he stood to don the new shoes left by the door. Flashier than what he would usually wear, Topher guessed Oliver had been sent out to buy them.

Topher immediately knew Annaliese was correct in saying this new branch of the city government didn't hold the power yet. There was a reception area, but even from where he stood at the desk, Topher could see how short the hall of doors was beyond—only three offices from the looks of it and the open area of hushed cubicles at his back. Josh's attention was on the humans behind them as Topher explained to the receptionist who he was.

The man's eyes widened, and he stood so fast that his chair seemed in danger of tipping over. "But d-do you have an appointment?"

"No. I just thought it would be good to introduce myself," Topher said, sheepish. If this didn't work, he might have to use his charm to get his meeting with Campbell. "It'll be so quick."

Josh snorted softly, feeling the brush of charm Topher didn't mean to slip out. Oh well. It worked in his favor. The secretary turned down the hall without another word, ducking his head into the last office on the left. Josh quieted his breathing as the two of them listened to the whispered exchange.

"Um, Christopher West is here. Christopher West is *here*. Like not hiding out anymore and in our office. No one has seen him in weeks. Why is he here?"

Something clattered on a wooden desk. "Micheal! How should I know? I am not prepared to talk to him!" More scuffling. A hissed curse. Josh's shoulders were shaking with laughter.

"You only have to ask him the vampire questions, right? You just did it with his maker!"

"But Kate isn't here."

"She'll be here in ten minutes. I'm sure he'll wait." The receptionist, Micheal, leaned back to look at Topher down the hall. He ducked right back inside Campbell's office when their eyes met. "But I don't think we should make him wait."

"Why are you pushing this?" Suspicion crept into Campbell's look. Josh stepped closer to Topher's side.

"He doesn't seem like someone we should say no to. They say he's the most powerful vampire in the city."

"Did he charm you?"

"No. I don't think so. I felt it when he walked into the

office. Everyone did. If we want a vampire on our side, we should do what we can to ensure he trusts us."

"Vampires don't need to trust humans, and we cannot trust them."

"I think you should talk to him," Micheal insisted.

"Fine. Have him wait in the interview room. I'll prepare, and we'll get started when Kate arrives."

Micheal hurried back to the desk and waved for Topher to follow. His pale skin was flushed, eyes not quite meeting Topher's. Micheal frowned when Josh moved to follow but didn't say anything. Topher was surprised enough to glance back. He was not expecting the scowl on Josh's face. The crossed arms or tipped-up chin.

Topher spoke too quietly for anyone else to hear. "You don't have to—"

"I'm going in, Topher."

Like Michael, Topher had no desire to argue with this stubborn version of Josh. He shrugged. It could be Campbell's problem if he wanted to kick the werewolf out of the meeting.

The room they were taken to was the same one Lana had been in the night before. Gray walls and cheap blue carpet. A metal table in the center of the room had two chairs on either side. Topher sat, expecting Josh to settle in next to him, but he waited against the back wall like the lowers had been expected to do during leader meetings. His eyes went to the camera, blinking above, and Topher thought about Chance potentially watching from the other side. It was comforting.

Topher drummed his fingers on the table and listened carefully to everything outside the room. He mentally ran through his arguments and goals for this conversation. It had been so long since he'd asked for anything he wasn't confident he could get his way without charm. Outside, Campbell was on the phone with this Kate person. She showed up only a few minutes later, and they shut themselves in Campbell's office, but not before Kate mentioned the presence of a werewolf. So, this Kate was a supernatural. Topher suspected as much when Lana's charm hadn't affected her. Josh caught the woman's scent first, being closer to the door. "She's an alphaless wolf," he said, surprised.

Topher and Josh shared a look, ready for Campbell and Kate to enter, but they waited another five minutes before opening the door—a power move. One Lana would have performed. Topher sighed, then wiped all thoughts from his face as Campbell sat down. Kate leaned against the opposite wall, a mirror to Josh. Her expression wasn't pleased.

"You're rumored to be the strongest vampire in New Brecken, Mr. West. I wouldn't have thought you'd need a member of Nora Morales's pack for protection detail."

Josh spoke before Topher could open his mouth. "I'm not from Nora's pack."

Campbell leaned back in his seat. "Gould's then."

Even the humans knew Topher wouldn't associate with Gabriel. Josh nodded.

"We prefer to meet with supernaturals one on one. If you would like to do an interview for our records, feel free to wait outside."

"I'm not leaving."

"Listen, Mr…."

Josh gave a thin smile. "Gould."

It was the first time Topher had heard Josh use his name and connection to his alpha like that and it gave Brett Campbell pause. He tried to hide the stumble by straightening his papers. "Right. Mr. Gould, everyone else we've met with has—"

"No one else has been through what Topher has. I'm not leaving him alone for you to try and sink your claws in like every other person with an ounce of power in this city. If you get a werewolf to watch your back, so does Topher. You're lucky it's only me. I had to fight his sister off, and she would have brought Nora along. I'm staying."

Campbell raised an eyebrow at Topher. "You can't take on one werewolf and a human yourself?"

"I'm not taking you on. We're talking," Topher said. Exhaustion was already pulling at him. "And humans are capable of causing just as much damage as—"

He broke off when the door opened again. Topher caught Annaliese's scent as she stepped into the room, an apologetic Michael at her back. "She insisted, and you said—"

"It's fine, Michael. Annaliese, what can I help you with?"

"Oh, I'm just emotional support for Topher," Annaliese said. Brett's eyes widened. She paused to bump fists with Josh before taking the empty seat next to Topher.

He glanced back, wondering if the two of them had coordinated this. Josh looked surprised but pleased. His shoulders relaxed as Annaliese took control of the room.

Annaliese looked at Kate first. "Nora smelled you on me. She said she's still taking pack members if you want to talk to her."

Kate looked almost affronted. Campbell was displeased. He enjoyed having a supernatural on the roster too much to appreciate Nora's invitation. He turned to Annaliese. "This is a one-on-one interview."

"This is an informal talk, and Topher has been through enough," Annalise said, echoing Josh's words from earlier. Topher rubbed his temples, uncomfortably coddled. Yet not enough to protest. "You're lucky I convinced everyone else to let me come alone. You could have Nora Morales where Josh is, Zayn glaring at you where I am, and our witch friend giving you a magical tickle to distract you throughout the conversation. Not to mention his—"

"—Sister. Yes, we've gone over this." Campbell frowned between the three of them, deciding.

Annaliese shifted on the chair, pressing her knee into Topher's. With her presence and that one small point of contact, all the tension caused by Topher's disappearance and self-isolation vanished. Josh's heartbeat was steady at their back. A fissure cracked open in Topher's chest. A warm flood cascaded into his core, soothing the rough, broken edges and filling the emptiness he'd lived with for weeks. It seemed to swirl with the dark, shadowed love always waiting to be summoned.

Topher had never felt stronger. Supported and believed in, he straightened his shoulders. "They aren't leaving," he stated.

Maybe Campbell was willing to argue with a lower werewolf and a fellow human, but he hesitated at Topher's tone. "Very well. I do have questions for you now that you're here. Are you willing to answer them?"

Topher nodded.

"How were you turned? Lana wouldn't provide details, though she didn't deny it was done without you going through the legal processes required."

"Those processes are proven null and void if the subject is dying," Topher said, the defense of Lana falling out of his mouth without thought. He cleared his throat. That wasn't how he wanted to start the meeting. He wanted this, to be honest.

"You were dying?"

"Sorry. I've been instructed to always say that. I was dying, but I didn't want to be made."

Campbell's eyes widened. This was the most Topher had ever said publicly about his making. There were stories and rumors aplenty about what kind of turning would create someone like Topher. He'd had never confirmed or denied anything.

"She turned you against your will?"

Topher nodded. "But I'm legally registered now. It's water under the bridge, and you'll have no luck trying to reprimand her now. She had Grace's permission at the time, and, like I said, I was dying."

"Why were you dying?"

Topher's body locked up. Memories flooded, chilling any warmth he'd been experiencing. Annaliese opened her mouth, but Topher spoke before she could. "It's difficult to talk about."

Josh stepped forward, a hand coming to rest on Topher's shoulder. Annaliese squeezed his knee. Emotional support indeed. Topher closed his eyes, focused on those points of contact, and told a stranger about Hunter's gang, Dylan, the drug deals, the warehouse, and the witch and the demon.

"Demon?" Campbell asked, startled. He bent over a paper from the files he'd brought in. "Our first reported demons were dated months after your attack."

It was a relief that Campbell had moved so quickly past Topher's story, but Kate stared at her coworker like he was heartless. Topher supposed if Campbell really did study supernaturals all day, Topher's tale wasn't the worst he'd heard. It wasn't great for New Brecken, but only New Brecken had laws keeping their supernaturals in line.

"I think it was one of the first summoned." Topher hesitated. Did he talk about Tiff Jennings without clearing it with Poppy first? Should he mention Beth? He needed Campbell to know the threats the city faced, but he didn't want to bring it back onto the witches entirely when their ratings were already low. But… Beth didn't deserve protection. "Before the demons were used by Beth Kallow to help Reelings create what we call the drainers."

Campbell had been taking a sip of his water. He spat it out at the names dropped. Josh let out a startled laugh, and Annaliese's eyes widened, her hand gripping Topher's knee even tighter.

"Beth Kallow is the sorcerer?" Campbell asked once he'd caught his breath.

Topher leaned forward. "She needs to be stopped. I think humans will be the best way to solve all our problems. We've lost the other werewolf packs in New Brecken. We've lost vampires to the werewolves. We've lost witches to sorcery and demons. Yet, for every one of us, there have been multiple humans who have died or disappeared. I'm willing to be honest and tell you what I know in exchange for your support as I try to rid New Brecken of Reelings and Beth Kallow."

Campbell's eyes sharpened with interest. "Your species is historically unforthcoming and uncooperative. Why can't you do this on your own?"

"We aren't—" Topher stopped himself from going full Poppy on the man and giving him a biology lesson. "Because I'm not Lana, and I won't be the next Reelings, no matter how much power I gain. Lana has human allies." Topher leaned back, draping his arm over the back of Annaliese's chair. "I have human *friends*. Human family members in New Brecken. I'm not here to gain power over the city. The last thing I want is to be here right now. Secretly, I think Josh might be here to ensure I keep up my word because what I want aligns so well with his alpha."

Josh made a protesting noise, but Topher pressed on. "It has to be me. I hate it, but I know it. No one else has the power or the allies."

"So what's your plan?" Campbell asked. "How would aligning with you benefit me?"

Topher took a breath. Once these words were said here, recorded here, once Josh and Annaliese heard them, he would have to go through with it all. "Happenstance is still in disarray. The vampires are so unorganized that humans are afraid to frequent the place. I love what we built with the Alpha's Den, but they don't need me there. Fourth Street does. I'm going to take Fourth Street from what remains of the Big Three. I'll run Happenstance for myself, placing me close enough to Solas and Patter to keep an eye on them and the rest of the vampires."

"You can't walk into a business and declare it's yours."

Topher raised an eyebrow. "Can't I? Fourth Street is under vampire rule. Legally. It was given to us and follows *our* laws.

Our laws adhere to hierarchy and power. If I go in and prove I can run the place, it's mine. Simple as that. If I do it, I'll be taking a lot of work off your hands in ensuring the humans are safe, but I'll need something in return."

Campbell leaned toward Topher. "I'm listening."

They left the interview, Josh hesitating on the sidewalk outside. Topher sighed. "I know you have to go tell Henry what I said."

It shouldn't have hurt when Josh nodded. They exchanged a long look, Topher swallowing the words to beg Josh to stay and wait until morning. Josh left without another word. At least Annaliese stuck to Topher's side. "Can we talk?" she asked.

Nerves fluttered in Topher's gut. Every feeling was intensified after weeks of nothing but depression and sleep. He and Annaliese hadn't been alone together since she'd tried to get him out of bed in those first days after facing Reelings. Topher knew Annaliese thought he blamed her for what happened, but he didn't. It was Annaliese's plan that got them out of that situation mostly unharmed. He was grateful to her, but she hadn't left the confrontation untouched.

Topher still didn't know how to handle the fact that she was immune to his charm but not his bliss or his strength or the danger associated with his status in the city. He was even more fearful now of bringing anything worse to her doorstep. A fear that built and spiraled and consumed right alongside his grief until he hadn't been able to look at her when she visited. How did he explain something like that?

From the expression on her face now, Topher knew she felt the same as she had back then. Maybe it was a mistake, but he followed her when she turned and walked up the block. She continued until they reached campus and then the apartment she shared with Nora.

Matt's scent lingered. Topher stifled a hiss of displeasure.

They went upstairs, Topher tensing and more nervous than

he'd ever been around Annaliese. He hesitated at the threshold, noting Nora wasn't home and hadn't been for hours.

"Need an invitation?" Annaliese asked, then appeared annoyed with herself for being unable to contain the vampire joke.

"No, but I want to make sure it's okay."

Annaliese considered him. Arms crossed, eyes hard, every braid of hair and painted nail and piece of clothing in perfect alignment. She was always neat. Always certain she could control her surroundings. Always at ease within the structure she created for herself.

Topher wished she'd share that steadiness. He craved it more than anything. Denied it for himself more than anything.

"What did you want to talk about?" he asked, keeping his voice even.

Annaliese frowned and moved to the sofa, pulling a striped, pink throw pillow into her lap and patting the cushion next to her. Topher sat and angled himself in her direction. He owed her his full attention after all the weeks of silence and avoided eye contact, but his grip on the back of the couch was white-knuckled outside of her view.

"What's going on with you?" Annaliese asked. It was such a broad, unanswerable question that Topher snorted. Annaliese's eyes narrowed, unamused. "Seriously. We don't hear from you in weeks and now you're planning on taking on all the vampires in the city?"

Topher ran a hand through his hair, frustration bubbling up from his core. "Isn't this what you all wanted?"

"What do you mean 'you all'? None of us want you unhappy."

"But you'd rather me in power than Reelings."

"You can take out Reelings without taking over Fourth Street."

"Can I, Annaliese? Tell me how?"

"Get rid of him!"

"And then?"

"Then you return to normal, and the city owes you a favor!"

Topher stood, agitated. Feeling too much. "We've talked about this! I'm not some superhero in a comic, Annaliese. It doesn't work like that in the vampire world."

"Then how does it work?"

"I've told you! I've told everyone. Lana's power games may seem like she's just keeping herself entertained, but she's tame compared to the other makers. Compared to how Grace was and how Solas and Patter are now. There is loyalty between vampires, but we are monsters. We are creatures of the night with our own laws and rules and checks and balances. I can't take out the biggest threat to the city and be left alone any more than Nora could break out from under Gabriel and be a lone wolf in the city as an alpha. This path in front of me is settled. I got a reprieve, but this was going to happen since the day I challenged Reelings."

"But—"

"There isn't a way out for me. There's only hope for you all."

Annaliese's jaw set. "You made a choice when you confronted him. We're making our own decisions now. I accepted an internship at Campbell's office, and the city will keep changing. Why can't vampires?"

Topher ignored her last question. "What does your internship involve?"

"Mostly running their socials like I've been doing for Alpha's Den. We are going to get the humans on your side and help the city. It isn't all on you, Topher. It never was. Maybe you'll have to get into power to change Fourth Street, but that doesn't mean you can't dismantle the structure after. We can make this better. But that means you can't shut us out. Not even us weak, useless humans," she finished bitterly.

"I don't think you're weak or useless."

"Then why don't you talk to me? Why don't you include me? Why is Josh the only one allowed in?" There was anger behind Annaliese's words but worlds of hurt, too. Topher had put that raw edge there.

Topher dropped to his knees in front of Annaliese. He couldn't stop himself from touching her, curling his fingers around her thighs. "Don't you see how it ruins people?"

"Two people," Annaliese agreed, a twist of the knife. "*Two* people, Topher. Tiff Jennings killed one, and Reelings turned the other when he found her on the streets."

Topher raised an eyebrow. "You make it sound innocent. Julia smelled like me, Annaliese. I let her walk around without protection, angry at me. She went toward Fourth. She got attacked. Purposefully. Because she carried my scent so deeply from all the feedings. That didn't just happen. That was a targeted attack."

"How do you—"

"I traced her scent. I found where she was changed. I found Reelings's smell all over that place, but I didn't have someone to tie it to until I met him."

"Then why hasn't he attacked me?"

"Because of Nora. Because my scent isn't tied as deeply. I can't know, but the more time we spend together, the riskier it is."

Annaliese placed her hands on the backs of his, slotting their fingers together. She leaned into Topher's face. "I don't fucking care, Topher. I want to be there for you. I want..."

Topher could read the rest in her eyes. This was the language his body understood above any other. He slipped a hand free, reaching up to cup her cheek. *God.* He'd forgotten what it was to feel this much. The dams had burst in Campbell's office, and now...'Annaliese, I can't. I can't give you all of me. I gave it to Dylan, and it—"

"I don't care. I'm not going to give you all of me. I like

myself too much. But I want something. I want to explore this.”

“You would settle for so little?”

Annaliese rolled her eyes. “I’m not asking for a ring, Topher. I’m not asking you to forget Dylan or Julia. Right now, I’d settle for seeing if you can even get me off.”

It was a sensation like blood roaring in Topher’s ears. He finally let himself acknowledge Annaliese’s heat, her smell. The arousal in the air. His position between her knees. The challenge begging to be accepted in his veins. He swallowed. “I can’t promise you anything. Dylan was the only person I was ever faithful to, and we only had a few months together.”

Annaliese dipped even closer. No, Topher had risen on his knees. He’d shortened the distance between them. “Topher. I’m not giving you every one of my nights. I’m not sacrificing my days like Oliver is willing to for Zayn. I want to give you what I can and take what you can offer. I want you to—”

Topher didn’t let her finish. His body knew this dance, this invitation, and he had never, ever been any good at denying this part of himself. With a soft growl, he closed the distance between them, sliding his hand behind Annalise’s neck and fully capturing her to his lips.

He refused to open the seam, but Annaliese took what he gave. She tugged at him until his body was on top of her own, boxing her into the couch. Already, she was moving against him, seeking friction and pleasure that Topher was starved to give her. But not without warning.

He separated their lips, just a breath. “There’s going to be a lot of bliss.”

“Bliss sounds good. Really good.”

“Sure, but let me know when to go only hands. I don’t want you to—”

Now, Annaliese cut him off with a kiss, latching onto his open mouth, diving in with her tongue, and moaning enough to set Topher on fire. He moved from Annaliese’s lips, allowing her to acclimate to the rush. Her movements slowed, touching, petting, luxuriating as his bliss tamed some of her fire. Topher couldn't have that. He dragged his lips down her jaw, her throat, nibbling at her pulse enough to speed up her breathing. She reached and pressed his head more firmly to that spot, but he grabbed her wrists, pinning them above her head. She gasped.

There it was. The wildness came back in a flurry of squirming movements. Annaliese held, contained, messy, asking for more. No, begging. It was more than someone as weak as Topher could resist. He transferred her wrists to one hand and lifted himself off of her, everything hardening at the sound of her need and protest. Topher dragged a finger down her neck, leaving a line of red with his nail.

"God, Topher. Don't stop. Don't you fucking stop."

"I'm going to undress you now," he said, voice rough and husky and full of uncontrollable charm that didn't work on her.

"Please do."

Topher took his time. Button by button. A zipper tugged below. He used his vampire strength to lift and maneuver, and Annaliese was putty in his hands. If there wasn't that sharp gleam in her eyes behind the bliss, Topher might have slowed.

Soon, Annaliese was bare below him. Her hands under his shirt, nails digging in as he examined her. "You wanted to know if I could get you off?"

"Topher, shut up and get to work."

He grinned. Her breath caught. Topher kissed her once more before traveling downward.

Annaliese's over-hot skin pebbled wherever it touched his coolness. She hissed and moaned at the sensation, and Topher played into it, letting his cold fingers stroke her in more sensitive places, even drawing out a giggle when he touched the dip of her waist too lightly. "Please, Topher..."

He couldn't say no. He was too far gone. She was perfect

when she wasn't begging, and this version of her? It was heaven. Irresistible. He stopped with his face at the juncture of her thighs. Annaliese squirmed and gasped, seeking her pleasure. "Be still," his voice was all command and she tried to listen.

Remembering her reaction to his cold, Topher leaned in and blew gently at her core. It was enough to draw out a cry from her lips. "So reactive. So sensitive."

"Just for you..." Annaliese panted. "I've never felt like this."

Topher wasn't possessive or proud, but that sent his sluggish and stolen blood racing. He gave Annaliese no more warning before he dipped his head and sucked her into his mouth.

Annaliese arched off the couch with a sharp cry. "Yesyesyesyes."

Topher eased off, licking her from bottom to top, then refocusing his efforts on the bundle of nerves that sent her writhing beneath him. With one hand, he pressed her stomach still, the other scratched gently up her leg, hovered closer to her dripping entrance. "Topher, I'm already...it's too much..."

He backed away only long enough to assure her, "You can take it, Annaliese. If anyone can, it's you."

He slipped his finger inside, beckoning into her ceiling as he clamped his lips back onto her clit.

It didn't take much more than that, not with his bliss in the picture. Annaliese shattered. Filling the air with the smell of her tears and the sound of her chest heaving. Her body trembled under Topher's hands.

"Good girl," Topher muttered. She moaned, and he knew she could barely handle it when he started back in for another round, unable to resist her taste and feel.

She pressed the back of his head, forcing him closer. "Thank you, thank you, thank you. God, I'm so happy you're back."

For the first time, Topher was too.

CHAPTER 21

The shower was running when Nora got home, but the evidence of what had occurred in their shared space still hung in the air. Nora waited with a glare, keeping away from the couch, when Annaliese stepped out of the bathroom in her robe and hair twisted into a bun on top of her head. There was no shame in Annaliese's grin when she caught sight of Nora's expression.

She spoke in a cheerful, sing song voice before Nora could open her mouth. "Topher said you aren't allowed to be annoyed after what he smelled on his front door."

Nora's glare slid away, blushing as she broke eye contact with Annaliese to make coffee. But then the words processed. "It was Topher?"

Annaliese shrugged, still smiling. "Honestly, I see the vampire draw now. That spit of theirs is pure magic." Annaliese sat on the stool at the counter, more relaxed than Nora had ever seen her.

"Please stop talking. You and Topher really…?"

"Well, not all the way. He just ate me out for a long time. Like a really—"

"Too many details."

"I'm giving you the bare bones. Just because you smell more than I'm offering doesn't make it my fault."

Nora opened the window pointedly. "You sure this is a good idea? A couple of days ago you weren't very happy with him."

Another shrug from Annaliese. "I think we'll be okay. We communicated how low the expectations are. He knows I'm not giving up my day life, but he isn't jealous. He isn't going to get mad at me for not giving him enough time like everyone else I dated. Honestly, I'm pretty sure he's into Josh too, so he'll be plenty busy between that and Fourth Street." Annaliese said the words so casually Nora turned to stare.

"Does that bother you?"

Annaliese sighed. "Is the coffee almost done? I did not get enough sleep for this conversation."

Nora was glad to have something to do with her hands.

Despite her words, Annaliese kept talking, puzzling it through out loud. "I don't know what it is about Topher or this whole situation, but I couldn't deny him anything. I'm so worried about him finding baseline happiness that I couldn't imagine limiting his resources to find it, even if that means he dates more than one person. And I know I'm human. I know I have limits, even if I think they are beyond what you and Topher expect. If there were ever some big fallout on Fourth, I wouldn't put myself in the middle of that, but I wouldn't want him to be alone."

"But you'd expect Josh to be there?"

Annaliese nodded. "I've never gotten the sense that Topher is some fuck boy, but he also doesn't seem like the type to commit fully to one person."

"What makes you think Josh isn't straight? And what about Poppy?"

"Last night, during the interview, Josh watched Topher in a very non-platonic way. He seemed reluctant to leave Topher to report to Henry. Then, Topher stared after him. I don't know what's going on with Josh regarding Poppy or if he and Topher are just bonding over their grief, but seeing them together so much lately makes sense."

Nora had to agree. Something was going on there, whether Topher or Josh realized it was another question.

"You'd really be cool with it?" Nora checked.

Annaliese laughed a bit. "I know you were raised in a traditional setting, Nora, but you have to know these things happen. I don't mind the thought of polyamory. I don't think I'd want more than one partner, but I've also never liked the idea of having a monogamous boyfriend demanding all my time and attention."

Nora poured them both coffee. She almost dropped the mug she handed Annaliese when her friend said, "Plus, as long as he's capable of giving head like *that*, I don't care what else he gets up to."

"Annaliese!" Nora backed away, grimacing.

"Prude." Annaliese laughed. "Wait until Colbie gets her hands on you. It probably runs in the family."

"That makes no sense. Why would it? Ewww. All I needed a change of clothes. You will not see me back here until that smell is out of the couch."

Nora started to turn away but then remembered why she'd rushed upstairs. "Oh, also, I smelled Matt outside."

Annaliese feigned surprise. It was so obvious Nora froze. "Did he talk to you?"

"I mean, he tried to. I wasn't interested. He wanted to know what was going on at Poppy's house. Well, not the house in particular. He seemed to think we were in that area to spy on Gabriel's pack, but he can't figure out why I was there with Josh and Topher."

"What did you say?"

"Nothing. I told him to fuck off, or I'd call you."

"And how did he seem?" Nora couldn't stop the question even as she feared Annaliese's answer.

Annaliese studied Nora, weighing how honest to be. That look said enough. Nora wasn't surprised when Annaliese replied, "He looks like he hasn't slept in weeks."

Nora nodded. She wasn't ready to forgive Matt for making her so small, or even before that, how he wasn't there in her deepest days of grief. Now that she knew more about her father's death, she couldn't control the sinking suspicion that Matt had known more about it than he let on, and that was why he hadn't been able to look at her.

But even so, she and Matt were so young. Their childhoods were so intertwined. They had once been each other's best friends. Nora now had Colbie and Annaliese and everyone else. She had all these new perspectives to learn from. All Nora could imagine was darkness and secrets when she pictured Matt's current life. She was happy she'd left but hated the thought of leaving the boy he'd once been behind.

Not certain Matt deserved such thoughts, Nora pushed them away and went to change.

Poppy smiled. It was a rare night in their apartment. Topher came out of his room without Josh, and Colbie left hers without Nora. Ru was at the house, so it was the three of them.

There was too much tension in Topher's face when he realized this, but he tried for a light tone when he said, "Just like the old days."

He walked around the couch and took a seat next to Poppy, leaning his head until it rested on her shoulder. Colbie sat in the armchair with a grin, body sinking into the cushions. "Updates?" she asked her brother.

He obliged, explaining how the meeting with Campbell went and how he should know soon if he would be registered as a maker with Colbie under his name.

"What else?" Colbie knew he was holding back.

It took Topher two tries to answer. Poppy's heart sank,

suddenly feeling like this was a goodbye of sorts. "I'm going to go to Fourth and get the vampires in line."

"We knew that already," Poppy said. "Why do you say it like that?"

"Because I can't rule Fourth from here," Topher said, gentle and hoarse, leaning closer into Poppy's warmth. "I don't know how long I'll have to stay there or how often. Once I take it, I'll have to monitor them until I know how deep Reelings's charm truly is. I told Campbell I'd fix Fourth and keep the humans safe in exchange for my no-questions-asked registration change."

Colbie was glaring at the carpet, trying to think through this. Topher spoke even more softly to his sister. "I don't expect you to come to Fourth with me. I think you could be like a liaison between me and Twenty-Fifth Street. Spend your time mostly south of the river and—"

"I'm not leaving you alone on Fourth, Topher," Colbie said quickly. "The most I'll do is half and half, and still, Nora spends most of her time with her pack anyway. She has to. It'll be fine. Don't worry or even think about me while getting into this."

Topher's whole body lifted and sank with a sigh. "I'll have to explain to Raven."

"Raven loved the Maker and being on Fourth. Returning won't be a problem on her end."

Topher had just woken up, but this conversation seemed already to be taking a toll. Poppy's hand moved to pick up her phone, wondering if she could discretely text Josh without Topher noticing.

She stilled. Since when had Josh become Topher's source of comfort? Or was he simply motivation? Poppy remembered being jealous of Josh when she'd heard of his first flirtatious interaction with Topher and then seeing it afterward. Yet even in this post-Quinn state, Josh was a burst of light and energy that Topher needed.

Poppy had liked Josh. She'd found comfort in him too, probably taking it for too long without giving it back, but the feelings had never compared to what Poppy had felt for Topher that first year of living with him. And now, Poppy had too much to focus on with rebuilding a coven and saving the witches in the city. Vivienne was talking to Kallow, trying to get Poppy a meeting with her without Lana involved, but the Mother was still too upset over Lana's demands that she banish Beth from her coven. Poppy hoped recent events would have fixed that missed alliance, but Mother Kallow went quiet instead of taking action against her daughter. If Poppy got a meeting, it would be the first time Kallow faced someone outside her coven in a month. Even Vivienne struggled to go in and out of her childhood coven with the wards Kallow had thrown up and her new suspicion of her daughters. Vivienne only alluded to this, but Poppy assumed it was why she'd chosen her freedom at Margot's side.

"Topher…" Colbie started slowly, brows pinched.

The vibration of Poppy's phone interrupted. Poppy shifted on the couch, jostling Topher as she freed the ringing device from her back pocket. She was ready to dismiss the call in favor of this important conversation but stopped short when she saw Ryan's name on the screen. Heart in her throat, some magic thread already warning her to worry, Poppy answered. "Hello?"

"Poppy, I… Maybe this is too early to worry; sometimes she takes a while to get back to me, but Amelia still hasn't answered or stopped by like I asked. I don't have a good feeling about it."

"I don't either," Poppy muttered. She couldn't be sure, but it was almost like their old ties as a coven were slowly reform-ing. Poppy had a new *sense* of each of her siblings. Her grip tightened on her phone. "I'll head your way, but have Ru—"

"She's already watching for Amelia's wards to fall."

"Good. I'll be there—"

Poppy was interrupted again, this time by Topher when he

snagged her phone out of her hand, barely even noticing the resistance of Poppy's death grip. He hit the icon to put the call to speaker. "Have Ru watch, but we'll spread out in the city and try to smell for a summoning. As soon as she has a location, text it to the group message I'm going to add you to. It'll have Nora's pack and my friends. Someone should be close enough to act once we're positioned in the city."

"Are you sure? What if I'm wrong?"

"I'd *rather* you were wrong, but just in case, we're going to be ready."

"Okay… yeah, okay. That's a good idea. Should we spread out, too?"

Topher considered. "It's your choice. Usually, the demons are drawn to the spell—" Topher didn't even pause as Josh walked into the room, but Poppy felt him relax. "—so you should be safer than usual if they already have a witch in their grasp, but if you have any doubt in your wards, I wouldn't risk it."

"Alright, thanks. I'll let everyone know and text if Ru sees anything. If this is a false call, I'm sor—"

"Don't apologize," Topher said. He ended the call, pulled up Ryan's contact information, and added the number to his phone. Topher started building a group message as he stood and crossed the room to Josh.

Josh raised an eyebrow, and Topher quickly explained. Seconds later, Josh's phone was at his ear, and Poppy hated the witches' self-imposed solitude more than ever. How many witches could have been saved if they trusted other supernatural groups? If they had people who could be in the city while they sought out failed wards from the safety of their covens?

It took little convincing for Josh to get Henry to send his pack out. Colbie called Nora, and it took even less for her and her people to hit the streets. Topher called Zayn, who had a strangely attuned sense of smell for the summoning circles. In minutes, the city was crawling with supernaturals. Topher stared at the phone in his hand. "I wish I already had Fourth," he said like it was some new weapon he wanted to get his hands on.

"This will be enough. It's more than anyone has ever had to stop a summoning," Colbie assured him. "Let's go. We're the only ones north of the river right now."

"I'll go closer to Fourth to check, but don't go higher than Fifth," Topher warned his sister. Josh made no move to leave Topher's side as they turned to Poppy. "Are you coming?"

"I'll stick with Colbie," Poppy said. It made the most sense. Topher and Josh would be fine together, but Nora wouldn't be able to focus if she thought Colbie was hunting alone. Topher nodded, and they swept into the night. Poppy was strangely reassured by how the shadows seemed to cling to Topher once they hit street level. He barely waited for Josh to shift before they took off. Colbie went to Poppy's car. "You driving?"

"Why do I feel like we're replaying the night we found Ru?" Poppy asked, staring after Topher and Josh for too long.

"I hope we are. We kicked ass that night," Colbie said before ducking into the car and starting it up. Bolstered by the vampire's confidence, Poppy ran around and jumped into the passenger's seat.

CHAPTER 22

Nora ran on four legs through the streets, pacing herself only enough to ensure she didn't miss any scents. She felt the pinpricks of the threads to her pack members as they spread out into the city. Nora didn't often run in New Brecken as a wolf and never without a destination to focus her path. The wolf drew too much attention. Her human legs carried her far and fast enough.

Tonight, she needed the extra strong senses, the speed, the animal resolve for the hunt, and the muted emotions that kept her worry for her people at bay. She'd instructed half her pack to stay in human form so they could have their phones on hand for any updates. Nora wished they could do this search as a unit, sweeping the streets as one intimidating group, but the goal here was to cover more ground and have someone be close enough when Ru Saw her sister, wherever that may be. Once her wards fell, Amelia wouldn't have much time.

Nora sniffed out a lot of information she had missed as a human these past weeks. She often caught the scent of leaderless wolves, but not as many as this. They seemed to be everywhere. Hiding. Waiting. Nora thought she'd spread the word that she was accepting members fairly well—the very name of

Alpha's Den should be bringing them in at least to talk—but too many stayed away and unclaimed. The alpha in her bristled at the realization.

Nora didn't have time to think about this now, but each alphaless werewolf nagged at her as she ran deeper south. Nearly to the city's outskirts, Nora ducked into a dark parking lot to shift. The strap of the crossbody bag she'd tucked her phone into was far too long once she was human, but Nora didn't adjust it, having no plans to stay human and naked for long. She checked the group message. One of Henry's pack was closer than Nora expected and would stay there to wait. Nora frowned at the number of wolves texting their locations. They were spread almost perfectly throughout the city, from Topher on Fourth to this point in the south where Nora stood, but that wasn't the only supernatural territory in the area. On a hunch, Nora shifted and continued running, only stopping once she reached Golden Spring National Park.

Poppy and Colbie parked halfway between Fourth and the river. The engine was idling gently, the windows all down so Colbie could smell. Poppy texted Ryan advice on how to keep Ru's power from faltering and tracked the updates flooding the group message. It seemed they were perfectly spread out, everyone focusing on prowling their sections as the frequency of texts petered out. They waited. The entire city was on alert, even though, according to messages, the nearest werewolves were still at Henry's and the Alpha's Den.

No part of her wanted Amelia in danger, but Poppy hoped Ru could find something soon. Poppy remembered when Tiff's wards fell. It had been during the day when Poppy was too distrustful of her roommates to help her anyway. For Amelia's wards to drop at night would mean greater immediate danger for her sister but also more protection. Poppy had no doubts now. As soon as they got the location, Topher would be one of the first people there. It didn't matter where Amelia was in the city; Topher was fast. He'd get there.

If he could survive checking Fourth Street unharmed and unhindered.

Topher walked slowly, unprepared for how familiar Fourth Street would feel after all this time. He felt disconcertingly at home. This place had been all that could distract him once from Dylan's death. Under Lana's guidance, Topher had learned the clubs and alleys and other vampire-tailored businesses dotting the block like it was all that had been keeping him from falling apart at the time.

The air felt light. And Topher's breathing easier than usual in the darkness. They passed the remains of the Maker, and Topher reached for Josh as the smell of it hit him. Josh gave no reaction aside from pressing into Topher's side.

Topher hoped Ru's bracelets held up and blocked their scent from the other vampires. Fourth was not a safe place for a lone werewolf, although Topher doubted anyone would be focused on Josh when Topher was right there.

A turn toward Third Street took them into a hedged backyard behind a modern mansion. Topher led Josh into the bushes and crouched. He hated the waiting. As everyone found a block to patrol in the group messages, even Topher's phone went silent. The shadows crept in and Topher resisted the urge to try and shift them to his will. It still felt like some ability he'd dreamed of and couldn't be capable of in his waking hours, though he knew that wasn't the case.

After a few minutes, Josh shifted out of his wolf form. Topher quickly took off and offered him his hoodie. Topher was taller than Josh, so it covered everything Josh might not want exposed, even with his lack of modesty being a werewolf. "Do you think her wards will fall tonight? Is it smart to already have everyone out, or should we be staggering shifts?"

"If Ru can watch all night, so can we. The witches have a bad feeling. Maybe Poppy's Sight isn't particularly strong, but I've also never known her to be wrong in a situation like this."

Josh nodded, accepting that. He craned his neck to peer at the home at their backs. "Do you know who lives here?"

"Grace did."

Josh started. "I thought all the vampires lived on the upper floors of their clubs."

Topher nodded. "It's easier that way, and Grace usually stayed there, but…"

"But?"

Topher cleared his throat, his maker's-maker's secret still hard to expose. "Grace had a human family that lived here. He disguises it as a place for his favorite blood donors, but his wife lived here too."

"What happened to her? After he died?"

Topher frowned, hunching deeper into the shadows and wrapping his arms around his knees. "I've always been too afraid to ask."

Nora entered the forest, knowing none of her allies were nearby. Not even her mother remained to prowl its depths. She wasn't afraid, but everything leading up to slipping between the trees added to the tension she carried as she distanced herself from her pack.

Keeping low and moving fast, Nora began sweeping the forest. She didn't expect to find Reelings here. The Park had always been werewolf territory. Sometimes, the witches came to cast large spells in privacy, but there weren't enough humans and too many wolves to hold the vampire community's interest. But no one had seen Reelings in New Brecken. Topher only caught whiffs of his scent on the streets. So, if he was nearby, there was a chance Gabriel could have shown him the forest and hid him in it.

The thought made Nora see red in her more territorial form. She shook her head and focused on her search, but the alpha was rearing for a fight.

Even so, Nora stumbled when she caught a scent, disbelief pausing her steps. It was a hint in the air that her brain might have dismissed if she weren't searching for it. Similar to the smell of magic Poppy would let out when she felt safe and her wards slipped. When she wanted her supernatural friends to be aware of her presence. Nora turned quickly toward the metallic odor confused when there was no tang of the sweet demon rot or Beth's sulfuric magic tainting the air as well.

Following the scent further into the forest, Nora still couldn't believe she'd never picked it up before, especially when she came across tire tracks where the smell was more condensed and inexplicably surrounded by Gabriel's. By Matt's. Nora put on a burst of speed, sure she had found Poppy's sister.

Nora was so used to passing Poppy's wards that she was in the clearing before realizing she'd just shaken some off. When a witch burst out of the cabin in the center with her hands wreathed in flames and stark terror in her eyes, Nora understood her mistake.

Their aimless driving eventually led them too close to the apartment building where the drainers had once been kept. Colbie let out a frustrated huff. "I can't smell anything but demons and drainers here."

"Recently?" Poppy asked, looking up from her phone and the number of people waiting for an update from Ru.

Colbie shook her head but seemed to reconsider. Sticking her head further out the window, she drew back in with a whispered, "Yeah, actually. Recent."

They shared a long look. "Should we…" Poppy didn't want to go back into that building. She didn't even want to suggest it, but maybe following the demons would lead them closer to Beth and, therefore, Amelia. Maybe Reeling and his people were using the scent of the drainers that used to live here to hide the making of new ones.

Poppy read the same hesitations in Colbie's eyes. "But Lana would see on the cameras if the drainers or demons were in the apartment."

"Maybe she hasn't been checking," Poppy said. "Or maybe she's hiding something else. Especially since Topher has been avoiding her. Understandably, but he would be the one to keep her in line."

"Shit. You're right." Colbie's hands tightened on the wheel. "Are we going in then?"

"I kind of think we are."

"Okay. Let me text Nora first. I don't want to panic Topher, but someone should know."

"Nora might panic even more than he would," Poppy pointed out.

Colbie's smile was soft. "Yeah, she might. But she's also wolfed out right now. She won't check her phone for a bit."

"Does that help us then?"

"It's better than not telling anyone." Colbie threw the car into park. They were still a couple of blocks from the apartment, but it was easier to sneak up on foot.

The building was as abandoned and overgrown as it had been in the spring. Colbie stepped in closer to Poppy as they neared, her expression tight. Poppy grabbed Colbie's hand as they crept up along the fence to the side of the building, Colbie explaining in barely a whisper that they were in the camera's blind spot. Poppy tried to feel for danger, but as usual, her premonition was lacking. She Saw nothing to warn them if a threat approached. Hopefully, Colbie would smell or hear something before they were attacked. As far as Poppy could tell, the building was empty. She heard nothing. The curtains remained drawn in place over all the windows. Her only hint that Colbie might be able to tell something else was with them was Colbie's stillness between steps and her intent expression. It slowly shifted from concentration to disbelief to horror. Poppy dug deep into her magic, throwing a ward around them as Colbie searched for her voice and shook her head in shock.

It didn't take long for Topher to regret bringing Josh to Fourth Street with him. As soon as Topher admitted he didn't know the fates of the humans who had once lived in the house at their backs, Josh whipped off the sweatshirt, shifted, and prowled closer, all thoughts of finding Poppy's sister put on hold in his need to determine the safety of the humans. Topher swore under his breath and followed.

"Josh, stop! You can't—"

He broke off when Josh growled. Of course, it was then that Topher smelled vampires getting closer. Fear for Josh's safety began to consume and Topher felt himself disassociating. Danger was here. It was closing in while Josh was distracted. Even worse, Topher could smell the humans inside. No doubt the reason Josh was so determined to keep going.

Then, unexpectedly, Josh moved away from the vampire scent drifting toward them, backing Topher into the shadows of the bushes once more. He shifted, pulled on the discarded sweatshirt, and crouched, breathing too heavily. Topher hated to do it, but he reached around to set his hand over Josh's mouth to muffle the sound, already holding his own breath.

Josh took the hint. He leaned into Topher and tried to quiet. It wasn't appropriate for Topher to press into Josh's warmth. Relief that Josh had listened, had turned to him instead of danger, was making appropriate behavior hard. He pulled comfort from the knowledge that Josh could shift in a breath and run from whatever situation approached. Fight if necessary. But for now, they were safe.

They stayed frozen as the grass gently gave under footsteps

approaching. Topher could barely see out of the shadows surrounding them, but he let his charm pulse out—an urging in the air to look the other way. He didn't know if his charm was compelling without being seen, but he could manipulate people without words, so he had hope they could get through this unnoticed.

"It's nothing, Rachel."

Josh went even more still at the sound of voices. He hadn't smelled the vampires approaching or heard their near-silent footsteps. On Topher's wrist, the bracelet Ru had given him started to heat. He shifted so it wasn't pressing against Josh's cheek.

"I *heard* something, Kai."

"Just an animal. That heartbeat isn't human, and I can't smell anything. Come on, we'll be late if we don't go now."

Rachel didn't respond, but the two vampires didn't move either. Topher's eyes slid shut. Out of everyone on Fourth Street, Rachel was one of the vampires he least wanted to face. Rachel's and his grief had sung together just months ago. She was one of the few Topher wouldn't mind talking to—in a different context. The scent of the other vampire lessoned with his retreating footsteps, but Rachel moved closer to their hiding space.

It was a risk, but Topher removed Ru's bracelet for a second. Rachel took a sharp breath, footsteps halting. "Topher?"

He didn't respond. Rachel was smart. She would know what it meant that he was on Fourth Street again. She would know that if he didn't come out to talk to her, it was because he needed to stay hidden. And Topher knew if he left his hiding place and asked, Rachel would take him to her maker for a meeting. He could test the boundaries of Reelings's charm and see if fixing it would break a vampire's mind like it had Julia. By leaving this hiding spot, Topher could have Fourth Street under his control within hours. Or, he would learn if he'd overestimated his powers and charm and be dead by morning for daring to challenge them.

Rachel stepped even closer and spoke in a whisper. "If you can, we need help, Topher. I don't know what's happening with Solas and Patter; they won't talk to us. Two humans have died from excessive drainings, both at Happenstance. Honestly, I wouldn't be surprised if more were hidden. Two of Grace's seconds are dead, and I don't even know how many lowers, but I know the makers that used to be under him are making too many more without registering. Lana needs to take it over. Or you. Something has to give before more people get hurt. They're meeting in the basement of Blue Blood tomorrow night. Grace's seconds have been told to attend, but everyone is at each other's throats, and I can't imagine it turning into anything but a bloodbath as they try to take Grace's spot or even surpass Solas and Patter. Please, come. Or ask Lana. Anyone else at this point. Please. Fourth Street is falling apart. It's time."

CHAPTER 23

Flames shot up, surrounding Nora close enough to make her yelp. As the circle crept in, Nora had no choice but to shift to her smaller form. Sweat instantly coated her skin. Naked and human, she lifted her hands. "Stop! I'm here to help!"

The witch stepped through the circle of flames, fury darkening her features. She had the same green eyes as Poppy and looked more like Tiff Jennings than any of her other children that Poppy had met. "I'm going to burn you to a—"

"I know Poppy. I know you're being hunted by werewolves, but I'm not—"

"I have no reason to believe you!" Amelia screamed. Nora could smell Amelia's terror this close and with so much magic pouring into the flames surrounding them. She also smelled blood.

"You're hurt. I can help. Please, let me help."

Poppy was Nora's friend. Colbie's best friend. Poppy was one of Nora's people, and that extended to her siblings. Nora, all alpha, reached out and grabbed Amelia's arm, turning it to see the extent of the damage. Three lines of thick claws had slashed across Amelia's bicep. Nora was already mad, already seeing red, but scenting Matt in the wounds was almost enough to make her shift and leap through the flames.

Amelia's question halted her anger. "You've taken Poppy, haven't you? That's how you know her name and why I can't see her." The realization, though false, caused enough pain to cut through her anger. The flames flickered, and Nora tightened her grip on Amelia's arm.

"Don't you dare drop your wards. No, they don't have Poppy. You're being chased by another pack. Not mine."

But Amelia's face had paled. She barely heard the words. "First, Natalie. Then Poppy. Jane. Ru. I thought Margot and Ryan were… but they've vanished too…"

Amelia swayed. Poppy became aware of how thin the wrist she held was. How dirty and exhausted Amelia looked. And then, over the sound of her dying flames, the growls in the trees surrounding them.

Nora yanked Amelia closer. "Listen to me now. Poppy is a strong witch and has surrounded herself with even stronger supernaturals. Her wards must be too thick for you to See her, and she brought Ru into them months ago. Then she found Margot and Ryan earlier this week." Nora couldn't tell if Amelia was listening. There wasn't time left to convince her. "I'll prove it, but we have to get out of the forest first. Use my strength, pull in your wards, and *move*."

Maybe it was the alpha in her voice or the promise of hope, but Amelia finally focused on Nora's face. Then, the forest beyond as Nora turned to meet the threat head-on.

Since their last confrontation, Nora had contemplated over and over again what she should have done differently when she challenged Gabriel that night in the warehouse surrounded by shadows. In some variations of her imaginings, she shifted and told him, human face to face, exactly what he'd done to her. How much he'd taken from her, starting with her father's death, then seizing the pack, then chiseling away chunks of Nora's confidence until he'd made her so small she'd ended up in his bed unable to fathom a life spent with Colbie. She would tell him how much better her new life, pack, and lover were. How much better she was without him and how little she'd deserved what he'd done. She would do everything she could to tear him down with one conversation like he'd done to her with years of work. But Nora wasn't good with words, so most of her fantasies simply involved her staying in wolf form. She would let him feel the power of her alpha, and that would say all he needed to know about his place.

As the flames died and Amelia's face shuttered with concentration, Nora lost all those fantasies in one go. Turning and facing Gabriel again was nothing like she'd expected. She wasn't prepared. Her concentration only held steady when she conjured Colbie's fierceness in her mind. Nora could be that. Colbie had taught her.

Shoulders back, Nora watched Gabriel shift. She smirked, noting how long the change took him. For Nora, it was instantaneous—half a thought between two legs or four. Gabriel changed as quickly as Patrick and Heather. What about him even qualified him to be alpha?

The smirk died when Amelia sighed in relief. "Gabe."

Nora turned back to Amelia, completely nonplussed, but the witch had her eyes on Gabriel as she moved as if to walk around Nora and to his side.

"Milly," Gabriel started. Nora's lip curled back at that familiar, placating tone. "I told you to keep your wards up. You know I'm the *only* werewolf you can trust. They're on their way now."

So Amelia couldn't hear the growling in the trees. She didn't know they were surrounded by Gabriel's pack already. She didn't know Gabriel was lying, and his own people had tormented her into hiding here alone and far from help. Nora's hands fisted.

"What's going on here?" Nora asked, voice low. She needed him to say it.

Gabriel's eyes lit with poorly concealed mirth, but he was too tense to give into smug amusement. Good. He wasn't as confident as he was pretending to be. He was afraid of Nora. The realization was a heady rush. "Amelia's being hunted by demons and werewolves. Werewolves like you and your pack. She has my protection, and you need to leave. Yesterday, I heard of wolves sneaking around her old home. She used to be our neighbor, did you know?"

"Ryan." Amelia gasped, face paling even further.

Gabriel looked at the witch but kept his body angled toward Nora. His wolf was unable to turn from the threat she posed. "Why didn't you answer my calls, Milly? Why didn't you call *me* before exposing yourself to her?"

"There's no electricity out here. My phone died."

Nora tried to reach for her own phone discretely. She only needed to place one call or pin her location, but wearing only the loose crossbody bag, it was hard to disguise her movements.

"Take that from her," Gabriel ordered Amelia.

If Nora hadn't spent so much time around Ru and her easy use of magic, the snap of Amelia's fingers that sent Nora's bag into her hands might have startled her.

"Now, step away. I need to protect you. We can't trust anyone else."

Gabriel began to lower himself into a crouch. The aura of his alpha filled the air. Nora didn't bother to copy his movements. It would be a fight as soon as she shifted, and they couldn't risk injuring Amelia.

"My phone doesn't have a passcode," Nora said, eyes still on Gabriel but speaking to Amelia. "There's a text thread right now. Ryan was worried when he couldn't reach you. Everyone is looking for you. If you need proof that I'm not lying to you and Gabriel is, it's right there in your hands."

"Don't listen. No doubt her pack is hunting you, so you'll be the next victim," Gabriel snarled.

"Fine. Open my messages with Poppy and call her. Call

Ryan's number from the text thread. I don't have it saved yet, but if you know it, it'll be there. Either way, it's at least proof your siblings aren't dead."

Amelia opened the phone before Gabriel could stop her. Her eyes narrowed on the screen. "Who is Colbie? What's the drainer apartment, and why is she following the smell of demons there?"

Nora froze, eyes going to the phone in Amelia's hand as worry for her girlfriend flooded her. It was a mistake. Too much distraction. Too much concern for Colbie with another alpha facing her. Those words were enough for Nora to momentarily drop her guard.

Gabriel shifted and lunged. The wolves in the trees howled at the challenge. Amelia swore, and the last thing Nora saw before Gabriel's teeth collided with her human form was how Amelia's eyes widened, backing toward the cabin and away from the wolves in the trees.

Poppy was wrong about the drainer apartment being empty. So, so wrong.

"I'm going to kill Lana," Colbie muttered.

Poppy nodded. She hadn't found her voice. She reached for Colbie's hand instead. Colbie had taken the initiative to get them inside the building once she'd smelled whatever put the horror on her face. She had bashed in a ground-level window with a stomp of her foot and then jumped inside without waiting to see if Poppy would follow. Poppy had to magic the remaining jagged glass smooth before lowering herself in after her friend, and by that time, Colbie had already run through the hall of chainlink storage units and reached the base of the stairs. With her heart in her throat, Poppy chased after her. She couldn't hear anything. The whole building was dark, and the air felt stale. The halls contained few memories, but the ones

Poppy possessed were visceral enough to lift every hair on her arms.

Hoping Colbie wasn't trying to be covert, Poppy conjured an orb of blue light to guide her. She'd mastered these glowing balls when she strung them up over her plants. The soft blue cast only served to make the hallways even more eerie as Poppy reached the first floor and continued upward.

She and Colbie stood on the third floor now. The door to Julia's old apartment was unlocked and Poppy had found Colbie standing in the living room, staring down at the couch.

Where Julia currently slept.

"What do we do?" Poppy finally found her voice to ask.

"I don't fucking know!" Colbie had never sounded so distraught before, whisper shouting at a high pitch. She slapped her hands to her cheeks and began pacing, jerking steps back and forth. "Poppy!"

When nothing more was forthcoming, Poppy took a shaking breath, checked her wards, and knelt before Julia. Tentatively, she shook her shoulder. "Julia?"

Colbie froze, staring at Julia's prone body as they both waited to see if she would wake. Poppy tried again, shaking her harder. "Julia!"

Julia's eyelid fluttered. It startled Poppy so much that she fell back onto her ass and hit the coffee table behind her, and yet Julia slept up. "What the fuck?"

"She's alive. Poppy! Poppy, Topher said she was dead. Oliver said she was dead! Topher thinks he killed her! Why does he think that if she's right fucking there?! Why is she sleeping like this?" Colbie extended her arms to point at Julia.

Poppy shook her head. "I don't know! What happened that night? Did anyone ever say?"

"I thought it had to do with Topher's charm, but I don't know what his charm does to people. I was never there. Should I call Zayn?"

"I don't... no."

"You don't know or no, don't call him?"

"I don't think we should call him."

"Why not?"

"Give me a second."

It was suspicious that Julia still wasn't waking. Poppy reached for her again, this time letting her hand hover above Julia's body. She closed her eyes and tried to read the magic, dark and crackling as it was. Poppy had never been this close to a prone drainer, so she didn't have Julia's current state to compare anything to. She tried to feel for Beth's influence first. The corrupt magic instantly rose to the surface, bringing a sulfuric taste to the back of Poppy's mouth. She gagged but tried to continue, tried to read it. The magic was dark and unfamiliar and fought against Poppy's power. She instantly developed a headache, and by the time she'd moved on to try and determine Julia's health, black was crowding her vision.

Poppy dropped her hand, gasping. She reached into her bag, clutching a vial of her latest brew. Likely, it wouldn't even work, but it helped provide a sense of security this close to the unknown. She only then realized Colbie had come to crouch at her side, an arm around Poppy's waist keeping her up. Poppy let her head fall against Colbie's shoulder. At some point during all this, she had started crying. Colbie was trembling but couldn't cry herself. This meant so much, and yet… "She isn't there. Or she's as much there as she was before whatever happened. I don't think she can wake up. I don't know how we would wake her up."

"What do we do?"

Poppy hated it, but it was the only idea she had. "I'm not strong enough to figure out exactly what Beth did. I, I don't like it, but I think maybe Ru would be Julia's only chance. No one can parse out casts like she can."

Colbie went quiet. She knew what bringing Julia to Ru meant. It was a last resort. Thus far, they'd done everything they could to keep Ru out of their supernatural business and out of danger. But Topher needed this. He needed something good. They all did. If Ru could figure out how to help the drainers past what Poppy thought her brew might accomplish, it would be just that.

"I don't know if it'll work. I don't know if we should tell Topher and get his hopes up or upset him more with her being stuck like this."

There was another long pause from Colbie, but eventually, she dropped her head to rest it on Poppy's and nodded slowly. "I don't know how to keep a secret from him."

"He'll be so busy. If we don't bring it up—"

"He should know she's alive, Poppy. He deserves a say in this."

"A week. Give Ru and me a week with her at the house. Even if we can't figure anything out in that time, we'll tell Topher."

"How are we going to get her out without Lana knowing?"

"And what's Lana going to do? Tell everyone Julia is alive and get mad at us for taking her?"

Colbie's jaw worked for a beat, but then she nodded. "Okay. Let's go then."

Julia was horrifyingly light when they finally got around to moving her. There were no blood bags in the fridge and no hints as to how Lana was sustaining the drainer, but their priority was simply getting her out of the apartment building. They'd figure out the rest later. Poppy slipped one of Ru's bracelets onto Julia's bony wrist so that no one could track them and Topher wouldn't smell Julia if he happened to use the car. Colbie took Julia's feet and Poppy her top half and they carried her down the block. Once they'd shut Julia into the back seat, Colbie and Poppy stared at each other for a long time.

"This is fucked up," Colbie repeated. "When are our lives going to stop being this fucked up?"

Poppy regretted the answer as it left her lips. "When Topher stops Reelings."

Colbie scowled. "It isn't all on him, you know. Topher might be stronger, but that doesn't mean we couldn't all figure out how to take Reelings. If Topher doesn't want to do this, you have to stop looking at him like he has all the answers. He's done and suffered enough." For emphasis, Colbie pointed at Julia.

"He can fix so much, though," Poppy insisted. "We'll help him, obviously, but the safest outcome will only occur with him involved."

"You say that like you've *Seen* it."

Poppy tipped her chin up. "It isn't clear. Nothing with vampires is, but Ru has *Seen* the city stable. She's *Seen* a version of New Brecken that isn't wreathed in shadows, but she didn't See it until Topher left his bed. That's when she stopped having nightmares. He's going to step up. He's going to do great, incredible things. Your brother was not meant to hide from power or love or risk or us or Reelings. You can't seriously want that of him."

Colbie looked away first, blinking and hugging her arms around her waist. "I'm afraid to lose him again. I'm afraid the next tragedy will truly break him."

Poppy grabbed Colbie's shoulders. "Topher is stronger than you give him credit for. He takes care of himself and knows his limits. His power scares him, but he'll use it in the end. Everyone, Topher included, will be better for it."

"And then what?"

"What do you mean?"

"What happens when Topher is ruling Fourth Street, Nora is running her pack, and you have your coven? What then?" Poppy thought she heard Colbie's unspoken questions there. *What do I do then? What happens to us as a whole?*

"Colbie, we can't go back to how things were before. Whether we want to or not."

At that, Colbie shook off Poppy's hand and moved to open the driver's side door. "I don't want to talk anymore."

"It's not like—" But Colbie slammed the door before Poppy could reassure her. Was it even reassurance Colbie needed? Poppy had never seen this side of Colbie. She wasn't used to seeing such stark fear in her best friend's eyes.

Slowly, Poppy rounded the car and got in on the other side. Colbie started them off and put on music. Poppy didn't know what Colbie needed from her, but when Poppy grabbed one of her white-knuckled hands from the wheel, Colbie let her take it. They clutched each other's fingers the whole drive to the Jennings house as Poppy called Margot and pestered her to have Ru pause her search and take the phone. Poppy quickly explained the situation, crying again when Ru interrupted Poppy's apologies for asking this of her to tell Poppy it was okay. She'd do whatever it took to help Topher and would get a room ready.

CHAPTER 24

Topher removed his hand from Josh's mouth when Rachel left the yard, but Josh remained where he was. His back pressed to Topher's chest, bodies aligned perfectly. The sounds of the night filled the silence, chirping bugs and cars driving and the ever-present pulse of the clubs. Inside the home before them, someone turned on the kitchen light and opened the fridge.

That finally broke Josh from his stupor. He turned on his knees to meet Topher's eyes. "There are humans in there."

"Yes."

"Their blood smells like bliss. They're being fed from too much."

Topher nodded. He didn't feel entirely present as reality caught up to him. His voice was distant and flat when he responded. "Probably by Grace's seconds. His house would have gone to them by vampire law."

"Topher…"

"I know. I, I know." He needed to act. Sooner than later. It was far beyond time. People had died while he hid. Lana had written Fourth Street off when she created the Alpha's Den, and Topher had gone along with her. If they'd stayed, thrown their hat into the mix, they could have claimed Happenstance. Lana might have kept Grace's other seconds in line. No one would have suffered.

Or, she would have killed them off so she could create her own club hierarchy and trust the hold she had over her lowers through charm. It was easy to imagine. Harder was picturing Topher doing this same thing. But he had to. Vampire brute force was the only way to gain Happenstance and the compliance he needed. He could keep *everyone* in line. Waiting any longer was a waste of life. Waiting would only allow the guilt to swallow him again.

Topher started to stand, but Josh grabbed his shoulders, holding him in place. "Do it tomorrow. When they're all together."

Closing his eyes, Topher shook his head. "I can't keep putting this off." He could barely breathe as it was. If he waited any longer…

"You can for one more night." Josh's hands shifted from Topher's shoulders to clasp around his neck.

"Josh, there are humans at risk. Humans *right there* at risk. I have the power to help."

"Do it tomorrow," Josh repeated, leaning forward until their foreheads touched. "I hate it when your voice gets like this. When your face closes off. I feel like that'll be who you become once you step forward and take your place among them."

"Who else could I be?" Topher asked. Half of him wanted to push Josh away. Embrace the monster and strike at the clubs at his back. The other half longed to lean in closer. Topher fought to keep his thoughts straight with Josh leaning in so close, sharing his warmth and air and touch. As a result, his voice was as toneless as it had been before.

Josh tightened his grip. "Not with me. Don't be like that when you're with me."

"Josh… I think, I think it's who I am. It's the vamp—"

Josh kissed him.

The press of unexpected, warm, firm lips cut off the words, the thoughts, the monster at the quick. The taste of Josh flooded Topher. Josh's gasp when the bliss hit was enough to make Topher groan, inviting Josh in deeper as his tongue swept out. Josh's hands gentled, even as his mouth claimed and demanded. Josh's hands were in Topher's hair, rubbing his back, comforting as he *took*. Just when Topher thought he had nothing left to give, he happily let Josh tug him in closer, angle his chin to deepen the kiss. Topher lost himself and surrendered control. Josh's hesitations, his strength, his want yet careful movements—the contradictions made Topher's head swim like he was falling for bliss himself.

Topher didn't know how much time had passed before Josh remembered himself and broke the kiss, keeping close and staring at Topher. Topher watched how quickly his werewolf blood metabolized the bliss and cleared Josh's eyes. The panic that had settled when Topher gave up control began to turn in his stomach as the real world crashed back in. He tried to pull away, but Josh's arms kept him close. Far more confident than his expression.

"Was that the first time you've kissed a boy?" Topher asked. He aimed for light, almost teasing, but his voice shook too much.

Josh winced. "Yes. I need a second to process that."

Topher couldn't give him a second. He had to focus on this, on Josh, or everything else would pull him under. "How long?"

"Have I liked boys?"

"Me."

"It's the same answer, I guess," Josh said. He was starting to relax, his fingers moving. One of his hands touched Topher's face, a gentle tracing of his features that Topher never wanted to end. "I liked it when you flirted with me, but I didn't understand what it was I was feeling. Then, when you disappeared, I was so worried. Especially when I realized how much time you were spending alone. Not even Annaliese was there. When I thought you two were together, it was an excuse not to examine my feelings. You were already taken."

"Josh, I slept with Annaliese after the interview with Campbell." The words were hard to say. Topher didn't want this to end with Josh so quickly and didn't want to hurt him. It wasn't loyalty to Annaliese that spurred them, though. It was loyalty to this half of himself that Colbie had encouraged him to explore. Topher didn't know what to think about it yet, didn't especially love this part of himself for what it might do to others, but if he was going to kiss someone, they had to know. "Colbie says she thinks I'm poly?" It was too much of a question. Topher needed to think about this more, just as Josh needed to examine his feelings for Topher. If only they had the space, the time, the ease of life to sit with things. Instead, they were stealing a moment in the bushes. "I do have feelings for Annaliese, but I also want to explore these feelings for you. I'm selfish. I want both."

Topher almost sighed in relief when Josh's expression went thoughtful instead of hurt or angry. "You want both," he repeated like it was some simple fact he was trying to get his head around.

"You both... I'm a different person with everyone. I like what each of you brings out in me. I like what both of you offer. Annaliese is strength and support and honesty and fun. Not just that, but I don't know how to describe it."

Now Josh was starting to look hurt. "I'm not?"

"No, you're... comfort. You're an outside perspective. You're like sharing the same air with someone in a way that makes it lighter. You're putting me first right now. I would never expect that of Annaliese, even though I know she'd do anything for me, if that makes sense. It's simpler with you." Topher winced, hoping that didn't sound bad.

"I don't know if I understand."

Topher only realized he was gripping Josh's hoody, *his*

hoodie, when he let go to cover his face. This wasn't the place to have this conversation, hushed and confined to their shadowy hiding spot. "It's like… I love. I love a lot. Multiplication and not division, as they say. It's not something that gets small for me. I'm grateful whenever someone makes a place for me, and if I can, I want to do the same for them. It's like all these places in the city. Annaliese makes me feel powerful, like the version of me I have to be on Fourth and at the Alpha's Den. You make me feel like I'm home. Like I'm warm in bed and waking up with something to look forward to that night. Not that people are locations, but it's like not wanting to spend all your time in one place. No, I don't mean it like that. I just—"

Josh's hands resumed their trailing touches, but Topher was too afraid to meet his eyes. "I guess it's like the pack love," Josh said, saving Topher from his messy attempt at an explanation. "Nothing is more intense than the love and loyalty I feel for my packmates, but gaining a new member doesn't diminish what I feel for the others."

Topher's shoulders dropped with the relief of the comparison. He nodded.

"I guess, well, I mean, Annaliese is great, but I don't feel the same about her," Josh said.

"She said the same. I'm not asking for a throuple, just both. For me. Selfishly."

"Stop saying that," Josh said, pulling Topher's hands down so their eyes met again. "I'm not expecting much yet. This is too new for that. But, if we continue and you and her continue, I want to know when I get your time. I don't want to beg for scraps of your attention."

"Don't worry, I'll be doing that for Annaliese's time. But when I take over Fourth—"

"You'll make it a safer place for everyone. I won't make demands, Topher, but I need communication. And, like I said, it's still new. Maybe this won't even work out. I want to make sure—"

"What happens between us is special and only for us," Topher agreed. "I can do that. But I am still hurting over Julia and Dylan. Some nights, I might not be able to handle *any* of this. Colbie wants me to move past the guilt I feel when it comes to how easily I fall into romantic feelings, but it won't always be simple. Also, if I'm around you and Annaliese at the same time, I don't know…"

"It's different." Josh laughed softly. "It's complicated. I get it. We can see what it feels like in the moment, okay? Take this night by night."

"Okay."

"Good. Then I think I need to try kissing you again. Make use of our last night before you take Fourth, and make sure this is worth it." Josh grinned around his last words, already tugging Topher closer. He'd won that fight, and he knew it. Topher would wait another night.

Topher rolled his eyes. "I think the fact that you've put up with me this long says it all."

"Just to be sure," Josh said, a twinkle in his eyes. He pulled off the hoodie, and Topher's mouth went dry. He forced himself not to stare at Josh's bare chest. It was suddenly a view of possibility and utterly different than twenty minutes ago. Josh was still talking, "Let's get out of here first, though."

Josh shifted and ran. Topher gave chase, more than happy to leave Fourth Street behind for one more night of freedom.

Gabriel clamped his jaws around Nora's waist. She didn't even register pain as she shifted to wolf, but his mouth stayed clamped with the movement, stretching the wound and finally drawing a yelp from her. Gabriel tugged back and forth, snarling in bursts of effort as Nora tried to twist and fight back, but even without the full pain hitting her, she had this dreadful knowledge that he'd hit something vital. She could barely reach him as she twisted and snapped her jaws and fought to move away, knowing her best chance right now would be to put space between them. Gabriel sensed her intent and made the most out of his current positioning. He shifted his weight onto his haunches, swiped with his front claws, and raked down Nora's side repeatedly until black began crowding her vision. The pain was flooding in, taking over, drowning. For the first time in wolf form, Nora knew fear.

With one hard shake, Gabriel threw Nora. She hit the side of the cabin with a thud hard enough to lose her breath. She refused to slow and pushed to her feet, but her ribs were aching and her steps were unsteady. She could hear her blood splattering the ground at her feet, too fast for her healing abilities to keep up. Her side was hot and wet, and the fight hadn't truly started.

The sound of her old family barking and celebrating Nora's pain nearly crumpled her resolve to fight back. It was so *cruel*. Gabriel had always been able to make Nora feel smaller, weaker. As she ached for help, for him to let up, for none of this to have happened, he and his pack succeeded in doing so yet again. But Nora bared her teeth, the alpha rejecting her human insecurities. She let the wolf take over, and when Gabriel lunged again, Nora was ready to meet him head-on.

The last time the two of them had fought, Gabriel had been sharing his power with Beth, unable to concentrate while he tried to change Annaliese into a drainer. Now, Gabriel gave all his energy and focus to defeating Nora. She understood for the first time where his strength came as an alpha. It was physical and violence and ruthlessness that gave him the ability to lead. And this was his challenge.

They circled briefly. Nora was losing blood rapidly and knew if she was going to stand any chance in this fight, she would have to end it fast. She struck and managed to clamp on with her teeth, going for Gabriel's throat but hitting his shoulder when he moved at the last moment. He got a paw up and clawed at her front leg and then at the injuries he'd already inflicted, and Nora wasn't strong enough to stop herself from cringing away. She tried to snarl and cover the moment, but as they began to circle each other again, Nora's limp grew more exaggerated. Victory lit Gabriel's eyes. Blood loss was making Nora's movements too sluggish. Her heart was pounding, and she imagined the blood spurting out of her in synch with it. That's what it felt like.

Gabriel rose up, and Nora met him for another snarling row of clawing and biting. He backed away this time with a yelp when Nora managed to slash at his face, but it was only a feint. In the next second, he faked one direction and then pounced on the wound Nora exposed without thinking. Gabriel bit down, a claw catching in her skin and ripping low until Nora blearily imagined gravity spilling her insides into the grass. Gabriel danced backward, howling with victory.

A red wolf inched closer, eyes on Nora and hackles raised. Coming to help Gabriel finish her off or to defend her? Things were so broken between her and Matt that she had no way to know. Gabriel pushed off the ground and head-butted Nora, sending her flying while she was distracted by Matt's approach.

Breathing ragged, Nora tried to rise again. A figure jumped in front of her. It took Nora's failing brain a moment to realize it was Amelia. She shouted, "Protect us!"

Amelia's magic flooded the air. Nora let Amelia draw from her dwindling stores of energy, Amelia's back straightening with shock at the power. Gabriel snarled and jumped, glancing off the wall of magic with a yelp. Nora tried to focus on healing herself but was giving Amelia too much. She couldn't even make the change to tell Amelia to run. They were trapped in Amelia's ward. As soon as it fell, the wolves would strike. Amelia's power would be converted to drainers until the corrupt magic took too much of her life, and she died for Beth's sorcery. Nora wouldn't survive to even feel guilty for failing.

Despair was fast encroaching. Nora looked beyond

Gabriel's circling form to the wolves coming out of the forest. Tio Marcus. Adriana. Matt. Greg… all of them waiting for Nora's downfall. They would follow Gabriel after he killed her, just like they'd followed him after her father died. Was this her legacy? Her father's? Failure with every attempt to save a city that couldn't love them back?

Nora searched for the strength to stand. To exit the ward and give one last push to end Gabriel. At the very least, she needed to buy Amelia time to run. Her efforts were interrupted by a snarl from the other side of the clearing. Gabriel turned and froze when the enormous white-blond wolf stepped out of the shadows. Nora's whimper held pain and relief.

Nora's mother hadn't come alone. Henry was there, too. Somehow, they had come. Gabriel knew better than to face his pack's former beta or start a war with the largest pack in the city by going after Henry. To start a war with the witches now that he had witnesses outside his pack. Gabriel didn't have the element of surprise that had allowed him to take advantage in his fight against Nora. More than that, Gabriel was a coward, so it surprised no one when he turned immediately and ran. His pack protested, but when Helen and Henry gave chase, there was no choice but to follow. Nora could read their reluctance to fight Helen Morales swimming under their shock at her arrival. She had been their beta longer than Nora had been alive, and they all knew now what had happened to her husband.

As soon as the wolves left, Amelia dropped the ward. Without that drawing Nora's strength, she was able to shift, knowing her human form had a better chance of getting medical care and transportation.

Kneeling before her Amelia's hands fluttered over the ravaged mess that was Nora's side. "I have a car. Where do we go?"

Nora barely got out, "Alpha's Den," before the world went dark.

CHAPTER 25

They were finalizing the wards on Julia's room at the Jennings home, blocking in her scent and keeping everyone else out, when Colbie's phone rang. She looked relieved by the name on the screen, so it must either be Nora calling, who would calm her guilt over this sudden secret, or Topher, whom Colbie was always slightly worried about.

Yet, when she answered, the immediate reaction led Poppy to conclude it was neither. "Why do you have my girlfriend's phone?…What?!" It was the second time Colbie had used that distraught tone in one night. When she dropped her phone from her ear, Poppy snapped to send it into her hand.

"Hello?"

The person on the other end was quiet long enough that Poppy thought they might have hung up. She checked the screen. The call was still going, so she tried again. "Hello? What's happening?"

The voice on the other end was small, familiar, and broken. "Poppy?"

"*Amelia?*"

Ryan, Margot, and Ru all turned from double-checking Julia's door to stare at Poppy.

"Hi, um… is this werewolf really your friend?"

"Nora? Yes. Why do you sound like that?" Colbie's eyes were fixed on the phone in Poppy's hands.

"Because she's hurt. She told me to take her to the Alpha's Den and—"

Colbie took off running. The night was full of repeated instances as Poppy sprinted after her and tried to pay attention to the story Amelia was recounting in her ear. What Poppy heard made her blood run cold as she motioned for Colbie to get in the passenger's side of the car. Even with her vampire reflexes, she was too upset to be driving. Poppy slid behind the wheel as Amelia detailed Nora's injuries. Colbie grabbed her phone back, and Poppy started the car. "Keep pressure on her wounds… If they won't let you in the room, then make sure that's what they are doing!"

Colbie hung up. Her breathing was too rapid, her hands fisted on her knees. Poppy drove as fast as she could toward the club, grateful they were only about five minutes from the place and the late hour meant few cars were out to cause traffic. By the time Poppy turned onto Twenty-Fifth, Colbie had called Topher and told him to meet them there.

Poppy let Colbie out in front of the Alpha's Den and quickly found a parking spot. She ran inside and then up the stairs, following the sound of shouting. Colbie stood outside the conference room beside an enraged Annaliese. Patrick, Chase, and Heather blocked the door.

"—us in! You know Nora wants us in there!" Colbie was desperate enough that her voice carried charm.

It took Poppy a moment to notice her sister standing silent and blood-soaked a few steps down the hall. That much blood —Poppy couldn't think about it. Colbie stepped forward. She practically vibrated with emotion. "I will fight you. I will do everything I can to get to her side. I know I don't stand a chance against a pack of werewolves, but you won't stand a chance when she wakes up and realizes what you've done."

Colbie's words lisped, her fangs dropped. She wasn't lying. She would fight her way into the room.

"What the hell is going on down here?" Lana exclaimed from the opposite side of the hall. "Why do I smell blood?"

Colbie ignored the maker. She crouched, ready for battle, when a weak voice behind the wall of werewolves called out, "Let them in."

Nora had never sounded like that. Small and cracking and uncertain, yes, but never like this. Vibrating with pain. Breathy with exhaustion. Poppy saw why as soon as she, Colbie, Lana, and Annaliese ran into the room. Annaliese swore violently, but the vampires didn't pause at the sight of blood. Janelle stood over Nora where she lay on the table, trembling and eyes blown wide. Poppy could barely see Janelle's hands through the blood where they were pressed into Nora's side.

Nora's eyes went to Colbie first, but Colbie was all vampire. Poppy readied her magic to make a wall to protect her friend as Colbie grabbed Janelle's arm and yanked her aside. The werewolves in the room let out a collective growl as Colbie crouched and Lana went to Nora's top half, leaning over her throat. Nora's eyes fluttered shut as the vampires began licking, sucking, and sinking in their fangs into her wounds. Poppy held her position at their backs, magic flickering in her palms and Amelia joining her, ready to defend against the murderous and disgusted werewolves. Luckily, the shock of seeing the vampires drinking their alpha's blood had momentarily left them frozen, but Poppy didn't waste her spare seconds as she constructed a wall between them. She remembered too well how Nora had joined Matt to try to get Topher away from her dying little sister.

Colbie made a frustrated noise, and Lana leaned away from Nora to gag and heave out some of the werewolf blood. Poppy examined their progress with a sinking pit in her stomach. Nora's wounds were now exposed, but Colbie's saliva was barely making a dent in the gashes on her side, let alone the deeper cuts raked into her skin.

"Gabriel did this?" Poppy asked Amelia. Somehow, after all he'd done, the extent of his violence was shocking.

Amelia nodded. "I… I thought I could trust him."

The room went silent save for Colbie and Lana's efforts.

"What do you mean?" It was Lupe who asked.

"I sometimes saw him growing up when we were neighbors. He'd flirt with me. After Mother broke the wards and I went into hiding, Ryan and I would meet at home to talk sometimes. Last month, Gabriel saw me leaving and asked for my number. We've been texting. He told me yesterday I should leave the city, that the other wolves were hunting for a new witch for the sorcerer. I told him about the cabin and how Ru and Jane had gone there. Even though they've gone dark, I'd hoped to find them and that we could ward ourselves. Gabe drove me to the cabin and told me it should be safe to stay there alone."

"They were going to use you to make drainers. He probably hoped to find Ru and Jane there too to make more of them, but Nora found you," Poppy concluded. Three witches. Reelings, Beth, and Gabriel must have been planning something huge.

"He… he was going to kill her. I tried to save her, but we were losing power, and then two wolves showed up and chased him and the others away."

Lupe looked ready to ask more, but the door opened downstairs. It was too late for customers, so Poppy expected it to be Topher, but when Patrick let the change rip through him and ran down the stairs, it wasn't Topher's voice that shouted.

"Please! Patrick, I'm sorry. Is she okay? Please tell me she's okay."

Colbie slowly lifted her head, gaze going to Janelle. "Get that fucker out of here."

It was Annaliese who moved, Matt's name already on her lips. Chase lunged forward, testing Poppy's wall to try and reach Nora while she was distracted. It barely held, but Ricky stepped forward to take Chase's arm. "Look! They're healing her. Colbie wouldn't hurt Nora. You *know* that."

"*Colbie is a blood-sucking monster*," Chase hissed back. Poppy winced for Colbie, but Colbie was too focused on Nora, her movements getting more frantic as Nora didn't wake up and continued bleeding enough for a steady drip to fall from the table. Poppy wished she had the magic to help, wished she could do anything but give Colbie space as she tried to keep her girlfriend alive.

Topher finally arrived. Everything shifted, and Poppy sucked in a breath. She heard him first, his voice woven in charm as he addressed Matt over the sound of Patrick snarling and Janelle and Annaliese shouting. "Shut up, sit down, and wait until we can deal with you."

Matt instantly quieted and then Topher was there, pushing Chase aside like he weighed nothing. He patted Poppy's shoulder as he passed through her ward and then moved Colbie out of the way. Colbie let him, finally pausing in her healing attempts and bending to heave up the blood that wasn't intended for her system. She managed only a weak "Save her" between gags.

Poppy noticed then that Zayn had followed Topher in. He took Lana's position while Topher set to work on the more severe wounds.

Whatever magic Topher possessed, Poppy thanked the Mother it was present and condensed so thoroughly in his saliva. The fight had left even the pack as they stared at him. Poppy knew they must be hearing something horrible if even Poppy could tell Nora's breathing was getting more difficult. Annaliese was crying at the door. Josh wrapped an arm around her, face tight. Poppy started a bit when their eyes met, but he quickly slid his gaze back to Topher. With Nora dying on the table before her, Poppy couldn't think about anything else. She could only hold Colbie and beg the magic, beg Fate and the Mother, beg Topher's shadows, beg anything to save her friend.

Topher woke up confused and in a room he didn't recognize, but it smelled like Josh, so no panic set in. Shortly after that realization, Topher smelled Annaliese, too. Then, their whispered conversation.

"And you? You're okay with, uh, sharing?" Josh asked so awkwardly that Topher could perfectly imagine his wince. His hushed voice floated down to Topher, where his head rested on Josh's thigh.

It was Annaliese's warmth on his other side. Topher waited for her answer, taking in how he was nearly hot pressed between their bodies in what must be Josh's bed. Annaliese's quiet was considering. She had one of Topher's hands in her own and was tracing the bones of his fingers. Josh's hand was in Topher's hair, idly stroking.

If Topher died right now, he would have no complaints.

"When's the last time you dated someone? Like actually labeled as a couple, not whatever situation you were in with Poppy," Annaliese finally asked.

"I… haven't. Poppy is probably the closest I've gotten, and I only felt free to do so because Henry was serious about putting roots down here. We moved around too much before to think dating outside the pack was an option."

"But you wanted to date?"

Josh twirled a strand of Topher's hair. "Yeah. I've always loved romance and wanted it for myself."

Annaliese snorted. "God, we couldn't be more different. If anything, I feel like that's the only real indication I have that this will work out."

"Why? What about you? With the dating question?"

"Couples, dating, romance, and love stories have always given me the ick. I've had crushes on the quote 'bad boys' before, but mostly because they were out of reach. When my dad died and my mom got remarried, it shook any faith I had that love was real or, if it was real, that it was worth it. I, I don't think I want the love in the movies. I don't want a marriage like my mom has. I don't want the obsession Nora feels for Colbie. Topher understands that. He's happy with what I have to give, and I've felt more for him than I thought myself capable of, but it's still less than what I've always thought a real relationship would mean. It's easier this way."

"You think this all could be that? That it could be easy?"

"What are you imagining here?"

It was Josh's turn to gather his thoughts. His voice was quiet and stilted but directed right at Topher as he spoke, hand moving from Topher's hair to brush his cheek. "I'm imagining getting to know Topher. Helping him. Letting him help me. Healing with him. With the pack, most of the older people have known loss before. Quinn's death was horrible for them, but life is going on. Topher made me feel like it's okay to feel like everything is over, to make yourself move on in a different way. I like the freedom he gives me to feel everything. I want to keep feeling like that, spending time with him, and fighting to improve this city. I want to set down roots here, and I want a partner as I do it."

"But, you'll have a life separate from him. Stuff you have to do with your pack and during the day."

"Yeah. Right now, Henry is being lenient. When he saw how Topher was helping and realized Topher was reentering the city, he told me to take as much time with him as I needed. Once this settles, though, I need to go back to all the pack bull-shit and help Henry since he doesn't have his beta to ease the load. Daniel still wants to attend UNB as a werewolf next year, and we have to figure out what exposure we want the pack to have. There are so many other details that Henry can't figure out on his own."

"I have a lot happening, too. But from the human side. I'm going to take that internship. I even think my major in sociology will help me with that. If Topher takes Fourth, Henry stays, the assessors get their footing, Poppy unites the witches, and Nora builds her pack… New Brecken would be so much better for all of us getting along. Topher's power ties so much of it together, but how openly he lets people in also helps. I think that's what I'm so attracted to about him. He doesn't judge. He understands hurt. He isn't sparing with his attention. I trust him to take care of both of us. With how busy we all are, it should work."

"He needs us," Josh agreed softly.

Topher had been in such a dark place for so long that it took him a moment to identify the fluttering in his chest. The ache. He felt, somehow, happy. Until the mention of Nora made the night before came rushing back. Topher sat up. "Is Nora okay?"

His last memory was trying to staunch her bleeding while the sun worked to pull him under. He must have collapsed as he was healing her. Topher's eyes went to Annaliese. Why was she here with him when she should be with Nora? That must mean—

"She's okay. She hasn't woken up yet, but after you fell asleep, Colbie took over again, and by the time she passed out, most of Nora's wounds were basically closed. We think the blood loss is mainly why she's still resting, but the pack won't let us in to see her. They let Colbie stay, but we brought you here for the day when we saw it was pointless to argue."

Here as in Henry's apartment building. Topher nodded. He wanted to fall back into bed and curl up between them, but his night was already too full. "We should go check on her."

Standing was a mistake. While werewolf blood wasn't necessarily harmful to vampires, it didn't settle well. Apparently, this was especially the case in large quantities. Topher barely made it to the trash can to the side of Josh's desk before he vomited scarlet.

"God. I hate that," Annaliese said, voice tight. "Hate seeing how much she bled."

Topher spat, grimacing. There was a quiet that indicated they were all thinking the same thing. Nora should not have survived last night. If she were human or even less powerful as a wolf, she wouldn't have. Topher stared into the trash, mind spinning through the possibilities. Nora could have *died* last night. Facing Gabriel all on her own. He couldn't get the panic in Colbie's voice over the phone out of his head. Topher had run as fast as he could to get to her. Thank god he had his phone last night. If he hadn't—

"Breathe, Topher."

Topher hadn't realized he'd been knelt, staring into Nora's blood, letting out wheezing breaths until Josh was there. He pulled Topher away from the bin and into his arms. Josh held him tight. Annaliese remained on Josh's bed, and Topher couldn't stop himself from checking her face. He relaxed into Josh when he didn't see anger or discomfort there. Feeling steadier, the night began to press in. Always an issue in need of his attention, not to mention the meeting on Fourth later that he intended to crash. His last night of freedom with Josh hadn't gone to plan, but there couldn't be any more procrastination. "We should go check on Nora. And I need to see Poppy and Jay."

"And what time is the Fourth Street meeting?" Josh asked carefully as if he hated to remind Topher that it was happening that night.

"Probably later, but it doesn't matter if I'm not on time as long as it's still going when I get there, and I'm sure they have a lot to talk about."

· · ·

Lana closed the Alpha's Den for an entire night. Nora's pack was being too protective of their space and no one felt up to customer service with the alpha still unconscious upstairs. They kept the lights low and Poppy muttered a ward to keep people from seeing in but allowed them to watch the street outside. Everyone had been going in and out all day, offering help to Nora's stubborn pack and checking on Zayn and Lana, who were sleeping on the couches in the basement. Now, as night fell, they waited for the vampires to wake. Raven watched people read the sign on the door and paced in the cocktail lounge. Poppy tried to ignore her movements, keeping an eye on her phone and the stairs. After the vampires had fallen asleep one by one, Nora's pack had kicked everyone out of the upper floors, though no one had said anything about Colbie sleeping beside Nora. Hopefully, the pack had deigned to tuck her into bed with their alpha for the day. Colbie wouldn't be happy waking up anywhere else.

Ru texted an update on Julia and Amelia, but there wasn't much to report. With all of Poppy's remaining siblings accounted for and safe, Poppy was finally free to give her full attention to their next steps. They weren't as strong as they once were, numbering seven and with a Mother to guide them, but Poppy was confident if push came to shove and her siblings were willing, they could make a difference in the battle brewing. She'd completed her first goal. It was time to perfect her brew and organize the other witches. Then, hopefully, once the witches weren't focused on survival, they could direct their attention to fighting back.

Poppy needed to speak to Mother Kallow. Viv was still trying to get Poppy a meeting. They all knew Kallow was Poppy's best bet at getting an introduction to the other witches in the city. Tiff had mentioned three main covens negotiated when the laws came into effect. Mother Kallow would know of the Rosenfield coven, and having an alliance with those two covens alone could make all the difference. *If Kallow would let Poppy talk to her.*

But that was a problem for later. Poppy checked her phone and relaxed when she saw Topher had finally answered the group chat, waking earlier than anyone expected. Her eyes immediately slid to Matt, seated at one of the high-tops across the room. Someone had given him a glass of water, but that was as far as their hospitality went while he waited for Topher to return and lift the charm.

Down the bar, Oliver showed Chance his phone with the update that Topher was on his way. Poppy nearly started. Chance had a way of blending himself into their group. He didn't say much, but he was always there these days, with Jay often at his side like they were now. The two of them became their own little bubble on the outskirts.

Moments later, Topher used his key to enter the front door of the Alpha's Den. He bared his teeth at Matt and moved to the stairs, reaching back to grab Annaliese's hand. They disappeared up the steps with only a wave hello from Annaliese. Josh made sure the door was locked behind him, pulling Topher's keys out of the door. Then, he stalked across the room and pulled out the stool across from Matt. He sat, leaning his elbows on the table and scowling into the other wolf's face. "Henry said your alpha turned tail and ran pretty quickly once he realized Nora's mother was part of the picture again."

This felt like a werewolf conversation, but everyone went quiet, listening intently.

"Where is Helen?" Matt asked carefully. He didn't seem at all like he wanted to see her.

"She and Henry are looking for something in the city."

"Looking for what?"

Josh raised an eyebrow in a "wouldn't you like to know" expression. "Any and every way to take out Gabriel."

Matt's face drained of color. "We're trying to *save* the city. Gabriel is the only one who knows what's at risk."

Josh rolled his eyes, but their conversation was interrupted when the speakeasy door opened. Zayn and Lana walked in, their faces making it clear they had heard everything. Zayn looked thunderous. Lana feigned nonchalance. She stepped closer to the table. "Explain," she said, snapping her fingers.

Matt glared at her, unfazed by her attempted charm.

Almost lazily, Josh said, "Topher's going to be asking next with Nora at his side to hear the answers."

"Nora will come around," Matt said, crossing his arms. He looked so young at that moment. It was easy to forget Nora wasn't even twenty-one yet, so Matt likely wasn't either. Most of their group wasn't. With Poppy, Colbie, and Oliver being the oldest among their friends, life had made everyone grow up too quickly. Even Chance, only another year younger than Nora, seemed to be in a completely different generation after his mostly standard human life. His biggest loss was his siblings being made vampires, but even so, he had them back now.

"You sure about that?" Nora's voice came from the stairs, as hard and angry.

Colbie was at her side, Topher and Annaliese behind, and the rest of the werewolves filling the stairs. Colbie's eyes were only on her girlfriend. Nora had never looked so tired. So drained. Her power was working overtime to keep her standing.

Poppy moved, reaching into her bag for the potion she'd spent the morning brewing. She wasn't sure how well it would work, but it was a take on her sunlight brews that replenished her own magic. Nora barely spared Poppy a glance with the enemy werewolf in their midst, but Colbie gave Poppy a small, grateful smile as Nora threw back the potion without question and almost immediately regained the color in her cheeks. There was enough of Topher's spit in the vial to dull the worst of the pain she must have been in, not that Poppy would tell Colbie or Nora that.

"Let me explain," Matt pleaded. He glanced furtively around the room. "Alone."

Nora took the third stool at the table, accepting the hand that Josh offered to help her up. All three of the werewolf packs represented. "No. You'll just explain."

His focus shifting from person to person, Matt seemed to recognize who all had gathered. Witch, werewolves, vampires, humans. Comfortable in each other's presence and staring at him like he was the scum of the city. Whatever Gabriel was trying, it wasn't going to work here. Matt cleared his throat and wiped his palms on his jeans. "Reelings is going to strike on Fourth. We'll finally rid the city of the vampire leeches." He'd lowered his voice, but if Poppy could still make out his words, no doubt the vampires in the room could. "You can't think they're worth defending."

Nora leaned back into her seat, resting her head on the shoulder Colbie provided as she stepped in close. Their movements had become so aligned in the last weeks. Every mannerism mirrored and supported and known. "Your job right now is to convince me that you and your pack are, Matt."

His eyes widened at the casual contact, his lip curling. "Once the vampires are taken care of, we can return this New Brecken to the werewolf haven it once was."

Topher scoffed. Matt shifted to glare at him. "What? You think the vampires have made the city better?"

Topher rolled up his sleeve, pointing at the rosebush tattoo, then the scars dotting his inner elbow. "Do you know what the werewolves did to keep their power before Fourth Street was established?"

Even Nora turned to Topher with a question in her eyes. He surprised everyone by turning to the older members of her pack. "Heather? Remember what you did for work?"

Patrick stepped forward, teeth bared.

"Chris… I only worked as protection, I didn't—"

"You didn't sell the drugs to the humans?" Topher tilted his head. "You really going to take a moral high ground? You think the people you worked for were better than Fourth Street?"

"We worked for whoever paid. The city wasn't welcoming of werewolves and—"

"If your vision for the future is supposed to be better than your past, what is it? Exactly what we're trying to do, but without vampires in the picture?"

"This is a human city. It should belong to the humans again."

Topher didn't look impressed. Poppy couldn't blame him. Humans hadn't treated him much better than the other groups of New Brecken. But it was Annaliese who snorted. "You just said the words *werewolf haven*. Humans choose to go to Fourth Street. Humans voted in favor of the laws. Humans—"

"Are susceptible to charm and can't make their own choices in the matter! I've seen it."

"And experienced it," Josh put in pleasantly, gesturing to where Matt had sat the entire day, waiting for Topher to release him.

Matt's face paled, losing his footing in the argument. Annaliese let out a laugh. "It seems I have more of a right to speak on this topic than you do, Matty."

Matt's brows pinched. "What do you mean?"

"Whatever dark magic Reelings and Gabriel were throwing at me last spring made me immune to even Topher's charm. Should I tell you my opinion on vampires and Fourth Street now that it's decided I'm the only one with a valid stance in this room by your logic?"

"Just because one vampire can charm me doesn't mean he can charm Gabriel or that I'm wrong. We need to get rid of the vampires in this city. That means letting Reelings take control and then taking him out of the picture."

"It won't be that easy," Annaliese protested. No one looked at Topher, refusing to give up his plans to take Fourth and painting a target on his back. But Poppy saw how Nora and Topher shared a look. The vampires were disorganized and vulnerable and Topher couldn't fix that in one night. For him to take Fourth meant she would have to distract and handle Gabriel while Topher gave all his energy to getting the vampires in line.

And Nora had to win this time.

CHAPTER 26

Topher and Josh escorted Matt out of the Alpha's Den. Poppy couldn't tell what they talked to him about once outside, but they were determined when they returned and answered the questioning looks they received. "We know where the next human cult meeting will be and that Reelings will be there."

"What does that mean?" Lana asked. She had yet to hear about the cult Reelings created to gain human support, but no one bothered to answer her.

Topher instead turned to Jay and Chance. "Do you two know anyone who—"

"Stop, Topher," Chance interrupted. "It'll be us. Obviously. With Ru's protection, we'll be fine."

Topher hated it. His jaw worked as he tried to think of a protest. But Chance's expression must have swayed him. The fight bled out of Topher. "Fine. Make sure she knows to block our scent from you but keep you smelling human. Talk to Colbie about how to act charmed. And Poppy?"

She started at being so suddenly addressed. "Yes?"

"We need to know where Reelings is hiding. We can track him after the meeting."

"You and me?"

"I was thinking more we'd ask your grandfather to go," Topher said, a knowing look in his eyes. Poppy had so much guilt about the spying last spring and what had come of it that she dropped her eyes and agreed before she'd fully considered his plan.

"Okay. I'll summon him tonight."

Topher checked his phone and winced apologetically. "The meeting is in an hour."

That was how Poppy found herself and Ru parked down the street from the human cult meeting. It was not how she'd expected her night to go. But with Jay and Chance waiting in the backseat, she took Ru's hand and searched for that sleeping bond that connected her to her grandfather.

Jay let out a yelp, and Poppy turned. Gus sat in the back between the two humans, looking largely displeased. It was too easy to summon him. Since she and Topher had banished Gus from Poppy's life, she'd tried hard to convince herself they had severed the bond she had accidentally formed with the poltergeist.

This was not the case. "Penelope."

"Gus."

Jay's eyes widened when Poppy addressed him, but Poppy barreled on. "How much have you seen lately?"

"Shadows." Gus was usually more talkative. His short response was enough to raise the hair on Poppy's neck.

"Well, you should know I've found all the Jennings witches, and we're very close to ending Reelings's reign on the city."

"The demons?"

"Are under his control. We end him, we'll take them out."

"Are you certain?"

Poppy and Ru shared a glance. No, Poppy was not certain,

but she couldn't let Gus detract her from the issue at hand. "We need your help."

Gus only raised an eyebrow, so Poppy explained how he needed to follow Reelings for them. "And if the sorcerer is there?" he asked. "She's seen me before."

"Then don't let her see you this time," Ru answered.

Up the road, cars parked and people spilled onto the sidewalk, entering the midsized home to the left. They carried desserts, casserole dishes, and bottles of wine. People laughed and walked hand in hand, excitement brimming. Poppy's insides went cold. Whatever she expected to witness here, it hadn't been joy. Not excitement and cheer. It was like they were going in for a holiday dinner with friends.

"Please. You know this is important information. My mother—"

"Was killed. By the people you want me to help."

Ru scoffed. "You were with my mother for her power and the freedoms she allowed you. Not any sense of true love or loyalty. I don't feel that your current being is capable of such feelings."

Gus affected a pout, crossing his arms over his chest. "I—"

"Go with Jay. Poppy and I will be watching. Follow Reelings, and don't alert him to your presence. Or do we need to call Topher here to ensure you stay in line?"

Gus's eyes widened enough to show Ru's threat landed. Ru was twisted in the passenger's seat, staring him down. The standoff lasted until Chance shifted in his seat, the only one unable to see the poltergeist in their midst.

"Fine."

Ru smiled. All teeth. She'd been spending too much time with vampires. "Fine."

Mother above, Ru was becoming terrifying as her confidence and power settled in.

Poppy gave the humans tight smiles. "Remember what you're supposed to say?"

"We met Matt a week ago near campus, and he gave us these," Chance answered, holding up the business card style invitations Topher had slipped from Matt's pocket. His lingering scent around Nora and Annalise's apartment gave them the rest of the recruitment story. Poppy hoped it would hold up.

As Jay left the car, Ru adjusted her grip on Poppy's hand and sent them into Gus's field of vision.

Jay stepped closer to Chance as they approached the house. They glanced back at Gus, confirming the ghost was following. Chance brushed their fingers with his own. "It'll be fine," he promised.

Jay snorted. "I thought you hated the vampires. I would never have believed if you'd told me we'd ever do something like this last summer."

"Well, I have to get Topher's trust somehow. Now, quiet. They have good hearing."

"At least pretend you're excited to be here," Jay said. "They all are." Gus floated before them, providing a view of Jay's forced smile.

"If I seem reluctant like you dragged me along, they might try harder to win us over," Chance argued. "We might get more information that way."

"I don't think I want any extra attention."

Just like that, Chance's eyes widened with feigned anticipation as he took in the building. When the two were greeted by a couple making their way inside, he seemed almost shy, letting Jay do all the talking. The werewolf at the door, one from Gabriel's pack that Poppy had seen going in and out of the Den, barely even glanced at their invites. Was this too easy? A trap waiting to be sprung? Or were Reelings and his people really so confident?

A quick search showed no sign of Beth, so Gus remained close to Jay and Chance as they moved with the flow of people to the large living room and kitchen area. Attendees sat on the couches, dining room chairs, stools at the bar, on the kitchen counter, on laps, and even on the floor. Chance and Jay took up their positions, standing against the wall by the bathroom. They looked nervous but so did others around the room. They fit the energy humans often took on when around the supernatural for the first time. There seemed to be an even split of people who were at ease, comfortable like they'd been attending these meetings for years, and newcomers like Chance and Jay. One girl in particular looked nervous enough to be sick. She wore a scarf around her neck that she kept touching while the two friends next to her giggled and whispered with excitement. She must have been dragged along.

Finally, those in the kitchen hushed, and the room turned as one to watch Gabriel stride in with Reelings at his heels. Gabriel looked primarily unscathed. There was a bandage on his neck and a scratch on his forehead, but he moved easily compared to Nora's current state.

At the front of the room, he seemed to bask for a moment under the rapt attention. "Welcome!" He smiled, showing slightly pointed canines. Even the nervous girl on the couch lost her hesitation as she stared at his mismatched eyes and tall build. "I won't waste your time with introductions, but I wanted to say how pleased I am by the turnout tonight. You are all taking steps to make change and to be part of something bigger. Together, we will make this city a better place. Now, here is the man of the hour, Anthony Reelings!"

Gabriel stepped aside. There was a smattering of applause, but it fell off when Reelings took his place and sent out a pulse of charm. Everyone stilled, and eyes glazed. Luckily, Chance and Jay were behind other people standing, so their acting didn't fall under too much scrutiny as they hurried to flatten their expressions.

The look of power and arrogance that crossed Reelings's

features was terrifying as he held the room in his palm. "Good evening. Thank you all for being here so late to accommodate my schedule. Let's get to business so you can get to the rest you need. At this point, I have convinced you all to my cause, a progressive, idealistic plan to better the future of New Brecken for all humans and supernaturals, placing us on an even playing field, sharing wealth, and keeping everyone safe." The humans nodded. Chance's eyes widened, and Jay grabbed his hand. "You will convince your loved ones that I am in the right and tell them to petition the city government to end the reign of the current vampires on Fourth and to out witches who use their magic in secret to only better themselves. You want to force them into open positions to aid humans and save lives. You will request more access and freedom for werewolves to police their fellow supernaturals. You want me to become the voice of supernaturals everywhere. You trust me to keep you safe. You will never speak a word against me and convince as many people as you can to attend my meetings. You will say I never feed from you or charm you. You will say the vampires can't be trusted, with myself being the only exception, so you trust me to deal with them and the damage they have caused on Fourth Street. You will proudly join a movement of humans against vampires, your goal being to dismantle the unnatural laws that gave us access to your blood. Without the laws in place, you think it is right that my power rises until it is unchecked because I need the freedom to keep other vampires in line, starting with Christopher West. Only I can save you from the demons and other creatures of the night that these laws allowed to spring into being. Only I can make you more powerful than any of them if that is something you desire. You want me in total control, first of the supernaturals, then you will begin to think I should run the entire city, though you won't state that blatantly.

"Those with special invitations in the front row will stay

behind. The rest of you can leave. Take pictures on the way out and post them on social media with the appropriate hashtags. Vote in my favor for every poll and be vocal about your support of me."

Humans turned to leave. Gus remained behind while Jay and Chance disappeared from view. It took a while for all the humans to file out, grabbing their uneaten dishes and wine bottles and taking selfies with huge smiles and hope-brimmed eyes.

Poppy was vaguely aware of the car she sat in shifting, Jay and Chance's incredulous voices, being led into the backseat while someone took her spot and started the engine, but she and Ru stayed in the shared vision of Gus.

Everything was going to plan. It was time to follow the vampire maker to find out where Reelings had been hiding.

Reelings took in the ten people left in the front row. He snapped his fingers at them impatiently. "Phones."

The people offered up their unlocked phones. Gabriel and Reelings went through them, comparing the frequency of messages, the emails, and the social media presence. Eventually, they narrowed the results to one man left on the couch.

They were so charmed that the humans watched without expression. Reelings dismissed everyone but the man whose phone he held.

"He'll do," Reelings said, tossing the phone carelessly back onto the couch. "When will Beth be ready? Is the witch secured?"

Gabriel cleared his throat. "We lost the Jennings witch. We need to find someone else."

For the first time, the shaky foundation of Reelings and Gabriel's alliance was exposed. Gus faced Reelings. He saw the way Reelings's expression flashed with a deep, animal rage before smoothing with uncanny precision. "What do you mean, you lost the Jennings witch? You said she trusted you."

"Nora found the cabin where I left her."

"And when you killed her?"

Gabriel shifted on his feet. Reelings snarled, turning and striking with blurred movements. Suddenly, Gabriel was pressed up against the wall. "You said you could handle her!"

A growl ripped out of Gabriel. He threw Reelings off. "I had it handled! But her mother surprised me."

Reelings stilled. "You said Helen Morales wasn't in the picture."

"She hasn't been. I can't explain how she came back. Or why she was with Henry Fucking Gould when she saved Nora."

Reelings turned. "Helen could ruin all of this for you. Do you understand that?"

"She's not—"

"She was as respected as her husband. She was friends with the alphas. She probably knows where the packs hid."

"The other packs left the city." Gabriel sounded so sure.

"How would you know? You have failed me over and over again. Find me a witch in time for the full moon. We need an army. One that doesn't succumb to Christopher West. One that my controlling means control of the city. You know how important this is. Stop Helen, find a witch, and keep your pack under control."

Reelings turned and snapped at the human. "In two nights, meet us here. If Gabriel succeeds, you will get all you want."

The man blinked, the charm lifting. He smiled. "Thank you, maker. Thank you."

Without another word, Reelings left. Gus shadowed him but lost the connection as he stepped out the back door. There was only a glimpse of Beth in the passenger's seat of the car parked there.

She did not look well as she waved a hand at Gus. The shadows swallowed him.

Poppy surprised Chance by asking to be taken home when she and Ru came out of Gus's vision. Her mind spun with all the questions she still had. She couldn't get that glimpse of Beth out of her head. She texted the group chat all they had learned, including the knowledge of where Reelings was going to meet their next victim on the full moon, and then let herself focus on the mystery of the drainers. They had the means to determine what Beth and Reelings were trying to achieve. What the two of them were promising all those humans gathered. As soon as she entered the Jennings house, Poppy double-checked the wards. Only the witches and Julia were home, as Poppy had hoped. Ru followed Poppy upstairs and to Julia's side. Ru's silence seemed wary.

Poppy hated that she was probably proving Ru's anxieties valid when she spoke, the two of them standing over Julia on the bed and Margot looking up from where she'd been sitting, keeping watch. Their arrival quickly brought Ryan and Amelia. Maybe Poppy was imagining it, but she felt stronger than she had in ages without the help of a potion. The Jennings witches together, back in their home wards. The absence of Jane and Natalie was cutting, yet it still felt almost like it had before Tiff broke her tie to them. Like Ru might have been correct all along. They had lost the Mother of their coven, but maybe not their ties to each other.

"Reelings is making more drainers. No witch has even attempted to look at what Beth has been doing. They're too afraid of the demons that usually show up wherever the drainers are. Even after all this time, I don't know how the demons are tied to this. If they're being used to hunt us because they feel our magic, if they're a byproduct of Beth's sorcery, or if Reelings needs them to make the drainers in the first place. But without the threat of them here, this is an opportunity no one has had before. If we can help Julia and the other drainers, or at the very least try to study Beth's magic within them, it'll be the first step toward finding answers. I'm worried Reelings has been busier than we thought in the last few weeks. I'm worried he might have been building an army of sorts. No humans were reported missing, but now we know why, and who knows how many he's recruited?"

Ru's eyes slid shut. She hadn't wanted Poppy to say it aloud, but she'd come to the same conclusion after seeing Beth and realizing what Reelings was doing with his cult.

"The magic surrounding Julia…" Ru paused, searching for a way to describe it. "It's dark, but that's not all it is. It resists my attempts to parse it out, probably the vampire and were- wolf influence. But I'm going to keep trying. I have a theory about how it's constructed, but I need to look more closely at what happened to Annaliese and Topher."

"Topher?" Ryan asked, brows bunching.

"When Mom killed his boyfriend, she intended to use Dylan's potential to power a spell to compel the demons to her. To help her control them. Dylan willed the spell somewhere else, though. He gave that power to Topher. It's why Topher's so strong. He's not a drainer, but the cast was similar enough that his strength is comparable. I think Topher might be what Reelings and Beth are trying to achieve with the drainers. Creatures that strong but under their control." Ru glared at their siblings, realizing how much she'd revealed. "Not that anyone here will ever repeat that."

"Of course not," Margot quickly agreed. Everyone else nodded, but Poppy couldn't shake the chill that had come over her at Ru's words.

Ru had moved past the distance of their childhood. It had never been as bad for her as it was for Poppy. A big part of Poppy believed her siblings only gave her attention because she'd earned their respect with her wards. If Poppy hadn't had that skill, if she was simply brewing and managed to find them all still, would they have stopped long enough to listen to her? Would they have already abandoned her again? Was Ru what kept them here? All eyes were on the youngest Jennings, and Poppy was acutely aware that she'd never been looked at like that. With respect and a desire for guidance.

But did that even matter? Didn't Poppy look at Ru the same way when it came to magic?

"I'm sure Topher and Annaliese will let you study them, but please, be careful how you ask," Poppy said.

Ru nodded. She'd seen how hard Topher had struggled to rise above his shadows. She would be as gentle with him as she needed and keep Julia a secret. "I will. And I'll keep examining Julia. I'm getting close."

"Okay." Poppy turned to Margot, who straightened under the sudden attention. "I need to talk to Vivienne."

"She's home right now."

"Then tell her to open the door when I get there."

"What do you m—"

Poppy had already left the room. Her car was at the Alpha's Den. She opened her phone to get a ride share, but opening the front door, she found Chance and Jay still parked on the street. Even from here, Poppy could see they were engaged in an argument. Shame was already crowding in, but Poppy hurried over and knocked on the window, earning herself an incredibly uncomfortable ride back to the Alpha's Den, where she beelined straight to her car. She spared a glance at the building, hoping Nora was okay, that Colbie wasn't too worried about her girlfriend, that Topher was there and not already on Fourth, but she knew none of that was the case. Nora had been mauled by Gabriel. Colbie had never looked so wretched, and it would take a long time before she comfortably let her girlfriend out of her sight again. Something that might be a problem when Nora's pack no doubt felt the same way.

And Topher... he was on his way or already on Fourth Street. Taking control of the vampires that Reelings wanted to target and painting the last strokes of the bullseye on his back.

Hopefully, if Poppy could similarly unite the witches, she would stand a chance of blocking the attacks.

CHAPTER 27

Poppy reached Mother Kallow's in record time. Armed with all the information that she had gathered on Reelings and her newfound confidence in her wards, Poppy knocked on the front door. Hopefully, Vivienne was ready on the other side. Hopefully, Mother Kallow would listen this time when Poppy spoke to her about Beth and her dark magic.

It wasn't Vivienne who opened the door, but Mother Kallow herself. She appeared an entirely different woman from the last time Poppy met with her. No longer was she running for mayor. No longer leaving her house, judging from the pale hue of her skin. But the regal, unimpressed stare she leveled at Poppy was all too familiar. Was mastering that look a requirement to become a Mother?

Poppy cleared her throat. Straightened her shoulders. Hardened her stare. "I'm here because I know what Reelings is planning, and I've figured out how to make wards that keep the demons out. In exchange for this information, I need something from you."

A beat as if Kallow was thinking this through. As if she hadn't expected Poppy or the news she shared about wards.

Vivienne would have told her, though, and the lack of surprise came out in her ready answer. "And what is that?"

"I want you to step forward to represent the witches again. I want you to support Topher's bid to lead the vampires and Nora Morales as the werewolf representative. I want you to meet with Brett Campbell and make him feel he has a significant role in the supernatural community."

Mother Kallow bared her teeth. "His little branch was *my* idea to begin with."

"Then support it. More and more people are realizing I'm a witch, but you're the only one of us fully exposed to the supernaturals and the humans. It should be you. You have the experience and are more—"

"I won't."

Poppy blinked. Mother Kallow waited, still holding open the door but making no move to invite Poppy in. It was enough to make her throw up her hands. "I don't understand! I don't know how to make sure the witches have a place in this city if we can't even talk to one another! My own siblings wouldn't talk to me, and I was the only one who could keep them safe."

"You have a lot of confidence for a girl who got lucky. Maybe it isn't your wards, but the company you keep. No one is convinced the demons and monsters aren't answering to Lana and Christopher W—"

Poppy's mouth dropped open. "Your *daughter* is summoning the demons and making the drainers!"

Kallow stepped forward. "Until my daughter is returned safely to her coven and is able to tell me for herself who forced her into sorcery, I will trust no one."

The door slammed in Poppy's face. She whirled with a huff, even as something cracked in her chest. She would never have a mother defend her like that. Never know a mother's love. All that had never been a possibility, and any hope of a relationship like that had died with Tiff Jennings.

But Poppy had Colbie. She had Topher and Ru. People

who believed in her. She couldn't let them down. Poppy had taken it upon herself to rally the witches, and she would do so. Maybe Kallow wouldn't put her into contact with the established covens in New Brecken, but while she was the most obvious and safest route, she was not the only option.

Poppy pulled out her phone, chest hollowing in anticipation of the call she needed to make.

Josh picked up on the fifth ring. "Hey, Poppy." He sounded stiff, but he'd answered. It was enough encouragement for Poppy to keep talking.

"I need your help."

Josh looked as tense as he had sounded on the phone when he met her on Second Street. The clubs along Fourth were distant enough that few walked here, but those that did had been shooting looks in Poppy's direction. She had stopped by their empty apartment, pet Mouse enough to hope he wasn't feeling abandoned, and stocked her bag with potions. Its bulging weight on her shoulder drew the looks. Most of these people knew what happened on this street. Cars stopped at old, multi-story homes similar to the Jennings house, as if the space between the two neighborhoods had erupted into a city and separated them with modernity. People went about their business with cautious glances, hurrying into houses without bothering to knock. Some came back out quickly, others stayed shut within, but no one lingered on the street. Another reason Poppy had drawn so many looks while she waited for Josh.

They would only continue to draw attention as Josh jogged to a stop in front of her. He stepped over the puddle nestled in the curb onto the cracked sidewalk. Crossing his arms, he waited for Poppy to explain why they were there. Why she'd needed him.

Poppy cleared her throat awkwardly. Suddenly, everything began to catch up with her, and her social energy faded. Her confidence plunged out of her grasp. "I needed someone to watch my back. I used to come here alone, and it was always too risky."

"So why me?"

"Nora's pack wouldn't leave her side tonight. Same goes for Colbie. I couldn't ask a witch or a human, and Topher is busy. I knew you wouldn't be with him."

"Zayn?"

Poppy blinked. She hadn't thought about Zayn. Zayn belonged to Oliver and Topher and Lana. They were friends, but Poppy couldn't think of a single time she'd called him. "Right. Sorry. I can call him instead."

Josh sighed. "I was just making a point. I'll go in."

"What was your point?"

Josh made a tired, cutting gesture. "Forget about it. It's fine."

"No, what was your point?"

"That you've always found it easier to call me. To ask me for things. I didn't mind before, but now I've grown to resent it, I guess."

"I won't call you again—"

"No. It's fine. We should be friends. If what I have going on with Topher keeps… going on, I'll be around too much for us not to talk anymore."

Poppy was afraid to ask. "What *is* going on?"

A blush immediately bloomed over Josh's cheeks. He dropped his eyes, looking younger. And Poppy didn't expect the crack of pain in her chest. She'd halfway anticipated this happening after her conversation with Topher and Colbie about grief and non-monogamy. It hadn't hurt so badly as a hypothetical. It hadn't hurt so badly when she thought they were talking about Annaliese. "You said his flirting wasn't real. I thought you were straight."

They were silly arguments to cling to, but the pain insisted she protest.

Josh ran a hand through his hair. "I don't know what happened. It was sudden. Out of my control but in the best way. But I also want to apologize. First, for blaming you when Quinn died. I decided not to tell Henry about the drainer apartment. I was distracted by you. None of that was your fault. I'm sorry. And second, I'm sorry that I dismissed your feelings for Topher when you had them. I shouldn't have tried to convince you that he was just a friend."

Just a friend to him or her? Poppy couldn't meet Josh's eyes as his words sank in. She turned her head and blinked, the old feelings resurfacing. Nothing felt fair about this. But she also couldn't deny that it made a certain kind of sense. "Don't apologize. You were right. I did have a crush on Topher, but I couldn't do his style of relationship. I wouldn't be able to share."

Josh smiled. She'd half meant the words as a jab, but it really didn't bother him. Poppy couldn't understand it. She was *always* jealous. Comparing herself to others in the habit of her mother. She was working on it, but the idea of having someone who made her the priority, who loved her the fucking *most*, was a dream. "How?" The question slipped out. She didn't want to know. She had to know.

Josh shrugged. "I've been thinking about it a lot, and I guess it's easier for me specifically because I grew up in a pack. Jealousy happens, but it's on the same level as being annoyed with someone, as a fight, as frustration, as sadness. All these other emotions are mundane and accepted. As a wolf, they are quickly dealt with. As a human, it's easier to talk about and work through. It's very *human* to think jealousy is the one emotion to be avoided at all costs. It's not as consuming in a pack mentality where we share affection and resources as a way of life."

And Poppy had grown up fighting for any scrap of attention and love. Witches were jealous, competitive, and fiercely loyal, even to their own detriment. Poppy nodded. Josh's words at once confirmed she and Topher would never work *and* that she and Josh wouldn't have either. Even Colbie, who was so confident and happy in all her relationships, was struggling with the pack aspect of Nora's life.

"I hope it works out for you both," she said, words too flat, but she'd work on it.

"Me too," Josh said, shoulders relaxing. "Now, what are we here for?"

Poppy indicated to the houses lining the quiet block, wondering how much of the magic Josh could sense in the air. "We're looking for witches. Welcome to the Black Market."

Topher approached Blue Blood alone. His eyes went to Happenstance, far too quiet down the street. Whatever happened in this meeting with the other makers, he'd have to go there next. Do all he could to breathe life back into the place when he had so little to share. No part of him wanted Colbie or Josh or Annaliese or anyone else to deal with this.

Every part of him wished he didn't have to do this alone.

Zayn had wanted to come. Colbie looked ready to offer, but it meant leaving Nora behind. Topher told them both to stay on Twenty-Fifth. Just because he was reentering Fourth Street didn't mean he had to drag them down with him. If Topher was grateful to Lana for anything, it was getting the people he loved out of these clubs.

The vampire manning the door was one of Sarah Patter's seconds. Everyone called him Fang because he'd lost one of his canines before his making. Topher had never spoken to him, but his vicious reputation proceeded him. Fang was kept on a tight leash. Even humans shied from him and his stumbling, aggressive charm. He was all power and bloodthirst.

This would be the type of vampire Topher was aligning himself with. The type of vampires he would have to keep in line even as they resented and hated him. Makers in their own rights, who had made vampires out of humans as vicious as they were. A whole culture of blood lust and physical feats and unchecked charm.

Topher hated how the challenge in Fang's eyes made his instincts sing in response, but he let them rise. He met Fang's gaze, infusing the eye contact with a command. When Fang ducked his head and opened the door without question, a smirk crossed Topher's mouth without his permission. But he let it linger as he stepped into the club, bypassing the protesting line of humans and drawing the attention of Fourth Street purposefully for the first time.

From there, it was crossing the floor, taking the stairs to the basement, and another quelling look to get him past the vampires on guard. Topher took one last breath before entering the meeting room. He fisted his hands and made himself move. Quiet fell. Topher's arrival interrupted what sounded like an argument on the verge of escalating.

Against the far wall, Mia Solas stood with her four seconds, all of them glaring and angry. Sarah Patter was to the left, an amused glint in her eyes as she watched one of Grace's former seconds hold Mia's lower by the throat, fangs bared. Grace's other seconds remained against the last wall, torn between joining in or letting the competition get himself killed.

"Seems like a productive conversation," Topher said. His appearance was shocking enough that the second dropped Mia's lower, who scrambled to stand behind her maker again. Topher knew everyone in this room by name but had never been around them on his own. If he'd hung out with any of them separate from Fourth Street politics, it had always been by an invitation that Tamera, Brady, Muscles, or Jaeger had received. It had always been with Zayn at his side. Or he'd been hiding behind Lana's audacity. He'd never tried to make friends, always on the outskirts and only interacting with Lana's other lowers.

Topher couldn't decide if his mystery was a good thing,

making the other vampires unsure how to react to him or if it meant he'd missed his chance to build friendships and trust with the people he was now moving to lead.

"What are you doing here, Mr. West?" Solas asked, trying for airy and unbothered.

"I'm here to find out how thoroughly Reelings has you all under his charm."

Laughter rang out, but as Topher stood unmoved, it began to die out or sound too forced. Patter stepped forward, speaking as if to a confused child. "While Reelings was our Maker, no charm lasts after death."

"So you haven't caught his scent around our city recently? Because I have. He isn't dead."

"He is," Solas argued, but her tone was off. Too mechanical.

Too charmed.

Doubt crossed Patter's face. She'd heard it, too. "Explain."

"I'd rather get to the bottom of the issue," Topher said. His next move, if successful, would do far more than uncover Reelings's current influence. It was Topher's last chance to back out. Last chance to leave the city. No one knew how big of a threat Topher was to the vampires' shaky balance. There were whispers, rumors, but in the moments where he'd shown the most charm, no one had told of the feat.

He could still walk away.

But Topher's reasons were too solid. Colbie's helplessness, watching her girlfriend bleed out. How worried Zayn was that Fourth Street would reach its claws down to Twenty-Fifth and put Oliver at risk again. Henry wanted an ally in Topher, so he needed power to offer if he was going to be a worthwhile partner. If he was going to hold Josh's interest. Annaliese wanted Topher to take his power, believing in him and what he was due.

It was cowardice that prodded for Topher to turn around. Even his shadows and charm wanted him to step forward.

Dylan wanted revenge on this city that had given them so little choice.

Topher crossed to the center of the room. He faced the united front Solas and Patter were willing to present to their opposition. Meeting their eyes, Topher dove deep into his charm and spoke, "Listen to me over Reelings."

Solas and Patter's expressions went blank. Horrifyingly empty. Topher's heart sank like a heavy drop. Had he broken them? He blinked the black out of his vision, trying to get a feel for how much of Patter and Solas remained, his memories too full of Julia's blanked face.

But, as he pushed, his charm met Solas and Patter's, their defenses already reforming as they breathed heavily and shook off his words. He hadn't used enough in his fear of hurting them permanently.

Patter found her voice first. "Impossible." Topher didn't know if she meant his strength or what he'd said about Reelings.

Solas's voice was entreating, the charm leaving her more shaken than her counterpart. "What did you do? Tell us what you know."

"I will. Reelings—"

Patter had heard enough. She'd felt enough of his charm. She knew what Topher's presence on Fourth meant without Lana. Knew what it meant for Topher to show his cards. She struck, defending her place on Fourth before Topher could explain.

Josh was quiet at Poppy's side. If he were a wolf, she had no doubt his hackles would be bristling. This was not the scene for one of Henry Gould's notoriously law-abiding werewolves. This was not the scene for anyone but the lowest who still lived in New Brecken, separated from routine city life by the line of vampire dwellings and clubs that few dared to cross.

This was the scene for those who wanted to remain hidden. Who thought the risk was worth it.

Poppy knocked three times on the door. This house was the one that sold potions. It was the most heavily frequented but also the house most left empty-handed. Poppy only knew the address because she'd found it written in one of Tiff Jennings's calendars with an appointment time. Poppy had come here looking for her mother after the wards fell and found a way to survive in New Brecken on her own instead. Now that she knew more about what Tiff Jennings had been up to, she likely came to Second Street while looking for ways to summon demons to her. With that chilling reminder of the knowledge the people who owned this business possessed, Poppy waited for the door to open.

And waited.

Poppy knocked again, glancing at Josh's tight features as worry crowded in. What if this wasn't the right place? What if the people she'd seen were just the new residents of this street and the Black Market had relocated? What if the laws had swept so thoroughly into effect that the Black Market became irrelevant?

The door finally opened. An older woman that Poppy didn't recognize peeked out. Poppy lifted her bag, jangling it so the woman could hear the vials within. "I'm selling," she said as confidently as possible.

"We'll be the ones to decide that, love," the woman said as she stepped back. It wasn't quite a welcome, but Poppy nodded her thanks anyway as she walked inside, Josh directly on her heels, the woman's appraising eyes a heavy weight.

The older woman led them upstairs, her gait painstakingly slow as she shuffled one foot up and then the other. Poppy wasn't surprised at all when Josh stepped forward, offering his arm.

And was promptly swatted away. "Learn some patience,"

she said, then cackled as Poppy and Josh slowly followed her, sharing glances for every step.

At the top, the woman's pace picked up dramatically enough that Poppy began to suspect the snail's pace on the stairs was for her own entertainment. It made Poppy smile and alleviated the worst of her nerves. The woman walked past the first two doors. Poppy remembered this well. From the murmured voices within, deals were taking place. Behind each door was a remodeled former bedroom. All turned into offices where the workers of the Black Market conducted deals. Most doors had a guard in position out front. Poppy had heard stories of what went on behind other doors and even in the basement of this house, but she didn't want to know the full details. From what she'd gathered, one house on this block was the last, clinging remnants of the city's drug problems. A solitary holdout for those who didn't want to switch their escape of choice because they distrusted the vampires. Another house peddled illegal weapons. When Poppy first did business here, she was asked if she would be willing to sell anything a bit more deadly. Poppy didn't want to meet the witch willing to broker a deal like that. The stories had been enough to keep her away after Topher's tips from the Maker opening were enough to live off.

Someone coughed aggressively behind one of the doors. Poppy's heart gave a pang. Far more often than someone coming here to sell magic, someone arrived searching for a cure. There were bounds to Poppy's potions and vampire saliva, but she still always wished she had the time and resources to help more of those who were desperate enough to stop here. Poppy thought of Oliver and his hopes to use his medical experience to incorporate vampire saliva into modern cures. If he successfully lessened the taboo, half the business on this street would likely dry up.

"This room here. The broker will be with you shortly," the

woman said, stopping at the last door on the left and opening it wide.

Josh and Poppy exchanged another look. Josh didn't want to be here. Poppy had no idea what he smelled or what his wolf instincts were telling him, but he looked ready to make a run for it. Lifting her chin, Poppy ignored her own instincts and entered the room ahead of him. Josh sighed. With no other option aside from abandoning her, he followed.

The room had a locked wooden cabinet to the left, a window with maroon curtains drawn on the opposite wall, and an ornate desk in the center on top of a paisley-patterned burnt orange rug. Poppy took one of the two chairs facing away from the door. Rather than take the second, Josh lingered at the wall. Poppy suddenly felt like she'd brought a personal guard more than a friend, although maybe that was why she'd called him specifically. It explained his annoyance and tension. He knew this was how the night would go.

The door was eventually pushed open again. Poppy twisted in her seat. Her mouth dropped open when eight women entered. Josh gave a warning growl as one stood on either side of him, smiling and batting their eyes. The younger woman reached up to touch his hair, and Josh jerked back. "What is this?"

Poppy swallowed. The women were all so similar in appearance: olive skin, loose black curls, dark eyes. Even Poppy had heard of them. Her mother had often mocked Rosenfield's use of the same male to father all her daughters. She'd been convinced it had spread the life magic far too thin, but as the coven's presence filled the room and made Poppy's head spin with the force of it, she had to disagree with that theory.

"Penelope Jennings," Mother Rosenfield said. "I've heard about you stirring up trouble."

Poppy blinked in shock. She'd never seen another coven. Hadn't imagined there was a complete coven left in all of New Brecken. She didn't even protest when one of the daughters stepped forward and grabbed her bag, presenting it to the Mother, who ruffled through it and frowned, unimpressed by the contents. Poppy felt her shoulders hunching, the disappointment too similar to Tiff Jennings's.

Josh's narrowed eyes were what Poppy needed to shake off the smallness.

"You're Eileen Rosenfield?" she asked.

Josh hid his surprise well when Poppy voiced the witch's name. The Mother said nothing. Poppy tried again. "You run the Black Market?"

"Is that the name you gave this place?" Rosenfield asked, amused.

"It's what everyone calls it."

The Mother raised an eyebrow. "You speak as if we're a popular establishment. Very few people know the truth of what my daughters and I do here. Even fewer supernaturals." A significant look toward Josh and back to Poppy for bringing him here. "We remember when you first sold potions to us. They were simple yet impressively potent. I thought you might have fallen to the darkness in the city when you didn't return."

Poppy didn't know what to say to that. It seemed the tone of the conversation was shifting, but she had no idea where she stood. Instead, she glanced at Josh. Unhelpful. He looked equally as baffled by the situation.

"Sit down. Both of you," the Mother ordered, snapping to angle the chairs more invitingly. She rounded the desk and sat, her daughters leaning against the walls. "You know who I am?"

Poppy nodded. "You were one of the three Mothers who helped with negotiations. I don't know your stance, though."

Rosenfield studied Poppy, and Poppy couldn't say where the sudden bravado came from, but she studied her right back. She'd gotten over the shock of the moment. Remembered herself and her accomplishments. Poppy wasn't just some witch. She had a coven of her own again and the backing of powerful supernaturals throughout the city.

Rosenfield broke first. "If you can get one human friend to vouch for you, I will tell you my stance."

Poppy blinked. "A human friend?"

Rosenfield's expression began to sour. Poppy recovered from her surprise enough to pull out her phone and hit the first contact. A text from Oliver asking if she'd heard from Topher since he left for Fourth Street.

He answered, sounding groggy. "I was trying to sleep, Pop."

"You're on speaker, Oliver." She quickly told him, cutting off him mentioning Zayn or Topher in front of the witches.

Rosenfield leaned over the phone. "Are you human?"

"Um… yes? May I ask who's asking?"

"Never mind that for now. Is Penelope Jennings a good friend of yours?"

"What's going on?" Oliver no longer sounded sleepy. "Are you okay, Poppy?"

"I'm fine," Poppy said quickly, hoping it was true. Oliver didn't need more to worry about.

"I'm here too," Josh put in to reassure him.

Oliver only sounded more confused. "Why are you with Poppy, Josh? I thought you went with—"

"He wanted to go alone," Josh cut in before Oliver could name anyone.

"Zayn left to find him," Oliver said quietly. "I thought you'd be there too to watch their backs." Oliver's displeasure was apparent.

The Mother watched the interactions with great interest. "You're all close friends," she said, surprised. Into the phone, she said, "Poppy will call you back later."

"What's—" Rosenfield hung up the phone, shutting off Oliver's question.

Poppy still couldn't read Rosenfield's face. She didn't like the whispering of the daughters at her back. "Call another," Rosenfield said.

Confused, Poppy opened Annaliese's contact. The latest messages were about Annaliese's shift that evening at the human mediation office. She had some choice words about one of Solas's seconds. Annaliese answered quickly. "Hey, P. What's up? Any updates from—"

"I'm calling human friends at a witch's behest," Poppy stated plainly. Annaliese wasn't as prone to panic as Oliver.

"Sorry, who are you again?"

"Not funny," Poppy said flatly, though Josh snorted. "Just vouch that we're friends."

"Definitely friends, but do you have anything for Nora? I think she's still sore." Her words were a reminder of everything that happened last night and the urgency of Poppy's current quest. She'd come to the Black Market to try and get into contact with more witches. She needed to focus and play her cards right.

"I think Colbie should have pain relief covered," Poppy said. "But I have to go. Bye!"

Annaliese didn't bother responding. Oliver was trying to call Poppy back, but she ignored the notification and pulled up another contact before Rosenfield could ask for it.

"Hey, Jay. You're human, and we're friends, right?"

"Not much longer. I swear to all things holy, something big had better be happening. You and your nocturnal friend group need to get it in your heads that I work at a fucking coffee shop! If you all don't stop calling me in the dead of night—" Poppy hung up and scrolled for the next contact.

Chance answered right away. "Have you heard from my brother?"

"Uh, no. Sorry." Poppy was beginning to think she should be more worried. Topher had been confident he wouldn't have a problem charming the vampires on Fourth. He'd made it sound like that would be all it took to sway them to fall in line. But if that was the case, why wasn't he answering his phone? Why hadn't anyone heard from him or Zayn? "I'll check up on him next, but I'm in the middle of something. Can you confirm we're friends and you're human?"

"Am I friends with you all?" Chance sounded oddly touched when he asked.

"Of course. I have to go, though. I'm sorry. We'll talk later." Poppy hung up, feeling guilty and making a silent promise to herself to get to know Chance better. He might be closer to Ru's age, but that didn't mean she had to treat him like he was just her best friends' brother.

Poppy opened Raven's contact and was about to call when Rosenfield's hand stilled her. Everyone was staring at her, but Poppy had been too caught up in the conversations to notice the shift in the attention she was receiving.

"You have many human friends," the Mother stated.

Poppy shrugged. "We're an inclusive group. And I go to UNB. It's hard not to meet humans there."

Rosenfield blinked. "You've been out in the open this whole time?"

It was the perfect opening, but Rosenfield kept talking before Poppy could make her pitch about exchanging her knowledge on warding for information and alliance. "I heard the rumors of what Tiff did to her coven, but I had no idea her daughters decided to live among the humans. I didn't think any of you would have survived this long in the city."

"Not all of us did. I've only recently found my other siblings."

Rosenfield's eyes narrowed once more. "So, your coven was destroyed, you came here shortly after to make some money, and then you…"

Poppy didn't see any help for it. She filled in the rest of the story, answering a vampire ad, moving in with them, etc. It was a practiced recap at this point. The disbelief on Rosenfield's and her daughters' faces was as potent as it had been on Ryan's, Margot's, and Amelia's. Then, Poppy got to the part in the story where Reelings returned. "You knew what he did though? This whole time? Kallow remembered he wasn't dead."

"I knew." Rosenfield nodded. "But my focus has always been on the humans. Humans like my husband and his relatives. If I'm honest, I didn't care much what happened with Reelings so long as the Big Three stayed in line, and they did for years. Then, when the witches were being attacked, I needed to keep my daughters safe. We pulled in our wards and haven't left Second Street. Luckily, very few demons make it past Fourth. Aside from some emails from Kallow and your mother, I've heard no news from the city."

Poppy and Josh shared yet another look. It was so easy to revert to their old comfort. When he nodded in response to Poppy's silent question, she turned back to Rosenfield with her chin held high.

"I told you one of the vampires I moved in with is Topher West. Have you heard of him?"

"Of course."

"He's currently claiming Fourth Street as his own."

That captured the attention of the room. Poppy kept going. "You know Nora Morales?"

"I've heard of her father."

"She's going to challenge Gabriel. He's been working with Beth Kallow and Reelings to create the drainers, letting Beth pull from some of his werewolf abilities to make them more resistant to magic and charm. Once Nora takes care of him, she'll be one of the most powerful alphas in the city and Colbie West's girlfriend."

Rosenfield seemed about to say something, but Poppy didn't let her. "We know Reelings has created an underground cult in this city, charming human members at meetings and using them to build his drainer army. That's what he has on his side, but we have Henry's pack, Nora's pack, and when Topher succeeds, all the other vampires in the city. The only way to ensure the least amount of damage is for us witches to do our part."

"And what do you imagine that is?"

"My siblings are already working on it, but we'll need help, and when the time comes, we'll need more witches. We will figure out what makes the drainers and try to save them. We're going to protect the humans in the city from reaching the same fate."

"Keep talking."

CHAPTER 28

Topher didn't want this. He didn't want to be here. He didn't want to dive back into his charm and hook his shadowed claws into more minds. He didn't want to be a vampire, let alone rule them.

But he didn't want to disappoint his people either. Topher couldn't fail. But god, it shouldn't have been so hard to muster the strength to put up his hands and stop Patter from clamping on to his throat. It shouldn't have been so hard to summon the words and lace them with his dark magic.

And that lack of motivation almost cost him. Topher stumbled back a step when Solas threw her weight into the mix. He made eye contact with Solas long enough to bring her up short. Holding Patter at bay physically and Solas with his charm, Topher knew how little it would take to lose this fight.

Topher pictured it. He had been fighting for an escape all his life, and sometimes this led to thinking about where Dylan might be. Where Topher might go after this. He realized he'd never been in a situation like this on his own. Topher had always had someone watching him, and that had always been enough to keep him from slipping up. But now, here, there was no one. And if he succeeded, he'd remain alone. Sure, there were humans on Fourth, but Annaliese didn't want this life of nighttime. Josh wouldn't be able to stand being surrounded by vampires even if Topher made things better. Colbie was with Nora, and Nora would feel the same as Josh. Zayn had Oliver and a way out. Topher would be stuck with the people who attacked him now. His life would become Fourth Street. It would become New Brecken.

Patter broke his hold. Mindlessly, Topher ducked and dodged and struck as she attacked. Something kept tempting him, kept him from truly fighting back—a quiet, gentle memory. Topher thought of his dreams with Dylan. Whispered plans to move away. To start life over. Dylan hadn't wanted to leave his father, but if Topher could have convinced him, he would never have ended up here. Never have been without. Wouldn't be dreaming of finding Dylan now in the darkness. Maybe even searching for Julia with an apology ready on his lips. Funny, Topher had never thought much about what came after this life, but as Patter landed a swipe of her nails across his stomach, he almost thought he could see it. A glimpse beyond the Veil that the witches talked about.

And shadows rose in response. From along the walls, they crept in, causing shouts of alarm. The first one seemed to caress Topher's cheek. His throat tightened as it had when he possessed the ability to cry. These shadows, this curse, this gift, had come from Dylan's life and Tiff Jennings's magic. It was enough to make him pause alongside Solas and Patter as they took in the creeping darkness with wide eyes.

Topher loved these shadows and this lingering sense of Dylan. If he died, where would the shadows go? What if that was all that was left? What if Topher accidentally ended them both?

The question was enough to make him think about fighting back. Enough to make him consider what that would mean. Yes, his life would be Fourth Street, but Josh wouldn't abandon him to it completely, would he? Would stolen nights and moments with Annaliese be sufficient? Would Colbie visit him often enough for the darkness to stay at bay? He'd be able to leave, right? Once he was in control, he could spare a few hours on Twenty-Fifth, here and there.

And what if… what if he really could make a change? Oliver came to mind, the most hopeful person Topher had ever met. He truly believed he could alter medicine by bringing in vampires to heal and ease anxious minds like his own. Oliver thought, even if it went unaccepted everywhere else, he could make New Brecken and medical centers here a type of utopia with the laws to allow it and citizens knowledgeable enough to consent. Oliver believed that eventually, their developed medicines and cures would spread.

What if Topher really could help him? Help everyone? Would that be enough to make up for the damage he'd done? If he fought back, fought for what was right and what people like Oliver dared to believe, could Topher change New Brecken?

If he trapped himself here, could he make it somewhere he didn't long to escape?

That line of questioning while being circled by some of the strongest vampires in New Brecken felt like taking a breath of fresh air. And if he was feeling what could only be called hope, didn't that mean he should keep going? Didn't that mean he wanted to?

"That's enough," Topher said. The shadows melted and pooled at his feet in response.

"You aren't a vampire," Patter said, accusing.

"I am. But, I'm also more. I'm what it will take to save you all. To save Fourth Street and keep the laws intact."

"The laws aren't being threatened," Solas scoffed.

"They are. By Reelings."

The two makers shook their heads and joined in the laughter of the lowers and seconds in the room.

"I'll prove it," Topher promised. His charm already gathering, right alongside the familiar fear. Trying to unlock their memories could kill them. Topher didn't want to take Fourth Street in that manner, but he had to take it either way. He braced himself for the possibility of adding more blood to his hands.

A crash against the door made everyone jump. Solas and Patter turned, distracted as Zayn rushed into the room. Topher seized the opportunity and slashed through their defenses, throwing his charm at the makers with all he had.

Topher had never charmed this intricately before and never to two people simultaneously. Even as he captured and stilled their minds, he hesitated before diving in deeper.

"I'm here, T," Zayn whispered, coming up behind him and placing a hand on his shoulder. "I'm with you."

It was all Topher needed. Not to be alone. He had so many friends when he let himself be happy about it rather than anxious. He wanted to be with them for years to come. And that meant getting himself and Zayn out of here alive.

Topher closed his eyes and focused on the shadows, the way they connected him to Solas and Patter while keeping the rest of the room at bay, silenced by his charm in the air.

Reelings's charm was too strong to undo without a spoken command. "Tell me what happened the night Luis Morales died."

He started there, waiting as Solas and Patter spoke over one another until the moment their voices flattened. "Then, Morales killed Reelings."

"Did he? Tell me the truth."

They stayed silent. Topher's eyes were closed, but he could feel the confusion in their minds begin to build. It was his command against Reelings's order to forget. Topher gritted his teeth as he sent more charm along the trailing shadows connecting them. "Tell me the truth of what happened that night. Remember it."

"We…" Patter trailed off.

Solas tried. "Reelings spoke to us before he died."

"What did he say?" That was already more than they remembered moments ago. Topher pushed harder, swallowing fear. He didn't want to ruin their minds. He would if he had to in order to take Fourth, but he hoped they could handle this. "What did he say? Tell me." He had to tag on the commands for the charm to strike true. His head ached, his hands shook. Thirst roared for attention, and only his extensive practice allowed Topher to shove the ache aside.

The basement fell quiet for so long Zayn shifted closer to Topher, thinking Topher was losing control. The shadows stayed strong. Topher felt them working through the knots, overpowering Reelings's grip. Topher thought he could smell cigarettes, laundry detergent, and the hint of cucumber deodorant. All that his human nose had been able to smell of Dylan. Topher breathed deeply, centered himself, then clenched his fists.

Solas and Patter cried out, both falling to their knees, hands clutching their heads. Solas recovered first, blinking up at Topher in shock. "He's alive?"

"And he's coming for us."

"What do we do?" Patter asked. Her voice shook with fear. Must be horrifying to realize your mind was altered, the effects lasting for years.

"I can take him. I broke his charm. I'm stronger. And that means—"

"We submit to you," Solas finished. She didn't like it, but it was the vampire way. "What do you need from us?"

"I'll start with taking Happenstance. I don't want to stay in this basement a second longer." Topher hated basements.

Not a single vampire in the room protested. They trailed after Zayn and Topher as they turned for the stairs, memories hurrying their steps. Solas and Patter followed cautiously. Usually, when a vampire gained control of a group, it was a violent process. No other vampire would let Solas and Patter live after what they had done, turning Topher, Lana, Zayn, Colbie, and Grace over to Gabriel those months ago. If Lana was in his position, no doubt Solas and Patter would be without their heads if only to avenge Grace fully.

Topher didn't dispel their worries. He needed them as compliant and fearful as he could keep them. He needed them in line. But he also needed them. He didn't want to run Fourth Street on his own. The music in the club was as loud as it had been when Topher first passed through the room, but the vampires working and interacting with humans were silent, making the room seem still and hushed. The humans followed the vampires' gazes, eyes instantly glazing over from the charm Topher still expelled. He tried not to look at them as he ensured every vampire in the room knew who they now answered to.

Rachel stood across the room. She smiled when she met Topher's eyes, ducking her head in a nod. The movement was copied by the nearest vampire and soon swept across the dance floor, behind the bar, and to those on the upper-level balcony that outlined the room. Compliance, at least in this club. At least for now.

Patter's lowers were his. She was stiff behind him but didn't try to retake control.

Topher turned to Zayn. "Make sure every maker knows to meet us at Happenstance in thirty minutes."

"And… Lana?"

Topher sighed. He was still so angry at her. Betrayed that she hadn't kept up her end of the deal with Julia. Uncomfortable with how she'd treated him, touched him, acting like it was her right since she was his maker. In his time among the vampires he'd seen so much worse, but it didn't make him forgive her. It motivated him to improve things on this street now. The worst part was that even with all these negative feelings toward her, there remained a slice of gratitude. A sense of loyalty. She'd supported him, Colbie, and Poppy by giving him a job at the Maker. She'd hidden Colbie for as long as she could. She'd handed Colbie and Nora a future by chasing her ambitions and opening the Alpha's Den. If Lana hadn't changed him, Topher would have died by Tiff Jennings's hand and the injuries her demon had wrought on his human body. Dylan's death and shadows would have only brought harm to the city. A waste of his goodness and potential. Some days, Topher resented Lana for that, but he'd *just* chosen to live. He kept choosing to live no matter how bad things got. Didn't he owe everything to the fact that she'd taken the choice from him when he'd been the closest to giving up?

Maybe not, but this was still her world.

"Her too. Every vampire in the city of consequence should be there," Topher spoke loud enough for everyone to hear. He walked with his back straight and mask in place out of the club, into the fresh air of Fourth Street and the life it carried in the darkness, and on to Happenstance, the tallest of the clubs.

He could immediately see where Grace's attention to detail no longer kept the place to its former glory. A neon sign was flickering, advertising a type of beer on tap. The trash beside the doors was full, the ashtray on top overflowing even though few smoked when vampire bliss was readily available. Most of those butts were probably Topher's from months ago. He eyed them hungrily. He'd been so lost, so empty, he couldn't remember the last time he bothered to smoke. The craving struck again. He needed an outlet for his nerves—something to do with his clenched hands.

Humans sat where the line had once wrapped around the building, all too blissed for Topher's comfort. And that was the front of the club. Circling around the back, he found broken glass, the smell of decay, and a dead lower vampire.

Topher stopped, staring down at the girl's twisted form.

Brady had been found in the same place. Topher didn't know her, but she had the smell of Grace's lineage. Topher turned to Grace's former seconds, those who used to be Lana's equals, still following behind him. He gestured to the girl. "Who is this?"

"Was," one of the seconds corrected with a smirk. The four of them remaining laughed. The others had no doubt been killed similarly in the power struggles. Topher watched them and knew it had been too long since they'd been forced into line. Grace had been tight-fisted. Patter and Solas were, too. They'd had to be after working so hard to pass the laws and work with the other city leaders. But these vampires had turned feral. There was nothing akin to humanity in their eyes as they shared amusement over the young vampire's misfortune.

"Whose lower *was* she?" Topher asked through gritted teeth and lowered fangs.

Two of them shrugged. One was still laughing and nudged the woman next to him. "Looks like the one Ian just made, doesn't she? Makes her yours."

"Please. You know Smithy has a thing for redheads. Probably William's second's then."

William protested. They fell to arguing, almost cheerful in the accusations and misbehaviors of the makers they had let run wild. Zayn and Topher exchanged a look, Zayn slipping his phone away. Grace's former seconds couldn't even keep track of their lowers. Didn't bother to keep track of the makers beneath them. They were openly, laughingly, flaunting the laws.

And the laws were explicit. Vampires had to keep their lowers in line or allow the werewolves to do so. No werewolves had been watching Fourth, not with the shaky alliances. Gabriel had steered clear, hoping Fourth fell to disarray, and Nora still building her pack. It was on the vampire leaders to keep their people in line.

After Topher's show at Blue Blood, it was on him. Zayn nodded when their eyes met, following Topher's line of thinking. Topher sighed again. When he turned back the bickering vampires, his fangs were out. They might have connected months ago. Might have rebuilt the ties Lana had once felt to them. They were family in the vampire sense of the word, but the dead girl at their feet needed justice. As did every other dead body Topher was certain he'd find in the nightclub. Topher wanted the laws to stay in place. It was his gruesome job now to follow them.

By the time Topher and Zayn entered Happenstance, there were four more bodies in the alley. Hissing rose when the doors shut, and the smell of the dead on Topher and Zayn's hands filled the space.

Topher called out around his fangs. "There's a new leader on Fourth. Submit to me now, or join your makers."

Humans were pushed out of the way, the sound of glasses crashing on the floor and screams rising like a tide. Topher let his charm sweep out enough to calm the humans and make them leave.

Topher knew Solas and Patter were slowly following on purpose. They wanted to see if he really could handle leadership here. If he was more than his charm.

The first wave of incensed and untamed vampires struck, but Topher and Zayn had been dealing with demons and drainers for a year. Sure, these creatures were more calculating, but the dark didn't power them in the same way. Most were smart enough to back away after they saw Topher tear out a throat with his teeth and Zayn rip a lower's head off with his bare hands. They moved with more caution. Not that it would save them.

Topher purposefully didn't use his charm. He wanted them to be afraid enough to follow him without relying on it constantly.

Zayn was unstoppable. He was known as one of the physically strongest vampires, but no one had seen him take advantage of his strength like this. He'd always held back, the same as Topher.

By the time Solas and Patter saw fit to join Zayn and Topher in the upstairs conference room, they had left thirty-one bodies in their wake and the direct order not to clean the club or allow any more humans in until the next night. Topher waited until every vampire of significance reached the conference room, their faces drained and the atmosphere muted after walking through the massacre. Then, he explained what he expected from them and Fourth Street. Even Lana was subdued, sitting alone and nodding like the rest. When Raven arrived with the contracts Topher had asked her to print out earlier that night, they all signed like civilized individuals and not the base monsters they had allowed themselves to become. Then, Topher began with his charming. He went from maker to maker and drew out promises that he enforced with his magic. He was nearly through half the room, enough makers sworn to him to defend him if any of them found the urge to rebel when the sunlight claimed him. Raven had orders to shut the blinds and lead in the closing down for the night as all the vampires slumped under the sunlight, knowing when they woke in the conference room, it would only be to continue this conversation.

Bodies. Charm. Oaths and plans. If the makers wanted a show of power, who was Topher to deny them? When he rose the next night, it would be with Fourth Street at his beck and call. He didn't know if he was ready, but he knew New Brecken was. It had been waiting for him all this time.

CHAPTER 29

Leaving the Rosenfield coven behind to discuss Poppy's proposal, Josh stuck close to Poppy's side. They were silent, heads spinning over all they had learned and, against all odds, had accomplished. Poppy was barely paying attention as she walked toward her car. She didn't notice the intent stare of the human approaching until they stopped in front of Josh and Poppy. "You have potions, right?" they asked, but it was more of a demand.

Poppy fought the urge to clutch at her bag. "No, I—"

"I know you have them. The alpha told me you did."

A chill scuttled down Poppy's back. Something was off about the human. "I don't," Poppy repeated, firm. Hating the lie in case this person was innocent and needed help. But instinct told her to stand her ground.

The man seemed disappointed in her. "Please. Come with me." He glanced up toward the lightening sky. Poppy's heart dropped, realizing the time. Her phone had been on the table the whole time she'd talked with Rosenfield. Poppy hadn't gotten any notifications. No updates on Nora or the attempts to help Julia or if Topher had returned. "My son. He needs help."

Josh stepped forward. Those words and he was convinced, and Poppy had no choice but to follow the two of them. The man cut through a yard between two houses as he headed toward Third Street. Poppy wanted to stop, but if she could help, she should. If Josh wanted to go, she owed it to him to stay by his side. She swallowed, hurrying to keep up as Josh followed the man behind the building.

Then yelped. The sound was followed by a heavy thud that sent Poppy running around the corner, only to trip and go sprawling, her bag spilling across the grass of the yard. Poppy looked to her feet and swallowed a scream when she realized it was Josh's limp form she'd tripped over. There was a gash on his forehead, but he was still breathing. That reassurance was all Poppy needed to look around, heart stopping when she saw nothing but the human walking away as if he hadn't heard anything happening behind him.

"Stop!"

The man ignored her. Hands already shaking, Poppy rose to a crouch, looking around frantically and muttering to her wards. Whatever had attacked Josh had to be fast. Fast enough to catch him unawares and vanish before Poppy turned the corner. That left a vampire, explaining why Josh hadn't smelled them, or a drainer. The monsters had been getting faster and more monstrous as Beth perfected her cast.

Still, Poppy found herself hoping it was the latter. If their attacker had been a vampire, that meant they weren't someone connected to Fourth Street. Topher would have taken up all their attention by now. And that left Reelings. Poppy wasn't ready to face him on her own.

She twisted on her heels, reaching back to shake Josh's shoulder even as her eyes continued to scan the yard, trying desperately to see through the darkness of early dawn. When Josh stirred, she turned her attention to the faintly glowing potions scattered in front of her. Luckily, none of her glass vials had broken, but Poppy had only brought one subduing potion and searched for it now. She hadn't intended to sell it or share it with the world yet. Not until she'd tested it. There. The white glow was a few paces away. She swiped it up and pocketed it quickly. She unstoppered a daylight brew and went to swallow it when the grass rustled at her back. Twisting, Poppy was already too unbalanced when the body slammed into her wards hard enough to send her flying into the porch railing. Her breath left her in a painful gasp as her magic walls shuddered. Barely drawing anything in and unable to find her feet, Poppy slid down the railing, clutching it with her free hand. Somehow, she'd kept hold of her daylight brew, though most of it had spilled. Her eyes fixated on that as she struggled to breathe and force urgency back into her movements.

Josh was waking up. The sound of him grunting centered Poppy. She blinked the stars out of her eyes in time to see a drainer stop in front of her. Too fast for her to follow, its hand was suddenly at Poppy's throat, rank breath in her face. It had breached her wards far too easily.

Her heart froze in terror. The punishing grip cut off her airways when she was only just able to breathe again. Its hold tightened. "Where is Topher West?" it asked, voice low and too smooth.

When Poppy didn't answer, the drainer leaned in, far too close. Its tongue trailed up Poppy's neck before its face twisted. It spat to the side. "Witch blood," it said in disgust.

It shouldn't have been a relief. The creature didn't need to drink her blood to kill or hurt her. But as the night around her grew even dimmer, the reference to the light magic Poppy carried in her veins reminded her of the vial in her pocket. She withdrew it. Not bothering with the cork, Poppy shoved it hard enough in the drainer's face for the glass to shatter.

It immediately let go with a scream, falling to its knees and clutching its burning face. Josh staggered toward it. He was bleeding in multiple places, his features twisted in a hatred Poppy never would have thought him capable of, and he was limping heavily. The bodies of three other drainers Poppy hadn't even noticed were sprawled behind him in the grass, body parts flung across the lawn. Josh was intent on adding this one to the pile. Poppy threw out a hand. "Wait!"

He turned, eyes widening with angered disbelief. The more Poppy stared, the more she cringed from the tears in his clothing and the dark, spreading bloodstains. Why hadn't he shifted? The wolf could have handled this far more easily.

"What?" The growl in Josh's voice indicated how close he was to shifting now.

"Ru and I can help them."

Josh's face curled in disgust. "Poppy, these monsters aren't—"

"They were humans. Changed against their will. We know how Reelings is finding them now. We know how deep his charm goes."

The drainer slowly stopped crawling toward Poppy. Its face was covered in splattered burns, bloodless, oozing a white substance that was too thick to be an equivalent to blood. Poppy gagged at the smell, lifting her shirt collar over her nose. She watched her potion take hold, pride ballooning in her chest as the drainer collapsed, chest still rising and falling. It hadn't been subdued as quickly as she hoped, but the potion worked.

It worked.

"They aren't human anymore, Poppy. They have no conscience. Killing them is the kindest thing we can do for the human they were once."

Josh wasn't close to being swayed. Claws had replaced his fingernails, and his jaw kept clenching and shifting around with the urge to let his muzzle take over his features. The empty hatred in his eyes wasn't anything Poppy had seen on him before. Suddenly, Poppy knew why Josh could handle Topher's blank, black mood. Their emptiness was different shades, but the hurt ran equally deep.

Josh's just sang for revenge while Topher's begged for escape.

Thinking of Topher, Poppy's heart sank because she knew what it would take to convince Josh now. He might have separated himself from her and the rest of their group, but he'd spent more time with Topher lately than he had any of them.

"It's for Topher," she burst out. Josh had been stalking toward the struggling monster, but he froze as Poppy predicted he would. "Lana was supposed to kill Julia and get rid of the body after Topher broke her mind, but she didn't. Colbie and I found her. We didn't tell Topher because we don't want him to grieve Julia all over again if Ru can't fix her but Ru thinks she can. She thinks whatever happened to Julia's mind is something Reelings did to keep Julia from finding her humanity again, but that the humanity is still there. If we get rid of the magic Beth infused his charm with, she'll wake up how she was before Reelings charmed her. At least, mentally."

Josh stared down at the monster with dawning horror on his features. "You can save her?"

"We think so. And others. Look how it's sleeping. I've been working on this potion for weeks. It'll keep the drainers alive and subdued while we finish the cure."

Josh was trembling. He seemed more ready to make the change than he was moments ago. Slowly, his claws crept back into his finger. He clenched the human fists, dragging his eyes up to Poppy. "He feels so much guilt for what happened to Julia. Even before he thought he killed her."

"Yeah."

"He'd do anything to make it up to her. To make her happy," Josh's voice was flat. The emptiness was replaced with conflict as dread and guilt and none of the hope Poppy would have expected entered his eyes.

Poppy stayed quiet, waiting. Josh made a noise of disgust and yanked off his sweatshirt. In a matter of minutes, he had the drainer tied up. "I'm not trusting you all with it," Josh said.

Poppy winced but nodded. She needed Josh's help and for him to keep a secret. After all the progress he'd made with Topher, it was probably already eating at him that he had to keep Julia from him. "What do you want to do with him?"

"We'll take it to the apartments. I'll go in and talk to Henry. If he isn't okay with guarding it, we're killing it. I won't keep this a secret from my alpha, and we won't keep the drainers you want to study somewhere they might get discovered and let loose. If Ru needs to look at it, she can come by."

Poppy helped him carry the drainer to her car and child-lock it in the backseat. At no point did the drainer stir. Silently, they drove to Twenty-Fifth, watching the sunrise and glancing back to see the harm it caused the drainer. Neither wanted to know the other's thoughts.

Nora woke up to Colbie's gentle, cool breathing on her neck. At some point, someone had put Nora's hair up, probably away from all the blood. She thought she had showered before going downstairs to confront Matt, but must not have washed her hair. All the events of last night were cast in a fog of pain. Nora barely remembered going back to sleep. She felt better now. Stronger upon waking than she'd been last night, but the thought of reaching up to wash her hair was enough to make her moan. Colbie didn't stir at the sound, so it must be full daytime.

Nora should bundle up the motivation and get up to shower. Check on her pack. See if anyone thought to follow Matt when they let him go and make sure he didn't try anything. See where her mom and Henry had vanished after saving Nora's life.

But that line of thinking reminded Nora of what happened. She turned in Colbie's arms, gathering her girlfriend up close and burying her face in Colbie's neck. It was inexcusable. She'd been so scared for her girlfriend that she almost let herself get killed. Nora hadn't been able to fight Gabriel off because one text had tipped her world so abruptly when she'd needed her complete focus. Two years ago, Nora would never have thought she'd be in her current position. She'd been so wrong about so many things. Dreaming of being Gabriel's mate and helping the city by his side. Even then, she'd known he had big plans for New Brecken and a bigger hatred for its vampires. She would have followed him without hesitation if one look at Colbie's smirking lips hadn't altered Nora's entire brain. What if she'd found another vampire that night in the Maker? What if she'd brought them home to the Den and killed them without hesitating? Where would she be?

Nora knew the answer. She'd be where Matt was.

Nora hated how easily it could have happened. She tightened her grip further on Colbie. Never more grateful that Colbie had *saved* her. Colbie had saved her from Gabriel's pack and then, through loving her these past months, Colbie had saved Nora from her own self-hatred. It was too easy to berate herself for how blind she'd been to Gabriel's manipulations, but Nora was figuring out how to forgive her former ignorance. The downside to this? She couldn't stop the pity for Matt. She couldn't help but think if he came around, she'd forgive him too. Maybe, like Nora needed Colbie to show her a new path, Matt needed someone to do the same for him. Maybe he needed Nora.

Colbie murmured, "Nora." The word was a sleepy sigh and nothing more.

Nora's heart felt too full, too fragile. She wished she could ward like Poppy, throw all her strength into protecting this precious bubble that was her and the girl she loved. Was it selfish to risk her new pack, to risk her city, with this weakness? When she'd heard Colbie might be in danger, Nora had forgotten about her pack, about Amelia, about Gabriel across from her. All she knew was that she'd lost too much and couldn't lose Colbie again. When she'd felt her hot blood rushing from her body far too quickly, all she could think about was how little she wanted to hurt Colbie. How Nora's death would… well, Nora didn't know. Colbie knew loss, but not like Nora did. Not like Topher and Annaliese and Poppy and Josh. How would Colbie react? Nora couldn't even stand holding the question in her mind. The very idea of Colbie's eyes dimming was untenable.

Nora felt like her line of thinking was going somewhere important, but she couldn't get there with Colbie warm in her arms. Sighing, she carefully extracted herself from Colbie's grip. She went to the bathroom to wash her hair. Alone, Nora let her face wince, her steps shuffle, and her breath shake with pain. She'd have to put her alpha's mask back on as soon as she faced her pack. Maybe it was asking too much to expect the pain to be gone already after being on death's door, but Nora couldn't afford to slow down. She'd been lax with her training and paid for it. She should have listened to Patrick when he insisted they needed somewhere to go and practice fighting in both forms. So far, Nora's alpha's instincts had been all she needed. She'd grown confident. She'd started listening to everyone who told her she was powerful.

She felt so foolish now, limping, bruised, and with her chest tight with hurt from the brutality of her former alpha. She tried to ignore the sense of betrayal over Gabriel's actions. It shouldn't have been so shocking, but her head was a mess. The buzzing thoughts intensified with every step she took away from Colbie. Nora spent most of the shower fighting and then giving in to tears.

Shutting off the water, the murmuring voices of Nora's pack in the bedroom made Nora brace herself. She flushed with an irritation she'd never felt toward them before. She wanted privacy. She wanted the door locked, a rooftop escape. Only her girlfriend's presence was welcome, and even then, Colbie was unconscious and didn't know how much Nora cried. Nora wasn't ready to work through this with other people. Her grief had always been something she traveled on her own, and her feelings after Gabriel's attack were too close to that. She hadn't moved to anger yet. She didn't want to face them until that happened.

Without much choice in the matter, Nora took her time drying her hair, letting the splotchy red around her eyes fade. Nora changed slowly, wincing as she pulled on a simple black skirt that belonged to Lupe and a band t-shirt of Chase's. She hadn't paid enough attention when she grabbed clothes on the way to the bathroom. Nora watched her face in the mirror until the raw hurt was gone, and something resembling calm took over her features. Nora opened the bathroom door and froze at the sight that greeted her.

When there weren't any outsiders around, her pack was an affectionate, loving huddle in these private rooms. Nora had gotten used to heads on laps, fingers in her hair, sniffed pulse points, and forms both wolf and human layered on top of one another. It was ordinary, familiar, vulnerable, pack behavior. But Nora had never seen them come close to acting like this with a vampire around.

Until now. Janelle had taken her place across the pillows, having lifted Colbie's head so it rested on her stomach. Ricky lay aligned with Colbie, his head on Janelle's thigh. Chase's legs rested across their stomachs, and he sat propped up against the wall. Heather was under his arm, and her legs were angled over Colbie's. Patrick was in the process of lifting everyone's feet to get his legs under them all. Lupe sat on the floor in front of the bed, head leaning into the mattress where Ricky's hand idly stroked her hair.

Colbie's sleeping face was flushed with warmth. Had such a sight ever been seen before? What had happened while Nora was unconscious for this monumental shift to occur? Nora wanted to take a picture for Annaliese to post as proof that vampires and werewolves could get along.

Fearful of ruining it, Nora chose not to address the cuddling. "How did things go for Topher on Fourth last night?"

Glances were exchanged. Heather reached for Colbie's hand as if she wanted to offer comfort. Nora's heart swelled. "No one has heard yet," Heather said.

"Zayn left to follow him," Patrick picked up. "Oliver is…"

"Frantic," Ricky finished, voice hollowed by the events of the past couple of nights. "He was sure Zayn would call."

Nora's heart was in her throat. "I should—"

"Regain your strength," Janelle interrupted firmly. "You won't be any use to Topher until you can walk without a limp."

Nora scowled. She thought she'd done a better job hiding her pain. "I'm fine. But Topher…" Nora's eyes found Colbie again, the sight of her giving Nora strength. The conflicting feelings crept up again. She was an alpha. She shouldn't need to borrow strength from someone else. She shouldn't be considering invading Fourth Street because she'd fallen in love with the West siblings and couldn't stand the thought of Colbie's worry when she woke.

Nora should be making decisions for her pack. Only her pack. Yet she couldn't find it in herself to care. What did that make her as an alpha? She'd never felt less like she deserved this strange title.

"Topher can handle himself," Heather said stiffly, too worried to be convincing. "If he's in danger from the vampires, nothing is happening to him right now. They're all asleep."

Nora threw up her hands. "Then what am I supposed to do?"

"Rest," Chase said, matching Nora's disgruntled tone.

A phone started to buzz. Janelle lifted a pierced eyebrow, gesturing to where Nora's phone was charging on the nightstand. "Answer that."

Nora almost didn't in a fit of stubborn pride, but she saw Henry's information on the screen and went to pick up, aware that every wolf in the room was listening in. "Hello? Are you with my mom?"

"I'm here. Are you alright, Nora?" Helen's voice was tight with worry. A flare of resentment filled her. Maybe Helen hadn't accepted this pack yet and didn't feel the need to be within five feet of her injured alpha at all times, but as a mother, Nora couldn't imagine what was keeping Helen away.

Her eyes went to Colbie again, and Nora pulled in a breath. "I'm fine. Where are you?"

"We need to talk in person," Helen said. "Can you come?"

"Yes." Helen didn't notice how Nora bit out the word. She rattled off an address as Nora's pack began to get up. Nora didn't argue with their intention to join her, but when Patrick shook Colbie's shoulder, she made a sound of protest. "She won't wake up," Nora said.

"She told us to wake her when you tried to leave," Janelle said, shrugging.

Nora almost laughed. "She needs her sleep. Let her be."

It was the first order as an alpha that her pack ignored. Nora watched in wonder as Heather started smacking Colbie's cheek, and her girlfriend's eyes fluttered open. "Wherewe-goin?" she mumbled sleepily, rolling to rise onto an elbow. Blinking slowly, she met Nora's eyes. The sleep began to clear, stubborn will settling into the blue.

Nora was so stunned she answered. "My mom wants us to meet her in Southside."

Colbie nodded and reached for Nora, ignoring Ricky's offered hand. Nora went to her, heart thudding with surging emotion, as she helped Colbie up and let the vampire lean heavily onto her side. "Lead the way," Colbie said around a yawn. "Oh, babe, you're limping."

Before Nora could respond, Colbie's lips were on her neck, fangs slipping into her skin. Nora was more stunned by the approval in her pack's eyes than the casual bite. The bliss instantly began to ease the pain. Nora took Colbie's weight as she healed the punctures from her fangs like nothing was amiss. And nothing felt amiss in that moment. They clung to each other with mutual need. Any feelings of conflict, of doubt, vanished as Lupe helped Colbie into her shoes and Chase laughed as he straightened Colbie's bun.

Nora had been thinking only of her pack. Of how she should be putting them first. All the while, they'd been bringing Colbie into their ranks, making her one of them. To push Colbie away would be the exact opposite of an alpha's purpose. Nora turned her face into Colbie's hair, breathing in the pack's scent all over her, stomach tumbling with warmth and love. She wanted to smirk at the people here who had been in her old pack, laughing over the fact that they too had fallen for Colbie's charm. They'd come a long way toward understanding Nora's actions, but this felt like the final step.

CHAPTER 30

Colbie dozed in the passenger's seat of Lana's car. She'd been the one to slip upstairs and steal the keys. Now Nora drove them across the city, her wolves causing a stir in the streets as they followed. Nora couldn't stop looking at Colbie's relaxed form. She fixed the visor when she saw how the sun was hitting Colbie's chin. Silly, beautiful, stubborn girl. And she'd chosen Nora. She was Nora's. It was still surreal that Colbie had insisted on being here in the daytime. While Colbie was grabbing the keys, her pack said Colbie made them promise to bring her along if Nora left the Alpha's Den whether they could wake her up or not. When Nora asked her pack what the point of that would have been, they simply shrugged. They hadn't argued with Colbie enough to get a reason.

It was ridiculous and amazing. Nora reached over and grabbed Colbie's hand. The returning pressure was invitation enough for Nora to speak without worrying about waking her. "You're so…" Nora couldn't find the word.

Colbie's lips quirked up at one side. "Badass? Sexy?"

"Stubborn."

Colbie leaned across the console between them to

awkwardly rest her head on Nora's shoulder. "Did Topher come home?"

Maybe he had gone to the apartment and no one was there to greet him, but Nora still thought he would have messaged if all was well. "No."

Colbie's head bobbed in a shallow nod. "He'll be okay. He has to be."

"You're so sure?" Sure enough to be with Nora instead of searching for him?

"No." Colbie shifted, hand squeezing Nora's. "Nora, I'm keeping a secret from him. I feel like it's going to consume me from the inside out."

Nora froze. That was huge. Colbie was closer to Topher than anyone else. Nora honestly hadn't thought Colbie capable of keeping secrets from him. "What is it?"

"I can't tell you and not tell him, but Lana did it to start. I can't fucking stand her. Or the smell of her in this car." She turned, pressing her face into Nora's shirt. "Help me replace it? Make her mad?"

"How?"

It was the correct answer. Colbie sighed, relaxing fully into Nora. "You'll see."

They didn't have much opportunity to talk past that. Nora pulled up to the office building matching the address Helen had given her. Luckily, the directions included a code for the underground parking garage, hiding Colbie from the sun. Nora slowly drove toward her mother, who was waiting around the bend.

"I might stay in here," Colbie admitted. "If you scream, I'll wake up and come help."

"You really think you're going to, what? Fight off Gabriel if he attacks again?"

Colbie sniffed with indignation at Nora's tone. "Maybe. He won't be expecting it. But, even if I am no help, my saliva can heal you awake or not. I don't want you bleeding ever again."

Nora raised an eyebrow. "Are you going to control my periods now?"

Colbie's eyes smoldered. "I'll lick those up, too; don't tempt me." She made a show of licking her lips.

Nora gagged as she threw the car into park, but Colbie's wicked smile turned the heaves into a laugh. "You're depraved."

"You're delicious," Colbie replied, fangs bared. She snapped her teeth.

Nora fought a shiver. She leaned over, stole a quick kiss, and left Colbie in the car. A look at Chase and Ricky had them hanging back with the parked vehicle, ready to defend Colbie in her vulnerable state. This was a stupid idea, but Nora was grateful for Colbie's supportive presence at her back as she approached Helen and Henry. Too many other smells were in the air to let her guard down.

Too many wolves. But not all Henry's. Nora's pack closed in, a few rumbling with anxious growls. Nora stopped walking, refusing to move further from Lana's car and the half-asleep vampire.

"What's going on?" she asked. The worry in her voice was embarrassing, especially given the way it was amplified in the mostly empty garage.

Henry didn't seem able to move past Colbie's presence. He was dumbfounded. "Is there a vampire sleeping in your car?"

Nora shrugged. "She wanted to join us."

"But she's not even awake…" This came from Rory, stepping out from between two cars with her twin, Cora, at her side. Janelle was closest to them and growled. Colbie was awake enough to flip her the finger.

Rory laughed, shaking her head. Friendship lingered from past soccer games and interactions with Josh. The tension in the room eased. Nora suddenly remembered Heather's story about Topher as a human. Hunter brought him along to negotiations and drug deals because he had a way of calming an entire room with his smile. Maybe this was another family trait. One that had skipped Chance and his nervous energy around strangers.

"What's going on, Mom?" Despite the lessened tension, Nora didn't want any more attention on Colbie than necessary, not with the unfamiliar werewolf scents underlying the smell of gasoline and mustiness of the parking garage.

"I've been doing some digging with Henry's help. It's bothered me since I returned that Gabriel is the only alpha still here. I've been trying to get in contact with the others."

"What did you find?"

"Not a lot, but it seems Gabriel was busier than we thought," Henry said, stepping forward. "Even before he became alpha."

He turned, beckoning someone into the light. More wolves come forward. Five of them, all older than Nora. Three looked to be in their thirties, the other two about her mother's age. Even from six parking spaces away, Nora could sense their open tethers. They were alphaless. Had been for a while, judging by the potency of the smell and their restless movements. Their eyes bounced from Nora to Henry, consumed by the knowing that alphas were in their midst. One was focused on Colbie, lips slowly curling in a snarl. Nora stepped into their line of sight. Just a look, and she'd convinced the werewolf to step back.

The werewolf in the center cleared his throat. "You're Morales's daughter?"

Nora nodded. She had no idea where this conversation would lead, but her alpha instincts were almost painfully thrashing for release. Their open pack bonds beckoned enticingly.

"And you're accepting members?"

Nora nodded again, slower this time.

Henry cleared his throat. "We've asked them to explain

what happened in the months leading up to the laws being passed."

"But they do need an alpha," Helen's words were gentler, but her eyes instructed Nora to do this. To build her pack. Build her power. A spark of the old Helen, the powerful beta, flashed in her eyes. Many of Luis's moves as an alpha had been made at Helen's encouragement, and together, they had built one of the strongest packs in New Brecken. Her mother wanted Nora to carry on the tradition of power.

It called to Nora. To the desires in her heart and the fears she pressed down. A bigger pack would keep more of her people protected. It would help in the days to come. If Topher could risk himself on Fourth Street, if Poppy could track down the siblings after they abandoned her, Nora could accept five strangers into her pack. Her alpha was strong enough to keep them in line. To flush out any secret plans they might have. Nora's side twinged with pain, Colbie's bliss wearing off too quickly.

She had to be strong enough. "So what happened?" Nora asked. "Why was it only my father at negotiations? Where did your alphas go? Why did your packs break up?"

The first man had become the group's designated speaker. "When Morales first approached us about the laws, he brought Gabriel. He was training the young man to one day lead his own pack. I don't remember seeing Morales without Gabriel during this time. It was always him, Gabriel, and Helen." A respectful nod toward Nora's mother. "Our pack was small, like most in New Brecken, only four of us under our alpha, Devon. It was common for smaller packs to be spread throughout New Brecken, most of us connected by family relations. We all worked together to keep the vampires at bay within our set territories." He explained this for Nora's benefit and waited for her nod before continuing. Nora remembered how the city used to be set up, but she'd been kept out of any disputes or vampire hunts. "The day after Morales approached about the changes he would be making within his pack, Gabriel came back hours later. He insisted on talking to Devon alone but had to have known we could all hear him through the door of Devon's office. He started by proclaiming he didn't want to say anything against his alpha. He didn't want to start trouble, but he could never align himself with the vampires. He could see Morales's point but couldn't imagine himself staying within a pack that refused to hunt the bloodsuckers. Gabriel framed his words as if he was asking Devon for advice, but I see now how he was trying to plant seeds of doubt. Doubt within all of us against these laws."

Another werewolf stepped forward. She was younger than the rest yet seemed far too tired and worn down. "He approached Parker the same way, but Parker was a huge supporter of Morales. He didn't want to hear it. Our pack territory was along First Street. The vampires were already staking their claim on Fourth in anticipation of the laws passing. Parker knew we wouldn't survive where we were if we didn't have the other werewolves backing us, and Morales was too big of an ally to lose. He kicked Gabriel out the first time he visited."

The first man sighed. "Devon listened. Gabriel called Devon and set up a meeting with the other alphas in the city, all those who seemed receptive to his misgivings about the laws. It was there that he explained his plan. Gabriel had met with a vampire who was also opposed the laws, and that vampire had enough sway to keep things from progressing. We were to attend the official vote, and then, having seen all the powerful vampires in the city gathered, we would betray the vampire Gabriel was working with and strike at his people when the laws failed to pass. But there was a meeting ahead of time. We still don't know why. The meeting where Morales was killed."

Voice thick, Helen took over. "We'd heard there was dissent, but we didn't know from what angle. We thought it was all Reelings and that, with Patter, Grace, and Solas on our side, we could convince him to align with us. Now that I've had years to replay what happened, I think Gabriel panicked. I don't think he received all the support he expected from the alphas and decided he needed to build his own pack instead."

The younger woman nodded. "He'd already attacked Parker. We found his body later in the forest. It was enough to spook other alphas away from meeting with him or agreeing to go to the vote. Most of my pack left the city. I went to my cousin's, only for her alpha to go missing too. The attacks happened in safe zones, neutral places only the werewolves frequented and always had Gabriel's scent on them."

"We think Gabriel was planning on building his pack by killing other alphas and still living under Luis's protection," Helen said. "Once Reelings killed Luis, he would pick up the tethers."

The first man spoke again. "It was Luis's death that convinced Devon to flee. The city had fallen to the Big Three, and Gabriel was too young and inexperienced to lead a revolution. It was only when Devon died last year, and I came back to New Brecken, looking for an alpha, that I found out the two had remained in contact. Gabriel is trying to set his plan in motion once more. He's contacting werewolves who kept in touch and inviting them back to the city."

Helen nodded. "Gabriel still struggles to claim the alphaless, but he's reaching out to the alphas that fled. With them on his side, he wants to retake the city and strike when Reelings weakens the current vampire leaders," Nora didn't bother interrupting to say Matt had told her this the night before. It felt good to have the plot confirmed.

"He's told them he will challenge you, Nora. He wants to take your pack and is convinced Henry will remain neutral. That since Henry isn't aligned with Lana, he will align with the werewolves once they swarm New Brecken and kill Reelings."

Nora had known Gabriel was responsible for her father's

death but hadn't ever considered the betrayal ran this deep. Hadn't thought any werewolf capable of murdering their kind, other alphas, for disagreeing. It was too human. Werewolves fought over territory, fought for power, not for schemes. Not to take over cities with little care for the damage they left in their wake.

Gabriel planned to stand back, let Reelings make the drainers, take Fourth, destroy the New Brecken's trust in the vampires, and then call in the former werewolves to save the day. "What if the alphas don't come?"

Henry met Nora's eyes. "Nora, we can't let it come to that. We can't let Reelings take Fourth Street to begin with. We can't trust the alphas not to answer Gabriel's call, and we can't trust a city taken over by Gabriel. We already know he'll target alphas who disagree with him when they aren't expecting it. He has a knack for getting them alone." A significant look at Nora's side. "We also know he'll spare little thought for the alpha's pack when he can't claim them. Gabriel would be a poor leader, an unstable leader, a leader who refuses to accept progress. This plan isn't thought out."

"So stop him!" The words burst out of Nora. She sounded like the youngest person in this room, and she was. How had all of this fallen on her? She'd thought her part in this was to take out Gabriel, loosening Reelings's grip on the city so Topher could strike. To maybe take out Reelings herself if the opportunity presented itself and avenge her father. She hadn't thought it went this deep. That the former alphas, all people willing to betray the Morales pack, would be returning if they didn't move fast enough. That she might have to go against an army of her own people.

"Nora, my pack is one of the largest in the country, but I don't think it'll be enough. I've told you before that I'm spread too thin, and I can't take on many more members. We'll stand by your side, but we need your gifts. With your power, you could unite the werewolves answering Gabriel's call. You could take out the alphas that betrayed your father. My pack and I will have your back, but only you are strong enough to do this. To stop Gabriel before he can make his move."

"I couldn't even take him in a fight."

"You were distracted. He attacked you in human form, something we now think he used to kill the other alphas. It wasn't a fair fight, and next time you'll be ready. I'll work with you, and for every member you accept, you'll gain some of their experience and knowledge."

Silence fell as Nora considered. She fought the urge to look over her shoulder, see if Colbie was awake, and search for what she should do in her girlfriend's face. Nora knew what Annaliese would say; her best friend the voice of strength in the back of her mind that loved the plan, hungered to take Gabriel, sweep the power he expected to accumulate out from under him. But Nora blocked out Annaliese's voice, didn't look toward Colbie. She was learning to listen to her alpha, to search herself for what she wanted.

And, as always, Nora wanted to be strong. To hold power. She didn't want to give Gabriel or the other alpha's a chance to even hope the city could be theirs. She wanted to control her own life. To keep her people safe.

Nora sent out the alpha invitation, flushing with strength and power as the five unclaimed in the parking garage immediately accepted, latching on as their features filled with happy relief. "I appreciate the answers you've provided. It's good to know Gabriel's motivations, but it doesn't change anything. We won't let anyone take our city, not him or the alphas that fled or Reelings."

Pride filled Helen's face. Henry nodded, almost as relieved as Nora's new pack members. Nerves swept up Nora's throat. The pain in her side reminded her how quickly she could lose it all.

CHAPTER 31

"Go home. I'll call Poppy to make sure the witches are okay with us taking rooms at the Jennings house and try to get our new members settled," Nora said, the order making her pack straighten.

Always the one to ask the questions, Janelle approached Nora while everyone else went to the new members, touching, scenting, and welcoming them to the pack. Nora didn't even know their names. Unease twisted Nora's stomach, almost overshadowing the flush of energy that came with accepting new members. "We're going to run out of room again at this rate. Even with the witch house," Janelle told her.

Nora nodded. "I'm going to have to get us more space." Somewhere close to where her wolves were already settling. Somewhere safe.

She needed the Den. "Mom?" Helen turned from her murmured conversation with Henry. Nora already had an idea of what was happening there, and she didn't like it but understood Helen's role. Understood where her mother felt she belonged. "Who was the Den left to when Dad died?"

Helen gave Nora a look as if she expected her daughter to

know the answer. "It's yours, Nora. It's all always been yours. Are you going to take it?"

And suddenly, this was all too much. She nodded at her mother and turned, almost fleeing the few steps it took to return to Lana's car. Colbie jerked awake when Nora slammed her door but remained silent as Nora sat, trying to catch her breath. They watched as the werewolves trickled out. Nora heard all their words of goodbye distantly. The werewolves were from New Brecken. They knew each other, knew the city, and had trusted Nora with it because of her mother's introduction and father's memory. Everything she'd dreamed of was at Nora's fingertips, but all she wanted was the quiet that fell in the car when the parking garage cleared. When it was just her and Colbie.

"How much of that did you hear?"

"Not a lot," Colbie confessed, yawning. "But your scent changed again. New members?"

"What?" Nora jolted in her seat, turning to Colbie.

Colbie smiled and reached over to play with a strand of Nora's hair. "You take on a hint of their scent when you accept them into your pack, and they all smell a bit like you. I don't know if it's something anyone else would notice, but I can tell."

"Gabriel wants to use Reelings to weaken the vampires and then bring in all the werewolves that fled to kill off Fourth Street and the drainers. He wants to use the battle as proof the laws didn't work. I don't know how far he'll let Reelings go so that he can step forward as the werewolf hero."

A beat passed as Colbie considered. "Poppy thinks she and Ru can save the drainers," she said. "Not return them to human, but help make them less… monstrous. It's part of the Topher secret, so I can't tell you more."

Secrets and drainers had never worked out well for their friend group, but Nora let it slide for now. "Gabriel wouldn't wait for a cure like that, but he'll help Reelings keep making them as long as it makes the humans afraid and lessens the vampires' popularity."

Colbie hummed in agreement.

"I have to build a pack big enough to take him on. I have to get to the returning werewolves before Gabriel. I'm the only one who can offer them a pack membership. We have to take Reelings on before it gets bad enough for Gabriel to call the other packs in."

"Okay. Sounds like a plan."

"It's not that easy."

"It's not," Colbie agreed. "But I'm barely awake, so I'm done talking about it. You should give yourself a break and stop thinking about it."

"I can't shut off my brain."

"I can," Colbie offered readily.

With a tug on Nora's hair, Colbie turned her head so they were face to face. Nora's breath caught, eyes going out the windshield. For the first time, she realized how readily her pack had cleared out. Colbie smirked. "Come here, babe."

Nora gave an inch but couldn't resist asking, "Babe?"

"I'm trying it out. Don't pretend it doesn't do anything for you," Colbie's voice was pitched low enough to raise goosebumps on Nora's arms as she gave an exaggerated inhale. Colbie's pupils were huge, only a ring of ice left of her irises.

And Nora still couldn't shut off her brain. "Here?"

"Here." Colbie stole a quick kiss and leaned back to throw off her seatbelt, the click of it hitting the window not nearly enough to break the moment between them. Nora couldn't look away as Colbie settled back in the seat, sent it backward to give her legs more room, then slid down, hair bunching, until she'd settled with her knees under the dash and her back arched down the lip of the seat. The sight of Colbie awkwardly and confusingly scrunched in that space should not have made Nora's mouth go dry.

"I love that skirt on you. I love that you aren't wearing any underwear. It's like you were thinking about this, too."

"About what?"

In answer, Colbie patted the seat on either side of her head. "Knees here, *babe.*"

Swallowing, heart pounding loudly in her ears, Nora crawled over the console and carefully positioned herself. There were rare moments where Nora found herself listening to Colbie, and she swore it was charm that blanked her mind. Just like when they met the first time. Nora hoped Colbie would always have this power over her.

Nora found herself eye to eye with the headrest, knees deep in the crease of the passenger's seat, with Colbie making happy noises between her legs underneath her. One of Colbie's fingers pulled Nora's skirt back so they could make eye contact. "You with me?" Colbie asked.

Nora's favorite phrase when it left Colbie's lips. A way to check consent, to make sure Nora was okay, to assure Nora that Colbie was equally as turned on as she was. Beyond words, Nora nodded. She might have been panting.

Then, the cold, searing bliss of Colbie's tongue parted her. Nora arched, clutching at the headrest. Colbie's tongue darted, it savored, it moved with precision and caring. Nora was a writhing mess in seconds. Her words incoherent, and thoughts unable to concentrate on anything but *sensation.* Every ache dulled when faced with Colbie's bliss consuming such a sensitive area. Nora had never felt so much, and all good. Any self-consciousness she may have experienced because of her extreme reaction and rocking hips was blanked by the sounds Colbie made below. It was as if it was doing as much for her as Nora. She couldn't even worry about her weight on Colbie's face with both of Colbie's arms snaked up around her thighs, pulling Nora down as if it wasn't enough. She held Nora in place, gave her no room to relieve any of Colbie's pressure.

One of Colbie's hands left her thigh, and Nora glanced

down to see Colbie touching herself. Her words shifted, encouraging, hurrying, world narrowing to the goal of waiting, waiting, teeth-gritting waiting for Colbie to come too. Finally, finally, Colbie arched beneath her, noises muffled and consumed by Nora's center.

The orgasm came then. A wild, hot, consuming rush. Nora returned to her body clutching the safety handle, slumped into the chair, and gasping as Colbie's tongue wrung out the last of her pleasure. Legs shaking, Nora started to climb off, but Colbie tightened her grip long enough to place kisses along the insides of Nora's thighs and one last on the bundle of sensitive nerves. She let out a breathless laugh as Nora yelped and jumped.

Her body felt liquid and sated as Nora fell into the driver's seat, legs still sprawled across the console as Colbie pushed herself up to sitting again, eyes and lips too wicked as she took in the state she'd put Nora in.

Her hands trailed up Nora's legs, corners of her lips rising. Her tongue darted out to lick her lips. "Delicious."

Nora shook her head. "You're…"

"Talented? Sexy? The greatest girlfriend ever?"

Nora couldn't believe she'd looked at Colbie earlier and wondered if it would be better not to have her in her life. Colbie West wasn't weakness. She was life itself. "Never getting rid of me."

Colbie lunged across the seats, crushing Nora in a hot, wet kiss. Nora's taste and warmth lingering on her lips. It made Nora flush with too quickly renewed heat. By the time they left the parking garage, Nora was having trouble concentrating. She was too relaxed after the two orgasms, too distracted by this new knowledge of what Colbie was capable of. How had Nora waited so long? Already, she was debating driving to her and Annaliese's place instead of the Alpha's Den to go again. It wouldn't be happening, though. With a sleepy murmur of, "I'm so glad we did this in Lana's car," Colbie's head lulled, and sleep claimed her as they entered the day-lit city again.

Nora couldn't help staring at Colbie at every stoplight. Her body no longer hurt, her brain no longer spiraled. She couldn't keep a smile off her lips, and after everything, it felt foreign to be able to grin so effortlessly. That was the magic of Colbie West. With one parking garage visit, everything was suddenly manageable.

Nora could breathe and think through her next steps, knowing Colbie would stay right there with her. The words left her lips unheard and unplanned but still so true.

"I fucking love you."

Nora had come down a bit from the high of accepting more pack members and Colbie's attentions by the time she parked Lana's car in the back of the Alpha's Den. Her voice was practically normal when Annaliese called and Nora answered on the second ring.

"Have you heard from Poppy?" Annaliese asked.

Nora almost laughed. Her world had been consumed by Colbie and her alpha duties. She hadn't had time to talk to the witch today. "Not recently. What's up?"

"She mentioned Ru wanted to see me. I don't know what about, but I don't have Ru's number and Poppy isn't answering."

"Did Ru get a phone? I can check Colbie's for her number."

"Can you come with me over there? The wards probably won't let me in."

Nora sighed, eyes on Colbie. Her face was turning red from the flashes of sunlight that managed to reach her, but there was no way Nora was risking making her angry. "Yeah. I can come pick you up."

"You can?"

Nora didn't want to explain. Her voice came out a mumble, "Colbie won't let me go anywhere without her today. We have Lana's car."

"And Colbie is…"

"Currently asleep, yes."

After Annaliese had gotten over her laughter, she told Nora she was at Vegan Your Day and would meet them. Annaliese laughed all over again when she climbed into the backseat and saw Colbie's sunburn. At Nora's scowl, Annaliese shed her sweatshirt and draped it over Colbie's head. Nora caught Annaliese up on the day's events as she drove, Annaliese blinking at the news of five new pack members being accepted so quickly.

"Are you not going to vet anyone like you did Janelle?"

Nora shrugged. "If they come to me, I don't think I'll have the luxury. I need the strength of numbers, and they need an alpha. If they turn out to be not great people, I can release them from their bonds."

Annaliese was quiet for a moment. "Should it be so easy?"

"I don't think it is for other alphas," Nora admitted.

Under Annaliese's sweatshirt, Colbie said a muffled, "Badass."

"So not fully asleep," Annaliese said.

"She has selective hearing," Nora replied, unable to keep the sappy fondness from her tone.

They arrived at the Jennings house in little time. Nora didn't let herself look toward the Den as the last of Colbie's bliss faded and anxiety returned. She went around the car, quickly pulled Colbie out of her seat, and carried her inside before she was too exposed to the sun.

When Nora let herself in the front door, the wards warming to her presence like the Alpha's Den's did, Ryan and Amelia stood. Margot remained lounging on the couch in the front room. They all blinked at the sight of the limp vampire, but Ru brought Nora's attention to the stairs before her hackles could rise at the attention on her vulnerable girlfriend.

"You made it! Come upstairs. I have good curtains, and we can toss Colbie in there," Ru said breezily.

Annaliese really couldn't get over this situation. Ru's referring to Colbie like a bag to be put off to the side had her laughing all over again, but Colbie remained silent in Nora's arms, forehead pressed into the warmth of Nora's neck. Nora didn't want to let her go, but she tucked Colbie into Ru's bed and followed her and Annaliese down the hall.

Ru paused in front of the last door. There was an absence of scent and a presence of magic coming from within that brought Nora's instincts to attention. "What's going on, Ru?"

The younger girl chewed her lower lip. "I'm realizing that I could have gone about this differently. Poppy isn't answering her phone. Maybe I should go try to talk to Colbie…"

Annaliese didn't give her the chance to back out. She stepped forward and tried the door handle, glaring at Ru until the witch sighed and gave in with a snap of her fingers.

The sight that greeted Annaliese instantly set Nora on alert. She yanked Annaliese from the door and whatever terror within that made her face look like that. Nora stalked inside before Ru could protest.

Julia slept on the bed. *Julia was sleeping on the bed.*

"Ru…" Nora's voice was pitched dangerously, and Annaliese nodded as if to encourage her. "What the fuck is this?"

Ru shuffled her feet. "I can save her. I think, I *can* save all the drainers. I'm so close to figuring it out. But, just in case, we aren't telling Topher we found her."

Colbie's secret. Annaliese's scowl could sizzle ice. "Like hell I'm keeping this from my—" She faltered. She didn't have a title for what she and Topher were.

Ru threw up her hands. "It's not my call! Talk to Poppy

and Colbie. They don't want to get his hopes up or make him go through losing her twice."

"Does Lana know she's alive?" Nora asked. She spoke more quietly than Ru and Annaliese. No part of Nora wanted to deal with an awake drainer.

"Lana had her at the old drainer apartment. Colbie and Poppy found her while everyone was looking for Amelia the other night."

Nora's jaw clenched, realizing Colbie must have gone into the drainer apartment after sending the text that distracted Nora enough to get attacked. Her response to the message felt valid now. Julia could have attacked and Nora hadn't been there to protect Colbie.

"She doesn't wake up," Ru said as if reading Nora's mind and attempting to reassure her. "I'm trying to wake her up or heal her or do something to curb the bloodlust that drainers experience, but to do that, I need to understand Beth's cast. I want to compare Julia's magic to yours, Annaliese. If I can feel where the spell is incomplete in you, I can understand how it built to make Julia what she is now."

"And reverse it?"

Ru hesitated. There was the question that had risen to most people's minds when the laws passed, and vampires stepped out of the shadows. What made them what they were, being the only *made* supernatural group, and could it be reversed? If Ru found out how to save the drainers, she could—

"I don't think so," Ru finally admitted. "Seeing you and Topher and hopefully examining you will allow me to confirm, but I think that whatever made the drainers, the spell is incomplete. I can't reverse it, but maybe I can alter it and complete it. Beth siphoned magic, Gabriel only gave enough for her to weave it into the spell and make the drainers resistant to charm, and Reelings does a bastardized form of the vampire making. Nothing going into the spell is in its full form. Nothing is enough to… well, I think Beth's cast is a variation of what happened to Topher. I think he is the fully formed version of what Reelings's drainers are; only Reelings made sure none of them are strong or sound enough to fight him."

"What are you saying?" Nora asked. It was too much. With Julia lying there, she couldn't keep up.

"There might be a way to complete the spell. To make them basically vampires, only I don't know what Gabriel and the sorcery's influence will be entirely. I don't know if I can make them safer to be around, but I'm hoping that will be the result, especially if whoever finishes their vampire change can charm them."

"But would that fix Julia?" Annaliese asked. "Will it fix how Topher's charm…" she couldn't finish that sentence either.

Ru winced. "I'm hoping if Topher is the one to complete her change, he'll have the ability to heal the damage. He described the charm that Reelings infused in her as being like a wall. I picture it more as some kind of sentient guard. It attacked when Topher got close to breaking it. I'm hoping if he gets rid of the guard, it'll get rid of the hold on Julia's mind that's keeping her hostage. It should free her and let her be the person she once was."

"You can feel that?" Nora asked. "With your magic."

Ru nodded. "It's a bit like seeing through the veil."

"How much can you see into other people's minds?" Annaliese asked, her tone casual but eyes sharp.

Ru dropped her gaze, moving forward to adjust Julia's blanket. The evasion caused the first stirrings of apprehension toward Ru that Nora had ever experienced. Sure, Poppy and everyone else talked about how strong Ru's magic was, but she was just a seventeen-year-old girl. Yet, when Ru glanced up, Nora saw her for what lingered behind that innocent mask. Something ageless, something all-knowing, something that could change the world with a snap of her fingers. "Not enough for you to be worried." In a blink, the teenage Ru was back with a sheepish smile. "I have to really concentrate and I can feel Julia's because it's tied with magic that I can parse out."

Nora went cold, unable to tell if Ru was lying.

CHAPTER 32

Nora didn't voice her hesitations as Annaliese considered Ru. This was Annaliese's decision.

"Okay. You can look at the magic in me."

"You sure?" Ru asked. "I'm not entirely sure how it'll react to my prodding."

Nora stiffened. "It might hurt her?"

"Nothing like this has ever been done. I'm stronger than Beth, but trying to undo another witch's spell is always risky. We all speak to the magic differently, and it moves for each of us in a unique way. Beth could have put protections in the spell without even realizing it if that was an undercurrent of thought, but in Annaliese's case, since Beth was using my mom and Poppy, the Jennings magic shouldn't fight me too much. It'll be riskier when I try this with other drainers." A glance at Julia. They didn't know which witch was used to power the spell that changed her.

"I'll do it." Annaliese was resolute. "If it'll save Julia and help Topher, I'll do it." *For him.* The words were unspoken, but the slightly desperate look in Annaliese's eyes said it all. No one wanted Topher to vanish again. No one liked the emptiness in his eyes, different from the mask he wore to keep his charm at bay in front of humans. For Annaliese, with whom he'd gone particularly reticent, it had been worse. She was just getting Topher back. Since the moment Annaliese had met him, met this entire friend group, she'd stepped up to have their backs. She'd always known her limits and taken the risks to help Topher. Annaliese had done what Nora wished she'd been brave enough to do months ago when she saved Topher from the Den's basement, but Nora knew herself better now. Nora loved Annaliese because she would stand by Nora in the hardest times and when it was too hard for Nora, Annaliese would do what needed to be done.

Nora found herself swelling with pride in her best friend. A year ago, it had been the two of them. Annaliese had been too impatient and irritated with the world to let in anyone else. She'd started her quest to make friends when Nora believed her shifting would cause a rift between them, and even when that wasn't the case, she hadn't balked from the new relationships they were building. Hadn't shied from the feelings she had for Topher. Annaliese was growing up. It was evident in her relationship with her family, in her acceptance of Nora's pack and Colbie's presence, in her spending time with Poppy, Oliver, Jay, and Molly. Annaliese was loyal and thoughtful and had a hard time sharing that with too many people in fear of spreading herself too thin, but here she was. Taking risks for Topher, standing tall in a witch's house, accepting internships to help other humans in this world of supernaturals.

Nora had always admired Annaliese, but she hadn't been paying as much attention lately. She couldn't stop a slight smile as Annaliese closed her eyes and faced Ru, muttering, "Do your worst." Nora was worried but stepped forward and took Annaliese's arm in silent support.

Ru sagged with relief and approached. Nora smelled the metallic, heavy scent of Ru's magic as she lifted her hands and rested her fingertips on Annaliese's temples. Her eyes slid shut, and her face pinched with concentration. Annaliese's body stiffened at the first prodding of Ru's magic, but with a deep breath, she relaxed a bit, leaning into Nora.

Then, they waited. And waited. The magic must be complex and difficult because Ru's brow furrowed and her breathing picked up. Her cheeks reddened with unseen exertion. Annaliese's heart was pounding. Nora swallowed a growl, fought the urge to yank Annaliese away from Ru's touch. It was agony, standing there with no idea what was happening. Nora's gaze flicked to Julia. What if that was Annaliese's fate? What if she—

Before the panic could fully set in, Ru dropped her hands and stepped back. Annaliese swayed, and Nora held her firm, searching Ru's face. "So? What is it?"

Ru shook her head. "It's too hard to describe. I need to think about it more and see what I can find out from Topher, but… from what the magic told me and Beth's patterns for the cast, I'm hopeful I could undo the worst of it." Ru beamed.

Nora's thoughts spun. This could mean so much for the New Brecken. For the laws and the humans and cutting Reelings off at the knee and never allowing Gabriel to strike. New Brecken could find balance once more. If Ru could figure this out, if she and the witches were willing to switch up the hunt, finding drainers in the night instead of waiting for the demons to attack, this could solve everything. It wouldn't be on Topher and Nora and Henry anymore. It wouldn't come to bloodshed and brute force.

As if she'd followed Nora's thinking on some level, maybe an invasive level going off their previous conversation, Ru turned to Nora. "I need to look at Topher, but I'm finding a thread of something else here. I have a favor to ask."

"What is it?"

"I need you to catch me a demon."

"Oh, absolutely not," a new voice said from the door. Nora whirled. It had been too long since she'd been snuck up on. She wasn't prepared to find Poppy standing there scowling.

Especially not with a split lip, bruised throat, and an even more beaten Josh hanging off her shoulder.

Josh's eyes skipped past Julia on the bed, finding Annaliese first. "Where's Topher?"

"We don't know how it went yet. He didn't text or call, and now he's sleeping."

Despite his injuries, Josh looked ready to turn and head directly to Fourth Street. Poppy grabbed his arm, hurt flashing when Josh yanked out of her grip. "We need to heal you and—"

"He doesn't want to be there," Josh said. "I shouldn't have let him go without me. And now we're all just standing around his—around Julia, keeping this from him." But the energy seemed to leave him all at once. Hands covering his face, he leaned back against the wall and slid back to sitting, knees curling up even though it pulled at the gash on his thigh, fresh blood spilling.

No one was more surprised than Nora when Annaliese was the one to step forward. She crouched beside him, one arm snaking around his back. "You won't be any use to Topher like this. Let Poppy use a healing salve on you and—"

"I lost my potions," Poppy cut in softly, eyes downcast with guilt. "The vials broke. I have more at the apartment. All my ingredients are there anyway, and it'll take me a while to brew more. He needs sleep. His werewolf abilities will do a lot of the healing in the meantime."

Annaliese didn't look happy about this, but Josh's bleak features were beyond reaction. He turned his face to her and whispered. "Do you think he's okay?"

"He's still alive. Okay isn't something Topher's been in a while, but he has support. We'll get him through this, too, but only once you feel better. Go get sleep, like Poppy said."

Josh was still far from relaxed. How long had it been since the boy had slept? Werewolves needed less rest than humans and vampires, but he'd spent nights with Topher and his days helping Henry get his pack back on their feet. That didn't leave much time for sleep.

"I can't ask Henry to send the pack to Fourth Street. I don't know who to ask if he's okay—"

"Zayn went, remember?" Poppy interrupted. "He'll wake up before Topher, and I'm sure he'll text Oliver. We'll hear from him."

Josh wasn't convinced. "Where is Oliver?"

Guilt flared in Nora's chest, realizing the human didn't know where the Jennings house was or that they were all here. She would call him next. Once Josh was sleeping. Josh wasn't Nora's pack, but he was a lower werewolf, and her alpha didn't like that he wasn't being cared for properly. Nora tried to be gentle as she said, "You really should get some rest."

"Fine." Josh didn't move from his place at the door. "But I'm staying here. If I can't help him, I'll make sure Julia is fine."

Annaliese winced, but Josh's stubborn side had been making itself known lately, and no one bothered to argue. They were all sharing looks, trying to decide if he'd be fine here with some blankets and a pillow when Nora's phone began to ring. She pulled it out and blinked at the caller. "Maybe we spoke too soon. There is someone who might know more than Oliver." Nora answered. "Raven? You're on speaker."

"Hey, sorry it took me so long to update you guys. Honestly, I forgot Topher asked me to do it before he passed out."

"Passed out?" Josh asked.

"Yeah, I mean, I'm still kind of finding it hard to keep my thoughts straight. The charm he was emitting last night... Zayn had to counter-charm me so that I could pay attention to what I was doing."

"Topher has Fourth?" Nora asked. The update sank her stomach despite it being the best outcome.

"Topher has Fourth," Raven confirmed, slightly breathless with excitement.

"And he's okay?" Annaliese asked.

Raven laughed. "There's barely even a scratch on him." Her tone sobered. "Can't say the same for Happenstance. He and Zayn… I'll just say it's a good thing vampires don't bleed, or my job running cleanup this morning would have been way more difficult."

Poppy paled, looking nauseated. Everyone else's expressions tightened. Ru's eyes went to Julia as if already planning how to make Topher feel better. Because Annaliese was right. Topher wasn't okay. His guilt ate at him, and killing vampires on Fourth Street would not help. "That's why I called you first, actually," Raven continued. "Can I borrow your pack to get rid of the bodies? Topher said if you want to claim the kills for the assessors and to make a statement, your pack can, as long as you say he's the one who gave you permission to clear out Happenstance once you saw how the humans were being treated."

"Wouldn't it be better for him to claim them? In the humans' eyes?" Annaliese asked. "I've been talking to Campbell, but he's still weirdly hesitant to register Topher as a maker."

Nora hated how political this all was. How deeply they had to think about using dead bodies to give them an advantage over Reelings.

"Topher said after humans start coming to Happenstance, he won't need to worry about swaying their opinion of him."

Right. Because he'd be there, feeding on them and keeping the lower vampires in line once more. Fourth Street would go back to the bustling haven it had been before the rumors of unclaimed vampires started spreading.

"Which brings us back to you, Annaliese," Raven said.

Nora angled her phone toward Annaliese. "What's up?" her friend asked.

"I need you to go to the assessors and inform them what happened. I know you said you were working on Campbell, but you need to press harder. Topher has Fourth, has vows from every maker to stay in line, and has 'allowed Nora' to clear out all the rot. He needs to get his registration in order before he can make me and others into vampires and start building his own hierarchy."

Annaliese didn't seem excited by the task, but she nodded and straightened. Annaliese took a second to stare at Julia on the bed. "Wait for me," Nora said when Annaliese patted Josh's head and made to leave. Her friend waited by the door.

"Can you send me Ru's number?" Raven asked next.

"I'm here, too. I don't have a phone yet," she said, shooting Poppy an accusing look that made Nora think of little sisters everywhere.

"Topher wants to start giving away your anti-charm bracelets."

"Of course he came up with an awesome name for them," Ru said with a laugh. Then, she considered. "I would be willing to sell them."

Silence in the room. Poppy raised an eyebrow. Ru set her hands on her hips, defensive as she continued. "They take real work. As much as I want humans protected, I need some type of compensation. I need to be able to afford things like a phone."

Raven considered. "I'm sure Topher will be able to pay generously with the clubs at his disposal. I'm more worried about you being able to make enough to make a difference."

"I can help with that," Poppy said. She and Josh shared a look, something akin to victory suddenly in their eyes. "I've been meeting with enough witches who are in favor of humans that we should be able to make plenty."

"And they work on vampires, too?" Raven asked. Calculating. Even Nora's gaze sharpened on Poppy. This would mean a lot for their chances when Reelings decided to make a move.

"Yes," Ru said.

"Between the Jennings and Rosenfield covens and Vivienne helping, we can get to work today," Poppy promised.

Even Josh looked happier when they ended the call. Nora turned to the Ru. "Can you teach them how to make bracelets *and* fix the drainers? That's a lot for one person to spearhead."

That scary, ancient look passed through Ru's eyes again. "Yes." There was no doubt in her voice. Nora nodded, unable to stop her smile. "Let me know if you need our strength."

"Having some wolves around to pull from would make this go much faster."

Josh nodded in agreement, already texting his alpha. Nora glanced over her shoulder toward the room where Colbie slept. "We need more wolves, then. As many as possible. I'm going to go out in the city. Please make sure Colbie calls me when she wakes up. Even if she's pissed at me for leaving her here."

Nora joined Annaliese at the door and walked out with her friend at her side. Topher had Fourth. Poppy had witches. It was Nora's turn.

CHAPTER 33

Nora and Annaliese paused outside the Jennings house, both looking down the street at the Den. It was Nora's. It should be hers right now. She wanted to walk through the familiar front door and soothe the ache that cracked her chest every time she looked at her childhood home.

"Why haven't you sought him out yet?" Annaliese asked.

"I just… I think I can use my time better looking for pack-less wolves. It took so much to get Chase, Patrick, and Lupe on board. And…" Nora pressed a hand to her side. The dull pain was back, Colbie's healing only going so far to injuries as bad as Gabriel had left. "I don't feel ready," Nora finished lamely.

Annaliese gave her a dubious look but didn't say anything. She waited for Nora to expand. Instead, Nora led the way to Lana's car. Annaliese took the keys, always preferring to drive. Once they were safely tucked inside, the action was so familiar Nora could nearly trick herself into thinking she was simply getting picked up from home a year ago. It was enough to loosen her tongue. Dropping her eyes to her hands in her lap, Nora admitted, "It was the look in his eyes. I could see he wasn't going to hesitate. He wasn't sad about the situation. He was determined, but also…Annaliese, I think he was enjoying it, and *that* terrifies me. I'm scared to see it again."

Annaliese didn't respond for a beat, putting the car into drive. Nora turned to watch the Jennings house grow smaller out the window. She regretted leaving Colbie behind.

"Do I need to tell you how I feel about that?" Annaliese asked. "How much I fucking hate him? How badly I want you to—" she cut herself off.

The venom in Annaliese's tone wasn't like her. She could be angry, she could be opinionated, and she was fiercely loyal, but Annaliese was rarely emotional enough to turn to violence. She was cunning and liked to have a plan, but she looked half a breath away from turning the car directly into the Den and hitting the gas.

"That's the worst part of *all* this. Ever since I met Colbie and everyone else who is horrified by Gabriel, it's been horrible because I agree with them. I think he is wrong. I hate what he's done. I keep getting these big thoughts in my head. Declaring to myself it's time. The Den is mine. It's *time* to fucking face him, but then I find myself talking with my pack, or kissing Colbie, or helping Poppy. I keep putting it off. Psyching myself up for it and then doing nothing again. I can't break the pattern. It's all thoughts. When he attacked, I couldn't summon the determination when I fought him. It was all self-preservation. I couldn't make myself want to kill him. I don't want to kill anyone, but when it comes to him, it's like the wolf remembers every knee he bandaged. Remembers moments with Matt when the two of them let me hang out with them. Remembers how badly I wanted to be his beta, and I can't *let it go*. When I'm not in front of him, I know what I have to do. When he makes me angry, I want to fight back. But when push comes to shove, I… lose it all, and it feels like I'm letting everyone down, especially myself. My younger self who needed someone to step in."

Annaliese didn't seem to have anything to say to that. But

she offered a rare show of physical comfort and grabbed one of Nora's hands. Eventually, she asked, "So, the Den comes later. Where am I taking you now?"

"You were going to the assessors, right?"

Annaliese nodded.

"I think I should talk to the wolf they have there. Seems as good a place to start as any."

"To start what exactly?"

"Convincing all the wolves in the city to get involved. To follow me and not Gabriel."

"You should talk with Campbell, too. Get him on your side. I can only do so much as an intern and through Alpha's Den's socials. Gabriel is still riding your father's coattails in terms of garnering favor among the humans, and he's used that plenty to get Campbell to talk with him, but that won't last if you come forward."

Nora wanted to roll her eyes. She hated this part of it, even if Annaliese was right. They drove toward downtown, and Annaliese changed the subject. "Do you believe Ru will be able to save the drainers?"

Nora shrugged. "A witch figured out how to make them. Without the demons hunting them, maybe one would have figured out how to help the drainers by now. If there's a witch that can, it's Ru."

Annaliese nodded. She lapsed into another quiet, this one more thoughtful.

"Are you worried about losing Topher if Julia gets better?"

Annaliese's expression tightened. It was the most anxious Nora had ever seen her over a boy. "Sure. I don't know what it'll do to him. To us. I'm a little worried he'd let Julia call the shots out of a sense of guilt and that she wouldn't be as open as we've been about him."

Nora quirked an eyebrow. The gossip was enough to dispel her thoughts on Gabriel. "*We've* been about him?"

Annaliese shot Nora an evaluating look as if worried about her judgement. "Josh and I."

"Josh and you what?"

"We've come to an understanding. With Topher and each other."

"He's really dating both of you?" Nora checked. "People can date multiple people at once until they decide—"

"Topher isn't going to decide. Just like I thought he wouldn't. He's not going into this thinking a choice is on the horizon. The choice is now, but for me and Josh. Whether we're okay with him pursuing things with us both."

"And are you? Really?"

Annaliese stopped at the red light and slumped back in her. "Honestly? It was a relief when he brought it up. When he spelled it out, I realized how little time he'd need from me. How much freedom I would have but still know he was there and cared about me. I don't know if I can see myself being happy with this five years from now, but it's perfect at this point, and I think I could be. I'm willing to see how it goes."

"And, you and Josh?"

Annaliese shrugged. "He isn't my type, but I've always liked him. We're friends."

Nora had so many more questions, but they were pulling to a stop in front of the assessor's building. It would have to wait, but she still appreciated the update. She stopped Annaliese before she could throw her door open. "I'm happy for you. Even if it's unconventional, it seems like it's working and good for you."

Annaliese nodded, eyes drilling into Nora's. "And how bad of a person does it make me that I don't want Julia getting better and ruining it?"

"All you can do is keep talking to Topher. It didn't sound like he'd been in love with Julia for a long time, even before he was made into a vampire. Maybe Topher will be ruled by guilt for a time, but it won't last. He'll come back to you."

"I don't know if I would still like him if he chose monogamy with her over what he and I have. I want to be chosen, even if it doesn't seem like that's what he's doing from the outside."

"He is. Julia will be okay, and I have no doubt that Topher would choose if you or Josh asked. He respects you enough to do that."

Annaliese nodded. "I need to think about this more. Aside from what it means for me and Topher, but for all of us if Ru figures out how to save Julia and the rest of the drainers." With that cryptic sentence, Annaliese left the car and didn't bother checking to see if Nora followed.

The man working the reception desk greeted Annaliese warmly enough to clue Nora into how much time her best friend spent there. The man pulled out his phone and asked Annaliese about the latest post he was trying to caption for the department.

Nora stood back awkwardly as they chatted. She could smell the unclaimed werewolf. Her scent was all over the place.

Annaliese explained the situation, and the receptionist made a quick call. "Kate will see you. Her office is the second on the left," he said, pointing behind him. Nora nodded and went in that direction.

Kate's office was sparsely decorated and far too cold. Nora didn't expect a lone wolf to have a family photo on her desk, but there it was. She knew that Henry's apartments were full of human spouses and children who laid low but hadn't gotten far enough to consider how she would house her pack if she brought in wolves with families. It made her feel in over her head as Nora sat at the desk and dragged her eyes away from the photo.

Kate waited, and Nora knew she should lead this conversation, being the one to request a meeting, but the words evaded her. Nora found herself wishing she'd asked Annaliese to come in with her, or that Colbie was awake, or that she'd at least thought to bring Janelle. She was so much more grounded when she had a pack member at her side.

Clearing her throat, Nora said the first thing that came to mind. "Hi, I'm Nora Morales."

The wolf narrowed her eyes. "I'm aware. You should be speaking with Brett, not talking with me first."

"But you're a wolf," Nora said, her voice lilting at the end as if asking a question.

"And so are you. Why would that mean you get special treatment from me?"

Nora twisted her hands in her lap, under the lip of the desk, where Kate couldn't see her do it. "I've been made aware of how many unclaimed wolves are currently in New Brecken and how many are in that situation because of Gabriel. I'm trying to fix that. I'm offering you a pack."

Kate jerked back as if offended. "Is it not customary for the unclaimed to go to the alpha? Did you not think someone like me, who is well aware of all the supernatural players in the city, might have already come to you if I was interested in your pack? This is quite presumptuous, Ms. Morales."

Nora tried to keep her features composed while inside, she felt shriveled like a scolded child. "Times are dangerous. There is a war brewing in the city. No one is safe, and a lone werewolf is at even higher risk."

"I am capable of taking care of myself." Kate glared fiercely as if to prove it.

Nora sighed. She'd never been good with words and knew a lost debate when faced with one. It wasn't as if she had enough confidence in herself currently to argue her case. She nodded, pushing back the chair, but didn't leave without the final word. "If you know anyone looking for a pack and wants to make a change for the better in this city, tell them to come by the Alpha's Den. I want to unite the supernaturals and the humans. Tell them that Gabriel will soon be sending out a call for the wolves to join under him, and his goals are the exact opposite of my own."

Kate's eyes were already on her computer again. Nora had the sense that something wasn't right here. She'd never heard of a wolf who didn't want an alpha but valued their human body. The fact that this department and Nora's goals aligned should have been enough for Kate to hear Nora out, but Kate ignored her. It didn't sit right, but Nora couldn't say why, especially not when Annaliese had so happily found a place here. If she trusted anyone's opinion about an institution, it would be Annaliese's.

"Schedule a meeting with Brett on your way out," Kate called before Nora shut the door to her office.

Nora didn't bother. She stopped long enough to hear the tail end of Annaliese's muffled voice in another office. Figuring her friend had it handled, Nora left. She needed to talk with her mom, ensure her newest pack members didn't feel abandoned, and ground herself. Then, she could try to think up her next steps.

CHAPTER 34

Topher stepped out of Happenstance and pulled in his first breath since he'd entered last night. Zayn was quiet at Topher's side. The two of them were exhausted. They had pushed their bodies to the limit the night before, physically and with charm, all without stopping to feed. They'd slept in Happenstance's uncomfortable conference room, then woke up immediately to start business again. Slowly, Topher released the other makers to work their clubs and return to their lives.

Topher locked the club doors, the building nearly empty despite the early hour of the night. He shot a look down the block. Blank Space and Blue Blood were open as usual, though the street had a subdued air. He would let things run as usual for the night and had sent charmed lowers in to check on their practices. Happenstance, however, was closed and getting a deep clean. Topher, Zayn, and Raven had spent the last two hours reviewing the numbers and inventory, charming anyone Topher hadn't gotten to the previous night, and checking for any places missed by the first round of cleaners and wolves who had come in during the day. Grace's seconds had been running the club to the ground and it would take more effort than Topher felt it was worth to get it back to its former glory.

Luckily, most everything had been figured out for the night when Lana found them and insisted she and Raven had it handled and Topher should check on his registration and Nora. In the eyes of the vampires and the city, Topher wouldn't truly be a vampire of consequence until he was registered as a maker.

Topher had a feeling Lana was hoping to gain Happenstance from him. He was ready for a betrayal but couldn't fear it after all he'd accomplished last night. He'd eagerly jumped on the excuse to go check in with his friends, maybe find Josh or Annaliese, and get Zayn out of Fourth Street. His friend was more than ready to see Oliver.

The fresh air was too nice after the last twenty-four hours. Rather than call a car or use any of the ones now available to Topher, they set off at a light jog.

Zayn upped the pace, and Topher knew he had to say something. He ignored how it hollowed his core. He hadn't expected Zayn last night. Hadn't expected him to stick around tonight, either. Zayn hadn't even mentioned leaving until Lana practically pushed them out the door. "Thanks for coming. I really… it meant a lot not to have to do all that on my own. But I don't expect you to come with me back to Fourth full-time."

Zayn nodded, but Topher knew him too well to take it as agreement. After a few paces, Zayn spoke, "You'll make Fourth a better place. Once Oliver is safe, I don't mind spending more time here. The Alpha's Den has been great, but it's nothing compared to the tips we made at the Maker. I never wanted Oliver to worry as much as he has been about money. I didn't realize until we were a couple days into our trip that he wanted to work on his relationship with his parents mostly to ask for help with his tuition. I cover our rent, but I forget how much the day-to-day costs for humans. He needs to get his eyes checked, his car insurance paid, and a friend of his is getting married. Oliver was going to back out of the bachelorette trip.

I convinced him to go, but it'll be tight. I don't want him going without."

Topher blinked. The reasoning was so human. "Sounds like you had some good talks while you were away."

"We did. It felt very adult." Zayn huffed a laugh.

"So, you'd rather work at Happenstance. Really?"

"As long as it's safe for Oliver to stop by."

"I'm going to make it safe." The promise held enough confidence that Topher surprised himself with it.

"Then, yes. I didn't mind working at the Maker. Before that, we spent most of our time at Happenstance. You know, some of us wanted to become vampires." Zayn smirked, teasing. "I feel the most myself on Fourth."

Topher's head went dizzy with relief. Zayn had backed him last night when it mattered, but Topher hadn't thought he could hope for more. His steps felt ten times lighter. Without discussing it, they both picked up speed, eager to see their loved ones again.

It was a weekday, so the Alpha's Den wasn't nearly as busy as usual. Entering the wards, Topher almost smiled. Everyone was in. Josh, Annaliese, Poppy, Colbie, Nora, Oliver. Even Chance and Jay's scents reached his nose. As soon as they entered, Zayn beelined for the bar, an apology for Oliver already on his lips. Oliver threw himself into Zayn's arms, smashing their mouths together in a kiss that Zayn had to temper in such a public setting. Topher nearly smiled again. If he could keep his promise to Zayn, he wouldn't lose either of them to his life in Fourth.

The desire to smile died instantly when he turned and saw Josh. "What the fuck happened?"

Everyone went quiet at his tone. Zayn pushed Oliver behind him, instantly on alert. Topher stalked across the cocktail lounge to take Josh's chin in his hand. His heart was not in good enough shape for the sight up close.

Josh leaned into his touch. "I'm fine. Just got taken by surprise by some drainers."

Topher's grip tightened. For the first time since finding out Julia was a drainer, Topher wanted to go on the hunt. These monsters had been plaguing the city for far too long. With a quick yank, Topher brought Josh's face down and licked heavily across the scabbing wound on his forehead.

Distantly, he heard the sucked in breaths of surprise, but he didn't care about anything but how painful Josh's face looked and how his eyes fluttered closed at the first touch of Topher's bliss. Another lick and his forehead was already looking like a weeks-old injury. Topher moved to the bruising, smaller licks and quick kisses, leaving everything looking better until Topher stepped back to look into Josh's eyes. "Where else?"

Josh looked dazed, a smile Topher had never seen before playing on his lips. "I'm fine," he said, and seeing that Topher needed it, he pulled him in for a tight hug.

It might have been enough to distract him, but Topher only let the touch last a moment before he spoke, "You limped."

"Are you going to take my pants off and lick my thigh in front of everyone?" Josh whispered in his ears.

"No." Topher ducked and tipped into Josh's waist, straightening with the laughing werewolf draped over his shoulder. "We'll be right back," he announced to the room. He barely took in the shocked expressions, Colbie's wild smile, and Poppy's hurt. He'd deal with all that later. Once Josh wasn't in pain anymore. He turned for the stairs without another word, ignoring Josh's protests that he could walk on his own.

Topher ran all the way up, dismissing the unfamiliar wolf scents in the hallway as he skipped stairs until he'd hit the top floor. Lana was happily immersed in Fourth Street drama for the rest of the night. The top floor was empty, would remain empty, and as the new top vampire in New Brecken, Lana's space was as good as Topher's.

He opened her door and went straight to the couch. The bed would be better, but Topher had no desire to go near it. Fortunately, the couch was long enough for Topher to lay Josh down fully. He met Josh's eyes briefly, consent asked and granted in that exchange of looks before he reached for Josh's belt. When Josh only settled his head back on the couch, eyes sliding shut, Topher took that as further permission and quickly slid it off. In the next breath, he had Josh in his briefs. *Briefs.* Focusing on the injuries, Topher set to work, licking at the wound across Josh's thigh like it had insulted him personally.

"You know, you did that fairly easily," Josh said above him, breathless.

Topher pulled up to watch Josh's skin close. He stroked the healing wound, and the angry color began to fade. "Does that bother you? That I've had lots of practice undressing people?"

"N-no. Does it bother you that I haven't?"

The mark now a light scar, Topher moved on, placing wet kisses on any other bruise he could find. Without being asked, Josh sat up and discarded his shirt. He was trying to look casual about all this, but Topher could hear how fast his heart was racing, smell the nerves, and hear Josh's quickened breathing. He gentled his movements, only touching Josh's bruises. Eventually, he made his way up to Josh's neck and hovered above his face. "No. Of course not."

Josh nodded but didn't meet Topher's eyes like he couldn't believe him yet. Topher touched his cheek, content to take his time to prove it.

Whatever time he'd be left. He sighed, dropping to press his face in the curve of Josh's neck. Josh reached up, wrapping Topher tightly in his warm arms. So strong he was able to take Topher's weight without even a grunt. And Topher was more than happy to be cuddled.

"How bad was it?" Josh asked gently.

Topher couldn't stop the shudder that wracked his frame. Josh's arms tightened. "It was horrible."

"I wish I could have been there."

Topher shook his head, nose buried in Josh's warmth. "I don't want you to ever see me like that."

Josh snorted. "You do know I'm half wolf? It would take a lot to scare me away after the animal behavior I've seen."

Topher pressed himself closer to Josh and let himself go through the memories, knowing full well that if he didn't, they would only come back to haunt him later. The words came out unbidden, but as Josh promised, he didn't flinch. "Zayn and I… we killed all the lowers at Happenstance and their makers. Lana and her line are the last of Grace in the city."

"Who's running Happenstance then?"

"We closed it for the night. I'll have to open it soon if we want to keep Fourth Street running. The only reason the humans wanted these laws to start with was all the money the vampire clubs brought in. I have to convince the assessors that I'm worth supporting. Campbell hasn't even cleared me as a maker yet. Annaliese texted to say he was still thinking about it."

"He'll clear you. He probably wants to make you sweat. He needs to show some of his power, especially now that you're in control. Patter and Solas will have to bow to him and his office if you do."

Topher nodded, conceding the point. "I'll have to wait him out then. Hope Annaliese can convince him." Topher shifted, reaching to touch the fading mark on Josh's forehead. "Now, tell me what happened. Really."

Topher wasn't expecting the conflict that darkened Josh's previously open expression. Josh looked away and swallowed. "I can't tell you everything."

"Pack business?"

"Not pack business." Josh sounded wretched. Topher raised himself onto an elbow to look down at him, fingers still tracing the line on his forehead, down to his temple, jaw, and back up.

"What's wrong? What is it? What can I do?"

"Poppy wants to keep it secret from you," Josh whispered.

Topher blinked. "I suppose… that's only fair." Except hadn't they all promised no more secrets? Why was Josh looking at Topher like he'd already said too much but longed to say more? Why was Josh in this position? Topher didn't like it but tried to keep the stirring anger directed toward Poppy down. "I've kept a lot from her."

Josh's jaw clenched. "It's not fair. It's awful and I want to tell you. I feel like just saying this is much crueler than telling you, but I can't—"

"Who all knows?"

Josh jerked away from Topher's touch, sitting up abruptly. "I can't say more. I—" His breathing turned ragged, and Topher knew what this was. He moved, shifting until he was straddling Josh's lap, Josh's face between Topher's hands. When Josh still wouldn't look at him, Topher slid his hands, got a grip of Josh's hair, and tipped his head back. Josh's eyes darkened as they met Topher's, but the conflict remained.

"Do you trust Poppy to keep everyone safe?"

Josh gave a reluctant, stilted nod.

"No one is going to end up hurt?" Like Quinn.

Josh's eyes slid shut. "You will."

"I don't care a—" Topher cut himself off at the glare Josh shot him. "I mean…" But Topher didn't know how to recover from that. He took a breath and leaned in closer. He was thoroughly addicted to the warmth coming off Josh already. "I mean, I trust Poppy to do what's best for me."

"It's not."

Topher let his forehead fall, resting on Josh's. "Maybe but I do probably deserve it. She wasn't expecting me to react like that downstairs. This is already hurting her, and she doesn't know the details."

"She knows plenty. But neither of us are doing anything wrong. She and I aren't together. We never really were."

"Yes, but she had feelings for both of us and got rejected

twice over. I might not have returned the attraction, but Poppy is one of my best friends. What I feel for you is worth working through things with her, but I also know she wouldn't do anything to hurt me purposefully. Thank you for the warning, but I'm sure it'll be fine."

Josh shook his head, miserable. It really wouldn't do. They'd so recently gotten together in any sense of the word. The first time Topher had Josh practically naked underneath him, Josh should not look so deeply unhappy.

Pressing forward, Topher touched their lips together. A quick, light brush. A question as much as a kiss. And Josh's answer was difficult to read. His body tightened under Topher's, his heart skipped, his breath caught—all very good indications that Josh wanted to keep going, but when he sat back and shook his head, Topher knew that was the movement he'd need to listen to.

Didn't mean he'd have to be happy about it. Physical release was something Topher couldn't give up, and he was more than ready to lose himself in learning Josh's body. "Why not?"

Josh smiled at the whine in Topher's tone, but it died quickly. "I can't while I have this secret in my head. I want this to always be honest between us."

If anything, that answer only made Topher want Josh more, but he nodded. He leaned forward to kiss Josh's cheek, then dismounted. In quick order, they had Josh dressed again, but Josh hesitated to follow when Topher turned to leave the room.

The smell of his arousal was still heavy in the air. "Can we not go downstairs yet?" Josh asked.

Topher went to him immediately, opening his arms. Topher held him tight because he could, because Josh wasn't in pain anymore, and Topher had done that for him. It reminded him. "If I'm awake and Poppy needs help going somewhere as unprotected and risky as the Black Market, you call me first. If

I don't answer, you call Colbie or Zayn. You shouldn't have been alone."

Josh's sigh ruffled Topher's hair. "I know. I do have a pack, and I'm used to getting help, but I thought I might be ready to talk to her about everything. I don't think I was, though. Once I saw her, I was angrier than I expected to be. I didn't like that she still thought I was hers to call."

Topher dragged his teeth up the side of Josh's neck. It didn't help with the potent scent of the werewolf's arousal in the space. "She knows now."

Josh stepped back. "You really don't feel bad?"

"I do a bit. But I also don't have much experience with jealousy. I can't fully relate to what she must be feeling. I don't want her to think I don't care because I do, desperately, about our friendship, but I also don't think you and I are doing anything wrong."

"The thought of facing her right now makes me want to crawl out of my skin."

Topher shot a pointed gaze toward the couch. "You know, when I feel like that, I find physical exercise helps a lot."

Josh's face brightened enough to make Topher think he might have changed his mind. "You're right! I think what we all need right now is a soccer game."

Topher had to laugh, loving the pleased look on Josh's face even if he hadn't put it there intentionally. He wrapped his arm around Josh's waist and tugged him toward the door. "You're a genius."

CHAPTER 35

Poppy couldn't stop staring at Josh and Topher. She couldn't stop replaying the look on Topher's face when he found Josh injured. In the span of their friendship, she couldn't think of the last time she'd seen him display so much emotion. Typically, Topher went numb in the face of pain. He hid charm-riddled smiles when he was happy. When he was sad, he looked drained and unsurprised. Face to face with Reelings, he'd been controlled and aloof. But when he was angry, apparently, he was terrifying. Who knew Topher was capable of looking possessive and vampiric?

Then, to be faced with Josh's pleased grin after Topher's show of emotion…it had been a lot. To get space from it all, Poppy sat beside Oliver on his blanket at the edge of the soccer field. Even he was running at a lower energy than usual. He'd been working more than ever, his night schedule often bleeding into days and then into their drama at Alpha's Den. Reelings's looming presence was wearing on them all. Oliver shifted, sprawling on the blanket and putting his head in Poppy's lap.

He squinted up at her. He was taking his night off seriously and had already drunk three seltzers since their arrival. "We haven't talked in a while. How's Poppy?"

Topher ran at Annaliese, picking her up and spinning her away from the ball while ignoring her delighted protests. Poppy was still waiting for Annaliese to say something about Julia and was shocked she hadn't yet. Poppy was here without any of her siblings because her magic wasn't strong enough to help Julia or infuse bracelets with the ability to block charm. Poppy had potions brewing at her apartment and the Jennings house, all set on low for at least another two hours to replicate the tested subduing potion she now carried everywhere. Poppy was dealing with all the anxiety of waiting for Rosenfield to text her back once she and her daughters had come to a decision.

Running a hand through Oliver's soft curls, she considered how to answer. Maybe the worst part about all the tension looming over New Brecken was knowing everyone was feeling it and not wanting to add to other people's burdens. Last night and today had been awful for Oliver. Zayn hadn't gotten back to him, and Raven took her time before updating them. The circles under Oliver's eyes were bruise-like, and not even Zayn's feeding had helped with the furrow between his brow.

"I'm doing okay. I have my siblings back, and we have a direction. It's better than weeks ago when none of us knew what we were doing or what Reelings was up to."

Oliver nodded. He turned his head, watching the game for a beat. His eyes followed Zayn across the field. "He's looking at Topher differently."

Poppy stiffened. Was Topher flirting with Zayn now, too? Was he—

"He's watching him like he used to pay attention to Lana. Whatever they did last night, things are different."

"You sound like you don't think it's a good thing."

"Topher doesn't want to be the vampire leader. He's only just getting better, and it won't be long before—" he cut himself off.

Poppy finished his thought, "Before distracting himself with Josh and Annaliese won't be enough?"

Oliver sat up, frowning at the bitterness in Poppy's voice. Nora was on their side of the field and looked at Poppy with a similar expression before her attention was taken by Daniel passing her the ball. Josh's younger brother didn't seem to notice the looks between Topher and Josh, or if he did, he wasn't surprised by them. The twins from Henry's pack were a bit more attentive, but there wasn't any disproval in the glances they shared.

"He needs ties to us," Oliver said.

"Colbie isn't enough? I'm not enough? You and Zayn aren't enough?"

Oliver shrugged. "Colbie has Nora and the Alpha's Den. She'll be busy. You have your siblings. Zayn, he'd rather be with Topher. He'd rather be on Fourth, where the real money is. It's all the same to him, just bartending at a vampire club. He doesn't mind vampire politics and power plays. He's strong enough not to be threatened, but his other abilities aren't enough to make him threatening. Zayn barely remembers being human at this point. His only worry about Fourth is whether I can visit him there, and he believes Topher will make it so that I can."

"If it's going to be so much better, why does Topher need a boyfriend and girlfriend outside of Fourth to keep him tied to… what? Us? The rest of the city?"

"His humanity," Oliver said. "And yes, the rest of the city. How often have you seen or heard of Solas and Patter leaving Fourth Street? It's not like they have to bop out for groceries. Humans are in charge of all the daytime errands. Zayn has talked about how things were for him before we started dating. The vampires live on or close to Fourth. The makers have rooms in the clubs. Everything comes to them, and it's night after night of running the clubs, keeping up with the dramas between vampires, and easy feeding. The fact that Topher left the first chance he got says how little he wants that life, but it sucks you in."

"Pick a different verb," Poppy said, but the joke was hollow. "If Topher doesn't want that, he doesn't have to live that way. Tonight proves he can leave."

Oliver nodded. "With Happenstance closed and him leaving Solas and Patter to see how they act without his charm. That's special circumstances. This doesn't mean he's not afraid we'll all move on. That with him spending the majority of his time there, he'll be out of the loop whenever he comes to visit us. That being around us could still make us targets for vampires who don't like how he's running things. Vampires don't historically live very long lives in this city. Maybe he'll distance himself, so it causes us less pain when it all catches up to him."

"But why would having Josh and Annaliese make the difference if we aren't enough?"

Oliver sighed. Then gestured toward the game. "Are you saying you can't see the difference they're making already? Just the fact that Topher isn't currently in bed is thanks to Josh. I wasn't sure about it at first, but Josh is helping. Annaliese has historically been great for Topher. They're kind, great people. I'm happy for him, and I think in time you will be too."

Poppy hated to admit it, but Oliver did have a point. She turned back to the game. Topher was listening to Colbie, her hands making big gestures as she argued the other team's latest point. Josh shoved her, laughing and disagreeing. Topher's smile looked unpracticed but as real as Poppy had ever seen. With Chance wearing a bracelet, there were no humans at risk. Their younger brother had followed along on his own tonight, refusing to say where Jay went when Annaliese asked. From the heavy stoop of his shoulders, Poppy could only guess the two friends had gotten into some kind of disagreement, but she didn't have the space to ask. Topher had stuck close to his brother's side at the beginning of the night because of it, but a competitive streak between Chance and Daniel became the distraction the younger boy needed. Chance was a collegiate athlete, but Daniel had the raw physicality of a wolf. The boy who stepped onto the pitch without Jay an hour ago was not the boy who stood laughing now with flushed cheeks and grass stains on his knees.

Likely adding to Topher's current ease.

"But all that being said, I understand you're hurting over this. I'm sorry," Oliver added carefully.

Poppy pulled in a breath, relaxing in the validation. She was being defensive, she knew, but now that she was acknowledged, her fight leaked away. "I mean... it doesn't feel great. But you're right. It does make sense for Topher and I do know how important it is that he's smiling. It stings, but I'll get over it."

Oliver rolled into Poppy's stomach to give her an awkward, squeezing hug. "You're a good friend. Once everything settles down, it'll get easier."

Poppy nodded and helped herself to one of Oliver's seltzers. After chugging the bubbly drink, she pulled Oliver off the blanket to join the game. She shouldn't have been surprised by how happy this made Topher or the encompassing hug he gave her. For the moment, it was enough to soothe the pain. The game was fast and breathtaking with Nora's pack here. Poppy threw herself into it, magic sparking off her fingers, determined to exhaust herself enough to stop her thinking.

Thirty minutes later, Poppy ran right into Janelle's back. Too late, she saw the game had paused around her. Ricky was quick to lend a hand to steady her, but he was only half paying attention. Three new people had joined them, standing by the blanket.

Three new vampires.

Colbie came to stand by Poppy. Zayn and Oliver followed her as they watched Topher jog across the field to talk with the newcomers. When Nora came to Colbie's side, she asked Zayn, "Are they friends?"

Zayn shrugged. "Rachel's great. Her partner was one of

the murdered vampires last winter. The other two work at Blue Blood. Topher asked them to report how the makers acted tonight."

"He trusts them?" Colbie asked.

Josh's familiar warmth joined their little circle. He had Chance protectively hidden at his side.

"Charmed them," Zayn corrected.

Colbie was staring at her brother. "I don't like that look on his face."

"You should be glad you weren't there last night then." Zayn didn't sound too disturbed by whatever had happened. It made his answer to Colbie's next question all the more surprising.

"How bad was it?"

"After we found a dead lower, he wanted all the Grace's makers dead. They weren't doing anything to keep their lowers in line. Raven's been finding bodies poorly hidden all day."

Josh began to pale. Chance's eyes widened.

"And the lowers who were doing all the killing?" Nora asked, voice hard as ice.

"All dead," Zayn stated.

Even Oliver looked shaken. "What do you mean?"

"We had to draw the line. Make a clean start. Topher's pissed Solas and Patter let it get as bad as it did, but he wants them to keep some of the authority so he's not running the entire block. He went into Happenstance, told them how it would be, and those who disagreed attacked. He always stayed a step ahead of me," Zayn rolled his eyes there like Topher had ruined his fun. "He would get in the killing hit or weaken them before they got to me. But we had to kill them all."

"Babe, your vampire is coming out," Oliver said. The eerie, ageless look in Zayn's eyes melted, and he reached for his boyfriend with a sheepish smile.

Colbie wasn't ready to drop it. She stared across the field at Topher as he spoke with the lowers. Even from here, Poppy hated the blank expression that returned to his face. "How many?"

"About thirty lowers. Four makers," Zayn said. "Raven's still getting the exact numbers. A few tried to run, but they didn't get very far."

Colbie frowned. "Why didn't he say anything?"

"What was he supposed to say?" Zayn asked, sounding genuinely confused. "You all knew he was going to take Fourth last night."

"Colbie!"

Colbie ignored Nora's call, stalking across the field and to Topher's side. She impatiently waited until he seemed satisfied by the update and pulled him aside. He wasn't happy that she drew the interest of the vampires he'd been speaking to, but they quickly cleared out at the sight of his frown. Once they were gone, Chance broke away from Josh and went to join his siblings as Colbie began shouting. "—without me!"

With a nod, Nora sent her pack into the night. The game and brief reprieve from the city's tension was over. Nora ran to stand behind Colbie. With a quick word, Josh sent Daniel and the twins away. Taking up Zayn's hand, Oliver approached the arguing siblings with his chin high. Poppy, Josh, and Annaliese followed, lingering at the outside of the conversation that Poppy felt had been brewing for weeks.

"Colbie, you don't want anything to do with Fourth Street, and Nora was hurt! I don't know why you're—"

"Because you could have waited! You have to stop excluding me from—"

"I won't! You didn't choose this! Any of it! It's not your problem to deal with!" Topher was yelling now, too. Poppy had never heard him raise his voice before, but everything was getting to him. The way his voice cracked at the end had everyone moving in closer, worry creeping between their brows. Poppy wasn't sure when she started thinking of Topher as fragile, but thoughts of Josh and Annaliese disappeared as she feared this conversation might send Topher back into his room.

Colbie let out a hollow laugh. "And you did?"

Topher clenched his fists. He tried to back away a step, but Josh was there and put a hand on his lower back. "I didn't," Topher said, more steady. "But something chose me for all this! I'm finally accepting it. I have to accept what it means for me. Can you?" Topher pressed on when Colbie opened her mouth to argue. "I don't want you on Fourth Street. I don't want anyone here on Fourth Street."

Colbie narrowed her eyes. Surprisingly, it was Chance who broke in. "It isn't your choice to make, Toph. If we want to be involved, you might as well include us, or we'll find other ways."

Topher's face twisted in heartbreaking confusion. "*You* want to be involved?"

Chance rolled his eyes. "Yes, Topher. I already thought I lost you and Colbie once. I'm not doing it again. I'm trying to be smart about this and consider our options."

"And what do you think the options are?" Colbie asked. It was a different side to the West sibling dynamic, one Poppy hadn't witnessed before. Chance was the smart sibling, the golden child. His older siblings looked to him for answers now.

Chance took a breath and straightened. "First of all, I should let you know I'm applying to transfer to UNB in the fall. So, whatever solutions we come up with, they're going to be permanent. I already talked with Fuller, my friend from high school, and we're getting an apartment together so I can move out of Mom and Dad's. Don't act like this is something you can argue," Chance said, pointing at Topher so he'd shut his mouth. "Now, for you two. Am I correct in assuming since you're now technically her higher-up, Lana would concede the Alpha's Den to you, Topher?"

Topher glanced at Nora. "Her shares, maybe. If I told her to."

"You don't have to do that. Get Colbie more involved there to the point where she and Nora could run it if they wanted to eventually. You guys need to start thinking about the future, and if Nora and Colbie keep working out, they could run the Alpha's Den together. And for you, Topher, learn how to fucking delegate. There's no reason you need to stay on Fourth all the time. Live in your current apartment, have your current relationships, and do enough random checks to keep your people in line."

"It's not going to be that easy. Right now—"

"Fine. It's bad now. Make it better, but have the plan to eventually take a step back. Just because most vampires are controlled by their thirst for blood and power doesn't mean you are. We already know you can last way too long without eating. Fourth Street won't consume you like it did Reelings or the Big Three. Have a little faith in yourself, for god's sake."

Chance clapped his hands on his brother's shoulders. "Look, your brain has always worked in absolutes and focused on the bad, but that doesn't mean it's really what the world is like. Trust us to help you see that and take a breath, okay? Running Fourth Street is a job. A managerial position with assistants beneath you to carry the brunt of the work."

It seemed they all held their breath as Topher considered. Finally, he gave in with a tight nod and let Chance pull him into a quick hug, whispering in Topher's ear that it would all be okay. They'll figure it out. Colbie looked like she'd be crying if she could. Her eyes went to Nora. They seemed to agree on the future Chance painted with that look. It left Poppy standing there, wishing Chance would turn his attention to her and spell out her own next steps so neatly.

When Poppy asked, Topher agreed to come by the Jennings house before returning to Fourth Street. They were all aware of the approaching sunrise, but Topher wasn't concerned. He was reluctant to return to Fourth and preoccupied with his younger brother's optimistic view of the future. Somehow, it ended up just being Poppy and Topher in the car.

Emotions were still high and raw for her, so Poppy was as content to sit quietly as Topher seemed to be for the first half of the drive. She still wasn't ready when Topher turned to her. "Are we good?"

Poppy nodded without thought. Topher stayed quiet, waiting for more even as the silence grew unbearable. Poppy knew he needed more than that. That *she* needed more than that. "Why?" she asked, and when he tilted his head in confusion, she forced herself to keep talking through the embarrassment rising in her throat. "Why them? Why all of them and not me? What's wrong with me that you never even considered?"

Topher sucked in a breath and blew it out. "I don't know. I met you too soon after Dylan, maybe? Or the apartment and life we built with Colbie was so safe and amazing that it was enough of an escape for me and I didn't need more? I just… It's like I don't have control of that part of myself, and I know that's a shit excuse, but I never had feelings for you in that way. I was too grateful you were there and friends with us and so easy to be around. I still remember the first time I laughed after Dylan died. It was the first time you teased Colbie, and she was so stunned… the look on her face was priceless but not as good as how proud you looked. It was like you'd been saving up that sassy side of yourself for the perfect moment."

Poppy snickered. "Well, she really is weird for making pictures with her hair and leaving them on the shower walls."

Topher laughed and shrugged. "She's been doing it for as long as I can remember."

Poppy glanced at him. "Then I stand by what I said; she should be better at it by now. There's no reason all of her pictures should be indecipherable."

Topher pointed in the air like Colbie would. "Abstract."

Poppy laughed. Topher relaxed into his seat, and only then did she notice how tense he'd been. Leaning against the window, he angled himself to better look at her. "Can this be enough for you, Pop Tart?"

Her cheeks heated under his scrutiny. She could sense how desperately he wanted her to say yes. Poppy gathered her courage. "It's enough, Topher," she said. "But I won't settle for less."

He stiffened and Poppy continued before he could get upset. "You have to factor Colbie and me into everything, even if it's hard. You have to come home sometimes. You have to keep us in the loop, and I want to be part of Fourth like I was at the Maker and Alpha's Den. I'm not strong enough to make a difference in the city like Ru is going to, but I can ward your clubs and work with you. I can protect myself against vampires. I'll be busy, you'll be busy, but we've always made time and been involved with each other's lives. I won't ask for more from you, but can you promise to try and stay my friend?"

"You want that? After everything? You'd go to Fourth with me?"

Poppy didn't hesitate. Her attraction had lessened, but she loved Topher West. "Yes."

He breathed out a sigh of relief, and Poppy knew she'd said all the right things. "Deal."

CHAPTER 36

They pulled up in front of the Jennings house. As he was sure they all did upon parking, Topher glanced down the street toward the Den. The house seemed quiet. Topher knew Nora had big plans for the next day, plans that Henry and Helen were helping her with. He hoped Gabriel wasn't ready for whatever Nora brought to his door.

Poppy's shoulders rose with tension as they walked through her wards and entered the chaos that had become the front room. Beads and strings and bundles of bracelets littered the space. Topher could taste the coppery tang of magic in the air and swelled with pride over all Ru had accomplished and organized in so little time.

They cut right and went downstairs before Topher could even ask why Ru had requested so cryptically to see him tonight. She was sleeping on the couch downstairs, visibly drained from all the casting. Topher whispered to Poppy, "We can do this another time."

Poppy shook her head. Face guarded, she didn't attempt to explain the urgency. A bad feeling flooded Topher's gut, remembering Josh's warning about secrets, but he only stood by as Poppy gently shook Ru awake. When Poppy offered it,

Ru accepted a vial of daylight brew. She threw it back like a shot and walked up to Topher. Despite his confidence that they wouldn't hurt him, Topher braced himself.

"I want to examine your magic," Ru said. Topher relaxed a bit. He'd been tempted before to ask Ru to find what made his shadows before. What was left of Dylan in his strength.

Topher didn't ask for more details, too fearful the answers would be lies after what Josh said. He nodded and held still as Ru stopped in front of him. She started to lift her hands but hesitated, glancing over her shoulder at Poppy.

Whatever wordless communication they exchanged didn't give Ru any more confidence as she turned back to him. "It might hurt. Maybe not, but this won't be comfortable."

"It's fine, Ru. I'm happy to help." With whatever they were after. Topher didn't need the answers. He closed his eyes and waited.

Ru's fingers were cold when they lightly connected with his temples. Her wards were so strong he couldn't smell her even this close. It was eerie. Poppy let out enough to have a scent like most humans would, but Topher realized this must be what it was like for other beings when they were around vampires. He didn't have long to dwell on the strange sensation. Ru's magic was a quick, sharp spear that distracted him immediately.

It felt like when he dove into his charm to use a great deal of it at once, only he was being *forced* to burrow into it. As if Ru's magic had taken him by the mental hand and dragged him with her while she explored. The shadows swirled, the layers of protection and his unnatural magic rising, but Topher quickly calmed it so it wouldn't strike against Ru's prodding. He heard her make a noise of surprise, but she kept going without a word.

He couldn't understand what Ru was looking for or what she read from all his inner forces. That feeling that came when Topher used all his power made itself known, the smell of Dylan filling the air, the faint warmth of embrace teasing and out of reach. When Ru started to draw out of those depths, Topher almost protested. Dylan was so, so close here. Ru's magic took a turn, and then, all Topher felt was Lana's influence. He shied from that place, and fortunately, Ru seemed satisfied with all she'd learned.

He opened his eyes when Ru's fingers dropped from his face.

"Is he there?" Topher asked, voice low and shaken.

Ru's smile was sad. "I'm sorry, Topher. The magic came from his sacrifice, yes, but what's left is more of an impression. It's your love for him conjuring those feelings."

Topher shook his head, unwilling to believe that. He stepped back quickly. "Do you need anything else?"

Ru looked drained, her eyes blinking slowly and a slightly green cast to her skin. "Not at the moment. I have to think about all I've learned, but I might need you soon."

Topher nodded, satisfied the answers would come even if he already didn't like the one Ru had given him. He stopped to give Poppy a quick hug goodbye and ran out of the house with the emotions fast on his heels. It was almost a relief to return to Fourth Street, to make his way to Grace's old room in Happenstance, and to have the memory of the dead maker fill his thoughts instead as the sun finally dragged him under.

Nora waited on the front pew, more than grateful to have Annaliese looking nearly bored at her side. This meeting had been a full day of work. Phone calls, drop-ins at work, emails, and even a couple trips to people's houses, but Helen Morales had pulled through. Following memories of territories and scents, she helped them gather all the werewolves she could convince to meet in the small church Henry had rented for tonight. The afternoon sun was streaming in hot from the high, stained glass windows. Annaliese tipped her head back, taking in the decor. "How much time have you spent in churches?" she asked.

Nora let out a laugh. After all their years of friendship, the topic had never been broached. "Honestly, with the laws and chaos before the laws, I didn't know New Brecken had any."

Annaliese shot her a grin. Helen was walking toward them up the aisle, looking satisfied. The smell of so many alphaless werewolves threatened to make Nora's head swim. Half of her wanted to take their tethers and draw them in without wasting her words. Half of her couldn't get that conversation with Kate out of her head. Was it presumptuous to assume the werewolves gathered here wouldn't be insulted by her invitation? Didn't wolves want an alpha, or had she been alone in her desperation? Was everything Henry told her about this process wrong?

Nora twisted to look at all the faces gathered. It was shocking that Gabriel had done this. He was the reason those who'd fled had returned, but Helen was why they were here now. Gabriel had been taking packs apart and dividing the city even before her father's death. All those secrets he wouldn't tell her, all the days and nights he spent away. All the whispered conversations she wasn't privy to. Somehow, she never imagined he was planning at this scale. Nora never imagined big enough. At least, because of this, Gabriel would never have anticipated Nora making this move. Standing in this church. This was beyond Nora's wildest dreams.

With a start, Nora realized her mother was waiting, and Annaliese was whispering her name. From the pew behind her, Janelle reached forward and gave Nora a little push. It was the encouragement she needed. Nora stood and moved to the front of the room. She felt young as she looked at the faces gathered. All grown adults who had been established in this city before the laws were passed. Some before she was even born.

What was she thinking?

But, as always, Annaliese stood by in support, and Nora

knew how much it took to gain Annaliese's confidence. If Annaliese believed Nora could do this, then she must be capable. Trailing that thought was the question she asked herself when she wanted to do better. What would Colbie do in this position? Colbie didn't bulk, she didn't falter, she loved and hated fiercely and wouldn't let anyone dictate how she should feel based on her age or experience or anything else. Nora wanted to be someone Colbie admired as much as she admired Colbie and Annaliese.

Straightening her shoulders, Nora addressed the room. "Hello. My name is Nora Morales and I am the new alpha of my father's pack. Some of you may have been against the laws when they were formed. You may be against more change even now. Werewolves are a group too centered on traditional values, a practiced, mindless way of thinking that I have had to unlearn and challenge. But every lesson I've taken in this last year has been so worth it. Times change. Just because the past has set an example doesn't mean we need to follow it."

The audience was wary, filled with closed-off expressions. Nora pushed on. "Maybe you don't support the laws, but no one can say we haven't benefited. New Brecken's openness is why we all live here to begin with. It calls to our human nature to find community—to be *known*. Nowhere else has caught up to New Brecken in that regard. The vampires might bring in the tourists and the curious, but we also benefit when open-minded people enter our city. We benefit from working together."

She might have already lost some of them at the mention of vampires, but Nora couldn't find it in herself to care. What she said was true. Everyone wanted their authentic self to be accepted. "The night before last, my girlfriend's brother returned to Fourth Street. Reelings is alive and left his lowers under a deep charm. Christopher West was the only one strong enough to break it, and now that he has, Fourth Street is his to control." Nora's smile caught the shifting werewolves off guard. "Fortunately for me, Colbie West is the most important person in his life and mine. Our alliance runs deeper than our competitors, and Gabriel won't stand a chance against us.

"I know my dating a vampire will make me an unsuitable alpha in some of your eyes. I know my dating a woman might sour me to you. But I also know which direction this city is moving in. Having his finger on that pulse has helped Reelings gather so many humans to his cause. Yes, he charms them, but they go willingly to his meetings to hear what he has to say. The difference between us is I believe what I'm saying. Let me be perfectly clear. I have seen the vampires feed, and I have seen how it benefits the humans. Under proper vigilance, under Topher, I support the clubs along Fourth Street and what the vampires can do for humans. The more we interact with the vampires, the faster New Brecken will progress toward the type of city the laws laid the foundation for it to become. Even the witches could step forward with some sense of safety should this happen. I've seen their magic at work. I understand why they fear being taken advantage of, but also see how much they could do for New Brecken. I know witches, and they are on my side. We've shared magic, strength, and goals for the city.

"All that being said, I believe this alliance, our keeping to the laws, our living in New Brecken as our authentic selves, will benefit no one more than it will the humans. We aren't super-heroes who need to take humans under our care to coddle, and we aren't their pets. We are simple groups with different strengths learning to live in harmony. Once that harmony is achieved, we will all be better for it."

Nora took a breath and wished for a glass of water. She settled for clearing her throat as she soldiered on, the faces before her blurring until she found Annaliese's. Her friend had never looked so proud. It gave Nora a straight path to the words she wanted to say. "I grew up in a pack that murdered vampires in exchange for the alpha's protection. My father changed his mind about that rule, but Gabriel kept it enforced. Gabriel wanted to take me as a mate when I wasn't old enough to legally drink, let alone make the shift. Gabriel told me to discontinue my human friendships, and my former pack members mocked me for being upset. Look at me now. Look at him aligned with demons, a sorcerer, and Reelings. Tell me who is in the right. Gabriel wants to dismantle the laws. He wants a bloody takeover of a city that has been striving for peace at every turn. I won't let him. Tonight, I will be going to my childhood home and pack. I will reclaim it. The house is in my name, and my father's pack belongs to me. Gabriel doesn't deserve the title of alpha. If he did, he'd be able to feel all the tethers that I do now. He would have offered a home instead of a battlefield. I'm offering connection. No games, no manipulations, no underhanded moves, or harmful alliances. I need a pack at my back when I go to the Den. I need a show of power to convince the city I'm the alpha to be reckoned with. Once Gabriel's power is gone, Reelings will be weakened and will have less human support as we strike alongside the vampires. Do any of you have questions?"

It seemed the wolves needed a moment to find their voice. Thus far, none of the tethers were reaching toward her, but Nora was willing to wait. Adrenaline was pumping after that speech. She felt ready to march on the Den with or without them.

Her pack members looked ready to follow. Heather beamed. Ricky bounced in his seat. Chase and Patrick had their heads bent together, eyes scheming as they whispered back and forth. In the center, Janelle's smile was fierce and supportive. Nora already knew she would name Janelle her beta. No one questioned Nora as justifiably nor supported her goals so completely. It felt good to have the decision settled, even if she hadn't yet asked Janelle. Hopefully, the answer was yes. Between her, Annaliese, and Colbie, Nora needed all the examples of unfaltering women she could accumulate so she had the constant reminder that no one could make her smaller.

Speaking of examples, Helen stood beside the dais, eyes brimming. She mouthed the words, "*He would be so proud.*"

"How can we trust you?" A deep voice called from the back. "I've known Gabriel for years."

"Then you've also known my mother. She helped me gather this information since she has returned to her human form. She wants my father's beloved city to fall as little as I do. Gabriel would raze it to the ground in order to rebuild it with the werewolves in charge."

Maybe it was wishful thinking, but it seemed as if some tethers were brushing against her power. Nora didn't invite them to grab hold yet, not until the wolves were sure.

There were more questions about Alpha's Den, the rumors surrounding Lana, and Nora's lack of experience. Someone had even heard about her and Gabriel's most recent fight. She admitted to being caught off guard in her human form, which startled some of the older, more traditional wolves into softening toward her. Alpha challenges were supposed to occur under the full moon and in wolf form. That he would attack her so blatantly was a mark against him and cast more doubt on Gabriel's strength as an alpha if he was resorting to such measures.

In the end, a woman stood up. She was holding a sleeping toddler in her arms. "I don't want to move into some bar. I don't want to uproot my life. I need an alpha, I admit, but I love the life I have built in the time I've spent away from the supernatural side of the city."

Nora blinked. "That's fine." Better actually. She was willing to search for more housing and claim the Den, but she wouldn't force people to move from their homes. It saved her some trouble if they didn't want to.

Surprise answered her quick agreement, and Nora worried she'd said the wrong thing. Maybe that easy compliance wasn't alpha. Nora shrugged. She was an alpha but also human and too logical not to see how this would help. "Keep your jobs. Keep your family homes. We can figure out when to run together and how to support each other. I want a community. A family. Nothing forced or toxic. We can figure out what works for us. Hopefully, tonight will be one of the only nights I need you to show up for me in wolf form and add to my strength. The goal here is a peaceful city and simple lives. You won't get that under Gabriel."

There was applause. Howls. Nods. Nora hesitantly opened her mind and power and watched relief sweep over the faces of the packless no more.

CHAPTER 37

Nora instructed everyone to come forward in a line so she could collect a list of her new pack members' names and if they wanted to find housing with her. Nora looked down at Janelle and Annaliese's handwriting as her wolves returned to their seats, talking animatedly about the approaching full moon and participating in a pack run once more. She was stunned. Most werewolves had no interest in changing their daily lives. A few mentioned throwing dinners once a week, but that was the most they asked.

Henry approached while Nora folded up the pieces of paper. "That was a lot of wolves, Nora," he said, studying Nora intently. Worriedly.

"Wasn't that the point of me doing this? To build a big pack and connect the lone wolves in the city."

"Yes, but I didn't think it would be so many. Not so many at once. You have at least thirty names there. How do you feel?"

"A bit… drunk? Maybe a little like I'm—" She almost said kissing Colbie, but as open-minded as Henry was, she couldn't imagine he knew what it was like to be blissed. "—high?"

"I've never heard of an alpha taking on so many members

at once. Your pack is as big as my own now, and even I struggle with how much it takes and gives to have that many ties. I'm worried you've bit off a bigger commitment than you were ready for."

"I'm ready to stop Gabriel and Reelings. If this is what it takes—"

"This is your life, Nora," he cut her off low and serious. "Gabriel and Reelings are only one moment in it."

Nora shrugged. "If, when everything settles and people don't like the commitment, or it's too much, we can figure out what to do then."

"You've already created the bond. You give it out too freely!" Henry was nearly yelling but wasn't looking at Nora when he said it. His eyes had gone to Helen.

"Then I'll remove it if anyone needs me to," Nora said, exasperated. Out of all the issues they had faced lately, why was this the one Henry approached her about? Yes, Josh was helping them, and she knew Henry's pack would show up if asked, but since Quinn's death, he hadn't actively helped them. He and Helen had searched for the werewolves, yes, but an adult voice would have made all this so much easier from the beginning. Why did he think this was his place after making it clear New Brecken was Nora's city to worry about?

"Nora. I've told you the only way to break out from an alpha is for another alpha to challenge them. For the bonds to weaken in that moment."

He *had* told her that. "But that isn't true," she said, thoughts muddling.

"It is—"

"I could let members of my pack go now if I needed. When they couldn't get okay with Colbie, I almost did for some of them."

Henry's mouth dropped open. Janelle stood behind Nora, watching all of this. She chose that moment to break in. "It's true. Being with Nora is a choice. We all feel how much control she has over our ties. If we asked, she could remove it." Janelle snapped her fingers to show how quickly Nora could do it.

Henry stared. "You can break the pack bonds on command?"

Nora nodded.

He shook his head, a smile quirking his lips. "All that power we felt from you… I wasn't sure how it would manifest in your abilities as an alpha. This is unheard of. You understand that, right?"

Nora shrugged. "Seems like everything happening in New Brecken these days is unprecedented. Something made us all as strong as we need to be." Maybe Poppy would call it fate. Maybe circumstance simply shaped them into what they had to become, but they had what it took to change things. Topher's strength, Nora's bonds, Poppy's potions and wards. They could do this.

"We're going to go now," Nora told Henry. She wasn't surprised when he nodded and stepped back into the ranks of his pack members present, but she was still disappointed he was again choosing not to join the fight.

"Good luck, Nora." Then, as if sensing her unhappiness with him, he added, "The Den is yours by right, but only you can be the one to take it."

"And after?"

"Call me with whatever you need. I'll meet with my pack and try to rally support for your cause."

It was a small promise after everything, but it was enough. Nora nodded and turned for the aisle. Janelle was at her back, Helen telling Henry goodbye behind them. The rest of Nora's pack filed out behind her, row after row of werewolves with one destination in mind. Luis Morales's old territory. His old Den, theirs by right. Gabriel would have to stand down or accept Nora's challenge. They shifted as they ran, the first glimpse of the full moon providing all the light they needed.

There was some new tension in the city as they ran. Nora's

hackles rose in response. It was as if New Brecken was holding its breath. As if the shadows had paused to watch. Nora knew the vampires were waking. She knew Ru and Poppy had plans to take what they had learned in the last few days to try and change Julia with the full moon's aid. There was change in the air, but Nora couldn't figure out why it was raising her hair when it was brought on by herself and her peers. This was their push. Their move forward. Finally. They were tired of the supernatural happening to them. They had Fourth and Nora had the wolves and Poppy was uniting the witches.

Nora's heart shouldn't be thumping with anxious dread. She was too aware of her phone left behind, of Colbie waking up without Nora, of Annaliese in the city alone. It felt too practiced to force her worries away from them all. To focus on the pack. Different than how she used to, but Nora knew how to put Gabriel at the forefront of her thoughts. This time would be the last.

Topher woke up slowly. He was comfortable and warm. His eyes snapped open when he remembered falling asleep in Grace's room. It was barely in better shape than they had found it in. Raven had been busy, and the bed had been replaced, but there was no reason Topher should feel so content upon waking here.

Rolling, he found Josh already awake and watching him. Without a word, Topher scooted closer, every tension melting when Josh wrapped him in his arms. Topher waited for the usual guilt, but all he could feel was relief at being held.

"Do I ever remind you of him?" Josh asked, quiet and cautious. Maybe Topher wasn't the only one unsure if he should be enjoying this as much as he was.

"Honestly? Not your personality, but sometimes what you bring out in me reminds me of what it was like with him."

Josh went quiet, considering. His hand idly massaging

Topher's neck kept him from panicking over whether he'd said the wrong thing. Eventually, Josh took a deep breath and pulled Topher in closer. "I think I like that answer. And how was Poppy?"

"We'll be okay."

"And what Chance said?"

Topher swallowed. He was far too aware of his duties below. Happenstance needed to open again. Topher needed to make sure the humans were in favor of the clubs and that meant the clubs had to return to being the city's main draw and money makers. He, Zayn, and Raven had already started discussing upping the entrance fees, an unspoken way to charge visitors for the bliss, which would mean each club needed enough vampires on hand to supply it. Raven had looked at Topher significantly, but he still hadn't heard back from Brett Campbell on his registration status. The roadblock had been a relief at first, an excuse not to delve into that part of his abilities, but now Topher needed to get to work. His patience was wearing thin.

Josh pressed his lips to Topher's head, bringing him back to his body and the comfort of Josh's arms. He remembered he'd been asked a question. "He's probably right. Chance usually is. But I'm not ready to focus on more than what's right in front of me yet. I have to take out Reelings and make all this worth it before I can figure out how to live around the consequences."

"Fair," Josh said. His hand moved up to play with Topher's hair. Topher melted further into their embrace.

His phone began to ring on the nightstand behind Josh. Topher protested when Josh let him go to reach for it but quieted at the way Josh stiffened at the sight of the caller ID.

"Who is it?" Topher asked.

"It's Ryan's phone," Josh said. His tight voice made even less sense. Topher had been getting texts from Ru from her brother's phone since she'd moved into their childhood home.

Josh didn't answer the questioning look Topher sent him as

he held out his hand. Dropping the phone in Topher's palm, Josh got out of bed. Topher barely had time to appreciate the view of him in only his underwear before Josh started pulling on the jeans.

"Hello?"

"Hey, Toph. It's Ru."

"What's up, Roulade?"

She laughed but wasn't as delighted as she usually was when Topher came up with a new nickname. When her laugh died, she took a deep breath. "I think… I think I've figured it out. The drainers. How to help them."

Josh was frozen, a sweatshirt gripped between his hands.

"That's great," Topher said, confused by the dread on Josh's face and the hesitance in Ru's voice. He was missing something. This should be good news, even if it came too late to help Julia. They had no way of knowing how many drainers Reelings had currently. No idea how many this full moon might produce. They could save so many former humans with this knowledge. "What about the charm block Reelings puts on them?"

"Well, I don't know for sure. I can't do this myself. I need your help."

Josh read something on Topher's face that had him at Topher's side in a blink. "I don't— Ru, I can't handle breaking any more minds. I can't compete with the charm that Reelings places on them."

"You can. Will you come to the house to try? We have a drainer here."

Now Josh looked horrified. He'd taken Topher's hand, but Topher couldn't tell who the tight grip was supposed to be comforting. But, he saw no reason to refuse. "Sure. I'll be there s—"

Josh took the phone. "We have one at the apartments. We should start there."

"Ryan and Margot don't want me leaving the house on a full moon. Maybe if you guys come pick me up—" There were protests in the background, Ru's older siblings vetoing the idea before she could finish voicing it.

Looking at Josh with even more confusion, Topher took the phone back. "Don't worry about it. If we have to go to you either way, we'll start with the one there."

"See you soon then," Ru said with that unfamiliar tense voice. Topher hung up before he could ask too many questions. He turned to Josh, letting all his bafflement show.

Josh shifted on his knees so he was straddling Topher's thighs. He took Topher's face in his hands. His eyes darted to the window. "I'll probably change soon, but I have to warn you—"

He was interrupted by Topher's phone going off again. This time it was a message from Colbie asking Topher to meet her at the Jennings house. Nora was moving against Gabriel tonight. Colbie had promised to stay out of it, but she wanted to be close, and she wanted Topher there. Josh read the message and sighed. His hands pressed closer to Topher's cheeks, but he seemed to think better than voice the warning. "It'll be better if Colbie and Poppy are there to break the news. I won't have time."

"The news?"

"The secret. It wasn't supposed to fall to you to do this, but if Ru thinks you're the only one..." he trailed off, struggling. Topher pressed forward to give him an assuring kiss.

"Whatever it is, it'll be fine. I'll survive."

Josh wrapped him in a hug in response, but they couldn't stay like this long. Annaliese was texting now, too, saying she would meet them all at the house for the same reasons Colbie wanted to be there.

Topher hurried to get dressed. He needed to make sure things were in order before leaving Happenstance. Lana was waiting in the sitting room outside Topher's bedroom. He hated to do it, but his phone was buzzing, and Josh was impatient to get this over with and twitching from his approaching involuntary change. Topher turned to Lana as he left. "I have to go deal with something. Will you make sure things are going well at Blue Blood and Blank Space?"

Lana smiled, too triumphant. "Of course, dar—Topher."

He glared at her for the near slip-up. "This is temporary. I'll be making more lowers as soon as I'm cleared, so don't get comfortable being back here."

She shrugged and moved out of the room. "We'll see."

Josh turned to Topher once she was gone. "You can trust her?"

"She knows what I want, and I know she wants to be here. She'll try her best to get into my good graces now that I've surpassed her. She's vicious enough to keep Patter and Solas in line in my absence. And, well, I don't mind risking her in a confrontation with them."

Josh was unfazed by that last very vampire line of reasoning. "Let's go then."

They ran. As soon as Josh shifted under the full moon's light, he couldn't shift back. He remained at Topher's side as they entered the Jennings house, making getting through the door slightly awkward. No one else found humor in the bumping shuffle. Topher's slight smile died. He didn't know if the strained silence in the front room came from Ru being so close to finding a solution or Nora marching on the Den down the road, but the looks on Colbie, Annaliese, and the Jennings's faces were enough to send anxiety roiling in Topher's stomach. He'd stopped to feed on the way here, and the fresh blood felt more hot and sickening in his stomach than usual.

Josh's growl startled everyone. Poppy's guilty eyes said she knew what it meant. Topher looked from her to Colbie, remembering what Josh said in Happenstance. They were supposed to break the secret now. Judging from the looks on their faces, he wasn't sure he wanted them to.

A breeze rolled between them from the open window as the silence stretched. Topher turned toward it, alarm in his voice as he asked, "Is that smoke?"

Howls rose in the night in response.

CHAPTER 38

Nora and her pack, now triple the size, ran through the park near her childhood home. Memories of her father assailed Nora as they broke in a current around the wolf statue in the center. Her mother was supportive and running at her side, but Nora longed to know what he would have thought about all of this.

They turned the corner from the opposite end of the block to the Jennings house, but Nora's eyes darted there first. It was like she had a reward in place for the end of this task, with Colbie, Annaliese, and everyone there waiting—a beckoning home of support for after one of the most difficult undertakings of her life. But with the full moon and the rush of new pack members and Patrick and Chase's crammed-in practice sessions and instructions, Nora was ready to see this finished. She turned her eyes to the Den and slid to a halt.

There was smoke billowing out of the open windows.

Helen was the first to let out a sound. A high keen filled with disbelief answered by howls from the rest who had called the place home. Nora recovered from her shock and ran full tilt. It couldn't be real. Instead of stopping in the yard and on the street as her wolves did, Nora pressed on, shifting so fast she lost her footing and had to force herself to her feet.

This was home. This was her home. Why was it burning? Where was everyone? She couldn't smell anything over the smoke. She burst in the front door. Nora ignored the tug of the pack bonds, fearfully calling her to return to them.

As always, Nora was torn. She was on the outside, looking in, and she could only see the loss. And, when she was within the doorway, she smelled Matt. The fire was consuming the kitchen and the living room, but only licked one side of the stairs. The other side was clean, aside from a smear of blood. That was where Nora smelled him. In a daze, unable to feel the heat or building ache in her lungs, Nora followed the trail of red.

She found Matt on the top floor. The attic. Her bedroom for her entire life. Even in her head after moving in with Annaliese, this was the image conjured when she thought of her room. Her bed. Her home. The familiar and comforting and forbidden. In front of the window she'd climbed out of so many times, Matt had collapsed against the wall. One hand on his stomach, the other holding his phone. Nora saw her own contact pulled up on the screen, still lit and awake while the person holding it was not.

Matt was still. So still. His head at an unnatural angle. Maybe he would have survived the stomach wound that he'd struggled up here with, but someone had—

Nora couldn't even form the rest of that thought. "Matt?"

He didn't stir. Even when a crackling crash sounded below, he didn't move. Nora knelt in front of him. She shook his knee. Then, his shoulder. He didn't move.

"No…"

But she couldn't deny it. She lost sight of him through her tears. Nora jumped when Matt's phone started ringing. She blinked down at the screen, unable to think as she pried it from his lifeless fingers. Nora accepted the call and wordlessly held it to her ear.

"I know what you're doing, Nora," Gabriel said. "But you have no idea how far I'm willing to go to save this city. It isn't about memories, or grudges, or idealistic dreams. This is the reality of war. Of being an alpha. Of being a supernatural. You're too human. You're too weak. No matter how many new pack members you bring in, it won't compare to us. To Matt. I know he spoke to you. Maybe one day, you'll be a strong enough alpha to deal with dissenters. Maybe that's how you'll deal with Lupe, who can't seem to stop telling Marcus all your movements. I've told you, Nora, again and again, that this wasn't for you. That you don't know what to do with power. You're not an alpha, but a little girl crying over her best friend like—"

The sound of Gabriel's voice was no longer in her ear. Nora followed the phone's path, still beyond reaction, as Colbie lifted it. "Gabriel? You've gotten a head start, but I'd run further. Not that it will help. Be ready to die tonight."

Colbie tossed the phone over her shoulder and held out a hand to Nora. "Do you want to come with or wait for me?"

Nora couldn't find words. Her hand remained on Matt. He still felt warm from the flames. Not from body heat.

Because he was dead. Her home was burning down around her, and Matt was dead.

"Colbie?" Poppy spoke from the doorway. Her hands were lifted, and she stood between Annaliese and the stairs. Nora distantly thought she must be casting. Keeping the flames at bay to buy Nora time. Annaliese was, for once, speechless, though the way her eyes filled was almost enough to jolt Nora into feeling something more than a numbed rush. It made thoughts too hard. Nora turned on her knees back to Matt. She really couldn't breathe.

Colbie's arms came around her from behind. She was trembling, or Nora was, and her hug was so tight it momentarily pulled Nora back together. She pressed her cheek into Nora's, her cool face calming Nora's burning skin. Nora must have been closer to the fire than she realized.

"I know you can't talk right now," Colbie murmured, "But the alpha doesn't anyway. I can pick up Gabriel's scent. I will kill him, but the alpha gets first dibs. Do you want to use your new pack and finish the night how we all knew it would go, or do you want me to make sure you never have to think that asshole's name from this moment on?"

Nora let her head fall back onto Colbie's shoulder and tried to find the animal. Colbie was right. Past Nora's numbed shock, something hot was building in her core. As soon as Nora acknowledged it, she felt the change beginning.

"Leave him here. His ashes will settle with the house," was all Nora got out before she let the wolf save her from all this. She jumped out the window, found Gabriel's scent, and ran. A vampire at her side, death at her back, and a pack on her heels, Nora hunted.

Topher paced in the sideyard, hands fisted. Colbie's parting words and Josh's form between him and the Den kept him at bay as he watched the Den begin to collapse. He stepped forward, and even Josh watched close enough that he didn't try to stop Topher. Where were they? Why hadn't they gotten out yet?

From the topmost window, someone finally moved. Nora, in wolf form, burst out of the glass. The drop might have seriously injured anyone else, but adrenaline was a powerful beast, and so was Nora. She rolled and was back on her feet the next instant, taking off down the road with a howl that her pack picked up as they joined her. Colbie moved faster than Topher had ever seen her to get to Nora's side. Again, Topher fought the temptation to join them, but Colbie's words... *Someone needs to stay behind and watch the witches. Something bad is happening.*

So, Topher stayed. Green light lit the shattered window in the Den where Colbie and Nora had exited. If Poppy was casting, then she and Annaliese were safe. Poppy knew her limits, and Topher knew she was capable of even more than she thought. She would get Annaliese out.

Topher turned to go back inside. The street was drawing too much attention now, and he didn't want to test the wards in order to stay hidden. Josh stayed so close behind, his nose bumping the back of Topher's thigh with every other step. Each reminder of Josh's presence was more than welcome. The witches were all seated around the kitchen table and looked up when Topher entered.

"What's going on?" Ru asked.

Topher explained that he'd seen everyone leave the Den but Poppy and Annaliese. No other supernaturals were in the area that he could smell. With grim determination, Ryan left to check on their younger sister, Margot and Amelia trailing behind. Topher set his hand in the warmth of Josh's fur and turned to Ru. "Where's the drainer then?"

Josh stiffened under Topher's hand. So this was the big secret. Had someone else Topher loved as a human been turned? Did they worry how far Topher would go to help? Why was this so unspoken and horrible between them all?

Ru stood up slowly. Her eyes flicked to the door. She was unsure about doing this without Poppy, but she kept pace when Topher moved to lead the way out of the kitchen. Ru took them up the stairs and down the hall. The old wooden floors creaked under their steps, no matter how light-footed Topher's vampire abilities made him. Josh panted with anxiety, his ears pressed back and eyes wide. Topher almost told him to wait there but couldn't get the words past his nerves. Ru paused at the last door at the end of the hall, her hand in the air to open it, but the uncertainty struck again.

Topher didn't give her time to change her mind. Stepping

forward too quickly for human eyes, he twisted the knob and opened the door.

And felt the world collapse around him. A black hole sucking in all light except what was used to illuminate the figure on the bed.

Ru spoke quickly, but how was Topher to follow her words? He stumbled back a step, bumping into Josh and flinching away. A secret. He'd called this a *secret*. It was a cruel joke. It was everything that was wrong with this fucking city thrown back in Topher's face.

Before the anger could sweep in, Topher felt himself shutting down. Ugly, familiar words rising from the dark place he'd always shoved them into. Of course, Lana would lie to him about this. She thought he was hers to control, hers to hurt, hers to play with, and he was, wasn't he? Just another vampire, a monster of the night who was only alive because his boyfriend had died. The world had always been hateful and cruel. Why would a light like Dylan survive it? Why would Topher deserve that?

Of course, Poppy and Colbie thought him too weak to handle this. He'd hidden himself away from them for weeks. They couldn't trust him not to abandon them again. Looking at Julia now, that was exactly what Topher wanted to do. It was too much. He needed the darkness of his bed and the emptiness of his room, or he would…

Of course, Josh hadn't told him. Josh was a werewolf, a good supernatural. The type that had always worked to help humans. Topher could never be something like that. He had been corrupt and worthless for years before that side of the city touched him. He was the shadows, the evil in New Brecken, the disgusting monster that lived off *blood*.

Topher was aware he was gagging. He wasn't breathing properly. Ru was still talking, stepping forward to touch his arm, but he jerked away again. He didn't deserve touches and comfort and soft looks like the one taking over Ru's face. He'd done this to Julia, and now he was making Ru feel bad.

He had to stop hurting those around him. The only way to do that was to listen and do what Ru said. After that, he could disappear.

"I'm sorry," Topher's voice was too flat even over the roaring in his ears, but he didn't have the capacity to worry about that now. "What do I need to do?"

Ru blinked at the sudden switch in his demeanor. He didn't need to imagine what she'd just seen happen to his face, going from shock and devastation to…nothing. The careful, practiced mask. They couldn't see his thoughts. It wouldn't make them feel better, and Topher didn't want to feel worse. Josh was already whining, a hitch at the end of each breath, keeping his distance after Topher moved away from his touch but unable to shift. He couldn't try to talk him through this. That was good. Josh didn't need to feel guilty when his words didn't help the pit Topher had reached in his spiraling thoughts.

"Well," Ru began slowly, questioning if Topher could hear this, but they didn't have time to wait until another full moon. "From what I can parse from Beth's casting, she's found a way to use sorcery, werewolf power, and a bit of demon influence to *pause* the shift to vampire. At its simplest form, that's what she'd done to make the drainers. If I can distinguish the werewolf strength and if you can," she paused again but pressed on, "if you can hold back the shadow magic, you should be able to pick up where Reelings left off. We should be able to turn them into vampires, holding the other influences at bay until vampire resistance to magic takes hold. The drainers are caught in a vulnerable state—when they're still too human, but the vampire is starting to take root. That's when Beth infuses the shadows, Reelings constructs his charm, and the werewolf resistance to magic goes into play. She stops it all there. But, if you restart it…"

"You can cast enough that they'll be vampires and protected."

"And the charm, Topher. You'll be able to deconstruct the intricate charm block that Reelings placed on their minds. I think only you can, but I also think that wall of charm is containing who Julia is and attacked her when you pressed too hard on it. I'm almost certain that if you remove it, Julia will still be there."

He tried to let that buoy him from the pit he'd sunken into. Julia could still be there. But in the end, she'd still have been forced into this world Topher had dragged her into. Even more permanently now. Hadn't a part of him been relieved when he thought she was dead and no longer a monster?

It was those feelings that made Topher even worse than Julia in her drainer form. Topher tried to keep the self-loathing thoughts at bay as he moved forward. He needed to get through this. He could wallow, or worse, later. Topher knew Julia. He'd known her for years and years. She would look him dead in the eye and say she'd prefer being a vampire to what she currently was, but… She would rather be alive and human and studying and living up to all her potential if she'd ever been given a true choice.

If she'd ever stood a chance in Topher's world post-Dylan.

He owed her this much. If she wanted to retaliate later, he would accept that. Topher dropped to his knees at the side of the bed, Ru circling it to stand opposite. Her jaw was set, and she reached into the bedside table to pull out a sunlight brew. Swallowing it in one gulp, Ru nodded at Topher.

"Feel for the shadows if you can. Try to get them out of her or will them to help us. Otherwise, it's a normal making."

A normal making. Topher let out a hollow laugh, the mask slipping. The only making he'd ever done was to Colbie. Another reminder of his worth, but it didn't help in this situation. He could barely recall the process of turning Colbie, only that he'd remembered himself at the last minute and stopped himself from killing her. After that, some vampire instinct kicked in to save her life. To doom her.

The ability was still there. Some willful change in the saliva and internal push of charm while feeding. Topher knew his vampire self well enough to know it would take over and handle this. He would focus on the shadows.

Topher debated a long beat and then rose up again. He couldn't do this from Julia's wrist. He needed the most blood he could get, or whatever counted as blood in her veins. He stifled a gag at the scent of her, calling on that change in his saliva right before he latched onto her pulse point on her neck.

The taste was worse than the smell. The feel of her lifeless, papery skin was worse than that. She felt and tasted like a demon. Even her mind in response to the charm he pushed out had nothing for him to hold onto or influence. What spark of life did Ru's magic feel for her think this was possible?

"The shadows, Topher. Push them back," Ru said, voice already strained by the casting.

Topher let his fangs sink in fully and dove into the darkness.

CHAPTER 39

There were moments that Nora felt it was only desperate hope she was following and not Gabriel's faint scent, but Colbie stayed steady, brow furrowed. It gave Nora enough confidence to keep to the trail as her mind began to fracture, trying to ask questions she couldn't examine right now. She shut them down and clung desperately to the red haze of anger and Colbie at her side.

Before long, they were weaving through the trees of the forest. Nora had no memory of getting there, but her pack released barks and howls of excitement. Running—no, hunting, beneath the full moon was an exhilarating call to the wolf within. Nora remained silent, leading almost faster than they could follow as Gabriel's trail thickened in the air. They passed the section of the forest where he'd met up with what was left of his pack.

"I smell Reelings, too," Colbie said, the benefit of having a vampire in their midst. "But I think he's already gone."

Heavy in the air now was the smell of magic. Of rotting. Drainers and sorcery. Lots of it. Too much for there to be no sign of the monsters within the trees. Only Gabriel and his pack at his back in a semicircle remained in the clearing where the dark magic took place.

Gabriel was naked. His human form was deliberate, his expression smug. He knew, unlike himself, that Nora wouldn't attack him in a vulnerable state. Her morals were the only thing holding her in higher regard than him for many of the wolves at her back. But oh, how she wanted to prove him wrong, to attack now and permanently wipe that look from his eyes.

At least his confidence visibly dimmed when Nora's pack fanned out behind her, and he saw Colbie at Nora's side. Whatever Lupe had told him, it wasn't the true size of Nora's pack. Whatever Lupe had thought or done before, it didn't change the fact that she was as angry as anyone else behind Nora. A constant snarl and a string of drool on her lips as she thirsted for a real fight, eyes narrowed on Tio Marcus. Betrayal stung through her pack bond alongside a haunting, drowning regret. The Den had been Lupe's home. Matt like a little brother. Their destruction was the final straw.

It took everything in Nora to get the courage to shift. To face Gabriel and her unfiltered, human emotions. As she straightened into human form, her eyes dropped to his hands. The hands that had snapped Matt's neck and lit her home on fire. She dragged her gaze back up to meet his eyes, not bothering to hide the roiling emotions.

"How could you?" the words ripped from her core. Colbie took a step closer.

"A pack needs to be loyal," he said with a significant look toward Lupe. Nora stepped sideways to block his view. "And we're in a position to do much better than that rundown shack." A pointed barb that fell on Nora without landing. She realized she didn't need his reasonings. It didn't make anything better.

But Colbie put it together. Her hand swept the clearing, indicating to the summoning circle burning into the grass and the stench in the air. "You used it like Tiff Jennings used her coven."

Gabriel's gaze sharpened. His pack behind him stirred, Adriana cocking her head in confusion. Nora looked to Matt for his reaction. Her breath left her chest when his usual spot in the lineup was empty.

Gabriel redirected his pack's attention. "This isn't a place for a vampire."

"A vampire was just here," Colbie said with a scoff. "This is New fucking Brecken. Get used to it. Oh wait, you won't be alive long enough. I'm surprised your own pack hasn't turned on you, or did they not realize what this was? Killing the boy set to be the second-most powerful in your pack, destroying territory that has stood for years and would for many more? It reeks of the destruction of potential. Beth used this to create more drainers. To turn the humans *you* and your pack are supposed to be protecting. What kind of twist of logic did you come up with to convince them this is okay? Or are they all as depraved as you are?"

"Who even are you?" Gabriel sneered. "Some lower vampire without any power in the city?"

Colbie laughed. Her cavalier attitude sank its claws into Nora's skin, infusing her with confidence. Fear was distant with such an angry, fearless presence at her side. Nora was so glad Colbie was here, standing tall, refusing to be made smaller. Looking at Gabriel like a bug that was lucky to be alive. "My name is Colbie West. You've met my brother. He controls Fourth now, did you hear? He's the only person who has constantly remained ahead of you in the polls."

"You're going to hide behind your brother?"

Colbie smirked. "One text, and I could have all of Fourth here. One other text, and I can bring in two covens worth of witches. Another, and I bring in my human friends. Maybe they're illegal and out of fashion, but guns still exist in New Brecken. They still land a hit. I don't have to text my girlfriend to bring in the biggest wolf pack, but Henry would answer my call if I wanted another one. I don't care that I'm not the strongest vampire. Unlike some people, I'm quite likable."

"Fourth Street won't exist for much longer."

"I don't know that. But I do know you won't."

Colbie glanced to Nora then, question in her blue eyes. *Are you ready?* Ready to talk, ready to fight, ready to end this?

Was she?

Matt's sightless stare in her old, burning bedroom. Nora stepped forward. "I challenge you, Gabriel." It was all she needed to say—the right words. Simple. Direct. Powerful.

Gabriel didn't shift. He narrowed his eyes. "I've already won our challenge. You know how this ends."

"A challenge results in a weakening of pack bonds to the point where I am no longer alpha of my pack. You didn't do that. Accept my challenge, or prove yourself a coward."

Gabriel sighed. "You don't get it, Nora. My one flaw as alpha is my inability to reach out to new potential members. You've played directly into my hand with this. Once you die, your pack is mine. You think your little bloodsucker will live after that? You think I won't reach all my goals? Killing Reelings, the drainers, and the vampires, once you hand me that power?"

"You won't win."

"You *can't* win. This is my last offer, Nora Mora. You know how this fight will go. Submit to me. Join me in saving this city from the problems your father started. Right his wrongs before they spread. New Brecken's wild ideas and laws must fail, or more cities will fall to this madness."

"God," Colbie said, an eye roll in her voice, "And I thought Reelings was dramatic in his tendency to monologue. You two need to hang out less." Colbie stepped in close, a hand on Nora's stomach as she bent in to press a kiss to the curve of Nora's throat. The bliss centering, Colbie always bolstering.

She whined loud enough for the werewolves around to hear, "Can you shut him up already, babe?"

Nora smiled. How she could smile at a time like this was a testament to Colbie's magic. "Anything for you." Louder, for Gabriel. "Do you accept?"

His shifted, the wolf answering for him.

Gabriel's front paws weren't fully settled on the grass by the time Nora was lunging at him in wolf form. She was tired of this. Of the threats and of what he could make her feel. He'd ruined everything. Held her back. Killed her father, Matt, vampires, and who knew how many more? As their bodies collided, Nora struck out with more than claws and teeth. She choked the bonds to his pack, offering a tie of her own. Gabriel yelped. Nora hadn't even landed a true scratch.

Adriana accepted without hesitating. She nearly had last spring and must have regretted sticking with Gabriel to reach back for Nora so quickly. Gabriel felt the snapping tie, and his shock slowed him. Nora raked a claw down his face, blinding him on one side. His mismatched eyes were no longer a trait that would draw anyone in as she ruined his blue eye. The physical pain shook his bonds further. Luis, named after her father, accepted Nora next.

Nora knew well now the flush of strength that came with gaining new pack members. She could only imagine what a blow it must be to lose them. Gabriel struck back, hard and fast anyway. His last hope was to defeat Nora and get those ties back, along with anyone else who would accept him. Nora dodged one blow, and then they were both on their hind legs, snarling for a bite, claws searching for fur. A hot pain bloomed on Nora's shoulder, but it was directly below where Colbie's kiss lingered on her neck, easing the ache that might have hindered her. Nora rolled on the shoulder, surprising Gabriel with the motion when he was confident that side must now be a weakness.

Too quickly, too late, Nora stood from beneath him, maw finding his throat. Nora clamped on and tasted Gabriel's blood.

Unbidden in that moment, the memories struck hardest. The bike riding lessons. The lost boy who had found her father and a pack even before his first change. The pride her father had showered on Gabriel as he grew and exhibited his alpha qualities. The quick mind consistently winning cards and board games. The hatred toward vampires that was justified after they had killed his parents and their pack. The crush in the background of Nora's childhood, always watching and admiring Gabriel. Dreaming of being his beta.

But it wasn't a crush. It was jealousy. It was longing but a longing to be him. To hold his power and her father's pride and the pack's loyalty. The real tension underlying every memory with Gabriel was the deception, how he did everything to break her so slowly that she didn't even know it was happening until Colbie appeared and started building her back together.

Nora couldn't let go. To do so would be to admit Gabriel was right about her. To do so would be to lose the pack she'd built with words and her unique strength. To let go would be to abandon Colbie in favor of Gabriel once more.

It took him too long to die. Long enough that by the time he finally stopped twitching beneath her, the emotions had caught up to Nora, and the adrenaline had faded. Not all of Gabriel's pack accepted her invitation, something she didn't need to extend consciously. She let Tio Marcus and the others go. They would leave New Brecken packless failures. There was no place for them in the city or Nora's heart.

Nora shifted as Gabriel drew his last breath. Colbie dropped to her knees beside her immediately. A cold arm turned her away from the death and gathered Nora close, her pack crowding in enough to block the moonlight as Nora was wracked with a sob—guilt unavoidable. Her head swam with disbelief. It was finally over.

CHAPTER 40

Ru was right. Topher could feel the shadows inside Julia. Feel that corrupt magic that Beth bent to keep these creatures to the most basic and rotted aspect of vampirism. Topher recognized the hunger, the insatiable thirst for conquest, the submission to a maker's charm, but Beth's spell tainted and twisted it. Already, her commands were weakening under Ru's prodding, weakening the hold enough for Topher to take control.

The shadows had been forced to succumb to Beth's will and the life magic she sacrificed to control it. But Topher had been forged by the shadows. He spoke their language, and they *knew* him. It took nothing to call the darkness in. It wanted Topher, wanted to belong to him and not the strict confines of Beth's cage.

Once he'd taken in the shadows, the world seemed to darken behind Topher's closed eyes, but he wrangled and expelled them with easy practice, Dylan's loving protection holding up against the assault.

The task was far from over, though the effort made Topher feel too heavy and sluggish already. He searched for any spark of life and found it dull and distant in the blood they had been forcing down Julia's throat to keep her alive in her current state. That, coupled with Ru's sudden bursting life magic twisted with his power, was enough for Topher to follow, to begin unspooling, as he discovered how far Reelings had gotten in the making process. Julia was more vampire than human, but Ru was right about everything so far, so Topher committed and pressed in the charm and venom from his fangs that would complete the process. Then, as he felt it taking hold, he backed away from Julia's neck enough to lift her top lip and watch the fangs begin to glisten there. He shoved his wrist into their sharp points, ignoring the sound Josh made.

This was the last step. If it worked, Julia would wake up starving. Topher would have to hold her under his charm enough to get her to someone willing to be fed off of. He'd have to take her to Fourth. But, if Ru was wrong and Julia was still beyond his charm, he'd have to kill her again before he risked loosing her on the city.

"Jules," Topher's voice was raw, throat still burning and wanting to gag after her rotten taste. It didn't matter. The charm still came out. "Come back to me."

He found the wall blocking his charm as he always did, but it was softer than before. Curious, uncertain, crumbling. It only took the slightest push.

Julia's eyes fluttered. As they opened, black faded to hazel. She met his gaze, blinking.

Her voice was even worse than his when she spoke…but she spoke. "Toph, what the fuck is wrong with your eyes?"

He blinked and tried to suppress the shadows further. Even that movement felt too hard; his whole body drained and aching from whatever form of magic he had performed. Ru was slumped and panting on the other side of the bed. She kept lifting a sleeve to her nose and dabbing away the blood falling. Fortunately, a witch's blood wouldn't call to the thirst Julia no doubt was feeling.

"You remember me?" Topher didn't recognize the hope in his small voice.

Julia made a face. A familiar face. The one she'd made countless times when he didn't understand an assignment or a social cue, and Julia had to explain it to him. Julia never hesitated to call him out, to call him dumb, but she'd always had the patience to explain. "How could I forget your ugly face?"

Topher wanted to sob. He'd done it. Saved her. Doomed her. It was done, and he could finally give into the—

Julia's eyes shifted, too fast, away from him and to the doorway. Annaliese stood there, face ashen with shock. She had a duffle bag under her arm that smelled like smoke and Nora. There were tear tracks on her cheeks that made Topher feel momentarily murderous.

"What's going on?" Annaliese demanded, unaware of the grip Topher had taken on Julia's wrists and the way her entire body beneath him began to strain toward the delicious scent of Annaliese's hot, flowing, life-giving blood.

"Leave, Annaliese," Topher bit out. "It's not safe."

Annaliese, as ever, stood her ground. Josh moved to stand in front of her. She dropped the bag and crossed her arms. Topher glanced at Ru and found the witch already mouthing a cast to put a protective wall between Annaliese and the newly formed vampire. "What. Is. Going. On."

"She's a vampire now. I have to take her to be fed."

Annaliese's eyes jumped from Topher to Ru, shock in her eyes. She was almost speechless, but that wasn't something that happened to Annaliese and didn't last long. "You figured out how to save the drainers?"

"I wouldn't call this saved," Topher muttered as he pulled his attention away from Annaliese to contain the renewed struggle beneath him.

"Topher, please, let me go!" Julia finally gasped. "I'm so hungry."

Her eyes, familiar and pleading, almost did Topher in. He

bent closer, cheek to cheek, and momentarily stilled the writhing vampire. "You have to trust me, Jules. I'll get you fed."

He glanced back to the door long enough to find Josh and Annaliese sharing a look. A look he read quickly. They were shaken by Julia joining the equation. Unsure of Topher, of what they saw.

Their doubt cracked what was already shattering in Topher's chest. He forced himself to speak, the charm heavy. "I'm going to let you go, and you're going to follow me to someone you can feed from."

Julia nodded eagerly, eyes glazed, without her own thoughts. Topher was beyond feeling. Numb to it all, he stood and went to the window. He couldn't face Josh and Annaliese again. Couldn't slip past their warmth. He threw it open, the old window pane fighting him briefly before scraping open. Outside, it smelled like smoke and death. It smelled like endings. Ruins.

Julia was a silent shadow. Topher rolled out of the window and onto the slanted roof. They hit the ground, Julia breathing hard through the smell of the surrounding humans.

"Keep up," Topher said. His last words before he took her hand and started running. Julia, who had stood by him as steadfastly as Colbie had through all his mistakes, remained by his side all the way to Fourth Street.

It felt even more damning than the look in Annaliese's eyes when she'd seen what he'd done. Topher didn't deserve Julia again. Once she knew what had happened to her, he would lose this too.

He was ready for the breaking. The punishment of it wouldn't be enough to ease the guilt, but it was something.

Nora wasn't sure where she wanted to go. In the end, her grief knew Annaliese's steady presence best. She went to their apartment. Nora kept a change of clothes stashed near the building.

Colbie untangled the bag from the bushes and handed it to Nora so she could duck behind the shadow cast by the branches and change. Colbie took Nora's hand as soon as she freed herself from the twigs and leaves. The pack left, brushing her with snouts and soft shoulders as they went their separate ways. Some to their families and roommates. Some to the Alpha's Den. Some to the Jennings house. Nora's chest buckled with pain, thinking about the state of that neighborhood. They should have been breaking off to the Den, too, but it was no more—just a burnt scar of a lawn. Nora's eyes welled, and Colbie shifted her grip, wrapping an arm around Nora's waist to steer her inside. At the door to their apartment, Colbie paused. "Do you want to be alone with Annaliese?"

Nora was careening toward codependency. She didn't have it in herself to care. "I don't want you to ever leave."

Colbie answered like it was simple. "Then I won't."

"What about Topher?"

That got Colbie to frown. Nora leaned against the door, not quite ready to go in and face the reality that would be Annaliese's expression. One she'd practiced often, comforting Nora through each blow. Colbie stayed close and pulled out her phone.

Nora didn't want to ask. "What is it?"

Instead of answering, Colbie let her head drop onto Nora's shoulder as she typed a response to her latest message. It was her first indication of fatigue. Nora glanced at the window at the end of the hall. Panic crawled up her throat at the sight of the sky lightening outside. She didn't want Colbie to go, not even to sleep.

"Babe, what's wrong?" Nora repeated.

"Everything is okay," Colbie said to the floor. "Topher and Ru made Julia a vampire. I don't know how he's feeling about it, but it's too late to do anything when he's probably sleeping. Also, Poppy and Josh can handle it until I wake up, so don't let it add to your plate."

Nora frowned. "I can check in on him if I need something to do."

Colbie lifted her head, smiling a bit. She reached out, fingertips running down Nora's cheek. "Will you be okay? I can stay up and—"

"I'll be okay. If I'm not, I'll come and try to sleep with you."

Colbie quirked an eyebrow. "I'll definitely wake up for that."

Even after these steady weeks of being together, Nora blushed. "I meant actual sleep. Like the kind where I snuggle up with you and don't have to think."

Colbie kissed her, fleeting and gentle. "I'll hold you all day if that's what you want, or I'll sleep in the other room while you talk to Annaliese. Whatever you need, I'm here."

Nora felt a twinge of guilt at that. Topher needed his sister, too, but Colbie's words implied she was putting Nora first. And Nora was far too pleased by it. The alpha preened at the attention. Her bruised heart managed a flutter.

"I'll start with talking to Annaliese for a bit."

Nora got Colbie a change of clothes and settled her into bed. There was something soothing in the motions of taking care of someone else. In giving a goodnight kiss and a lingering look in the doorway, knowing Colbie would stay and be waiting for Nora when she needed to take refuge here.

Annaliese came out of her room as Nora shut her door. She was gripping the strap of Nora's old duffle bag, the sight of it so out of place, not shoved into her closet at hom—at the Den, that Nora blinked. Annaliese held it out. "Poppy and Ryan held back the flames while I packed it. Amelia helped float us down through the window. I thought you might want this piece of home."

Annaliese seemed more lost than Nora had ever seen her. The night had been too hard for everyone. How long had her best friend packed in Nora's room with Matt's dead body right there?

Hands shaking, Nora took the bag. Inside were her favorite books, a couple photo albums, some clothes, her old stuffed wolf that looked like her dad and had been her favorite toy. Nora almost couldn't see the rest as she began crying again. By touch, her hands found her favorite blanket and Matt's sweatshirt beneath it, causing a sharp crack and intake of breath. It was the last one of his that she'd stolen and he'd yet to take back. The constant swapping had been a staple of their preteen and teenage years. It smelled like them and smoke as she pulled it over her head, sobbing and fumbling so that Annaliese had to help. The bag was left on the kitchen counter as Annaliese pulled her and the blanket toward the couch.

Helen let herself in as Annaliese tried to get Nora comfortable. Nora fell into her mother's arms and cried for all she had lost. Again. Annaliese made hot chocolate like she used to after Luis Morales died, and Annaliese hadn't known how to make anything else. Helen scratched Nora's back like she used to when Nora was young, unable to find words to express herself and choking on emotion.

She felt understood in this room. This place she and Annaliese had made for themselves. Colbie within reach. It slowly sank in as the tears healed and cleansed. Nora had killed Gabriel. He could no longer hurt her or the people she loved. She wasn't crying for him, but her best friend. The last time they'd met eyes, there had been some hint in Matt that he wasn't beyond saving. That potential was gone. The Den was gone. The family and future she'd clung to were gone. All of it used to make more drainers. Wasted in the cruelest way.

Gabriel was still capable of hurting her. He'd used his final night to better Reelings's position, never thinking he wouldn't survive to sweep in as the hero in the last moment. Now, it fell to Nora and her friends, as they always knew it would.

Nora caught her breath. Drank some water. Tucked her

hands into the long sleeves of Matt's sweatshirt. She sat up, out of the warmth of her mother's arms, and reminded herself how strong she was.

"Were you at the Jennings house to see what happened with Topher?" Nora asked Annaliese.

Annaliese's expression tightened. In a controlled tone, she said, "Yes. I saw them make Julia. They have a way to subdue the drainers. A potion Poppy's been working on. They asked Josh to have Henry and his pack find as many as they can so Topher can change them."

"Did he seem okay?"

Annaliese's gaze dropped. "I was too surprised by Julia's sudden reappearance and what it meant. The two of them left right after. He took her to Fourth, I'm guessing. Keeping her away in case she's not fully… better."

"Why do you look angry?" Helen asked.

Nora studied her friend. She did seem angry. "Are you jealous?" But that didn't make sense. Annaliese wasn't jealous of Josh; why would Julia be different?

"It's…the secrets. They're getting to me," Annaliese, always straightforward, always taking action, *would* be annoyed by that.

"It's almost over," Nora assured her.

Annaliese nodded tightly. "I'm going to go talk to the assessors."

Nora's heart dropped. "Annaliese, why? We're going to finish this. We should talk to the witches. Make sure everyone is ready to make a stand. There's no need to involve the assessors. We have a way to—"

"I don't know who this 'we' is. The humans get left out at every turn when all these choices and discoveries and secrets affect us the most!"

Nora blinked at the sudden venom in Annaliese's voice. "Think before you talk to them. What it'll do for Topher to have them breathing down his neck while he tries to get the drainers under control. What it'll do to Poppy if you expose her as the witch making the potions."

"Fine. I won't tell them everything, but they deserve to know there's hope for the drainers. The police have been shooting them on sight. They can at least stop that. The humans need an update."

With that, Annaliese left, slamming the door at her back. A horrible feeling rose in Nora's stomach. She wasn't sure where her phone ended up after last night. Instead, she went to Colbie and found hers on the nightstand.

Nora called Poppy, too tired to do this alone.

Poppy stood stiffly, ignoring her headache, and went to her phone on the counter. She'd left it there after making a cup of tea and didn't have the energy to summon it with magic. It was too bright outside for Colbie to be calling. Poppy's throat closed with nerves as she answered, unsure how delicately to speak with the person on the other end.

"Hey, Nora."

She was not expecting Nora's brisk tone. "Poppy, I think, well, I don't think she'll do anything to hurt us, but Annaliese is upset about the drainer cure and how the humans haven't been kept in the loop. I wanted to warn you in case..."

Nora wouldn't accuse Annaliese of anything outright, but Poppy felt her stomach drop in response to the unspoken. In case Annaliese named Poppy. In case Annaliese offered the humans access to the potion the witches were currently brewing if they weren't making bracelets to the point of exhaustion too.

"Thanks for the heads up," Poppy said. She wanted to end the call, but she could hear the raw edge in Nora's voice and couldn't get the sight of Matt's body out of her head. "I'll take care of it. Take the day and get some sleep, okay? I can have someone drop off a sleep potion if you need help relaxing."

There was a beat, then Nora's voice, slightly surprised. "Thanks. My mom's here, and I'll lay down with Colbie in a minute. I'm okay."

"Okay." They said their goodbyes. Poppy stared at her phone for a beat. She was tempted to call Annaliese and stop her from going to the assessors, but Poppy didn't want to assume the worst. Annaliese had a strict moral code. She wouldn't expose them.

Would she? Annaliese had gone against Nora's wishes to protect Topher once, but that was Topher, the boy she had feelings for. In this situation, he needed protected again. Annaliese couldn't feel so strongly that the humans were being wronged to throw him under the bus…Could she?

Poppy didn't know. She couldn't be sure. It was enough to worry her. She tried calling. When Annaliese didn't answer, the worry wormed in deeper, darker. Poppy had to know what was happening. What Annaliese would say.

Poppy checked her potions one last time. They would be fine for a bit, though Poppy was running out of room to store vials. Daylight brews, subduing potions, healing, and protective mixes. Nearly all of Poppy's plants had been sacrificed to her brewing last night, so she'd gone to use the power available at the Jennings house with the wolves there. She couldn't help but think it wouldn't be enough to help the city.

Grabbing her keys, Poppy ran to her car. She didn't have to drive far, but she passed the wreckage of the Den. Police were bent over to examine the ashes, and firefighters chatted beside their trucks. Poppy ignored them. She stopped at the nearest grocery store lot, checked her personal wards, and sent a silent summons.

When she turned, Gus stared at her from the passenger's seat, unimpressed and miffed.

"I need you to follow someone again."

When Poppy finished explaining the situation, Gus accepted her orders without hesitation. Tiff Jennings's goal behind her horrible actions was to stop Reelings and his drainers from taking the city. No one had dreamed there was an option for salvation. That Tiff's magic would create someone capable of swaying the shadows. This was bigger than Gus's petty arguments, and his taking the situation seriously only created more anxiety for Poppy, realizing the balance that Annaliese could tip one way or another.

Poppy slipped into Gus's vision with this uneasy knowledge.

Gus was able to reach downtown in a blur. He approached the Supernatural Mediation offices right as Annaliese pulled up to the curb. She paused, tipping her head back, braids spilling over her shoulders. She looked small beside the building. Too young with her blue hair, baggy jeans, and winged eyeliner in the concrete, polished glass, and maintained trees of downtown New Brecken. Annaliese hesitated, but someone else approached, holding coffees and greeting Annaliese by name. She followed him into the building, up the elevator, and into the office space.

Annaliese went straight to Brett Campbell's door and knocked sharply.

It was horrible, blunt, and startling. All told in Annaliese's calm. They had discovered a potion to subdue the drainers and it was possible for a vampire to cure them of the demon influences. Annaliese smiled, breathless at the end. "We can save the humans," she declared. "We just need the potion to keep us safe and give us time."

Campbell steepled his fingers, staring Annaliese down. "Vampires have tried everything to prove they are not the ones responsible for the drainers. Makers have tried everything. Who made the drainer you saw?"

The answer was already in the air between them. Annaliese paused, reading something in the gleam of Brett Campbell's eyes. Something they'd all grown familiar with in their time spent around vampires.

"Annaliese, you are right that this is important. It's hope for New Brecken. It's a new future. Who can we thank for it?"

Gus shook his head. Everyone knew there was only one vampire capable of such shocking feats. The name, when it left Annaliese's blood-

less lips, was damning. "Topher will do everything he can to help the humans. He'll save New Brecken."

Campbell nodded. He dropped a hand, drumming his fingers. Finally, he turned to Annaliese. "You understand Topher is not a registered maker?"

"What?"

"If what you say is true, he broke the law last night."

"No, he——"

Brett nodded. "The recording of this conversation is all the proof we need."

Annaliese rose from her seat. "You can't be serious!"

"The laws are very clear and very serious," said Campbell. That gleam was back, and it became recognizable. Even Annaliese stumbled a step away from it. "If Christopher West is an undocumented maker, the repercussions are severe. If he is making vampires without the city's permission... well, not even Lana Williams was stupid enough to try that."

"You're charmed. You don't mean this. He isn't——"

Brett Campbell addressed the werewolf woman standing at the door. "Arrest Christopher West while he's sleeping. We won't be able to bring him in otherwise. Tonight, we will go and question his people without him there to sway their answers."

"No!" Annaliese tried to bodily block the werewolf from leaving and earned herself a body check that sent her sprawling. Campbell stared down at her as he went to leave his office.

"You will remain for questioning."

Annaliese did no such thing. With the werewolf gone, only startled humans remained. Annaliese flung herself out of the office. Gus slammed the door behind her, gleefully throwing down the bookcase beside it to block Campbell's path.

Gus swept out the door, causing chaos, throwing papers, tipping coffee cups, opening windows, and knocking over trashcans. He effectively held back anyone who would have thought to chase Annaliese or stop her from escaping.

. . .

Poppy pulled herself out of Gus's eyes, lifting her phone and beginning to dial in desperation. Raven first, and when that went unanswered, anyone else she could think that would be near Fourth Street. But the city had been busy last night. Wolves were sleeping off the effects of the full moon, even Josh. Poppy drove as quickly as she could, but she was under no pretense that the assessors wouldn't have people positioned closer to Fourth than she was currently. She should have gone home. Their apartment on Sixth Street would have been so much better.

Thinking of places closer, Poppy called a number more recently programmed into her phone, heart in her throat. She talked a closely warded Rosenfield to Fourth, to Happenstance, and the rooms Poppy had only heard about upstairs.

Rosenfield, moving quickly, somehow didn't get there soon enough. The feeling that crashed into Poppy shouldn't be familiar.

"There's only a girl sleeping here. I'm sorry, Poppy. Topher's gone."

"Maybe he wasn't there. Can you check—"

"The sheets are messed up, and the nightstand is crooked. They weren't gentle. They took him. I'm sorry. I see the human impressions, but they look charmed if that's any consolation."

It wasn't, but Poppy had to voice her appreciation to Rosenfield for venturing onto Fourth. Poppy pulled over. Out of ideas. This all had Reelings's hands in it. The charm, waiting to be activated until Topher was vulnerable, and they had something on him. Something to report and ruin his high approval among the humans that Reelings was gathering to his cause. Poppy didn't know what she could do as her socials lit up with the news of Topher's crimes.

When Josh finally called back, answering was one of the hardest things Poppy had ever done. At least Colbie wasn't awake yet. Poppy had a few hours to prepare for that conversation.

CHAPTER 41

It was natural to gather at Fourth. Topher's Fourth Street, even in his absence, was a completely different place to the block Poppy had first gotten to know. She drove past the cleared, blackened place that was once the Maker, trying not to look at it. Trying not to think of a similar view south of town. Trying not to think about fire. Fire that wasn't hot enough to turn Matt to ash. Fire Ryan had to strengthen so bones didn't remain in the wreckage.

Down the block, after the parking garage, Poppy pulled to a stop in front of Happenstance.

This world was strange in the daylight. In the summer heat, the surrounding clubs looked human and oppressive. None of the drowning music, flashing lights, and occupied shadows that created the seamless world of vampires. A garbage can to the left was overflowing with food truck wrappers, though the truck was nowhere to be seen. There was a sparkling jacket discarded by the steps of Blank Space across the street. A pair of heels in a puddle lining the curb. The only activity was the humans going sluggishly in and out of the high-end hotel two doors down. The trimmed shrubbery and valet parking were wasted on the blinking, dazed humans who had dropped all their money for a chance to stay in the vampire territory, only to find the new world they had discovered ripped into the ordinary as the sun rose and vampires retired.

Poppy had never ventured past the Maker. She took her time examining the street. Cleaners were sweeping stoops, and a garbage truck rumbled nearer to empty the full trashes. The city didn't pay to maintain Fourth Street, but the vampires spared no expense to reset their businesses to pristine every day.

Sitting on the steps leading into Happenstance, Josh waited with his head in his hands. Raven was beside him, holding an ice pack to her lip. Poppy felt a wave of affection for the girl. Topher hadn't been entirely alone. Someone had been there, trying to defend him. She hadn't been enough, but there had been someone who cared. Raven stood as Poppy approached. "I can't wake anyone up. Lana sometimes can, but not this deep into summer. What do we do? If Solas and Patter wake up and he's gone…"

Raven didn't finish the thought. Even in the daylight, her world revolved around vampires and their pushes for power and schedules.

Josh took clenched, shuddering breaths. It struck Poppy how different he and Annaliese were. How could Topher compare them? Pick between them? He couldn't, and it had never made more sense. It was easy right then for Poppy to set aside every hurt feeling. They were flimsy. Healed. A remembered pain irrelevant to the current situation. Settling herself beside Josh, she slung an arm over his shoulder and held him in tight.

"I had to go update Henry. I wasn't gone that long. I don't know how—"

"They had people ready for this situation. They want to ruin Topher for the humans. They were probably waiting to have something on him since he asked to be registered. If Reelings could get him out of the picture and clear Fourth Street for himself, that was all he needed. To know where Topher was, to know he was contained and wouldn't appear again at the perfect time to ruin things."

Josh scrubbed his eyes one last time before lifting his head enough to look at Poppy. His lids were red-rimmed, but he wasn't crying like Poppy thought. He looked mad. "How are we supposed to find him? He doesn't have a scent to follow. Magic doesn't work to follow him?"

It was a strange full circle. On their first date, Poppy had been consumed with the very same questions. Poppy took a breath. "Ru's burnt out from the bracelets. She's napping and will look for him as soon as she can, but it might take time. I have someone looking." But the city was too large for one poltergeist to search on his own. He knew where to start every other time Poppy had sent him to follow people. His chances of finding Topher, even sweeping through walls and doors, were slim. They had no idea where Reelings slept during the day and had been looking for weeks. If he kept Topher in the same place, the chances were low that they would discover the hideout now.

If Reelings's orders were to keep Topher alive.

Miserable, Josh said, "Ru should keep working on the bracelets." Poppy silently agreed. Protecting the humans and vampires from Reelings's charm was too important.

Poppy's phone started ringing. Poppy pulled it out, stomach falling. It was Chance. He'd never called her before.

"Chance!"

Josh jumped at Poppy's loud voice, but his calling reminded her of other means available to them to look. Technology.

"What's going on? Why is Nora pissed and gathering her pack?"

"How do you know?" If Poppy hadn't thought to call Chance. She'd only worried they would break the news to Colbie. Focused on calling Josh. Chance wasn't around enough. He didn't insert himself, content to simply exist in his siblings' orbit and plan a new life around them.

"I was checking the cameras at the club. Seriously, what's happening? She looks upset."

Poppy drew in a deep breath and explained Ru's discoveries, how she and Topher had made Julia, and—

"Julia? Jules isn't dead?" Chance's voice broke, and Poppy cringed. She'd forgotten how ingrained Julia had been in Topher's human life. Of course Chance knew her and cared about her well-being.

"Not dead. Undead now," Poppy said. "But when the assessors found out, they had Topher arrested for making without being registered."

"How did the assessors find out?"

Poppy hesitated. She'd called Nora on her way to Fourth, and apparently, Annaliese had heard they were meeting here. Her car was turning onto the block, Nora and a good portion of her wolves behind her. "Doesn't matter. Do you think you can hack them again?"

"The assessors?"

"Campbell had to say at some point where they were holding Topher. We have to find him."

Chance pulled in a breath, but Poppy heard the click of computer keys. "I'll call you back if I find anything."

Poppy hated to do it, but she had an idea of what the rest of her day would look like. She didn't have the time to go searching for Topher. Not when Reelings would no doubt attack, using his drainers before Poppy and Ru could take them from him. "Call Josh. Do you have his number?"

Chance hummed the affirmative, already consumed with his task. Poppy hung up and turned back to Josh. He wasn't watching Annaliese's car but giving Poppy a grateful, tiny smile. "We'll find him," she assured him.

Josh nodded. He braced himself before he turned to face

Annaliese and Nora. And swiftly turned back to look down at Poppy on the stairs.

"I'm really mad at her right now," he admitted. "I'll go try and help Chance."

"Do you know anything about computers?" Poppy asked.

He shook his head quickly. "I'll bring Danny." Then he whipped off his shirt and was gone the next moment, a wolf running against the tide of the other pack.

Annaliese's face was devastation. Unlike anything Poppy had seen from her before as she exited her car. Even Nora was wary as she got out of the passenger seat, looking at her best friend as if she didn't know how to interact with this side of her. This guilt-ridden, trembling hands version of the girl they knew. Poppy crossed her arms and waited. Let Annaliese break the silence. Raven glanced back, clearly not liking this plan but following Poppy's lead.

And Annaliese dropped her eyes. She'd never looked so subdued before. "I'm sorry. I didn't think that this would happen. I thought the humans deserved to know. They deserved some hope. They gave New Brecken to the supernaturals and not even leader meetings have been happening. They had no idea what was going on, if they were in danger, or what the drainers were. They deserved some good news. I wanted them to know Topher was helping them. I didn't know they were charmed."

"They might have done this even if they weren't," Poppy said, voice hard with the trauma of witches. Humans had always distrusted them. Always made underhanded moves to put themselves in positions of power when they couldn't combat magic directly.

"No." Annaliese looked up, the fire sparking in her eyes once more. "You don't know that and talk like that is why I have to be the one in our group to think about them. You don't care about us. I can't imagine how it feels to be a witch, but you are the ones with power. You can't just—"

"And you're the ones with the numbers!"

"We're both being slaughtered in this city!" Annaliese stepped forward, pointing a shaking finger in Poppy's face. "No one will get anywhere if we hold each other down! If you could reframe your thinking and decenter yourself, how would you help the humans against the drainers?"

Poppy swallowed, hating this, hating the risk and exposure. Not to humans but of what lay in her core. Secrets, cowardice, and the desire to hoard what little magic she contained for herself and her loved ones. She didn't want to face this part of herself. Poppy believed herself to be a kind person. She felt her priorities were justified. Poppy was just getting to know this world that her mother had kept from her, and she wanted to believe she was a good addition to it.

But Poppy also wanted to be friends with Annaliese, with Molly, with her biochem study group from last spring, and that boy in her lab who was so effortlessly funny that she always left their experiments with sore cheeks. Poppy fed off the beautiful human life that filled the Alpha's Den and enjoyed the human accomplishments. She'd never had a better latte than the one made by Jay's hands at Vegan Your Day, an establishment that believed as strongly as she did that they could maintain the sanctity of life energy and sacrificing convenience for the better of all.

Suddenly, the contradiction struck. Poppy would do anything for her family, her friends, and animals she would never face. Her fear kept her from extending that care to the humans she loved to live alongside. And they would never know her, never love her back, if she stood down now and let them face New Brecken on their own. If she didn't throw everything she had into defending them.

Drawing in a breath that reached her core, soothing fear and hesitance, Poppy began talking. She began to plan. Something that would take even Reelings by surprise. Then, she called the covens. When Kallow didn't answer, she tried again.

And again. Poppy and the humans of New Brecken would not be ignored.

Grinning, Annaliese started to send out the texts.

Topher woke up surrounded by Reelings's scent. Unwarded, unhidden. There were no windows but fluorescent lights above, a bed in the corner, and the sturdy wooden table where Topher found himself. He blinked, straightening and wincing at the crick in his neck that quickly healed and soothed. He'd been sleeping sitting up, tied up tight to the thick wooden chair. The space was like an office, cold and sparse, with a few touches to make it homier—the patterned rug, the bed… a wall covered in post-its and plans.

This was where Reelings had been hiding. Topher's stomach sank as his nose picked up more information than he wanted to believe. Finally, his eyes found Brett Campbell on the screen of the laptop sitting on the table in front of him. Out of charm's reach and in the back of a car.

"Christopher West, you've been taken under arrest."

Topher didn't even bother to ask the charges. He pulled at the metal cuffs and winced at the newly discovered stiffness in his arms. They hadn't been gentle, getting him here. Though he'd been defenseless and unconscious, they had hurt his body, and he hadn't even woken up. There was a tinny sound ringing in Topher's ears. His breath quickened unnecessarily.

Topher battled the panic. He tried to remember the last time he felt safe. Falling asleep in Josh's arms. He drew in his first full breath since waking, momentarily settled.

"Don't you have any questions?" Campbell asked.

"Would it matter?" Topher tugged again at the cuffs. He thought maybe he could break them, but the heavy metal door opposite him didn't even have a window to shatter. Even in the bright, white light of the fluorescent bulbs above, shadows were crawling toward Topher. They lingered with him, heavier than ever. Topher tried not to watch their progress.

Campbell wanted to talk. Maybe he was a decent man, despite what his actions would do to Fourth Street by holding Topher here and leaving the vampires without a leader. And if Fourth fell, the wolves would be there to protect the humans, but who would keep the city afloat? Topher had seen the numbers. He'd realized how helpful the vampires had been. Free feeding and citizenship in exchange for clubs that almost exclusively funded New Brecken's economy. Money was funneled into UNB, charities, the roads, food banks, and social programs. More money than Topher had thought, more money than the humans likely realized. Suddenly, the control of vampires made much more sense, but in a strange twist of respect, Topher realized how little the Big Three had kept for themselves. They'd been content to have a place in the world. Topher had been so close to having that for himself.

New Brecken, this damn city, needed Fourth Street. And Fourth Street needed Topher. He again shook at his bonds, surprised by his desire to get free. Once he'd acknowledged it, it floated away. Emotions always too mercurial.

Campbell's following words reminded Topher of what he'd done last night. "We were told this morning you used your abilities as a maker."

Julia. Doomed to be a vampire, same as Colbie.

Topher's arms went limp. He stared at Campbell's face on the screen. The floors above his head were silent, but Topher knew where he was now. The Supernatural Mediation offices. He'd been above this room once before, not knowing Reelings was living in the basement. Likely, Beth had warded this space so thoroughly to keep Reelings hidden that no one would find Topher now.

Losing some confidence in the face of Topher's silence, Campbell pressed on. "You made without being registered. That's a breach of the laws."

"Yeah." There was no point in arguing. He was alone. Bound. Hidden so well he hadn't even been able to sniff Reelings out in this room when he'd been in the very building.

"We're going to Fourth Street now to see how many other laws were broken under your watch."

Topher recognized some of the buildings off to the side of the screen. Campbell was about to pass Patty's.

"Fortunately, we have a vampire willing to help us get your people in line."

Topher's eyes went to the bed. Reelings must wake earlier than Topher did. Had they been in here at the same time? The ringing began once more in Topher's ears. "So why are you filming? Why tell me any of this?"

Campbell blinked, and Topher knew the look. "He told me to."

"Reelings charmed you."

"No."

Again, it wasn't worth arguing. "So, you're just going to film the whole thing, making me watch while you destroy what I worked for?"

"Yes, I…" Campbell trialed off. He wasn't paying attention to Topher anymore, but the roads. "Why are there so many people?" he asked, the same panic in his voice that Topher felt wash over him. Charmed or not, Campbell cared about putting humans in danger.

Reelings was going to take Fourth tonight with an army of charmed humans, the assessors included. Too many people would be caught in the crossfire.

"Campbell, you have to turn back. This isn't safe for anyone." Topher found himself wishing for the ability to charm for the first time.

But Campbell wasn't listening anymore. He'd muted Topher and passed his phone off with instructions for the man to keep filming. They had double parked at a familiar street. Topher couldn't see much on the small screen, but he knew where the Maker once stood like he knew his childhood neighborhood.

Topher was surprised by all the feelings bubbling painfully behind his sternum. He was used to helplessness. Used to how it slipped to the numb. He didn't know this regret as he watched Campbell step onto Fourth. Topher, reluctantly, without even realizing he was doing it, had been planning. In the back of his mind, when he didn't catch himself, Topher had been dreaming up a future. He'd thought he'd have more time to mold Fourth Street. To thoroughly question Patter and Solas and find if he could trust them or anyone. He'd been remembering Lana's other lowers more and more as he witnessed the same comfort they'd shared in the different vampire factions. He'd wanted that again. In his own lowers. Topher had plans to figure this out, to take his spot. To save the city for Colbie and Chance and Poppy and Ru and Josh and Annaliese. He wasn't willing to let them down, yet the battle they had all been preparing for was beginning, and Topher wasn't there. He regretted the loss of opportunity. He missed his chance to finish this.

Topher was angry. He didn't want this one chance to finish this ripped from him. Didn't want Reelings to win in this, too. Topher had always thought that he would face Reelings. He would be there when it all came to a head, and then, he would either win or die. He'd never prepared to survive to see Reelings take control. He'd never once imagined leaving Fourth Street and his loved ones so vulnerable.

He watched as the humans gathered, waiting. Reelings joined them under the streetlight, appearing seemingly out of nowhere. The humans shifted, some fearful and nervous, some too charmed to do more than stare into the night.

"You gave me little warning, Campbell. I would have enjoyed more time to speak with the West boy if you had waited to move."

"You said to obtain him at the earliest possibility and position ourselves on Fourth. We didn't have anything on him until this morning."

Reelings frowned. "I understand that. But you could have waited to approach Fourth Street. My demons and monsters aren't ready to take the block yet. It takes time to summon th—" Reelings turned suddenly. Topher wanted to reach out and shake the screen. It didn't pick up the noises that Reelings could hear around him.

Topher had no warning when Zayn stepped into the light, face pulled into fake puzzlement. Topher knew the expression and easy stance was feigned, but none of those gathered knew Zayn as well.

Reelings turned, sickening kindness in his voice. "Can we help you?"

"We're looking for someone."

"Tell me who." Charm there.

"Our First."

Topher's jaw clenched at the term and obvious coaching. It had Lana's fingers all over it. First was once Reelings's title. Everyone under him his seconds. It was the genesis of the term they still used in New Brecken. Zayn used it purposefully to set Reelings off. Topher could only see the back of Reelings's head, but the way the vampire stalked forward had Topher yanking at his chains harder than ever, ignoring the fierce pain in his left shoulder.

He stilled when Zayn lifted his hands in an appeasing gesture. "We were wondering if you saw him." Zayn wore one of Ru's bracelets. Pretending to feel the effects of Reelings's charm.

"I'm sure you were. Who is looking, then? Tell me now."

If Topher still got goosebumps, the smile that Zayn shot Reelings at that moment would have made them erupt. It was a smile meant to test, to push. "I told you."

"Yes, your First. Me."

"You?"

"No one else can charm all the vampires in the city."

"So why can't you charm me then?"

"I am."

"Are you?"

Zayn was buying time. But putting himself at too much risk, and Topher didn't know why. Did he think Topher was coming? Was Nora on her way? Colbie? Topher yanked and yanked, but the events on the screen, so far away, played on without him.

Poppy turned away from watching Zayn. He'd gotten close enough to text that the drainers and demons were coming. Reelings had said so before they noticed the vampire in their midst. The witches behind the bar at Happenstance were ready. Rosenfield, Kallow, and Jennings. Even a few witches without covens who had stayed in touch with the Mothers. There was one Mother Poppy had never heard of. She came out of hiding at Rosenfield's behest and a promise that her little ones would be kept secret and safe at home. She kept rubbing her pregnant stomach, worry pinching her brow until Heather came over with questions about car seats.

They looked exhausted. Every witch had been brewing or trying to mimic Ru's casting to make bracelets. Neither was a magic form that they were used to, and the drain on their magic supply was immense. Poppy would never think of her magic the same way again. Not even her lingering childhood self-esteem issues could pretend the looks on their faces when she passed were anything other than respect.

They had shelves of potions and armfuls of bracelets to show for the day. The two groups stood at either side of Happenstance. Witches handed the drainer-subduing brews and bracelets to the vampires and humans in the two lines. The werewolves were on the other side of the expansive dance floor. They surrounded Henry and Nora as the two alphas coached their packs on what they would do tonight. Poppy gazed about the room, noting even Gus was there, passing vials to a perplexed Margot.

Never in her life had Poppy felt like this. Like she'd taken control. Wrangled sense into a desperate situation that no one else had prepared for on the same level as she had. Poppy had been brewing and experimenting for weeks. Half of the potions being distributed right now were hers. Humans shimmered with the dusting of her protection. Vampires listened to her directions. Werewolves looked proud to share their strength.

Maybe Topher hadn't had the time to bring Fourth Street in line as he'd hoped, but no one here wanted Reelings back in control. Solas, Patter, Lana, and Colbie ensured every vampire knew what was expected of them. They ensured everyone was fed and at full strength and listening to Poppy. Poppy, who stood before them as a witch.

The unexpected spotlight would once have made her shrink, but she was flourishing. Poppy had volunteered to lead this endeavor. Doing so exposed her irrevocably. The witches had brewed and cast the bracelets in private, and now they passed them out with humans like Jay and other Seers who lived in New Brecken, acting like they were all the same. Rosenfield's daughters had even cast to change their features enough so that they looked less like sisters. It had been a huge argument when Ru wanted to stand up here with Poppy. The fight only tapered off because Ru had done most of the casting and had to save what remained of her energy to help Topher make more drainers into vampires when they found him. Humans, vampires, and werewolves came to Poppy to ask about the potions and bracelets. Annaliese took pictures of them all working together, and Poppy allowed her wards to slip enough to capture her face. It was the most terrifying and thrilling thing she'd ever done.

When Zayn texted that Reelings had arrived, Poppy walked

out with the rest of the leaders, heart racing and with Colbie at her side. They couldn't find Topher. Josh and Chance hadn't had any updates. This thing with Reelings was finally upon them, and the void where Topher should be ached in the same way his absence while in his grief had hurt. But they were doing this for him. To end this for him so they could find him later. Everyone had rallied when the newly appointed First had gone missing. Humans with guns and tattoos of roses on their forearms, werewolves with protection detail experience, and even humans from soccer teams and high schools. So many stepping out of the clubs behind them.

Poppy prayed to the Mother it would be enough.

CHAPTER 42

Topher hated this older model of computer. Hated whatever shitty camera was recording on the other end. He couldn't see enough, yet saw too much. Humans and vampires stood behind a line of snarling wolves. The glint of glass vials, flasks, and water bottles in hands. But everything moved too fast for Topher to spot faces, to check that everyone he cared about was there or not. No flash of blue braids, no determined yet soft eyes in wolf or human form, no messy buns, or blue glow. He strained his eyes as if it would help, but the video grew even more grainy, and he growled in frustration, yanking at the metal cuffs on his wrists behind his back repeatedly.

A standoff settled on the street. From the hissing background noise in the speakers, Topher knew the drainers had arrived. Reelings gave a sharp command and stepped forward, keeping the creatures behind the assessors.

Topher caught a glimpse of Colbie and Nora as Reelings began talking in that specific tone he and Gabriel had shared. The one that said he was reasonable and they simply needed to listen to his explanation. The tone that hadn't worked once, so Topher had no idea why he kept trying.

"—and to show up with an established and beloved alpha's murderer!" he was saying. Nora flinched, but she was the only one to even blink at the accusation. The camera began to swing, briefly finding Annaliese and her bored expression before sweeping over the shadows behind the person filming. His breathing picked up, and Topher realized why. The shadows were shifting, and the hissing drew closer. Reelings's control was not complete.

And when Beth stepped out of the dark, the sharp breath of the camera holder spoke to how unreassuring her presence was. Beth looked worse than Tiff Jennings had toward the end. Her veins were blackened. The whites of her eyes murky gray. That was all Topher saw under the streetlight before she sneered at the camera and pushed it away as she passed. Topher saw her shuffling, stumbling steps before the man righted the camera, and she came to stand beside Reelings.

"This is more humans than we anticipated," Beth observed, looking out over the unimpressed and determined faces separating them from the three looming clubs down the block.

"We have even more supporters," Reelings said, sweeping a hand behind them at the charmed audience. Beth took in their dazed expressions and didn't look reassured.

"What do you suggest we do?" he asked, patronizing and obliging.

Beth shook off her hesitancy. "We finish this. End the laws and control the humans. No use dragging it out."

"I want my victory cemented. Unquestioned," Reelings reminded her, gesturing toward the camera. "Thorough."

Over their shoulders, Topher could see Poppy, Nora, and Colbie had their heads ducked together. Poppy seemed to be the only witch present. She looked horrified by Beth's appearance.

"So then take it. Take the clubs and go back to kill Topher. What are you waiting for? I'm tired."

Reelings's jaw worked. "Fine." He must have turned with his charm ready, pausing to listen to the sound of doors slamming at his back. Too many doors. Too many charmed and helpless humans picked their way through the darkness to stand behind Campbell's men. The camera took them in, proof of Reelings's influence on the city. The faces were blank. The features of the humans were far too relaxed, even as they held whatever weapons they could grab. Guns that Topher hadn't seen since his days with Hunter. Knives and flickering tasers. Before this night, this fight had been between the supernaturals. Magic was a threat, but even then, it didn't work well against other supernatural groups. Death had never been so blatantly readied. Humans were so fragile. Topher knew well how quickly a demon could kill one, but even that paled in comparison to gunfire. And when the camera turned back, he saw Reelings's people weren't the only ones in possession. Those gathered to defend Topher's territory were also armed. Humans would battle. Topher felt sick. Somehow, with the laws and bliss and shaking peace, he had thought New Brecken beyond the use of firearms. Crime had dropped so much. How could anyone think Reelings was doing good? How could Beth, the only one not charmed and with no plan to usurp him, agree with his methods?

There were too many lives at stake.

Topher was almost hopeful when Reelings called to his opposition, charm and confidence in his voice. "Move aside!"

But none of the humans moved. Topher's jaw dropped, realizing Zayn wasn't the only new person wearing a bracelet. They must all be prepared.

Beth didn't care. She was done with the stalemate. With a wave, she sent a flurry of demons crashing into the front lines. The camera barely helped Topher to know what was happening then. Wolves and demons collided. A wall of blue light flared into existence. Topher couldn't see beyond it but saw Poppy's outline at its center. The sudden attack, the release of demons, was so swift and heartless that Topher's stomach twisted. He was trembling, drowning in panic. Helpless to do anything but break skin and maybe bone as he tugged and tugged at the metal and ropes holding him back.

"Leave the witch's protection and step aside!" Reelings bellowed. Demons shied from the wall, and any that had made it past were already dead. The drainers edged closer but had enough self-preservation to keep from the light. They kept looking back at Reelings, but he gave them no direction. Topher didn't want to know how many daylight brews powered this show of magic, but Poppy wouldn't hold out for long.

"Your charm isn't working!" Beth shrieked. Reelings's charm had built this plan. It was something they counted on at all times. It hit Beth hard to see it fail.

"Solas, Patter, to me. Control your lowers!" Reelings kept trying.

Laughter on the other side of the flickering wall. Reelings ducked forward, squinting. Even Topher could already see how Poppy was flagging, but those gathered behind her were shifting on their feet, readying. Sending humans to the back of the group, Topher hoped.

"It's the bracelets," Reelings said. He was too fast, too clever. He'd once ruled this city and it wasn't through luck. Topher's heart sunk low. Halfheartedly, he pulled at his restraints again.

"No, no, no," he was barely aware of himself whispering as he watched Beth raise a hand and snap. Shadows whipped from the ground. She staggered but remained upright as the soft clatter of beaded bracelets hitting concrete sounded.

"Hold yourselves at the ready," Reelings commanded, too smug. Topher didn't know what he meant, but the charmed humans did. Guns and knives lifted, pointing at the temples and throats of their bearers. Reelings looked to Poppy. "Drop your wall, girl."

After a moment's pause, Poppy did. What choice did she

have? Topher could see past her well enough to note not all the humans were holding themselves hostage. Only about the first three rows. A testament to Beth's failing power that she couldn't take all the bracelets off.

Reelings looked to Beth again. "Send in the demons again. The wolves won't be held for long."

Beth did so, and chaos erupted. The demons ignored the still humans, attacking the vampires and werewolves, pushing them back as Reelings watched. Beth chanted, commanding the demons, keeping them focused and from running away. The first of the yelps filled the air. Topher knew he wouldn't be able to distinguish Josh's sounds as a wolf, but he tried to listen for him anyway.

Reelings looked at the humans. The humans stared blankly. Except one.

Annaliese had noticed what Topher did. She was pretending but could do little to disguise her sharp eyes as they swept to Beth. She had two choices. Go for Reelings to try and disrupt the charm, or go for Beth and stop the demons. Topher didn't want her to do either. He yanked so hard at his hand-cuffs that something finally shifted, but the pain of it took him by surprise. He tried to catch his breath, disentangling his freed arms as anxiety overpowered him, and Annaliese made her move.

With their focus on the demons, Annaliese moved too fast for Reelings to react through his surprise or for Beth to raise a hand to defend herself. Annaliese darted forward and landed a solid, quick punch to Beth's throat.

She'd chosen correctly. In true Annaliese wisdom, she'd gone for the weaker opponent she stood a better chance against. She'd gone for the option that helped the majority. Beth crumbled, clutching her throat, unable to breathe or control her demons. The closest demons turned to her. An unprotected witch in their ranks, werewolves, humans, and vampires forgotten. As a writhing mass, they jumped at her weakness. The camera swung away, the man holding it gagging.

Without Beth, the tide of demons broke, and any organization they had fell away. The wolves began to howl in victory rather than yelp in overwhelmed fear and pain. And the humans in the back of the line swarmed forward, grabbing hands and transferring extra bracelets to those caught in Reelings's thrall.

Reelings turned to Annaliese, sneering. *"You."*

Annaliese had run from the demons that swarmed Beth, panting. She straightened, eyes wide but brave mask in place. "Me," she agreed with a smirk.

Reelings took a step in Annaliese's direction, fangs dropped and expression murderous.

Nora threw herself from the chaos, blocking her best friend from Reelings's view. Topher drew in a breath, one arm finally free from the thick ropes. Unfortunately, it was the wrist he'd broken. He struggled to use his hand to free himself further.

Nora would never let anything happen to Annaliese. Reelings didn't bother to acknowledge her. He was a runner. He was a man who hid behind power. With a sharp look, he sent directions to the drainers and humans waiting at his back. Even the person holding the camera took up the unspoken command. The camera dropped. Topher saw feet. Nora's running after Reelings's, and then there were too many shadows. Not even the bursts of light from Poppy's hurled potions could make sense of what he saw.

Topher sank into the chair. Fear, pain, and despair threatened to consume him, but a second before the shadows swallowed the fluorescent light overhead, the door rattled. Again. Again. Then, with a bang, it flung open.

Topher pulled in a breath of fresh air, the shadows clearing as only Josh could make them.

He blinked, stunned by the sudden familiar face and Josh's

smile. Here. Not on Fourth being attacked by monsters. "You came."

"I'm annoyed you even seem surprised. Come on. They need us." Despite the urgency in Josh's voice, he paused before helping Topher break the remaining handcuff. He bent, his warmth fanning over Topher's face, and pressed a kiss to Topher's lips that eased all the pain and worry. Josh took in Topher's broken wrist and the shadows. He gently cupped Topher's cheeks. "They have a plan. Everything will be okay. We'll need you to organize the vampires and eventually make the drainers. This isn't only your fight, and Nora already called dibs on Reelings. Now, are you ready?"

Topher nodded, stunned into calm. With Josh's help, they were able to free Topher. Josh took a moment to check over his wrists with a frown before grabbing Topher's less injured hand and leading him out of the Supernatural Mediation building. Fourth Street couldn't have felt further away. Josh shifted quickly and started off. Topher followed, ignoring his throbbing wrist and the thirst burning his throat.

There weren't words to describe the relief and dread in his chest.

He tried to *run*. After bringing all this to her city, to Topher's street, and Colbie's world, the man dared to try and flee unharmed. And Nora, still in her human form, laughed.

The sound made Reelings stumble. They were deep within his gathered ranks of humans, and he hadn't expected to be followed. To be kept up with by a wolf in human form. "Shoot her," Reelings said, snapping at the nearest woman holding a gun. She was too charmed to hesitate.

It was shocking and numbing but not enough to stop Nora as her shoulder burst. She had another. She laughed again, and Reelings's eyes widened. Nora ignored the humans even as more began to lift their weapons for Reelings's next order.

Her mind was focused. She didn't need words for this, only the alpha already working to heal her wound. All Nora saw was her territory. Was Gabriel dead at her hands—only a teenager when Reelings sank his influence into Gabriel's mind. Still so young, he thought he could take on the vampires. All Nora saw was her father's gravestone, her mother lost in the woods, her city falling and falling. All Nora saw was the devastation Topher hid behind a mask, Poppy looking at her mother's dead body, Oliver biting his nails to the quick as Zayn volunteered to watch for Reelings's approach. She saw Reelings trying to charm Colbie like it was his right to do so and stalking toward Annaliese with his fangs on display.

This stupid, power-hungry man. Nora was sick of it. Of them all. New Brecken deserved better.

Nora deserved better.

The next bullet was deflected by a blue flash of light— Poppy at Nora's back. There were shouts of protest quickly shut off. Annaliese and Colbie slipped anticharm bracelets on the humans gathered as planned.

Reelings took it all in. He inched another step back, ready to pivot. To run. Again. Nora didn't give him the opportunity. Topher had let him go last spring, but Topher clung to his humanity more than Nora ever had. Nora was an alpha. She'd passed her childhood dreaming of this power. Of this ability to protect the humans of her city. To make her father proud. She didn't hesitate, the shift ripping through her so quickly that even the charmed humans stepped back in surprise.

Nora was upon Reelings before he could muster up more words. She didn't hold back, but he was strong. He'd become the vampire First for a reason. He caught her jaw before she could latch it onto his jugular, thumbs jamming into hinges and pushing into her throat. They struggled together, Nora feeling the upper hand as she stepped forward, forcing Reelings to give ground, but he kept her at arm's length so her swiping claws barely snagged on his shirt. Her teeth made no impact as he dug his thumbs into the soft part of her gums. It was a frustrating impasse, Reelings matching her even when she tugged backward. The wild look in his eyes said he knew exactly what would happen once his grip slipped. And it *was* slipping as Nora's thick saliva wetted his hands.

Nora couldn't say when she'd begun to know Colbie's presence. Without a scent, without body heat, with silent steps, it should have been impossible. But Nora looked up right as Colbie appeared behind Reelings, lip curled at how he held Nora at bay. Reelings stiffened, watching Nora's eyes move and knowing a threat was at his back.

Colbie lifted a hand, and Reelings made the riskier decision. With all his might, he threw Nora's head to the side, then dropped and rolled backward, stopping behind Colbie within one blink and the next. His voice was ragged but still oozed charm, too low for Nora to hear as he rested his hands on Colbie's shoulders and spoke in her ear. Nora circled, and he kept Colbie between them, matching her step for step, his hands too close to Colbie's throat. Too close to the place Nora preferred to kiss and nuzzle, marking Colbie with her scent. Making Colbie her own.

Reelings could no doubt smell exactly that as they circled, his smile spreading and confidence returning to his eyes.

"You have wormed yourself into quite a nice position among the real players, haven't you?" he purred in Colbie's ear. Colbie relaxed in his grip. Nora clung to the memory of last spring. It was all that kept her from worrying that Colbie was charmed. Colbie *looked* like she was utterly in Reelings's thrall. "Trusted sister of the vampire leader. Whore to the werewolf one. I'm sure you even have an in within the humans. Losing you, that's going to sting, isn't it? Enough to give my drainers a step up, do you think?"

"Yes," Colbie agreed, quick and flat. Nothing of her vibrance in her tone. Not a twitch of her expressive lips.

Nora's steps faltered. Colbie wasn't this good of an actor, was she?

"Turn around," Reelings said. Low and excited. Nora's hackles rose, painfully taunt. "I want to show Miss Morales how completely I own her precious vampires."

Colbie turned in his arms, pliant and sweet like she only was with Nora. Nora wasn't even circling now, just watching. Not daring to breathe.

"Kiss me," Reelings purred.

Colbie lifted her hands to his cheeks, thumbs sweeping his cheekbones softly enough for Nora to begin to lose all hope.

Then Colbie jammed her thumbnails into his eyes.

Reelings shrieked, tightened his grip on Colbie's throat, and flung her suddenly limp body to the side. Nora couldn't tell what he'd done to her—he'd moved too fast. She silently, desperately begged any force in the universe to make sure Colbie was okay as Nora took advantage of Reelings's shock and pain and struck again. This time, he couldn't see her approach. This time, her teeth clamped onto his jaw.

It felt too quick—one moment, he was screaming, charming the resistant humans to come to his defense. The next, his head was flying over the crowd, and his body was dropping into the blackened dirt where the Maker had once stood.

Fear too heavy to let victory invade, Nora turned to Colbie.

Reelings must not have wanted his humans dead. None of them ended up firing the guns or plunging in their own knives. Reelings *hadn't* commanded the drainers at his mercy to kill them all. His unspoken orders kept them on a leash, restrained in their attacks. He'd wanted those gathered, human and vampire, to belong to him. Only the werewolves faced battle. The rest were intended to become Reelings's empire.

That order not to turn Fourth Street into a blood bath went out the window once Reelings died. Everyone felt the moment the battle shifted. Any human still at Reelings's mercy threw their weapons away from themselves in horror. Many blinked, confused how they even ended up there. Poppy's eyes snagged on Brett Campbell when he stumbled, looking sick as he clutched his head.

The drainers smiled. All teeth. They turned to the humans with full black eyes. Poppy gripped her wards so close she was clenching her fists. If Julia hadn't been stuck to Poppy's side for the last ten minutes, bewildered but steadfast in her new body and the strange world she'd found herself in, Poppy wouldn't have believed these monsters could be saved. There was nothing human in their movements, in their blood thirst. Nothing even comparable to the vampires working with the wolves and humans to physically restrain the drainers long enough for someone to risk their hand pouring the potion into the monsters's snarling mouths. Zayn let one drop to the ground, pulling Oliver close to check his hand. Again. But Oliver was steady. His hands never shook when he poured. To lighten the mood earlier, he'd joked that he wished he had a needle and syringe. Zayn had fed from Oliver enough to calm any excess nerves, and his medical training had never been more apparent than when he focused on this task. He and Zayn made one of the most effective teams as they helped stem the tide of drainers.

That didn't help them for long. The potions were running out. Even after discovering the cult and how Reelings had covered his tracks, no one had counted on there being so many drainers. No one had realized how the demons would fall to disorganized slaughter once Reelings died. Half of the wolves had to run for the clubs to defend the witches hidden within as the demons scented their life magic. Even as Poppy glanced back, more wolves were heading that way to back up their pack mates. She thought she saw Daniel and the scar down his face, but it may have been Henry. Where was Josh? Where was Topher? Had Chance found him?

The street smelled of sulfur and blood. Screams were too loud, too real. The conflicts Poppy had been involved in had never felt like this. It was always a test of charm or magic or alpha abilities. It had never been about numbers. How many bodies each side could throw at the issue. The reality of it had Poppy fighting the urge to throw up more shields, but her magic couldn't support that.

She wanted this over. Poppy ducked behind Julia to drink yet another sunlight brew. She was running out of these, too, but her darts of sunlight were her most effective weapon against the demons seeking her out.

"Colbie hasn't come back," Julia shouted over her shoulder.

The sunlight brew hit hard as it dredged up more of Poppy's exhausted magic. She staggered to her feet, throwing a dart of sunlight toward the drainer taking advantage of Julia's distraction.

It was incredible Julia was even here. She'd woken without Topher, but Colbie took the time to sit with her and explain everything. They had waited for more blood thirst, failing memory, or inhuman—or rather invampire—strength. But Julia was acting as normal as Colbie. Feeding had been a strange experience, but she'd stopped when Lana told her to, charmed as any other lower would be by their maker's maker. The only remaining gaps in her memory were from her time as a drainer. When they'd first seen Reelings's army, Julia had shaken her head. "I wasn't like that, was I?" Her voice had been heartbreaking.

Now, she worked to save them like it could redeem any hint of what she'd been once. Maybe anger at the injustice of it all would hit later. Maybe she'd curse her vampire status by the end of the night, but for now, Julia seemed grateful to have been saved from the drainer's fate and determined to help the others. Julia was good. There was a reason she'd stuck by Topher and loved him so much. Poppy found her old jealousies assuaged, watching Julia hold her ground and fight back with unpracticed strength.

"She's with Nora. She'll be okay," Poppy said, though she did take a moment to stand on her tiptoes, scanning the crowd for a familiar messy bun of curling brown hair.

Julia grunted, but the mob shifted again and took up their focus. When Poppy had a second to think, she wished she could check her phone. Chance had promised to keep her updated on the search for Topher. They *needed* him. The vampires were tiring, looking toward Solas and Patter with shifting eyes. They needed to feed again. They needed firm hands leading them. Their respect for Solas and Patter had taken too big of a hit when Topher took charge. He needed to step forward again and soon.

As if the threads of fate felt Poppy's pleading tugs, a commotion broke out behind Reelings's drainers. Suddenly, Poppy wasn't fighting to get through his disordered lines. She planted her feet and tried not to be bowled over by drainers fleeing something coming from the opposite end of the block.

Then, like a gust of wind, a charm froze them all in place. The werewolves even shook their heads, resisting the strength of the unspoken command.

Poppy fell to her knees, the fight leaving and exhaustion filling every nerve in its place.

"He's here," Julia said, relief softening her features.

Poppy nodded, amazed as she looked across the suddenly meek drainers they had been fighting for what felt like hours. As quickly as that, Topher had halted the battle.

"Stop the demons. Heal the humans."

Poppy couldn't even hear the charm in the direction. Vampires and drainers turned, running toward the clubs to complete their new task and save the witches. At some point,

Poppy had started to cry. Sobs shuddered out of her chest. All the witches she had gathered would all be saved.

Almost as one, humans collapsed to their knees to catch their breath. The ones Reelings had brought looked more confused than ever. They had woken from his charm to find themselves in the fight for their lives against the freed drainers. Now, just as suddenly, the threat was gone. Cries grew as the dead and injured were discovered. Vampires did as Topher directed, licking wounds, desperately biting at gushing injuries. Even so, there were too many dead, including the drainers that had fought too hard for someone to get the subduing potion into them.

Shaking, Poppy stood. She could see over everyone now. The wolves were the tallest in the group, huddled in the center of the battle in the ruins of the Maker.

Where Nora was holding Colbie's limp form.

CHAPTER 43

Topher knew he should be running with his vampires toward the clubs. His territory needed defending. His people needed organizing. There were too many drainers in need of his making.

Even with all this responsibility on his shoulders, Topher approached Nora. He was flipping toward the numb darkness, this time so heavy he couldn't keep it contained. The shadows made the wolves shift backward nervously as Topher dropped to his knees on Nora's other side. She looked at him. She was ashen but tear-free. Her eyes too wide with shock and confusion.

"She won't wake up, but… I can't tell if she's breathing or if she needs to or, or what."

Topher's charm snaked out cautiously, and the terror dissipated at what he found. He turned, catching eyes with the nearest human. No words were needed. Raven stumbled forward and offered her wrist. Topher would have to apologize for the charm later. For now, only Colbie mattered.

"Drink," he said, charm spearing so deep that Colbie finally stirred. Her fangs dropped, but Raven had to press her skin into them.

Topher met Nora's eyes. "It was a big injury. Her throat is crushed. She should be able to get enough blood down. It takes energy to heal. Life energy. The blood will wake her up."

Now Nora cried. Clutching Colbie closer as his sister woke fully, sitting up to lean over Raven's wrist. He beckoned another human forward, watching Raven's face for the first sign of paleness.

A warm hand on Topher's shoulder alerted him to Oliver's presence. He would make sure Colbie didn't overfeed from Raven. Topher reached up to squeeze his fingers in thanks before he stood and turned toward the clubs. He paused long enough to take in all the drainers waiting on the road and dirt. Some subdued. Some fighting the control Topher had gained without Reelings's charm blocking him out. So many waited. So many human lives gone. The strength it took to hold their shadows in place made Topher dizzy. His eyes skipped over the number, welcoming the exertion and how it pulled him from feeling. Topher would more than replace all the lower vampires he'd had to kill when taking Happenstance. New Brecken would be missing too many humans, but the balance would be kept.

Topher stepped closer. He tried to focus. To steel himself for what he had to do. Daylight approached, and without Reelings, the drainers were far more easily charmed, but he didn't want them to live with the consuming blood thirst any longer than necessary. There were too many humans flocking the street, and the drainers were slippery and unpredictable. He could feel them even now fighting his commands, twisting his words with the strength that Gabriel lent. Some chased demons, hoping to get far enough away to find a human victim once they escaped the boundaries of Topher's control. His vampires were dragging them back, but they looked exhausted by the night's events. These vampires were used to lazing around in their clubs, their food coming to them willingly.

Tonight was a shock. Like nothing they'd experienced since the laws came into effect.

So Topher stepped forward to begin his final task of the night. He paused when Annaliese stepped into his path, bringing him up short.

For the first time, she wouldn't meet his eyes. She rubbed the knuckles on her right hand nervously. Topher bent, gently grabbing her fingers. He brought them to his lips, brushing enough bliss over the bruising to remove the memory of punching Beth.

Annaliese cleared her throat. "I'm sorry. I shouldn't have ratted you out."

"You didn't know they were under Reelings's charm."

"I shouldn't have done it at all. Even with that. I… I wasn't thinking."

"Yes, you were." Annaliese flinched. "You were thinking about the right thing to do. Giving the humans hope was the right thing. If you would betray Nora to save me from the Den, you think I can fault you for giving me up? It's who you are. The consequences could have been worse, all things considered."

Annaliese squinted up at him. "I don't think I agree. You'd feel differently if I put anyone but you at risk."

Topher shrugged. He didn't really care that she may or may not have wronged him; that was true. It left him without an argument. "We'll talk later?"

Annaliese wasn't satisfied, but she nodded. Topher noted how she couldn't meet Josh's eyes either as he came to Topher's side. Something felt broken between them all, but Topher couldn't think about that now. Instead, he focused on his gratitude for Josh's presence as he ran toward the other end of the block.

Topher's charm settled the drainers. There weren't many demons left, but Solas's tight expression tipped Topher off as to why. "Most of them got away. The wolves chased them, but…" She shuddered. "They were much tamer under the sorcerer."

Topher's eyes found Henry's. "You can call your people back. Contain the drainers. You can keep them in Happenstance once the humans and witches are out and we'll wait to open until I get them under control."

"But, the demons—" Patter began. Her right cheek was sliced with slow-healing claw marks. Everyone needed to feed. To rest. To process and recover. None of that would happen with wild demons flooding the city.

"Screw you, Tiff," Topher muttered under his breath, too quiet for anyone to hear. She had started all of this. The demons were still answering the enticing summons she had laid throughout the streets. Beth had picked up the call. Now, of course it fell on Topher to set things right.

It fell on Dylan.

Topher closed his eyes. He hated this connection, but the demons would never be this close and condensed again. He had to use the shadows before too many got away and hid. Reaching into the darkness brought him back to that night. To Dylan grabbing Topher's hand and twisting Tiff Jennings's spell so the shadows went to Topher, not the demons like the one that killed him.

The shadows that had only grown heavier as Topher drew them out of Julia. He dragged them out of the drainers brought into Happenstance now, pulling at any strength they could offer.

The darkness was heavy, consuming. It needed an outlet. Topher could get lost in it so easily, the singing call of numbness that resided in his being. Maybe that's what made him so inherently good at manipulating the shadows that he cast out.

Shouts and cries filled the night as Topher directed the lines of shadow into himself. It took mere moments, but in that time, Topher felt even his vast stores of energy falter. Josh's arms caught his fall, but the shadows swallowed all his focus.

He knew where he needed the power to go, what it had to do, but casting it out was too hard, too draining. Topher felt like he was unraveling. Like he'd found his limit finally and pushed past it too fast. Alarm rang in his head, and it felt like Dylan's panicking voice. Was Topher losing him? Losing himself?

A hand in his centered it all. "Tell me where to send it," Poppy said. And the shadows snapped back. They wanted her brightness. Could she handle them?

"To the demons. To overpower the demons," Topher gasped the words out, opening his eyes.

He saw Poppy's eyes widen in shock and knew he probably looked like Beth had, dark veins and blacked-out eyes. That would explain the dark shade the world was currently cast in. Poppy looked over Topher's shoulder, nodding at Josh. She pulled, the shadows going through the funnel that was Poppy's magic strengthened by Josh. The spears of power Topher cast out found direction.

Shadow was drawn to shadow. One by one, in his current state of darkness, Topher could feel the pits of black that were the demons in this bright city extinguish. Gasps to the right drew Topher's eyes. There was a demon on the ground they had thought was dead. Everyone surrounding him watched as the lines of its form blurred as the shadow filled it. Then, with a hiss of night, the demon vanished in a haze of darkness. Topher knew the same was happening to every demon summoned to New Brecken. Poppy's tilting lips said she knew it was happening too, even as she kept her eyes shut and focused on directing Topher's dark magic. She was undoing every wrong her mother had cast on their city, and Topher had never seen her look so sure or peaceful.

It took so much out of them both. Topher's blinks were growing heavy and slow as Poppy finished, but he didn't let himself slip into unconsciousness until Poppy let go and he could search his core. The shadows were lighter but returned to their state before he took them from Julia. A year ago,

Topher would never have anticipated the relief that swept through him knowing his power remained. Whatever Ru might think, Dylan remained. Topher summoned the feel of him and slipped into the arms of darkness, trusting Poppy and Josh with his physical body as sleep claimed him.

Nora held Colbie close. She kept a grip on Colbie's hand or waist as the hours passed, and they set about cleaning up the wreckage. Drainers were bound or fed the last bottles of Poppy's potion, despite growing subdued after all the darkness within them had flooded into Topher. People were still whispering about that, speculating what it might have been. Some form of charm made visible was the most popular theory. Poppy wasn't answering questions, and Topher had been sleeping next to the stairs leading into Happenstance with his head on Josh's lap since the demons had been ashed. A few brave humans had taken up the task of sweeping the demon remains off the street and dumping them in the blackened scar that had been the Maker.

The sun would rise soon. Fourth Street would hold little evidence of what had happened here. Campbell and Annaliese were loading the human bodies into ambulances. Henry and his solemn pack had already taken care of their two dead members. Somehow, Nora's pack had come out of it all with no losses. Lana, Solas, and Patter were taking care of the vampire dead. Lana had declared Topher would want a tally, but getting rid of the bodies was beneath him. Everyone had looked to Zayn for confirmation, and Colbie had laughed at the look on Lana's face when she realized her new place in the vampire hierarchy.

Colbie was flagging now, leaning into Nora as the sky began to lighten. She kept rubbing her throat.

"Where do you want to sleep tonight?" Nora asked her. There were almost too many options now with the clubs at their disposal, Alpha's Den untouched, Nora and Annaliese's apartment waiting.

But when Colbie said "home," Nora knew where she meant. "But not yet. I want to be part of this as long as possible."

Julia nodded her agreement. She'd spent the aftermath of the battle at Colbie's side or checking on Topher. There wasn't a place for her here, not yet, but Nora was amazed at her calm. Colbie wasn't. She'd declared Julia someone great at rolling with the punches. How else would she have put up with Topher all these years?

It seemed like between one breath and the next, everything was cleaned up, and arrangements for the drainers were settled. Nora met eyes with Josh, Solas, Patter, and then Annaliese and Campbell as they approached. They had slowly gotten the story out of Campbell. There was no way of knowing when he'd fallen into Reelings's clutches, but he truly had been passionate about supernatural mediation before Reelings returned to town. He knew what to do with this, how to tell the story, and most importantly, to throw his support behind Topher and Poppy. He'd keep the witches a secret and not villainize the vampires that had fought so hard to save their clubs. It would take a long time for the humans to forgive the death here, but hopefully, all the blame would fall on Reelings and not the laws.

In the end, Annaliese took the stairs to Happenstance and turned to face the crowd, with Josh and Topher nearby. Nora put herself and Colbie front and center as Annaliese spoke to everyone gathered, including the humans holding their phones, recording and live streaming.

"What happened tonight has been brewing for at least the last year, but the vampire responsible could not have known the resistance to his acts was growing simultaneously. Tonight, someone challenged our supernatural laws. Someone tried to take our city. With the law-abiding vampires, witches, and werewolves open to communication with humans and loyal to New Brecken, we were able to stop him. If the laws hadn't built us up and made New Brecken so strong, we would have fallen. Reelings could have attacked at any point, but without the sacrifices made by the supernaturals in our community to uphold our alliance—" A look toward Nora, Luis Morales in the air between them. "—we would have lost. The threats haunting New Brecken's streets have been dealt with. This may not be the last resistance to our peace, but in its aftermath, our bonds and leaders are stronger than ever. New Brecken will know balance from now on. Everyone will have a voice and a place here, no matter their supernatural gifts or lack thereof. This is a new day, and tomorrow will be safer for everyone. I have never been more proud of our city and its occupants. We can finally rest easy and enjoy the benefits of our laws without shadows hanging over us." A last, lingering look toward Topher, then Annaliese left the steps to allow the flagging vampires to pass and find the day's rest in the club.

Nora shifted her grip on Colbie. They waited for Poppy and Ru. Waited as Josh lifted Topher and held him close as he approached. Waited for Oliver supporting Zayn. Then, they went to the apartment on Sixth Street. The door was opened by Chance, already talking numbers of views and likes and shares. Mouse meowed and circled Poppy's feet. They each found a place to collapse, Annaliese following Josh and Topher into Topher's room after a moment's hesitation. Ru, Poppy, and Daniel took the couches, leaving Poppy's room for Zayn and Oliver. Smiling, Nora carried Colbie into her bed. They were safe in the Poppy's wards, secure in their city.

It was finally over.

CHAPTER 44

Poppy went straight from a frazzled-looking Topher putting out fires at the newly opened Happenstance and biked north. Frazzled was better than empty. It was better than hiding. It was emotion he was allowed to finally show given the delivery of Ru's bracelets that Poppy dropped off. Most humans wore them at the clubs now, though a few were dedicated to their lives as vampire prey and enjoyed giving up control. Poppy wouldn't understand that anytime soon, but Topher had corrected her when her face showed judgment enough times that she was working on it. Her problem, she decided, was about choice and her own fear of being power-less. But if someone's choice was to give up power in a safe place…well, it wasn't her place to condemn.

Her head was pounding, but at least the distance was short. Poppy had spent the night building wards with Topher and Nora. He took the safety of Fourth Street seriously and had an inspection tomorrow night. To Poppy's eyes, and even Nora's more suspicious ones when it came to vampires, the clubs were running perfectly. Topher would pass, the laws would hold and provide for the city, and Topher could hopefully trust his people enough to take a step back. No one had seen him outside of Fourth since that night when they fought for that block of vampire clubs a week ago.

It was Ru who was determined to get him away from Fourth. She shamelessly threatened to use Chance to get Topher to Patty's after the inspection to celebrate passing. As soon as Chance stepped onto Fourth, it was like Topher had an alarm to notify him. Chance was always greeted instantly by Zayn, Julia, or Raven. Always brought directly to Topher or Colbie if she was at the clubs. If he showed up and asked in person, they were fairly sure he could get Topher to take a night off. Poppy hoped it would work and Topher would show at Patty's, but having plans the next night meant she had more work to do today.

She stopped in front of the First Street building used to sell potions. She no longer called the street the Black Market. Poppy had learned each of the building names and what was sold within. She'd learned how many horrible rumors were meant to keep unwanted people away. There was no human contraband here, only the Rosenfield witches and their system of helping those who needed it. Over the last week, with laws and protections in place, word of mouth had spread of the doors opening along First Street. Business had picked up with each cautious human and witch willing to let customers into their wards. Poppy had no idea how it would come to fully affect New Brecken, but with each potion she sold to relieve a common illness, Poppy felt she was making strides to help the city in a big way.

She had several brews to prepare before opening. Margot and Ru were already inside. Ru sat behind the counter, beads littered on the wood before her and a string in hand. Margot was rearranging a shelf of protective potions, putting the ones that functioned as sunblock by order of strength. She had been Poppy's eager pupil since Rosenfield invited Poppy to help spruce up this neglected side of her business. Margot sold her shop deeper in the city. Too many years of hiding there in fear haunted the place. She had returned to her old room in the Jennings's house. Poppy and Ru took advantage of their older sister's good head for business. Margot sold her tarot cards around town and worked part-time at the potion shop. Poppy didn't know who was learning more, Poppy about business or Margot about brewing.

Poppy loved working here. She didn't even mind helping humans and openly discussing how she brewed. Security had gradually settled over her. Confidence in her wards. In her position. In knowing anyone trying to get to her would have to go through Fourth Street, would pass Sixth Street with her apartment, and Nora often over with a sleeping Colbie during the day. Annaliese had helped Poppy open some social media accounts. She posted her first timelapse yesterday and had a friend from class comment when they recognized her. Poppy was the younger, progressive face of the witches. She had coffee with Kallow twice to discuss how they would interact in the city. Poppy was busy and figuring out her place and so, so free.

She had no idea this was what she'd craved. Belonging and friendships and exposure and light and recognition. All things she had been deprived of by Tiff Jennings and the rigid structure of their childhood.

"Did you sleep at all last night?" Margot asked, hands on hips, as Poppy unlocked the shop door.

Poppy shrugged. "I'm used to weird hours."

"Well, go nap before we open. Viv is on her way over. The three of us can handle the morning rush."

Poppy didn't argue. Viv had proven to be one of the better brewers, more patient than the other witches with the time-consuming and delicate process. They wouldn't be busy for a while anyway. The tea shop gained the most business this early, and humans were mistrustful of witches; that wouldn't change in a week. Poppy was happy with the business they had gotten despite this, and Rosenfield assured her it was three times what they'd made on potions in the last month.

It had surprised her how much pride Poppy had already taken in the sales. In the routine of opening the shop and explaining magic as she knew it to curious humans. Each transaction was a risky victory. Colbie had been the one to note the happiness on Poppy's face after her biggest day of sales. "You look like you passed another semester with straight A's," she said.

The comment stuck with Poppy. She loved school. Helping humans, learning, testing herself, and facing new challenges. But it had all been safe. She'd done it pretending to be a human, but the rewards were as shallow as Poppy's disguise. She'd enjoyed learning to incorporate different elements of chemistry into her brewing, but this shop, this life along First Street, felt more real than any moment at UNB had. Poppy was still enrolled for the fall semester, but she was taking her time deciding if she wanted to go back. Nothing was as rewarding as this place. As the way witches swept in and out of each other's shops, sharing experiences and magic. Nothing was as thrilling as debating different ingredients with Viv or taking lessons in magic from Rosenfield with Ru. Having a patient teacher who was far more interested in receiving lessons from Poppy in return made magic something exciting and hopeful.

Poppy loved this street. She loved living among the witches. She loved her new relationship with her siblings. She loved continuing to be Ru's favorite. She loved the authenticity. She loved going home as Colbie stumbled out of her room and how they had an hour or so to catch up. She loved having Nora around and how Ru flitted in and out of the apartment to visit Mouse and escape the loud chaos of the Jennings household.

The bell above the door rang as Poppy moved to the office and its plush couch that was spelled to smell like lavender and never failed to provide the best nap experience. Poppy turned on the stairs. Rosenfield entered the shop, looking around with a critical eye. A part of Poppy still tensed at the sight of witch Mothers, but she was slowly growing used to Rosenfield—a witch who wasn't traditional. Happily married, having procreated with the same man, she was kind. She was like the human idea of a mother, not a witch building a powerful coven.

"Poppy, I'm glad I caught you," she said. "I need to talk to you now that your trial week is over."

Poppy's stomach dropped so hard it took her breath away. She'd forgotten she was running the potion shop only temporarily. "What is it?"

"As you know, technically, my mother has been running this place."

Poppy nodded. The older woman had trained Poppy. She'd been running the entire block for years, buying houses and building what Poppy had known as the Black Market over decades. She'd tried to give each house to a daughter, but only Rosenfield had shown any interest, leaving her to hire witches outside of her coven. Rosenfield's daughters had eventually helped pick up the slack, but Grandmother, as she insisted on being called by all the witches, had grown this place all on her own. She'd been what drew witches to New Bracken even before the laws.

"Is she ready to come back?" After two days, Grandmother had told Poppy to call with any questions, but not to have any questions, and left.

"No, the opposite, actually." Rosenfield smiled ruefully. "She told me this morning she wants you to run the Potion Coven."

That's what each shop on the block was called. Tarot Coven. Tea Reading Coven. Curse Coven. This street, to those who knew it, wasn't the Black Market but the Covens.

Poppy blinked, glancing at Margot only to find her sister grinning. "But I'm only twenty. I'm just a junior in college. I can't run a business."

Rosenfield shrugged. "Why not?"

"I was only twenty when Mother broke our wards," Margot said. "My shop did fine. And it's not like you won't have help. We'll all be here to support you."

Rosenfield nodded. Ru snorted. "Pop Rocks, if Topher can run Fourth and Nora can run the Alpha's Den, you can handle a little potion shop."

A sense of fullness went sprawling through Poppy's body, tingling to her fingertips. It was want. It was satisfaction. Poppy smiled, ideas spinning in her mind already. She could stay open late and bring in business from Fourth. Maybe tourists would want bottled potions with vampire saliva after experiencing the bliss.

This felt like the thread of Fate snapping into place. Her own coven. Her future and friends and connections settled. Helping humans, contributing to New Brecken, and living within the laws they fought for. Poppy nodded before she realized she'd made up her mind. She had time to consider returning to school but already knew she wouldn't.

Footage from the battle between them and Reelings had leaked. Poppy wasn't famous by any means, but she was recognized as often as Henry and Topher. People mimed shooting beams of sunlight when they saw her. She didn't want to go to school as a witch. She didn't need them to look into how she got accepted into UNB or funded her first few semesters magically. Poppy needed new levels of security and wards when she was among the humans now, but even that meant her siblings, Ru especially, had no focus on them. Campbell had already spoken to Poppy at length about how her potions could bring in more tourists and what kind of taxes she should expect to pay the city. Visitors would want to try real magic as much as they wanted to meet a vampire. And more witches would come this way when Poppy proved it was possible to live authentically in this world. Poppy didn't mind being an example, but she hoped any others would realize how much trusting the vampires and werewolves played into her ability to live this way. There was a balance in the city. An equilibrium of daylight and shadows that the humans could move between with ease. Poppy didn't want her influence to disrupt the balance, but she wouldn't change what had happened. This was her place in New Brecken, and it would take a lot to pry it from her fingers. Poppy finally found what she wanted to hold onto. It was her apartment on Sixth and her vampire roommates. It was her siblings that had survived. It was a community she'd never dared dream of.

Poppy smiled, and it felt more real than anything else she'd experienced in the last two years.

"What do you say?" Rosenfield asked. "Do you want to take your place in the Covens?"

"Depends," Poppy said. "Can I build a greenhouse in the backyard?"

Rosenfield waved a hand. "If you earn the funds."

"I'll earn the funds." Poppy would learn to trust this certainty in life, too.

"—so happy for you," Topher was saying as Josh stepped out of the shower. Topher smiled at his boyfriend. His boyfriend. Still so strange. So undeserved. But Josh had a stubborn streak, and he'd apparently saved it just for Topher. Even his uncle was surprised by how little Josh had let Topher argue with him. Josh had taken Topher to Henry's apartments two nights ago to meet his parents. His mother was Henry's younger sister, from whom he and Daniel had inherited their smiles and sunshine. His father was a human who hadn't been able to get a job in New Brecken until then. Topher had been stunned by their easy companionship, simple lives within the pack, and adoration of their sons. Topher had tried to stand in the background as they reunited, but Josh pulled him along, front and center. Henry laughed at Topher's compliance.

Topher had fought his smile in front of the humans. The last thing he wanted was to charm Josh's dad. As soon as Josh caught him pressing his lips, he pulled out an anticharm bracelet and snapped it onto his dad's wrist. He'd whispered a loud "relax," and the conversation continued to flow around them.

In truth, letting Josh call the shots was Topher's favorite thing. He'd been fighting too long. He had to keep fighting on Fourth. But with Josh, he answered all directions: "It's okay to smile." "Tell me about Dylan." "Stop apologizing." "Let's get out of bed now." "Show me how to touch you." Topher was Josh's willing subject and had never had a less complicated relationship.

Later that night, Colbie tried to talk with him about it. "Maybe it's a wolf thing. They know what they want. I thought Nora's taking charge was an alpha thing, but in bed, does Josh ever—"

"Nope. We need to set more boundaries," Topher had said, hand raised and ignoring the snickers of the other vampires behind the bar.

Oliver pouted, wanting all the details. Colbie crossed her arms. "You used to tell me everything."

"I was probably high," Topher admitted. Even that part of his history was getting easier to discuss, and Colbie's surprised laughter made it worth it.

Josh climbed into the bed now, dropping all his heavy, warm weight on top of Topher in the way he loved. He felt contained with Josh. Human. He didn't pause his phone conversation with Poppy, listening to her excitement about permanently running her own coven shop. When she took a breath, he glanced at the clock and reluctantly broke in.

"I'll help you however you need, Popcorn. Let me know. But I do have to do a final check of the clubs. Campbell should be here in an hour or so."

"Topher, you're ready," Poppy assured him. "Nora said the

Alpha's Den inspection was a piece of cake. You've got this, but I'll let you go because I can hear how anxious you are. I'll come by after, and then we'll go to Patty's?"

"Sure."

Topher hung up. Josh lifted his head to meet Topher's eyes. "Anxious, did she say?"

"Hmm." Topher pressed his nose into Josh's hair.

Josh turned his face, nipping at Topher's neck. His words were hot breath against Topher's skin. "Something I can help with?"

"More than likely."

Josh pushed up onto his elbows. He stared down at Topher, eyes soft and careful. "How do you feel today?"

Topher wrapped his arms around Josh's waist, trying to remember his first thoughts and feelings upon waking, but Josh had been there. Josh was like a siphon, sucking out every low sensation and replacing them with fuzzy heat. After a week of following Topher around the clubs, Josh was probably sick of vampires, the music, and the dim lights. Yet he hadn't complained and hadn't left Topher's side. Topher noticed him jumping at small noises. From the tidiness of his room and Josh's lingering scent, Topher suspected Josh rarely left his side during the day. Last week, no, the last year, had fucked with all their heads. Josh's way of coping was watching Topher and he claimed Henry had set him to the task.

Henry had too much on his mind anyway. He and Helen Morales were helping Nora make her extended pack work. Constant lessons on alphaship and meetings on Twenty-Fifth had kept the two so busy that Topher only saw them during said meetings.

Meetings. Spreadsheets. Schedules. Rumors. Bartending. Charm. Feedings. Josh. Since the night they had reclaimed the city, that was Topher's life. He couldn't complain, not when the alternative outcome would have been so much worse, and Josh was such great company, but Topher had found himself missing his siblings and friends. Zayn was a fixture at Happenstance, but Oliver's visits had been brief. Poppy came by to help build wards, but she was busy with her new shop. Colbie was Nora's Josh. And Annaliese…only silence. She hadn't returned a single call or text, and Topher couldn't get away from Fourth long enough to find her. Not that he should when she's so actively avoiding him.

"Toph?" Josh bumped their noses.

Right, he'd been asked a question. "I'm okay tonight."

Josh waited. Topher sighed, the force of his breath lifting Josh up and down enough to make him smile. Topher's answer killed the happy look and was precisely why he hated Josh's insistence that they do these check-ins. "I feel like the walls are pressing in. I've only been here for a week. I feel like—" Topher stopped. His words had gone reedy. Slightly whiney.

"What?"

Topher winced. "If you weren't here, I don't think I'd be able to breathe, but it makes me feel guilty. Like I'm trapping you here too because you can tell."

"*I'm* fine. I'm chilling. Sometimes, I find myself wondering how I could start liking boys like this so quickly, but then you enter a room all cool and unreadable, and it's so unbearably sexy I'm reminded how stupid a thought that is and how lucky I am to be here."

Topher blinked. "Lucky?"

Josh rolled his eyes. He got into Topher's face, so close Topher almost laughed. "*Lucky*. I feel lucky to get to do this." Josh kissed him. "I feel lucky that I'm cracking your shell, and you answer my questions even though you don't want to. I feel lucky that I'm dating a guy who cares so much about my happiness that you look like it's killing you to have me here even more than it's killing you to be here. I feel lucky that Topher West likes me. The most powerful and hottest vampire in the city picked me. I'm inexperienced and boring. I'm just a lesser wer—"

Topher covered Josh's mouth, giving him a look. "Don't talk about my boyfriend like that. He's not *just* anything. He's everything."

"He's lucky," Josh said, muffled by Topher's hand, eyes warm and soft and almost too much to look at.

"I'm really not—"

Josh slapped his hand over Topher's mouth so hard that he winced in apology before saying, "Don't talk about my boyfriend like that."

Topher melted and felt himself smiling into Josh's palm. When they played like this, flirted back and forth, it felt so gratifying. So unserious. Josh had caught Topher's eye the first time he saw him, smelling like Poppy and looking slightly lost in the new city surrounded by strange supernaturals. Flirting with Josh had always been instinctual, fun and effortless. It had reminded Topher of who he'd been before Dylan died. A bit of the smiling human he'd used to revert to in groups where he was comfortable. Now, being with Josh, Topher was reminded that he was only just technically old enough to bartend like he'd been doing for the past two years. With Josh, Topher felt young. He felt desired for more than the emanating charm and the shadows surrounding him. Josh stripped away all the supernatural dynamics, making them both human. His wolf side only served to cancel out any effect Topher's vampire abilities might have had on their relationship, even turning Topher's lack of desire for monogamy into something Josh could understand.

Topher swiped his tongue along Josh's palm, and Josh shuddered, the bliss making his eyes unfocus before he removed his hand and caught Topher in a long, deep, bone-settling kiss.

They would have gone further, but a knock on the door made Josh jump. He turned on the bed with a snarl.

"Oh hush, dog. I need to talk to your owner."

Josh relaxed at Lana's voice, but he and Topher shared a long-suffering look. "Should I banish her already?" Topher asked. He'd do it in a heartbeat if Josh said yes, but he had to admit she was doing a great job helping him run Fourth Street. Most nights, she and Zayn held down Happenstance while Topher popped into the other clubs or the homes along Third, checking to make sure none of the human occupants were too blissed or charmed.

Josh shook his head, rolling off Topher but remaining at his side. Topher didn't care enough about what Lana saw to do anything more than check if Josh was decent before calling for her to come in.

She scrunched her nose at the two of them. "First my car, now Grace's bed?"

"It's a new mattress." But Topher didn't know anything about her car. He wouldn't ask and give her an excuse to complain about whatever it was.

Josh growled, low and quiet, when Lana perched at the end of the bed. She pretended not to hear it. "The witch told me you have plans for later tonight? After the inspection?"

Topher nodded. He wasn't sure he was ready to face everyone, let alone leave Fourth Street unprotected in the busy, early hours of the night. But Ru had asked. She'd threatened to send Chance in to pick up him and Josh if they didn't go willingly.

"Are you leaving me in charge?"

Topher nodded again, less enthusiastically this time. "Just of Happenstance."

Lana straightened. She seemed to be readying herself, almost like she was nervous. Looking him in the eyes, she said, "Leave me in charge. Permanently."

Topher snorted. "You're too busy at Alpha's Den. I have to get ready for the inspection." He sat up.

"Just listen!" Lana put a hand on his leg, and he hated that he'd become so used to submitting to her that he instantly stilled. "Hear me out, Topher. You know I'm the better vampire because I want to *be* a vampire. It's been hard for you, I can tell, to rule here. You're good at it, don't get me wrong, but you hate charming people who won't stay in line. You hate physically subduing them even more. Every time you walk into the back door of this building, you wince, remembering how you and Zayn took this place. You never wanted to be a vampire leader. So don't. You're strong enough to transfer power to me. To delegate your responsibilities. Charm me however you need to, as long as I get at least Happenstance, but I'll take all of Fourth off your hands. All you'd need to do is back me up if I'm ever having problems, but the vows were made, and you charmed us all to follow you. You don't have to be here constantly. I want to be here constantly. Zayn and Raven want to be here constantly and have no problem working for me. I already talked to the Morales girl about taking over the Alpha's Den. She can have it. That place was never really my goal. Fourth Street as it is now with the laws and alliances was. I want this place."

Topher almost brushed off her words, but Josh reached and took his hand. Making him pause and consider everyone in this situation. Mostly, he knew he hated this idea because it was Lana asking, but everything he hated about Lana came down to her ruthless ambition and vampire instincts. She understood power moves and humiliation and what progress needed to be made to keep up in this world. No one human had ever come to harm in one of her clubs, and she knew better than anyone how much power Topher had. Lana had happily submitted to Grace. She had mourned his passing. She believed in vampire hierarchy and fought tooth and nail to rise in the ranks within that structure.

Topher hated Lana. He never wanted her to touch him again. Wanted her far away from his friends and family. But...

Topher shouldn't have looked at Josh's face then. Shouldn't have let himself see the hope there because that was all he needed to make this decision. It wasn't until he found himself speaking that he slowly began to realize what this would mean. "I'll need to talk to Zayn. He can manage Happenstance if you're watching all the clubs. You can do the inspection with me tonight and run point, but make it clear to everyone I'm still in charge. We'll do this on a trial basis and with Chance's cameras watching. If you set one foot out of line, it's done. You only get one chance. Now, leave." He charmed her with the last word, a reminder that he could.

She left without a word, but the smile on her face said it all. Topher didn't care. Josh's hand tightened on Topher's. "Does this mean you'll spend the day at the apartment?"

It took Topher a beat to find his voice again as his decision set in. "Or your place," Topher said, leaning over Josh to get the full view of his pleasure. And he *was* pleased. Josh had never said he wanted Topher to spend more time with his pack, but he rarely looked as relaxed as they had when they had gone to see his parents. Josh had fallen asleep at the meeting with Henry afterward. He'd been secure in knowing they were both safe, surrounded by his family. If Topher could give Josh more moments of peace like that, it was selfish not to. These thoughts had been building in the back of his mind since Chance's speech about the future and optimism, but Lana's words permitted him to put his dreams into words. Because if he was honest, he knew it was important for him to be here, but every day when he fell asleep in Grace's old room, Topher hated being unsure of where he would wake up and if Josh would be there when he did.

"I don't trust her, and I'll still probably have to spend most of my time here, but… things have been running well. Even my pessimism has to admit that. If anyone could handle Fourth, it would be her. Chance is right, you're right, everyone was right. This isn't a life sentence."

Colbie nearly upset the table when Topher finally made it to Patty's. She flung herself from their corner booth, the only one big enough to hold their whole group, and ran into Topher's arms. He laughed but buried his face in Colbie's shoulder before any of the surrounding humans could see. Not that it mattered. Ru straightened, looking smug because everyone in the diner wore one of her bracelets. Josh nudged Topher, already some unspoken language between them. It only took a look for Topher to notice, and his grin spread. With an arm around Colbie's shoulders, Topher turned them toward the table, but most of its occupants were already on their feet, waiting to greet the new vampire First.

Nora stayed where she was next to Annaliese in the corner of the booth. Even from where they sat, she could see how much lighter Topher appeared than the last time they talked. The opposite of how Annaliese currently looked beside her. Tension radiated from her body. Guilt had been eating at her since the moment Topher was taken by the assessors. Annaliese blamed herself entirely. Her strict morals and determination to do right had never failed her before. This last week had been full of soul-searching and phone calls in which Nora tried to reassure her best friend. The situation, every situation of the past year, had been complicated. All that mattered now was they were fine—more than fine. Even Julia had thrown herself into this new life with the same passion and thirst for knowledge Colbie said she used to show toward school. If Topher could get past dooming Julia to the world of night, Annaliese could move on, too.

Nora turned a bit, trying to discretely read her best friend's face as everyone sat and Chance took Topher's phone, showing him again how to check the cameras set up in his club, tsking and saying there was no reason Topher should be so bad at technology when he was so young. It was a running joke now. Chance had gotten all the technology smarts, while Topher and Colbie might as well be boomers. Colbie had just reopened her social media accounts and was racking up followers, but she preferred to spend her time playing the mindless fruit games Oliver introduced her to.

Annaliese remained closed off, but her eyes stuck to Topher. Nora remembered her former speculations that Annaliese was attracted to Topher's moody personality. Before Annaliese became immune to charm, Nora wondered if she would like the version of Topher that could smile and relax around the people he loved. The answer, no matter how Annaliese was trying to hide it at this moment, was a clear yes. Nora almost asked why she wouldn't say hi, when Ru grabbed Topher's wrist to get his attention and dropped it quickly at his wince. They'd seen the mess the handcuffs had left. How strong they must have been to withstand his struggles to free himself and help them against Reelings. The fact that his injuries were still bothering him meant they had to be extensive.

Annaliese looked like she was going to be sick. "I'm going to the bathroom," she rasped before leaving the booth as quickly as she could while having to scoot along the cracked red upholstery.

Of course, Topher caught her movement. He kissed Josh and said something into his boyfriend's ear before following Annaliese to the bathroom. Nora turned to find Colbie smirking, clearly remembering their own time making up in there. The filthy kiss that had been the two of them giving in to everything between them.

"Will they be okay?" Nora whispered to Colbie.

Colbie shrugged. "Annaliese feels terrible, but it's even worse because Topher won't ever be mad at her for what happened. He likes her because she acts like she did when she went to Campbell. He doesn't need to be put first; he just needs someone to put things in perspective. Plus, he has Josh filling any gaps if he does have moments where he wants to be the priority. I think they'll be fine."

Julia nodded. It almost made Nora laugh. Julia sincerely wasn't jealous. She'd taken to spending more time with Nora and Colbie than on Fourth Street, but she and Zayn worked shifts together, too. Everything Topher said about her not being jealous of Dylan had proven true. She'd barely blinked the first time Josh and Topher kissed in front of her. She had made it more than clear she'd learned she and Topher were better as friends.

"Topher's patient," Julia said now. "At least in love, he goes after what he wants. He'll look at you with puppy dog eyes and say he doesn't deserve you, but he'll take any attention and affection you give him. It's very hard to say no to that."

"Well, he has mommy issues," Colbie said breezily as if she didn't suffer similarly. Nora put her arm around the back of the booth, pulling Colbie in close with the reminder of how much her girlfriend melted for little touches like that.

Josh gave Julia a funny smile, but Oliver captured his attention with a question. Ru, Daniel, and Chance were bickering like the younger siblings they were. Poppy told Zayn about her new shop, asking him to help her move some furniture. Jay was sitting beside Chance, looking exhausted and on edge. It was clear things weren't right between the two friends, but Chance seemed to be ignoring Jay's discomfort. He was so different with his friends compared to Colbie and Topher's easy affection that Nora really couldn't get a read on that situation.

They quieted when their server came around, Nora ordering for Annaliese, Oliver calling the young man by name, and Josh leaning over to see if Nora and Janelle, Nora's newly announced beta, would share a couple appetizers with him. It was too much food, but with all four werewolves at the table, it would get eaten. The server looked relieved at the large ticket, even with the vampires at the table and Poppy's side salad being the only thing a vegan could order here.

Maybe Nora hadn't put enough faith in Topher. He and Annaliese left the woman's bathroom far sooner than she expected. Annaliese still seemed a bit tense, but she stuck close to Topher's side as he caught the server's arm on his way behind the counter and gave him his black credit card.

Annaliese tried not to look impressed, but her chin was lifted as she and Topher took the space in the booth next to Josh. Topher made it look too natural to put both arms over the back, hands resting on Josh and Annaliese's shoulders.

In the lull of conversation that came with Topher's arrival, Ru cleared her throat. Her eyes widened when it gained her the full table's attention, but she recovered quickly. "I wanted to make an announcement. I asked everyone to meet today because we're celebrating. One, Poppy's new coven shop."

Poppy grinned when everyone applauded. She looked settled and was faintly glowing blue with the high energy of the table.

"Two, Topher learning to delegate."

Topher rolled his eyes for his applause, but Josh snuggled closer to his side, looking so proud that Colbie let out a quiet "awww" beside Nora.

"Three, for my booming business," Ru said smugly. Her bracelets were everywhere and had more than funded the Jennings's expanded household.

"Four, Nora breaking ground on her new den."

This one was a bittersweet announcement. With the insurance money Nora had received from the Den's destruction, she had decided to rebuild. Her pack needed a place to live, and Nora didn't want her and Colbie to live in apartments and clubs forever. Nora missed having a house, a home full of family and memories. She wanted to provide that for herself, her girlfriend, and her pack. The biggest challenge would be convincing Colbie to leave her current apartment, but they would have years to decide when that should happen.

"Five, Henry's new beta and Nora's," Ru said, smiling at Janelle. Nora didn't even know how the witch discovered this one. She shared a look with Josh as they clapped, another pang in her heart. Helen had approached Nora just this morning, asking for their bond to be released. She and Henry had a long history and Helen longed for a position of leadership. Henry had offered her Quinn's old position, and it had been settled by lunchtime.

Nora turned to Janelle and they shared a smile. As soon as Helen left, Nora made the decision. Packs needed order, balance, and hierarchy. Josh had texted Nora to say thank you. He'd thought Henry was priming him to take up the mantle of beta and hadn't wanted it. He was too content at Topher's side and trying to help Daniel navigate his next steps to want to help run an entire pack. He would have done it if Henry asked, but Helen was the perfect solution. Nora would miss her mother's proximity, but after the years of separation, having her living with another pack down the street felt like nothing.

"Six!" Ru looked more excited for this one than any of the others. "To me and Chance and Daniel." She grinned at the boys, and they shook their heads, less enthused about the dramatics. "We got our acceptance information and will start at UNB in the fall!"

Poppy's mouth dropped open. "I didn't even know you passed your GED!"

"Well, I did! What do you think I've been doing with my time?" Noting her older sister's lack of excitement, Ru wilted a bit. "My wards are solid, Poppy. Everyone here is so busy. Margot, Ryan, Viv, and Amelia will keep helping me with the anticharm bracelet business, but I've made enough to pay for my first year of tuition." A grateful look in Topher's direction. "I want to figure out how to exist in this world. All I do is watch human TV shows and hear about college and human experiences. I know you understand that because you went to UNB for that very reason."

Poppy visibly tried to relax. "I know you're right. I just need to get used to the idea. What will you even study?"

Ru shrugged, all the happier for not knowing. "I'm unde-clared. As far as I'm concerned, I'm majoring in existing as a human. Maybe I'll do communications or something."

Oliver frowned. "You know, a lot of humans want your

spot because their actual futures depend on it and the degrees they're after," he said gently.

Ru nodded, deflating a bit more. It was a heartbreaking sight. "I didn't apply to any scholarships or use magic to get in. Maybe I'll find a real career I like or—"

"Or major in business since you're already running a very successful one but should know more about it," Topher broke in.

Ru grinned, looking at Oliver with an expression like *see?* on her face. "Business it is."

Colbie turned to her youngest brother. "So, you're officially transferring?"

Chance nodded. Jay stiffened. Maybe they were getting close to the source of the tension between those two. "I start summer practice with the soccer team next month. Mom and Dad aren't happy, but—"

"But fuck them. If you need anything, we have you covered," Colbie broke in. She looked so happy Nora resisted the urge to crush her in a hug. Nothing was more important to Colbie than her brothers. She'd followed Topher's lead after being made and let Chance go for his own safety. Now that it wasn't a problem, she'd been in constant contact with her youngest brother, trying to make up for all the missed time. Judging by his slowly growing smile, he was as happy for this opportunity as Colbie. Nora glanced at Topher. His smile wasn't as effortless, but it was there.

"We definitely have you covered," Topher told him. He could mean anything from covering Chance's tuition or paying his rent or taking a trip home to charm their parents into treating Chance correctly. He would never do anything to sway their feelings on himself, but he would manipulate them for Chance.

"I might need help with rent if I move out," Chance admitted. "Or a job to help cover it."

Topher looked at Nora. "He could bar back at Alpha's Den? Maybe for, like, fifty an hour."

They laughed, and Chance relaxed into his seat. Jay got up from the booth, ruining the moment. "I'm going to head home. I have work in a few hours."

Chance looked pained but didn't follow them out. He winced at the questioning glances. "I, um, told them I didn't want to be roommates. And they feel like I'm letting go of my dreams, leaving my Ivy League school and soccer team to come here."

"Ah, Chancy. Why don't you want to be roommates?" Colbie asked. She was far more gentle with him than she was with anyone else, Nora had noticed.

Chance watched the lights of Jay's car turn the corner. "Because I think they're in love with me, and I just love being their friend and people say not to room with your friends anyway."

A sad silence fell. They'd all seen the looks Jay sent Chance's way. Nora hurt for Jay but also for Chance and the friendship he was worried about losing.

Daniel slapped Chance's shoulder. "It'll work out. One thing at a time," he said. As Daniel grew more comfortable with their group, Nora realized he might be even more like a golden retriever than his older brother. With a sprinkle of frat boy mixed in that had Josh rolling his eyes constantly.

Chance didn't seem heartened by Daniel's confidence, but he nodded. Their food came shortly after. Ru questioned Poppy, Annaliese, and Oliver about their college experiences and kept the conversation going while everyone who was eating ate. Then, when Julia suggested it, they decided on a game of soccer.

When they hit the field, time passed so quickly that Josh barely caught Topher when the rising sun took them all unaware. Seeing that, Oliver ushered his boyfriend to their car before he'd have to do the same. From his place under Zayn's arm, he called his goodbyes over his shoulder. Zayn was far more focused on pulling Oliver in close to bother with the rest of them. Slowly, reluctantly, they cleared the field. Colbie grinned when Josh moved to take Topher to the apartment with them for the day. Annaliese and Poppy walked to Annaliese's car to head back, debating whether or not Poppy should stay enrolled at UNB, especially now that Ru would be there. Nora hadn't even known Poppy was debating dropping out, but Annaliese would be the person to talk to. Nora smiled. Whatever happened between her best friend and Topher, Annaliese belonged in this new family Nora found.

The sun was lighting the sky, but Colbie's eyes remained bright-eyed as Nora drove them home in Poppy's car, Josh and Topher silent in the back. A glance in the review showed the werewolf nodding off, and Nora couldn't help but wonder how much sleep he'd been getting. It was easier for them than for Oliver, but vampire schedules did a number on anyone dating one.

"I can't believe Chance is staying," Colbie said.

"Can't you?" Nora asked, teasing. It was probably the fifth time Colbie had repeated that sentiment since he'd announced his plans. Now that Ru confirmed, Colbie seemed shocked all over again.

"And you have almost all your people back," Colbie words were more cautious this time. They hadn't talked about Nora's new pack members; it brought too much attention to the ones missing. Nora was getting used to the gaps and additions. She and Henry had figured out the best way to keep her huge pack together as a community while allowing them the freedom to continue their lives. Everyone was happy with monthly runs under the full moon and putting money into a community pot to help support the pack members who simply wanted to patrol the streets or raise their kids. The Alpha's Den supported everything else, including the remaking of the Den where insurance didn't cover it.

Nora reached for Colbie's hand. She stopped at a red light and looked at her girlfriend. Her *girlfriend*. Sometimes, Nora still couldn't believe they made it here. "You're so…"

Colbie smiled, rolling her eyes and thinking Nora was finished there. It was where she usually lost her words.

"Amazing. I'm so happy with you. I love you."

Colbie blinked, turning in her seat to face Nora fully. They stayed caught in each other's eyes, Colbie speechless for once. The horn of the car behind them made them both startle.

Nora jerked forward, hitting the gas clumsily and making Colbie laugh. Cool fingers intertwined with her own, but Nora was determined to focus on the road. Even when Colbie's breath hit her neck, words breathed into her skin above her pulse point. "Love you too, Nora."

Nora tilted her head, pressing her neck into Colbie's lips. She smiled, her first smile since killing Gabriel. Since finding Matt. "You won't leave?"

"I won't leave."

"I don't think it's healthy how much I needed you to say that."

"Eh, I'm sure the rules for codependency are different for supernaturals."

Nora shot Colbie a skeptical look but grinned at the quirk on her girlfriend's lips. They finally pulled into the lot of the apartment, but neither moved for a moment. Josh looked beyond peaceful sleeping in the back, and these quiet moments were so rare. Colbie squeezed Nora's fingers. "It's going to be okay. It's going to be really good. Things will change, and we'll probably have more drama with supernatural politics, but it'll be good."

Nora nodded. Colbie's assurance made her want to cry. "I wish my dad could see me and New Brecken right now."

"Maybe he can. You made the city something he'd be proud of. His fingerprints are all over it."

Nora closed her eyes. She was tired. Days after everything

had begun to settle, it was like all the stress of the past year was hitting her like a freight train. She rolled her head, looking at Colbie. Steady, gorgeous, open Colbie. "How did this even happen?"

"Well, one time, a werewolf walked into the bar where my brother was working. I smelled her as she came up to me." Colbie lifted their intertwined hands, sniffing Nora's wrist with gusto. "It was the best thing I ever smelled. It gave me a head rush. I decided I wouldn't ever be able to get enough of it. Then I *saw* her, and everything was over for me."

Nora didn't even know she was crying until Colbie reached to brush away the tears. "I feel so messed up inside, but not about you. You're the only thing that makes sense."

"We have all the time in the world to figure out the rest, Nora."

"I miss Matt. I hate myself, but I even find myself missing Gabriel."

"It's not going to be easy, but you have us." As if on cue, Annaliese opened the backdoor of the car, nearly spilling Josh into the parking lot before she steadied him with a laugh that he was quick to join once he'd fully woken up. The two pulled Topher from the car, speaking in low voices. Nora was too curious to stop herself from listening in.

"What did he say?" Josh asked.

"He asked if he could take me to dinner," Annaliese replied, a bit of a smile in her voice. "I told him that's a weird way to ask me to let him feed."

Josh snorted. "You nerd. Go to dinner. He misses you."

Annaliese studied Josh for a long moment. "You're still okay with this?"

"He's my boyfriend," Josh said. "You can be his girlfriend, but it won't change that."

"No, it won't."

"You guys really don't do any threesomes?" Colbie asked, words slurring slightly as she fought to stay awake. Josh and

Annaliese jumped. They'd been leaning into each other, murmuring softly and in their own world. The way they stepped apart when they realized they were being watched felt like answer enough to Nora. She grinned. Topher matched Annaliese's cynicism and darkness; maybe they both needed a bit of Josh's glimmering sunshine to break up the clouds.

They got Topher out of the car and to the apartment door that Poppy held open. Nora turned to Colbie with a grin. "No answer seems like an—" Nora stopped talking. Colbie was already asleep, slumped against the window.

Poppy stayed at the door, holding it open while Nora approached with Colbie in her arms. "We're going to be okay," Poppy said, but her words tipped up at the end with a question.

"Colbie says so."

Poppy nodded. "She would. She came out of this all fairly unscathed. No dead family members, kept her apartment, kept her friends."

Nora frowned, defensive. "She lost the sun. Her human life."

"Do you ever get the sense she misses being human? I don't."

"Are you jealous, Popsicle?"

"No. Just, I hope I can get to her level of peace sooner than later."

They shared a look of understanding. It was confusing to mourn people who hurt you. "We can be better than they were."

"Sometimes I don't even think I'm sad my mom is dead. I'm sad she won't be here to see me prove her wrong."

Nora could only nod. She passed Poppy and took the stairs, sighing with each familiar ward she slipped through. The apartment still had a slightly abandoned feel after their hectic last few months and with Ru gone. Annaliese was gently ushering Mouse out of Topher's room. She winked at Nora before shutting his door. Poppy went to the stove, clicking the dials on and getting potion ingredients out, not ready for sleep yet. She called over her shoulder, "Want to go to Vegan Your Day in a bit?"

"Yeah. I need a short nap first."

"I will, too, but wake me up before noon."

Nora nodded. She held Colbie tight, grateful to her girlfriend for bringing her into this cozy apartment. Into this friend group that hung out as if they shared a pack bond of their own. She toed out of her shoes before dropping Colbie onto her bed. In short order, she had Colbie's shoes off. With kisses and whispered words, she coaxed Colbie slowly back to waking.

"Got enough in you to help me get these jeans off?" Nora asked her, fingering Colbie's waistband.

Colbie's eyes sharpened, her lips twisted. "Not even a little. I'll just watch."

Eyes on Colbie's face, Nora popped the button open and pulled down the zipper. Despite her words, Colbie arched her hips to help Nora slide the baggy jeans down. "You played soccer in these?"

"Not well," Colbie grumbled.

"Ah, need me to soothe your ego after that?"

"Please." Colbie dropped her head back into the pillows, hips shifting impatiently now as Nora helped her out of her underwear, yet, before Nora could lower her lips to her prize, Colbie pulled at her. "Come up here first. I want to feel close to you."

Nora crawled up Colbie's body. She settled her weight on top, willing all her warmth into Colbie's chilly form. Colbie reached up, wrapping her arms around Nora's neck. "You told me you loved me."

"I do love you."

"I thought I might have dreamed it."

"I'll keep saying it until you have no more doubts."

"No doubts. I like the sound of that. You too. I love you too."

Their lips met. Nora slotted her knee between Colbie's, and as the kiss deepened, they moved together. Easy, breathless, *right*. Nora couldn't believe she ever doubted, ever questioned. Her pack, her grief, it all flew to the back of Nora's mind.

There was only this. An apartment she loved. A girl she belonged to. In a city they pulled from the shadows. Power. Love. Accomplishments. Nora had everything she ever wanted. Maybe she hadn't gotten here the way she anticipated, but the girl who dreamed a year ago wasn't creative enough to come up with this place. Staring into Colbie's eyes, drawing out Colbie's noises.

There was only this.

ACKNOWLEDGMENTS

This series has been a wild ride. I want to start by saying the biggest thank you to my readers! I can't believe I'm at a point where I can say that, but according to my KDP reports, you all are out there! Writing can be so lonely, and self publishing can be disheartening, but almost every day someone is reading this series and that's just amazing. Thank you to everyone taking a chance on me and these books! I can't believe the reviews and support. You're the absolute best!

I began this series in 2019, quite a significant year for everyone. I was living with my mom and spending more time with my sister, who is ten years younger than me and had a very different view of the world than I did at her age. Through the freedoms allowed to me by my living situation (thank you Mom!) and with the pause on life the pandemic put on us, I began writing these books for my little sister. Quickly they became for me, but they started out of love and admiration for her. Anna, you have inspired me and changed my outlook on life. Thank you so much for that.

During this time, my mom received a scary diagnosis. Five years later we'll still going through the journey. There have been ups and downs, but no matter the state of her health, healing has been happening. Thank you Mom, for reading my books and being willing to do the learning. I know there are still a lot of conversations we need to have, but it's nice to be in a place where we can look forward to them.

This is getting long, but I have to shout out my other siblings and friends. Ben, thank you for reading the earliest drafts. You aren't the intended audience for these books, but the fact that you like them gives me a ton of confidence. Allison, thank you for loving book one and I'll forgive you for waiting until now to read Alpha's Den because you hate reading unfinished series. And Charlie if you ever get here, I'm impressed you've read your first vampire books and love you dearly. Thank you Linsday, Jake, Tami, Kat, Bridget, Hannah, Sarah, and everyone else I'm forgetting (sorry).

Love you all so much!

ABOUT THE AUTHOR

Kelly Cole graduated from the University of Wyoming where she studied English and Creative Writing. She is working on a self-publishing career and enjoying every step along the way. Kelly is most active on Instagram and enjoys sharing her latest and favorite reads. She recently moved to Minnesota with her dog, Maya. She spends most of her time writing and playing seemingly endless hours of fetch.

9 798991 037600